Also by Anna Cheska

Moving to the Country

Drop Dead Gorgeous

Anna Cheska

THOMAS DUNNE BOOKS
St. Martin's Press ⚏ New York

THOMAS DUNNE BOOKS.
An imprint of St. Martin's Press.

www.stmartins.com

Library of Congress Cataloging-in-Publication Data

ISBN 0-312-30040-9

First published in Great Britain by Judy Piatkus (Publishers) Ltd.

First U.S. Edition: June 2002

10 9 8 7 6 5 4 3 2 1

For Alexa

A big thank you to my lovely family, especially Mum and Dad, Luke, Alexa and the other Anna Cheska.

Thanks also to everyone who offered help, advice and insight, in particular, Pat James, Helen White, Claire Rodgers, Caroline Neilson, Jeannette Boniface and Rob Simons. Drop dead gorgeous, every one of them . . .

And to Teresa Chris for her perceptive eye, for her empathy and support and for *The Goddess Without*.

'This above all, to thine own self be true'
— William Shakespeare, *Hamlet*

'Beauty is the lover's gift'
— William Congreve, *The Way of the World*

Chapter 1

Imogen West took a shudder of a breath as she opened the door to Edward's study. His sanctuary. She stared into the gloom, almost seeing his figure, his hand . . . reaching up to pluck the *Encyclopaedia Britannica* from the top shelf of the tall glass-fronted bookcase perhaps. Almost hearing his voice. *Don't speculate, Imogen. Look it up. Every fact can be at your fingertips.* Every fact? Imo shivered. What about the fact of death? 'Don't give me all that stuff,' she said aloud.

Shadows weren't capable of emotional blackmail, but even so . . . In one swift movement, she reached for the light switch. Better. The bulky and the black became his mahogany desk, his bookcase, his favourite leather chair. Not so dark, she told herself, releasing her breath with a *pouf* of liberation. Not so unknown, though still a touch scary.

Solid, traditional, a little fusty – to be honest, rather like Edward himself – the furniture stared back at her, as though aware that its days were numbered.

Imogen didn't want to do this. She laced her fingers together, feeling the pressure of her wedding ring against her little finger. It felt too soon. The shock of his death had left her numb – functioning with only a part of her brain, doing the necessary tasks and forgetting all others, battling with divided emotions and wondering why she couldn't cry.

She glared around the room, hands thrust into the pockets of her jeans. But she had to do it. John Grantham, her smooth, dark solicitor, had asked her to sort out the paperwork. 'Get things moving,' he'd said. 'We have to get things moving.'

So Imogen moved. She straightened her back, pushed a stray hank of nut-brown hair behind one ear and strode into the study. It had to be. Her husband had died three days ago. Sooner or later, life without Edward must begin.

'Loosen up, Imo.'

'Mm . . . grmph.' Imogen was in a beauty salon a few streets west of Market Cross, the imposing stone structure marking the meeting point of East, West, South and North Streets in Chichester city centre. The salon was on the ground level of a three-storey building whose Georgian façade concealed a black-and-chrome interior that was, Imo thought now, thoroughly no-nonsense contemporary.

It was the following afternoon and Jude's fingers were gently but firmly massaging Imogen's scalp. Joe Cocker was crooning from a speaker above the black hand-basin about that elusive *Something* . . . and Imogen was trying to relax. She wasn't just here for a massage. Jude was both the owner of the salon and her closest friend.

'You're so tense, sweetie.' Jude's eyes were half closed in concentration, her honey hair hanging loose around her ample bosom this morning, displaying no hint or tint of the raven black it had been when they'd met up the week before. 'But who wouldn't be? It's dreadful, so dreadful.'

2

Rather like a dentist, Imo reflected, Jude could be relied on for continuous monologue if necessary. 'Edward . . . I still can't believe it, you know.'

Neither could Imogen. OK, his cholesterol level had been high enough for Edward to alter his diet – though not radically – and for him to consider having the tests in London that somehow he'd never quite got round to. But even so . . . The fact of his death, the cold, hard fact, was hard to assimilate, and Imo blinked agreement since she was too efficiently swathed in Jude's fluffy black towels to do much else.

'I mean, a massive heart attack. Out of the blue like that. He wasn't *old*.' Unthinking, Jude began to hum along with Joe, before stopping abruptly. 'How old was he anyway?'

Imogen breathed in the pungent scent of jojoba oil and mumbled an indistinct, 'Forty-five.' She might once have considered this a reasonable life span, but now, halfway through her thirties, it seemed painfully meagre.

'You poor love. What an awful shock. I suppose it hasn't sunk in yet?' Jude relieved Imogen's jaw-line of one of the towels. Her eyes were dark blue and sympathetic. But while Imo could believe in the sympathy – for Jude was one of the most compassionate women she knew – the colour was another thing entirely. Jude's collection of coloured contact lenses (not to mention hair dyes, mousses, sprays, hair extensions and wigs) meant that sometimes her best friend was hard to recognise, should Imo pass her in the street. But that was Jude for you – a woman of many different colours, Imo would be the first to admit, but with a heart of pure gold.

She sighed. 'It's the study I can't face.' For all her good intentions last night, she'd stood for ages in front of the mahogany desk, just staring at the wedding photo of herself and Edward, squatting in self-satisfied manner inside its silver frame.

She'd finally picked up the photo, scrutinised the Imogen and the Edward of ten years ago and wondered about love. Had she loved him? She'd certainly thought so at the time. The photograph showed a perfect couple, and perhaps that was why they had become one. They never argued, they listened to one another's point of view, they were kind, considerate and careful of one another's feelings. But love?

She'd replaced the photograph with a sigh. It was one thing telling yourself to knuckle down and get on with it, but the study was so much Edward's that moving anything felt like an intrusion, as if she were dismantling his life, dismissing his value. And that didn't seem fair.

Tentatively, she'd opened first one drawer, then another. Papers, folders, books, all neatly filed as per Edward's customary habit. Until the top drawer. She pulled at the worn handle. The drawer was locked. He'd shut it once, quickly, when she'd brought in coffee. She'd smiled and thought, Secrets . . . Now it seemed to have an invisible label on it – *MY LIFE. ALL YOU EVER NEEDED TO KNOW TO UNDERSTAND ME*, it seemed to say. That was it for Imogen. She had marched straight out again. Enough. More tomorrow.

She'd retreated to the bedroom, stripped off her jeans and jumper and wrapped herself in her old and comforting towelling robe. This was the room in which he had died. But it still felt kinder somehow . . .

'I'll help you one night after work, if you like,' Jude offered now, wiping her palms on the short, black shift she always preferred to work in. 'It must be ghastly.'

Imogen tried to shake her head but her neck was stuck in the constricting curve of the basin. 'No.' Jude had already offered her a bed in the crowded flat that she shared with her mother and daughter above the salon. She had offered a shoulder to cry on and a listening ear, not to mention this wash, massage and blow dry. 'You're a darling, but I can manage,' Imo told her. She had to do it alone.

But she appreciated the offer, appreciated Jude with her warmth and the big smile that helped a friend achieve instant perspective on her troubles. Imo reached out a hand and briefly squeezed her friend's. Was Jude everyone's confidante as well as the woman they expected to make them beautiful? she wondered, remembering yesterday's phone call. 'Come and see me,' Jude had said. 'I'll sort you out.'

Imo shifted in the squashy, black chair of Jude's unique beauty salon, *The Goddess Without*. She smiled, recalling the night she and Jude had shared a bottle of Beaujolais and come up with the name, one that suggested you could indeed simply walk in and emerge cheerful, transformed, attractive, desirable, what every woman wanted to be on the outside, what every man wanted to have . . . someone drop dead gorgeous. Huh!

Jude's capable hands were working away just above eye level, smoothing in the jojoba oil shampoo, lathering and moulding as if Imo's head were made of clay. Gorgeous? Imo frowned. The salon was good but it wasn't that good. Still, Jude's choice of decor had created a kind of well-lit cave. It drew you in. Like Jude, it seemed to promise the magic touch.

'Shout if you change your mind.' Jude reached for another bottle. 'I'm here if you need me.'

'Mmm.' Imo peered upwards but Jude's expression gave

nothing away. Was she remembering recent times, usually in Jude's flat after work, when they'd talked about Imo's leaving Edward? About Imo's taking the final step and becoming free and single once more. The parties and the clubs, the blind dates that Jude promised made you feel like a teenager again. The independence, the fun . . .

Imo breathed in deeply. Hair spray, nail polish and jojoba, underscored with bleach. Yes, she had begun to think of leaving Edward. She couldn't even remember the beginning of their end, just the time when she'd sat opposite him at yet another dinner party, in yet another little black dress, played the perfect hostess and thought, There must be something more . . . Just the time when her father had died and she had turned to Edward for support and found something missing. Some closeness. Something that had been lost or maybe never been there at all.

So she took a step back from him, then another. But it was failure, wasn't it, to admit defeat?

Imogen closed her eyes. She had never talked to Edward about all this, never broached the subject of separation or divorce. How could she have suggested such a final step without the dubious impetus of serial arguments, daily bickering or at least a good old-fashioned row? Something to propel her, as it were, from dissatisfaction into action. Half-wanting to be free . . . no longer in love . . . needing a bit of passion and plate-throwing from time to time, did not seem to be reasons enough.

Imogen sneaked open one eye. But, thank goodness, Jude had sufficient tact not to yell 'Hypocrite' as she lathered in the protein conditioner.

'How are you managing with the shop?' she asked instead.

'Okay.' Thank goodness too for *Say It With Flowers*.

6

Imogen's florist's business had always been her refuge, even more so now. 'I've opened the same as usual,' she added. Her assistant Tiffany was holding the fort this afternoon, and tomorrow was half-day closing anyway. 'It distracts me and gets me out of the house.'

Jude nodded sympathetically as she ran experimental fingers through Imo's hair. 'Best thing.'

'It feels so empty,' Imo blurted. As did she.

'It's been less than a week.' Jude's voice became brisker to match the movements of her hands. 'You know what they say about time and healing.'

Imogen was acutely aware of the pressure-edge of long finger-nails – in Jude's case acrylic and allegedly suitable for *An Active Life* – like a deceptively tender cut-throat razor against her skin. 'Yes.'

'And the funeral's tomorrow.'

'Yes.' Perhaps Imo was doomed to monosyllables for the rest of her life. Perhaps Edward's death was a punishment for all that singles-speculation. 'The singles market is a minefield,' Jude often said. Both materially inclined and extremely dangerous then.

Jude's fingers stopped their work and were still for a moment, poised above Imogen's conditioned head. 'Even if you didn't love him . . .' She broke off.

A strong jet of warm water hit Imogen's scalp making her jump with sheer shocked pleasure. You knew it was coming but it never felt exactly how you expected it to feel. 'What?'

'You still have to grieve, Imo. It's only natural.'

Even if I didn't love him? That was quite shocking. She was grieving, yes. That was what the feeling of emptiness was all about, the waking at four a.m. in a bed grown suddenly too

7

big, waking with night-sweat and a dry taste in the mouth. It was so damned quiet. Ridiculous – the grappling with silence, the talking to herself, the inability to open a locked desk drawer . . . 'But what am I grieving for?' she asked them both. 'Is it losing Edward? Or am I mourning what might have been?'

'Both probably.' Jude worked on. 'But what difference does it make anyway? Let the guilt trip leave without you, Imo. Grief can't be analysed.'

Ah, sensible Jude. Imogen closed her eyes once more. Outside *The Goddess Without* this grey December afternoon, she had paused in the drizzle to read the black lettering on the white board Jude kept as a permanent window display, surrounded by various beauty products, all claiming to transform your life. She changed these messages regularly. Imo had peered through the small square panes of the traditional Georgian bay to find today's.

TENSE? NERVOUS? HEADACHES? she read. *LET ME GET MY HANDS ON YOU.* And despite herself, she'd smiled. If the population of Chichester had any idea how good Jude was, there would be pre- and post-menopausal women queuing from here to Market Cross.

Imogen sank back slightly under the pressure of the glorious hot water. It was wonderful to come here for the pure luxury of feeling Jude's practised hands on her head, fingers working out the tensions in a hair wash and scalp massage that was so good it was otherworldly.

With Edward gone, Imogen felt split in two. There was one woman sitting here in Jude's beauty salon, dressed in black jeans and black sweater, with a pale face and no make up. (Jude had looked up disapprovingly as she'd walked in the door this afternoon, announcing, 'You look like a ghost,

Imo,' with not a hint of irony.) That woman had come here for comfort rather than beauty. That woman knew she must grieve. But looking down on her was another woman wearing a scarlet halter-neck dress. This woman had thought about leaving her husband, of paddling in the shallows of a single life once more. A woman no longer in love. Imogen gave herself a mental shake. Which one was she?

'I didn't love him enough,' she announced when the water stopped.

'Wallowing in self-pity won't help you either.' Jude wrapped one of the towels around Imogen's head, bent suddenly and kissed her cheek. Her honey-blonde hair brushed against Imo's skin in an echo of the kiss. 'But mahogany low-lights might do wonders.'

'What's that? Some sort of bizarre dining experience?'

'You know perfectly well.' Jude led her from the wash-basin to her usual chair in front of a mirror. 'Like I said, you're so pale you need some colour, sweetie.'

'Maybe I don't want colour.' Imogen peered into the mirror. The number of illuminated mirrors in the salon was frightening. Everything was on view and from every angle too. You were multifaceted and simultaneously naked. And her face was literally a whiter shade of pale.

'What's wrong with colour?' Jude, she knew, was trying to be patient.

'Nothing. I just don't want it.' Imogen basked in her own stubbornness. Colour was frivolous. If she wanted to be dingy for a while, she would be.

'You mean you don't want to be seen.' Jude eyed her critically in the glass as she dug her thumbs into the nape of Imogen's neck.

It felt like heaven. She groaned.

Jude continued her attack. 'You want to slink away from the funeral, pale and invisible. You want to be the grieving widow everyone feels sorry for.'

'Jude!' If she hadn't been trapped by her friend's steely fingers, Imo might have walked out. And if there hadn't been a grain of truth in what she was saying . . .

'But that's not you.' Jude sounded fierce now. Intent blue eyes met Imo's in the mirror. 'You're not some dry and dusty widow. You're going to be strong, Imo.' Her hands pressed harder.

She was right, of course. It had to be faced.

'Everyone will be staring at you even though you don't want them to. And although you do look terribly ethereal in black . . .'

'You're not touching my hair.'

Jude held up a strand experimentally and pulled a face. 'Lacklustre.' She peered into the mirror. 'I've got a marvellous new range, Imo. Barely streaking, they call it.'

But Imogen was used to her tactics. 'When I feel the urge to streak I'll take my own clothes off, thanks.'

'It's completely natural—'

'No.' Jude had wanted to get her tinting gear on to Imogen's crowning glory for as long as she could remember. She submitted to a makeover from time to time to keep Jude quiet – although even that went against the grain. And she had occasionally been lured into manicures and pedicures, though not nail art of the acrylic variety. But no, she would not submit to major changes such as body piercing – one in each ear was sufficient – or Titian over, under or anywhere-else-tones in her hair. Furthermore, since she was long and thin whatever she ate or drank, she required neither toning tables nor Jude's latest muscle-stretching and massage machine, known affectionately as 'the rack'.

Jude towelled and tutted. 'Do you fancy an hour with the sun-bed then? On the house?'

'Absolutely not.' But as usual Jude's ministrations were a tonic and Imogen was already feeling more cheerful as the door that led through to the back opened and Jude's mother drifted into the salon in a haze of old-fashioned cologne. She was the closest Jude had ever got to a receptionist. When Hazel wasn't around, Jude took the calls herself or switched on her answerphone. She was – as she liked to say – a one-woman operation, besides which Imo knew she couldn't afford any more overheads.

'Imogen, dear . . .'

'Hazel.' She took the proffered hand and allowed hers to be patted. To look at, her mother was about as unlike Jude as she could possibly be: petite where Jude was tall and well-rounded, fine-featured and small-bosomed where her daughter was all curves and dimples. She had grey hair coiled today into a neat chignon, pale blue eyes and an air of vulnerability that she never hesitated to use to her advantage.

'I'm so sorry, my dear girl. How are you feeling?'

'Not so bad, Hazel, really.' It was the constant sympathy, Imogen thought, that was the most wearing thing about becoming a widow. She flinched as Jude tweaked the damp towel from her shoulders and chucked it into a black tub by the back door. It was so hard being talked to when no one knew what to say. Even indomitable teenage Tiffany had been silent and wary at *Say It With Flowers* this morning.

Imogen longed for the briskness of her own mother who always seemed to be far away, globe-trotting for her

Intrepid Travel for the Over-60s articles. She was always, thank God, honest. And had never even pretended to approve of Imogen's choice of husband.

'Darling, surely not?' her mother had replied after Imo had placed an international call to Venezuela to tell her she was engaged to Edward West. Vanessa Vaughan's voice was as clear as if she were in the same room. 'He's sweet, of course, but . . .'

'I'm going to marry him.' Sweet? Her mother might as well have said he was boring as hamster food.

A long, breathy pause before, 'Is that wise?'

'Oh, honestly, Mother.' What did *wise* have to do with anything? Edward was hardly a vagrant she'd picked up outside the Odeon. He wore suits. He was respectable, reliable. He was sophisticated and knew his way around the world. And he had great timing – he had found her at a low ebb after a doomed relationship with the original Mr Anti-commitment. By contrast, Edward had swept her off her feet, showered her with gifts and compliments, made her feel desired and treasured and special and, 'I love him,' she'd said.

'Really?' Vanessa had managed to convey a wealth of incredulity. It was, Imogen concluded, all a matter of tone.

She heard herself growing hot and defensive. 'You hardly know him.' OK, she'd often heard her mother assert that it took just four minutes to tell if a man would become friend, acquaintance or lover. How long did it take her to assess sons-in-law?

'He's wonderful. He makes me feel safe.' Was she an invalid? Was she in-valid? Was she protesting too much? And what was ten years' age difference? A lot at eighteen, next to

12

nothing at twenty-five. Age was a great leveller. 'He makes me feel . . .'

'Quite.'

Vanessa was not a woman given to listening to the virtues of men. Neither was she swayed by love. She had loved Imogen's father in what she called *her own way* – selfishly, in Imo's book. She'd also admitted – since their divorce – that she'd made a lousy farmer's wife. Now she seemed to Imogen to have grown more cynical than ever.

'Edward is exactly what I need,' Imogen said. And if her mother laughed she would hang up and never speak to her again.

'Take what you need by all means, darling. But marriage?'

Hazel was still patting Imogen's hand. 'I remember when I lost my Byron . . .' she began.

Oh, dear. Mentally, Imogen prepared herself for the death scenario of Jude's father, a man she'd never known.

Jude squirted mousse and began slapping it on. 'Not now, Ma,' she warned.

Hazel contented herself with a sigh. 'Edward was such a *kind* man.'

Kind, yes. But something wasn't right. Imogen couldn't shake off the feeling that there may have been more to him than that. There might have been an Edward she never knew. There might be a whole lot of secrets locked up in a desk drawer. And if so . . . She wrinkled her nose and frowned. Wasn't it about time she found out exactly what they were?

Chapter 2

Alex Armstrong spent the first five minutes of the session rolling charcoal between the thumb and forefinger of his left hand and marvelling at the perfection of Marisa's body, as white and smoothly curved as an unused bar of soap. Now *there* was a clean and innocent image. He narrowed his eyes to examine every physical detail from an artistic point of view. Innocent? Hardly. But however many sexual partners this girl had enjoyed – and from his own experience with her he guessed it to be quite a few – he'd bet she hadn't been used by any of them. No way. Marisa Gibb was temptation personified. You couldn't resist touching . . . but you wondered how the hell you were meant to recreate any of it on paper.

Hence the delay and the black fingers. Alex smiled to himself. But black fingers were better for blending anyway, and it was good to have some thinking time. He had told his students that very thing as they sat goggle-eyed and useless in the Art Room, gazing at the spectacle of the naked Marisa for the first time. And *they* were paying for the artistic experience. Needless to say, Alex was not.

14

'You do realise it's bloody freezing in here, Alex?' Being a professional, Marisa didn't alter the tilt of her head as she spoke. Even the muscles of her bare, white throat hardly moved.

Almost reluctantly – once he'd started he'd be closer to finishing – Alex made the first strokes of charcoal on sugar paper. The sound was soft and grating, the result blurred. 'It's always freezing in artists' studios,' he said. 'It's the garret effect.' Though garage might be nearer the mark in this case. Alex's studio was a workshop on the end of a line of garages backed by a row of allotments. In its previous life – and he'd twigged this the second he first opened the door – it had belonged to a car mechanic whose idea of a paint job was rather different from Alex's. But a couple of rugs, chairs and a put-me-up had made it comfortable enough. 'The cold comes with the territory,' he murmured.

'Not in the college, it doesn't, and that's what I'm used to.' Marisa sounded very regal considering she had no clothes on. 'You might at least put the bloody fire on.'

'Maybe I want the goose-bumps.' He didn't comply. He wasn't teasing her; he simply wasn't interested in the perfect nineteen-year-old body all warm, pampered and cosy. Anyone could have that – the students at St Mary's Art College for a start. No, he wanted her bumpy and brittle because that was what Marisa was. What she had been since their first meeting at St Mary's, where Alex was artist in residence (though he wasn't in residence at all; he had a comfortable room and landlady, and to date two other jobs apart from his more bohemian – if artistically satisfying – one).

He too had been amazed when he first saw the college's life model. How the hell could the principal expect his male students (and perhaps some of the women too) to concentrate on the finer techniques of life drawing with that sort of nudity placed in front of them? But she was good. In life drawing what you needed in a model was a well-maintained position and rare lack of self-consciousness. And Marisa had both in abundance.

After the first class she had faced him, fully dressed now and even more beautiful, her clear green eyes unblinking. Instead of asking how she'd done and when she would be required again, she'd said, 'Do you like my body?'

Alex had laughed. Was this girl for real? 'Who wouldn't?' he told her. His background was rural Nottinghamshire – he wasn't one for compliments, only the truth.

She accepted this with a brisk inclination of the head. Her hair was strawberry blonde – the hint of red complemented her pale skin, and Alex realised he'd have to paint her in watercolours. With that colouring it was almost compulsory.

'So would you like to go to bed with me?' she asked him.

Thinking of this now almost made Alex lose his flow. It was the unexpectedness of it, he supposed, as much as the choice of words. A bloke expected a twenty-first-century woman to be capable of making the first move. But this wasn't so much a first movement as an entire sonata in a nutshell. And the total arrogance of it was staggering.

'To make love?' he replied, teasing her. They had barely spoken, after all.

She shrugged. 'Whatever you want to call it.'

The charcoal flew over the paper now as Alex captured the curve of Marisa's left breast. Goose-bumps apart, the nipple was standing proud as a flagship. Better . . . And she'd

16

been right, of course. It wasn't love. Since that afternoon (here in his studio with the electric fire on that time, on the put-me-up with the scent of turps, oils and drying paint hanging thickly potent in the air) there had been four more occasions. None of them love, differentiated only by the period of time they lasted. Alex shaded the thigh with the knuckle of his thumb and scraped the knee joint into place with the nail of his forefinger.

More time, each time. In direct correlation with the excitement he'd felt – man's awful irony that the more he fancied a woman, the quicker it was over, the less good it was for her. *How was it for you?*

He pushed the floppy brown hair off his forehead with an impatient gesture. There was a continued satisfaction though in playing the game of sex with Marisa – she gave herself up to the pleasure of it, and he appreciated that. She was feline through and through. Any man would want to stroke her and make her purr. But after a while . . .

'Poor old Imo.' Through the small panes of the salon window, Jude watched her best friend walk down the street towards her car. The tall, slender figure wrapped in a black wool coat seemed upright and purposeful, but Jude worried. Imo was suffering. And she was in shock. But who wouldn't be? Who was prepared to be widowed at thirty-five?

'Do you think she'll cope?' Hazel sighed. She was wearing a white blouse, a lilac cardi draped around her shoulders, and a navy pleated skirt. Neat as ever, Jude thought. Not a hair out of place.

'Case of having to.' Jude looked around. 'And where's Daisy?'

'In the back garden.' The phone rang, Hazel moved to answer it and Jude slipped through the tiny kitchenette at the back of the salon. She opened the back door on to the patch of grass they called a garden, and at the same moment something small and scampering in an orange puffa jacket and lime-green trainers shot past her.

Jude smiled as she filled the kettle. There was time for a quick coffee and a cigarette before she got to grips with a new set of *Fancy Fingernail* extensions for her next client.

'And funerals are so depressing.' Hazel was standing in the open doorway, one hand smoothing her grey hair from her brow. Her pale eyes were reflective. 'Wouldn't you think there'd be a pleasanter way of saying goodbye?'

'Will it be in church?' Daisy chipped in from her position crouched on all fours under the salon's reception desk.

Jude looked over Hazel's shoulder at her little blonde bombshell. 'The crematorium, darling.'

'Will Uncle Edward go to meet his Maker?'

'Er – sort of.' Jude spooned coffee into a mug. Perhaps it had been a mistake sending Daisy to a C of E school. They pretended the God stuff was just a sideline, confined to morning assembly and learning decent manners. But it seemed to be rammed down their throats at every opportunity, poor loves.

'Can I come?'

'Certainly not.'

'Why?'

'Because you're too young.'

'"Suffer little children",' Daisy reproached.

'Maybe next time,' Jude heard herself saying. *Next time?* The water boiled and she poured it into her mug. Strong and instant. *Tonight, tonight . . .* The words of the song spun through her mind. Who knew what tonight would bring?

Hazel eyed the coffee. 'Daisy, would you run up and fetch one of Granny's special Earl Grey tea bags?' She pulled the cardi closer around her shoulders.

Daisy — still on all fours — cocked her head to one side enquiringly.

'Fetch, Timmy!' Jude located her cigarettes in the deep pocket of her black shift and pulled one out of the gold packet. It was all very Famous Five, but if that was what made her daughter happy . . . And she needed to have a word with her mother about tonight.

Daisy shot through the kitchenette, whizzed through the back door and could be heard clattering up the outside staircase that led to the flat they shared then on to Florrie Hall's flat on the second floor.

'It's hardly healthy,' Hazel murmured.

Armed with cigarette, ashtray and mug of coffee, Jude eased past her and flopped into the nearest black chair. In her opinion, too many people obsessed over health — mental and physical. Weren't there more important things in life? Like having a good time, for example. 'Nothing wrong with a vivid imagination,' she said. For every hair extension and contact lens that Jude owned, Daisy had an animal — complete with name, personality and noise. And why not? Jude grinned. 'Let's face it, a girl needs a vivid imagination to deal with the opposite sex. Daisy'll have a head start.'

But Hazel clearly wasn't having any of this. Her arms folded and her light blue eyes narrowed in preparation for war. 'She's confused.'

'Aren't we all?' Jude drew hard on her cigarette. Not

19

now. She didn't want to argue with her mother now. But: 'There's nothing wrong with my girl,' she protested. 'She always becomes human again at mealtimes. That's what counts.'

Right on cue, Daisy dashed back in, tea bag thankfully in paw rather than mouth.

'Good dog.' Aware she was rubbing it in, Jude retrieved it and went to re-boil the kettle.

'Poor child.' Hazel let out a faint sigh as she sat down. 'If only there were a father in the nest.'

'Here we go,' Jude muttered under her breath. She stirred bag and water with rather more vigour than necessary and splashed in some milk. She didn't need this. All she wanted to do was think about tonight. 'Nests run more smoothly without the male bird.' Re-entering the salon, she slapped the mug down in front of her mother. 'He's well out of it.' And besides. Daisy's father had been married at the time of his affair with Jude, and far too busy placating those who lived in his other nest, to worry about who might be arriving in the new one.

Hazel put on her disapproving face. Below it, the white blouse was buttoned high to the neck. 'Don't tell me that men don't have the nesting instinct,' she argued.

Something about her mother brought out the worst in her, Jude reflected, feeling her patience disappearing fast. They helped one another, but although she subsidised her mother's pension, Jude always felt she herself got the better deal. Because who else would look after Daisy when she was working? In term-time there was after-school club, but women didn't want to be beautiful just in term-time, they rather fancied it in the holidays too. Still, her mother drove her to the edge – more often than Jude cared to admit.

Of course she loved her. But . . . And sometimes it was a big but.

She sat down again and stubbed out her cigarette. 'Most men enjoy having two women,' she told her mother. 'It's a desire buried deep in the male psyche.'

'Ears,' Hazel said.

'What?'

'Ears.'

'Oh, right.' Sometimes, Daisy's animal improvisations were so good that Jude simply forgot she was in the room and blithely broke all the Proper Parenting rules. She eyed herself in the mirror. Did it suit her, being blonde?

'God has ears,' Daisy said knowledgeably, returning to her position under the desk. 'Even Uncle Edward might be listening.'

Jude hoped not. She twiddled a strand of hair between her fingers and thought of him dying in the bedroom. How much more awful it would have been for poor Imo if he'd died during sex. God . . . what would you do? Where would you put him? What would you say to the paramedics? How did close contact with dead flesh actually feel? Jude shuddered and got up to tip the contents of the ashtray into one of her shiny black bins. But in Imo and Edward's case it would be most unlikely, she decided. Imo had always implied sex to be a rarity, foreplay a far-off dream and satisfaction a complete and utter fantasy.

Jude fetched a clean black towel and wheeled her manicure trolley from the back of the salon. Since *The Goddess Without* did everything from hair removal to nail art, and massage to makeovers, she had a separate trolley for each beauty procedure, lined up in a row, primed and ready for action. 'Ma, about tonight . . .' she began.

21

'Will Uncle Edward go to heaven?'

Jude positioned the trolley carefully. She would speak to her daughter's form teacher. Christian values were one thing, but paediatric brainwashing was something else entirely. 'Probably.' She crossed her fingers behind her back.

'And dogs?'

'Dogs?' Jude frowned. Perhaps her mother had a point, Daisy did seem confused.

'Do dogs go to heaven too?'

Ah. Jude leaned over and slapped her daughter's behind playfully. 'Only when they die, sweetie. And you have to vamoose back upstairs. Pronto.'

'But at least it'll be nice to see Vanessa at the funeral.' Hazel rose to her feet but only got as far as the make-up trolley. 'Is this a new pink?'

'Fuschia.' The friendship between her mother and Imo's had apparently begun during an amicable discussion of feminism at a meeting of the W.I. 'Friendly? Can you imagine it?' Jude had once joked to Imo. 'My mother saying women should be women, and yours sending her a doormat in the next post.' But despite their differences, the respective mothers had remained friends and Jude and Imogen, aged twelve and five, had soon followed suit. They were different, too, but in Jude's opinion shared the values that mattered. And that was what counted.

Now, Daisy was tugging at her arm. 'Can I watch *The Simpsons* on cable?'

'Sure you can.' Jude bent to kiss the top of her daughter's blonde head. It was reassuring at least to know that Daisy mixed an appreciation of *The Simpsons* with her missionary and animal tendencies. 'And . . .' she hesitated '. . . about tonight, Ma?'

Hazel sighed with the gusto of the true martyr. 'I might as well. What else do I have to do?' She wrapped her cardigan closer once more and shivered melodramatically. 'You go off gallivanting, I'll hold the fort.'

Jude swallowed her pride. 'Thanks.' Because that was the other thing about being a forty-something single parent. For some reason – despite everything she said and believed about nests running smoothly without men – she still felt compelled to spend half her spare time searching for a soulmate. And tonight was the turn of . . .

Jude grabbed her bag from the shelf, groped amongst the debris of tissues, mints, address book and lipsticks, and located a crumpled piece of paper: the ad cut from the *Heart to Heart* section of the local rag. '"Tall, slim, and solvent with OHAC",' she read aloud. 'What more could any woman ask for?'

'OHAC?' But Daisy was distracted, already halfway out of the back door, a flash of orange and lime green.

'Own house and car.' Jude blew her a kiss goodbye. It was bound to be an interview. If she had answered his ad then so had thirty other hopefuls. As he worked his way through the list his ego would swell to the size of a house.

'Name?' Hazel swiftly blotted her usual candy floss lipstick with a tissue and smoothed the pleats of her skirt as she followed Daisy outside.

'Rod.' A bad sign, Jude had to admit, shutting the back door after her mother and daughter and returning to the salon. If *Rodney* was a touch wimpish, did *Rod* indicate disturbing macho tendencies? She selected an aerosol from the back shelf and sprayed air freshener in wild strokes towards ceiling and far walls. She really shouldn't smoke in here.

Rod. What category would he end up being filed under? Just for a moment she slipped her black-stockinged feet out of her clogs and rested them on the cool tiled floor of the salon. Macho man, control freak or keep your goddamn' hang-ups to yourself, thank you? But there was always the possibility . . . Jude rested her hands on the back of one of *The Goddess Without*'s black chairs . . . that tonight she might fall madly, passionately, deeply in love. She stayed motionless for a moment, considering this, bending to frown briefly at her reflection before easing the crease from her forehead with one fingertip. Lines. Laughter lines were OK though – a good sense of humour was always essential. *Tonight, tonight* . . . Maybe her soulmate was only two hours away.

The front door of the salon opened with a reassuring tinkle and Jude straightened, restored her feet to the black clogs, flicked back honey hair and turned to smile a welcome at her next client. A dour face looked back at her. So if a good sense of humour was so essential, how come there were so many miserable-looking people in the world? she wondered.

Alex noted the tense shoulders and downturned mouth and wondered if it was worth the effort. After a while, you kind of lost the point. It was one thing joining bodies in love or sex or both depending on mood and personal definition; quite another being merely the instrument of someone else's pleasure. If that was it. And yet: 'Why are you angry?' he asked her. His painter's eye observed her dispassionately. It couldn't simply be because she was cold – if that were the case she would have walked out of the studio by now.

'What makes you think I'm angry?'

Marisa, he had found, often countered one question with another. Was she curious about the world she lived in? Probably not. Was she trying to hide her feelings? Unlikely. Alex was beginning to doubt she had many. More plausibly, perhaps she was using him as a reflector, to examine her own self-image. He laughed. He'd like to draw her as Picasso might have. With two faces. With a sort of cubist hauteur. Perhaps next time, he'd do just that. Give her one hell of a jolt anyway.

'Your mouth,' he said, sketching its shape. 'The sulk of it.'

'Huh.'

He waited, but the said mouth moved not a millimetre. Whatever her reaction, she was keeping it firmly inside. This made it harder – Alex was pretty good at reading body language. 'So?'

'So what?' Her face was partly in shadow now – the afternoons were drawing in and this place didn't let in enough natural light at the best of times. Alex had scrubbed at the nicotine and oil stains on the grubby window panes for ages when he'd first moved in; now he just accepted the light for what it was – extremely limited.

'Are you going to tell me what's wrong?' Some girls might complain that he hadn't called, that he wasn't an attentive lover, whatever. But Alex's attentions were reserved for those he cared about – and that rarely included girls.

'It's my mother.' Her lips returned to their original set. 'She's pissing me off, if you must know. Do you really want me to talk?'

'Yes.' No, if he wanted to carry on working, but he was done today. Alex flung down the charcoal. He was more interested in hearing about Marisa's mother because she'd never volunteered any information about her family or friends before. She had merely left after sex and a cup of tea (or occasionally a glass of red wine, depending on the time and if Alex had a bottle already on the go) with a rapid check of her diary and a light kiss on the cheek. Marisa did not go in for pillow talk, or in this case put-me-up-talk, and after sex she did not linger like her perfume. It was quite refreshing, Alex found.

Now, she shifted her position in a graceful stretch accompanied by a yawn.

'Your mother?' Alex prompted, watching her.

'She's doing my head in. Playing dirgey music, crying all the time, mooning round the house all day . . .'

Alex considered making a quip about bare bums but thought better of it. Marisa clearly wasn't in the mood and he could live without one of those looks of hers that made him feel like something the cat had brought in – or even up. Marisa was to venom what Marilyn Monroe had been to flirtation: a complete natural. 'What's the matter with her?' he said instead.

Marisa threw her cream fleece jacket around her shoulders. 'She's depressed, I suppose.'

He watched her move closer. Any second now, she would sit on top of him, let that fleece slip off those white shoulders and he would still know bugger all about her family background. All right, he didn't need to know, but neither did he need to feel quite so much like Marisa's plaything, for God's sake. A bit of communication and the exchange of the odd personal snippet might make these encounters less . . . well, perfunctory. Or was he kidding himself? He was a man, wasn't he?

'The change of life?' he suggested crossing one ankle over the opposite thigh to deny access temporarily. 'How old is she?'

Marisa neatly removed it, dropping it to the floor in much the same way that she had removed her clothes earlier on. She sank her perfect mound of a backside on to his lap. 'Forty-nine.'

She turned slightly, bent towards him, and he felt her tongue exploring the groove of his collar bone under his open-necked denim shirt. The scent of her strawberry-blonde hair was already deep in his nostrils. She never wasted any time. 'There you are then,' he said.

'What?' There was a hint of irritation in the clear eyes as she lifted her head to look at him.

'Could be the menopause.' Alex became aware of his erection, and, placed as she was, Marisa couldn't fail to soon become aware of it either. 'What's her name?'

'Her name?' Now Marisa stared at him in disbelief. 'What the fuck do you want to know that for?' She grabbed him, hard but not unpleasantly, with her right hand.

'I'm interested.' Yes, very interested, but she knew that too.

'Naomi. Naomi Gibb. Satisfied?' She took her time undoing the buttons of his shirt. She knew what he was thinking, he could tell.

'Just the two of you then?'

'What's it to you?' She completed the undressing of his upper half, slipped off his lap and began on his jeans. Alex wondered how long he could hold out.

'I told you, I'm . . .' All of a sudden it became difficult

to speak. He looked down at her and realised she was enjoying herself.

Marisa broke off from her concentrated activity. 'Do you want to meet her then?' Her lips parted slightly. He could see the pink, moist tip of her tongue.

'Uh?' Alex was so shocked at this turn-around, so taken aback that she'd stopped what she was doing, that he said, 'Why not?' before he had the chance to think of all the reasons. But it didn't matter too much. His mind – and the rest of him – was, at least for now, pretty well occupied elsewhere.

Chapter 3

Tonight, tonight . . . '"Love is in the air",' Jude sang as she nipped up the back stairs to check on Florrie. She had paused only to pull on black leggings and tracksuit top over her work shift because evening had already drawn in and the December air was damp and chilly. Florrie, an elderly spinster, lived alone, with relatives and friends never much in evidence. Living directly below her, Jude felt an obligation – no matter how hectic things were, and no matter who she had to meet later that night, she thought with a smile – to pop up and say hello, to see if her neighbour needed any shopping or a light bulb changed. Whatever . . . Knowing Florrie, she'd probably be too proud to ask.

Her rap on the back door was answered by a faint, 'Hello, my dear.' Florrie's face was white as a sheet.

'Florrie? Are you OK?' Jude tried to steer the bird-like figure towards the nearest chair. She seemed so fragile, as if the least pressure on an arm or shoulder would make her snap. 'What's up?'

'Nothing that a bit of a sit down won't cure.' Impatiently, Florrie brushed away her attentions. 'I'm tired, that's all.

I've had a visitor, and at my age they can be draining, my dear, even the helpful ones.'

'I know the feeling.'

'Come through and we'll sit somewhere comfy.'

A little unsteadily, Florrie led the way down the dark hall into her cluttered sitting-room. Jude had been here on countless occasions but each visit revealed new treasures: a twenties candlestick in the shape of a swan, a sepia print of Florrie as a young schoolgirl with soulful eyes, a Chinese tea service she had never noticed among the vases, pots, porcelain figures. You name it, it was in Florrie's sitting-room, coated with a faint film of dust and the unmistakable scent and shimmer of the past.

'His intentions might be good,' Florrie muttered, 'but too much concern can be stifling, you know.' She sank on to a brown, fringed velveteen sofa. 'Ah, that's the ticket.'

'Whose concern?' Noting that some colour had returned to Florrie's face, Jude crossed to the window. She spotted the familiar navy blue BMW immediately. Understated, classic; money but not vulgar money. 'Oh, *he's* been here. That explains it.' The car belonged to their landlord, James Dean, also known – to Jude, who reckoned she had him sussed from their first meeting – as Scarface.

'I'm not as young and strong as I was, you see.' Florrie tweaked at her tweed skirt with arthritic fingers. 'He's quite right about that.'

Jude's eyes narrowed. No, she'd never liked him. Property dealers were mostly sharks in her experience and this one probably owned half of Chichester. There was something unsettling about James Dean, though she couldn't quite put her finger on it. 'What's he been saying? Has he upset you?'

30

'Oh, no, dear, not really. I told you, I'm just tired.' But Florrie's voice rose and her fingers moved to the buttons on her fawn woollen jacket.

Jude dropped to her knees beside her. She liked Florrie. She knew from the stories she told and from the lines on her face – laughter lines curving from a generous mouth and fanning from her eyes – that her neighbour had seen life and enjoyed it to the full. Now she was old. And James Dean was just the sort of man likely to prey on the weak and vulnerable. Well, Jude was neither weak nor vulnerable, and she was not going to let him push Florrie around. 'It's all right,' she soothed. 'Shall I put the kettle on?'

Florrie shook her head. 'I've just had a cup, thank you, dear.' Her hair was pure white. The only colour, Jude thought, that couldn't be improved on.

'So what exactly did he say to you?' Jude persisted. Perhaps there was a problem with paying the rent. Perhaps Florrie was in arrears and didn't like to ask for help.

But the old lady's faded blue eyes had grown vague. 'I may not be as steady on my feet as I once was . . .' she began, staring down at her soft fluffy carpet slippers.

'Is that what he said?' What a cheek. Jude would like to see Scarface manage so well when he got to eighty.

'But I do so want to keep this place.' All at once, Florrie's voice was firm and her eyes focused. There was no doubting her determination on this score and no doubt in Jude's mind either what James Dean had suggested to his elderly tenant.

'He thinks you should move out,' she muttered. Florrie had been here for so long that their landlord was probably receiving next to nothing in rent. If he got her out and did the place up, he could charge a tidy sum for a flat like

Florrie's; it was a good area to be in, close to the hub of Chichester. He'd be raking in the dosh then.

'I need my independence.' Florrie's eyes were misted with tears. 'That's what you young people don't understand. I could no more go and live in a home—'

'You won't have to.' Jude grasped hold of her hands. The brown, mottled skin was thin, papery to the touch, the joints knobbly but with a surprising strength. '*I* understand,' she said. She had always known James Dean was a troublemaker – you'd expect it, wouldn't you, with a name like that? But she could deal with troublemakers, no worries. In fact, she'd enjoy the challenge. 'Leave it to me,' she told Florrie. 'I'll sort it. I won't let you be moved from this place until you're good and ready.'

Jude was no expert but she knew that Florrie's must be a protected tenancy. So what could Scarface do, if he wanted to get her out? Jude clattered down the outside staircase. He could go to Social Services – claim Florrie was incapable of looking after herself. But surely, so long as she didn't present a danger to others, so long as she wasn't damaging the flat, so long as she was paying the rent . . . ?

Jude let herself into her own flat through the kitchen door and followed the soft murmur of voices towards her tiny sitting-room. Everyone had rights, didn't they? She made a decision. She would visit the Citizens' Advice Bureau the following morning and find out exactly what Florrie's rights were.

She paused in the doorway to survey the scene in front of her. Her mother was sitting, knees together, navy skirt arranged to fall demurely over them, making deferential, *of course* and, *naturally we will* type noises. On the maroon and pine sofa opposite her lounged James Dean himself, late-forties, his dark hair brushed back from a rugged face that looked, she'd always felt, as if it had been around. Hardly a rebel without a cause. But still patronising her mother, drinking her tea, cashing in on old ladies' vulnerability.

He got up when he saw her – lazily, his body language a kind of languid drawl. Jude waited. There was a lot of him. He was big and broad-shouldered but in good shape, she conceded reluctantly. And the suits he wore always looked just that little bit too small for him. 'Mr Dean.' She kept her voice frosty.

'Miss Lomax.'

Hazel looked from one to the other of them, as if sensing the undercurrent of tension. 'Mr Dean was just asking if we could keep an eye on Florrie,' she said.

'Was he indeed?' Jude glared at him. So, not content with trying to chuck out his elderly tenant, he now wanted to enlist Hazel and Jude to help him in his dirty work. To tell him how hard Florrie was finding it to manage alone. That she'd left a tap dripping perhaps, or neglected to put her rubbish out. Well, if that was his game, he could find someone else to play it.

James Dean's brown eyes clouded and became more distant. 'If you have the time?' he added. 'I realise you lead a busy life.'

Was he sneering at *The Goddess Without*? He wouldn't be the first. 'As a matter of fact, I've just been chatting to Florrie,' Jude informed him tartly. 'And I can assure you that she's perfectly capable of managing for herself by herself.'

The other two stared at her in surprise.

'So you don't need to worry about a thing.'

33

James Dean opened his mouth to speak.

'She is a protected tenant?' Jude got there first.

'Er . . .'

Did he really expect her to believe that as a landlord he knew nothing about tenancy laws? 'She's been here more than a year,' Jude explained patiently.

He grinned. 'More than a year? I should say so. More like a lifetime.'

Jude ignored the grin. 'Precisely. And now . . .' She retrieved her worn black bag from the floor beside Hazel and found her purse. 'Can we get on? I presume you've come to collect the rent?'

'Got it in one.' Still looking amused, he moved away from his untouched cup of tea and followed her back into the hall.

But the grin had annoyed Jude. Clearly he found it funny – playing with people's lives. 'Wouldn't it be easier for me to pay by standing order in future?' she suggested, signing a cheque and handing it to him. 'To save you making the journey over here so often? Since we all lead such busy lives.'

'On the contrary.' Without looking at it, he tucked the cheque into the breast pocket of his suit, frowned and eyed her speculatively. 'I prefer to keep an eye on things myself,' he said in even tones. 'I like to have a chat with my tenants, see there are no problems, keep a finger on the pulse. That sort of thing.'

Oh, yeah? And more to the point check up on them. Like the way he was looking at her right now, as if he wanted to know every detail of her business. Jude was conscious of what she was wearing, that maybe she should have showered and changed the second she'd finished work. But what the hell . . .

34

To avoid meeting his eyes, she concentrated on the scar that had earned him his nickname. It ran from the edge of his left eyebrow to halfway down his cheek, and right now it looked livid, as if he was holding back his emotions with some difficulty. She didn't care. Whatever his plans for Florrie, she would fight him. All the way if necessary.

'Could I have a receipt?' Perhaps she was pushing it. But: 'I must get on. I lead a—'

He stopped her, one hand raised, muddy eyes crinkling into . . . laughter? Anger? 'Very busy life?' he suggested.

'Absolutely.' And Jude had no intention of giving away the kind of busy she was planning on being tonight.

Imogen locked up the shop, hurried to the car and drove back to the nineteenth-century flint cottage on the outskirts of Chichester, close to the City Wall, that she had shared with Edward.

There seemed so much to do. So much paperwork, so much battling with documentation, mortgage reports, bank statements, insurance and pension details. You name it . . . And while she battled with the paperwork associated with death, Christmas was already colouring the streets around her. Trees had sprouted lights and tinsel; garlands of crêpe, tissue and foil flapped across shop windows; Santas, snowmen and reindeer flew and flashed across roofs. And in the midst of this, she reflected, the shock and the grief went on.

It was raining quite hard now. She got what she needed from the car boot and took it into the cottage. She pulled off her coat, shivered, and opened the study door before she even checked the heating had come on, before she could change her mind. John Grantham, her dapper solicitor, was right. She must get on. And it shouldn't be too difficult, sorting out her husband's affairs, because Edward's affairs would be like Edward himself – well-regulated, compartmentalised, neat. He simply wasn't the type for secrets.

Imo had failed to find a key to the locked desk drawer so clenched the screwdriver she held in her right hand and rammed it into the gap between drawer and desk. It slipped, chipping the precious mahogany. Damn! She swore softly. Again, she pushed the narrow metal edge into the gap by the lock. She jiggled it back and forwards, eased it in further, snapped it down, and . . . The lock gave, the drawer opened, a piece of paper catching in the mechanism. Secrets . . .

She pulled it free. It was a bank statement. Nothing more sinister than that. She barely glanced at it. Putting it aside, she surveyed the drawer. It was stuffed with papers – stuffed in a very un-Edward-like way.

What was going on here? She picked up another bank statement and frowned.

'Do you think Amelia will get rid of the baby?' Hazel asked Jude, who was pulling on her knee-high black boots, guaranteed – she hoped – to make an impression.

Jude stopped mid-lace. She was trying to focus on the blind date she had lined up, but thoughts of James Dean and Florrie kept intruding. And now her mother . . . 'What?' She frowned. Who was Amelia? A client? A friend of Hazel's who had got herself into . . . as her mother always put it . . . trouble? Someone who had not obeyed the Nice Girl rules?

'Amelia.' Hazel clicked her tongue. 'Jeff's baby. You know . . .'

'Ah.' Unfortunately, Jude did know. 'Mother, I don't

have the foggiest idea. I don't watch the thing.' Sometimes she worried that *Streetlife* was taking over *their* lives. But she, at least, had a life to live.

'I did tell you.' Hazel launched into the latest cliffhanger. 'Amelia would never have looked at him if she hadn't been so upset about Davide.'

Davide? Clearly not the gorgeous Ginola. Jude pondered the French influence as she straightened her crimson skirt. Too long, too short? Just right? It was worth taking some trouble – who knew where it might lead?

'And you could blame her for getting involved with a married man—'

'Not necessarily.' Was James Dean married? Probably. His wife would wear designer suits and shop in Liberty's. Jude could just see her. She breathed in and glanced towards the mirror. It improved the line, but she'd never be able to stay like that all night. Every girl had to breathe.

'But of course he didn't tell her to start with.' Hazel wagged an admonitory finger.

Well, he wouldn't, would he? Jude checked her bag. She'd take her card and be prepared to pay her whack. Unlike her mother, she had long ago concluded that economic dependency could be seen to confer certain rights – both to demand and to criticise. Well, she wasn't having any of that, thanks very much.

Hazel caught her breath. 'And you know I don't approve of abortion,' she said.

Jude knew. When she had found herself pregnant – after forgetting to take only two pills, for heaven's sake – Hazel had begged her not to 'kill my grandchild'. That was what came of watching too many soaps, Jude decided. One developed a taste for the melodramatic.

But Hazel needn't have worried: the thought of having a child at thirty-five turned out to be an appealing one to Jude. So what if she were single? She wouldn't have wanted to marry Daisy's father in any case. And this way she got to make all the child-rearing decisions herself. It may have been both unexpected and unplanned, but Jude had no intention of passing up this chance of motherhood.

'But in this case . . .'

What case? Jude grabbed her coat.

'. . . who could blame her?' Her mother was clearly expecting a response.

'Who indeed?' Jude ran into the kitchen where Daisy-in-her-nightie was sitting at the counter on a high stool, coming to grips with a pot of glue, some cardboard and a tube of glitter. Her mother was going to love this. She smiled and kissed her daughter's upturned nose. ''Bye, sweetie. And don't make too much mess.'

Daisy sneezed loudly.

'Bless you.' Would she have this cold if Jude spent more time with her? Of course she would. She should take her own advice to Imo, Jude told herself, and let the guilt trip leave without her.

'Because she did give Jeff the option,' Hazel said as Jude re-entered the tiny sitting-room.

She peered out of the window. Was that a taxi? No one had come to the door, but sometimes they thought it was a laugh to wait for two minutes and then whizz off to the next call.

'And if you have an affair with a married man . . .'

Jude lost track. 'Rod isn't married.' Though it was a possibility. Rod was potential assailant, heart-breaker, married man, prince . . . The list went on and on.

38

She turned to find her mother shaking her head at her. 'Not Rod, silly, I'm talking about Jeff.'

'Jeff, yes, of course.' It was time to go.

'So who could blame her for making that difficult decision?' Hazel clutched hold of a maroon scatter cushion. 'And deciding to terminate?'

'Not me, Ma.' Jude kissed her on one powdered cheek. 'Certainly not me.'

She must encourage her mother to find new interests, Jude decided, as she sat in the cab and smoothed on another layer of Luscious Blackberry lip colour. How was she looking – under forty or over forty? The wrong side of forty was an abyss. All right she was in it and she didn't feel a whole lot different to tell the truth. But maybe that was because she was still clinging to the sides.

'Raphael's, was it?' The taxi-driver looked about fifteen – all mouth and acne. He braked, almost causing an unfortunate incident with the lipstick. 'Shit,' he pronounced.

Jude glanced at her watch. She would be ten minutes late which was about right – not late enough to risk Rod's walking away and not early enough to look keen. Singleton rules. Don't be early. Don't chase.

They drew up outside Raphael's and she snapped open her purse. 'How much?'

He told her, flicked the interior light on for a microsecond and then flicked it off again. He was tapping his fingers on the steering wheel, eager to be off. 'Haven't got all night, lady,' he muttered.

Jude took no notice. So what could her mother do? Ballroom dancing? Suitable – though there were always too many women, she'd heard, and she couldn't see her mother being the man. Bridge? Too sedentary. Hazel could do with something a bit more active.

Jude paid the cab-driver, omitting a tip, and paused on the pavement to check her hair. At least it had stopped raining. It felt good to be blonde, she decided – people said they had more fun, and she was beginning to think it was true. Men noticed blondes. Blondes had a certain panache.

She took a deep breath and swept into Raphael's, laced black boots leading the way with a confidence she didn't feel. The restaurant was one step up from a burger joint with red and white decor and lots of tables crammed too close together. But what did it matter?

Jude scanned the tables with mental fingers crossed, every sense alert, waiting for the moment of truth . . .

Chapter 4

As she drew level with the florist's, Naomi Gibb checked her purse. It always seemed light these days. But those white lilies in the tub just inside the open doorway of the shop were so pure, so perfect . . .

She pulled off her worn brown gloves, tucked them carefully in her coat pocket and flicked the clasp. There was enough change – just. She really shouldn't succumb; flowers were classed as a luxury these days, although Marisa frequently received scentless ruby rosebuds or huge cellophaned bouquets.

But lilies were special. And buying or not buying, it was pleasant to linger, Naomi thought. To catch the fragrance that lent this biting winter breeze an exotic sweetness. You could close your eyes and almost be somewhere quite different, back to summertime perhaps, back to a time when life was simpler, when she wasn't playing this . . . oh, this dreadful waiting game.

A customer left the shop, shutting the door firmly behind him. Back to summertime? Naomi sighed. What a hopeless romantic she was. Marisa often said that. But Marisa said lots of things – and should one listen too closely to a daughter? Flowers did so much for a house. She could do with a brighter day, a sharpening of the senses, a reminder of summer. Naomi sniffed hungrily but the scent was lost. Perhaps she could make a deal with herself? Forgo her weekend bottle of wine?

The shop, *Say It With Flowers* (a charming name, though what Naomi wanted to say to herself, she wasn't sure), seemed to be empty, apart from a leggy teenager with spiky white-blonde hair and an alarming amount of facial piercings. Not only did she seem to have been used as a pincushion and plugged into a thousand volts, but she had an attitude discernible even from Naomi's vantage point as she peered past the window display from her position on the pavement outside.

And then the tall brunette wandered through from the back. She was older, in her thirties perhaps, often to be seen here tenderly arranging blooms in wedding bouquets and wreaths. Weddings and funerals . . . Was it sad to deal with such combinations every single day? She knew nothing about the woman but instinctively Naomi liked her – because of the way her long sensitive fingers dealt with the flowers perhaps. With love.

Now that *was* silly. She shook herself as if to free her mind from sentimentality. Marisa had no time for it, perhaps that was why she was strong. But now, as always, the look of that woman – whose name she didn't even know – drew Naomi inside the shop.

'Hi.' The girl with attitude seemed even more abrasive close up. Below the shop overalls her legs were encased in skintight black and silver lurex. Naomi knew that lots of girls bleached their hair these days. And several rings in the ears meant nothing, though the nose was a little much and the eyebrow definitely over the top. But still, the brashness of it almost took her breath away. She fingered her own short curls — red, like pale gingerbread rather than carrots. The kind of hair that went inevitably with too-pale skin and an abundance of freckles.

The girl's face was white, her eye make-up black. Naomi tried a tentative smile. She felt over made-up in anything more than translucent pressed powder and a dash of lipstick. 'Hello.'

'What would yer like?' The girl drummed her fingernails on the counter and Naomi noted the black-and-white-striped varnish and pierced thumb nail. She winced. Goodness knows what *that* was trying to say.

'I was wondering about the lilies.' She addressed this to the girl but looked hopefully at the other woman — who might not think her daft to wonder about lilies. Naomi could no more march straight in and announce what she wanted than she could fly. Perhaps she needed some reassurance before she could justify the purchase. Or perhaps Marisa was right and she was just plain middle-aged barmy.

What was happening to her — truly? For so long she had been treading water, staying safely tucked in limbo, imagining the kind of happy ending that belonged to fairy-tales. And now, the worst thing was the not knowing, the waiting. She prided herself on never phoning him at work. But for how long could she stand *not knowing*?

She pulled her thoughts back to the here and now. The other woman in the shop was elegant, with striking, almost classical features, though today she was pale and her eyes drawn. However, when she smiled, her face was transformed. And she was smiling now at her lilies.

43

'They are lovely, aren't they?' She moved closer to the tub. 'I was just saying to Tiffany, I shall take some home with me tonight.'

'Will you? How nice.' And how fortunate to work in a flower shop, Naomi thought.

The girl called Tiffany tore off a sheet of cellophane. Naomi watched her. With those fingernails she looked capable of ripping someone's face to pieces too. 'How many stems?'

Naomi wavered. Her hand gripped hold of the battered leather purse more tightly. She had always known it wouldn't go on forever. What did she have to offer a man like him? What had she ever had to offer? And now this lurching uncertainty. It wasn't like him. And it was such bad timing, coming right on the heels of her redundancy like that. Some had families to support. Families . . . Naomi sighed. She only had Marisa. It was ridiculous to feel that you couldn't afford to buy yourself a few flowers, but hard, at forty-nine, to know quite what to do next.

'Four, five?' Tiffany was waiting. Like Marisa, she was probably thinking Naomi doo lally. Well, let her. The young didn't know about reflection, Naomi reminded herself. They simply acted, usually in their own self-interest.

But the other woman, obviously in charge, clearly did know about reflection, and maybe indecision too. She was bending forwards in rapt concentration, her long fingers caressing one white petal of an open flower. 'Just two would look dramatic enough,' she said now. 'If that's what you would like?'

'Yes.' Naomi felt absurdly grateful. The other woman seemed to understand so perfectly. 'That's exactly what I should like. Thank you.'

44

Tiffany raised her eyebrows (and one of her gold hoops) but made no comment as she wrapped the lilies.

Careful, Naomi wanted to tell her.

'Enjoy them.' The other woman accompanied her to the door. Her long brown hair was swept up today, she was dressed in black under her overalls, and she looked sad. On the third finger of her left hand was a wedding band; a lone amber ring shone on the little finger of her right. A fly in amber. Naomi's heart went out to her. There was something . . .

Naomi was not a fatalist. She had always believed that a person should take responsibility for their own actions, their own dreams. But now, with the heady scent of the lilies and this sense of some bond between them, she was almost tempted to ask her — was there any work available? Did they need someone for Saturdays? As if she had been meant to walk into this shop, as if someone had wanted them to meet, to establish some connection. But that was plain daft — there were already two of them working here, and the shop wasn't busy enough for more than two, it couldn't be. She turned to go.

Naomi was glad to leave the shops behind and round the corner into Chestnut Close. Theirs was a small house in a terrace of six — all painted in modest colours from dove grey to primrose yellow — bordered by a low brick and flint wall. Surely no one could take it away from them? Whatever happened next.

Outside the house a couple were lingering — Marisa and a young man, she realised. Naomi watched them. Marisa was standing slightly apart from him, not allowing him to enter the aura of self-sufficiency that always hung around

45

her, Naomi thought, rather fancifully perhaps. But she was getting her key out of her bag and moving towards the gate. Well, well . . . this was a surprise.

Naomi's steps quickened. Even inside the gloves her fingers were cold and her thin scarf seemed to offer no protection against the wind. Marisa had never brought a man home before. Because she was ashamed of where she lived, her mother's ordinariness? *When I get out of here,* she had said once, as if Chestnut Close were a ghetto slum, *I'm going up, just you watch.* Naomi knew there were men – from Marisa's throwaway comments, from the flowers and phone calls, the outings to dinner, the Festival Theatre, wherever. But there were so many men, that Naomi worried sometimes.

She drew closer to the house, her precious lilies cradled in the crook of one arm. The man with Marisa had thrust his hands into the pockets of his coat. He was tall and loose-limbed with longish hair. Casual bordering on scruffy . . . was that Marisa's type? The scent of the lilies swept over Naomi once more. She didn't think it was. Marisa had always expressed a preference for smart suits and expensive cars. And money of course. Marisa liked money.

Naomi watched them disappear into the house. Marisa had never been easy. Always so demanding, so strong-willed, so sure of what she wanted. Unlike Naomi, and unlike her father too . . . Sometimes Naomi wondered if Marisa had even engineered this distance between them, as if she blamed her mother for being a single parent, for giving in too much, for not giving enough, for everything. Children did that sometimes.

The lights went on inside the house as they shut the door behind them, not seeing her approach. It felt odd, as if it were no longer her house at all. Was Marisa in love? This man didn't look as if he was about to take her anywhere — at least not in an upwards direction. So why had she brought him here?

Naomi reached the gate. It was still open and she pushed it wider with one knee. All she wanted was for her daughter to be happy. But no, that wasn't all, was it? She would be lonely if Marisa left — *when* Marisa left. But then, in the future there might be grandchildren. They said grandchildren heralded a new relationship between mother and daughter. She could do with that.

She balanced her lilies on one arm and groped in her bag for her key. What was she thinking of? Grandchildren . . . Marisa was nineteen, barely more than a child herself. And when you had children then *up* was not the direction that came to mind.

But still . . . Naomi smiled as she prepared to meet him. She would hear something soon — she had to. And in the meantime, she was very glad that she had bought the lilies.

'How was it?' Imogen asked.

'It?' Jude shifted the phone to her other ear. She knew exactly what Imo meant. Last night's date had been uppermost in her mind all day — while she cleaned the kitchen and watched Daisy playing weddings with half a dozen kiwi fruit, while she painted her daughter's fingernails bright purple with gold glitter on top, and even when she agreed — with some trepidation — to let her loose in the beauty salon downstairs. That was where Imo had caught up with her.

'Or should I say how was *he*? Tall? Dark? Handsome?'

Jude watched Daisy's ghoulish expression as she dipped one of her fine brushes into a pot of liquid black eyeliner.

'Not exactly, no.' She could easily have overlooked the polka dot tie and the pink shirt (some men needed a woman to manage their clothes for them) and she knew that flares were supposed to be back in fashion. She could even have helped him with his problem skin – a tea tree facial for starters, plenty of water and cucumber, and a Chinese skin cream that was an absolute wow.

'Looks aren't everything,' Imogen said.

Jude recalled the way his gaze had been fixated on her cleavage. 'Talking of looks, he had some trouble looking me in the eye,' she told Imo. '*And* he sells vacuum cleaners.' Daisy had drawn black circles on each cheek. She was filling them in with yellow and creating an interesting marbled effect.

'Someone's got to do it, I suppose.'

Imogen was far too nice to be single, Jude decided. 'Yes, but they don't have to talk about it all night.' At least, looking on the bright side, she could now tell a suction hose from a no-nozzle output tube. It could be useful one day, but she doubted it. Her mother had always assured her that she and vacuum cleaners were not a match made in heaven.

'He didn't sweep you off your feet then?' Imo asked.

'Hardly.' Jude watched Daisy painting her lips bright yellow and silver. Her daughter's perfect elfin face was beginning to look like a luminous milky way. Rod had made it clear what he was looking for and Jude had made it clear that sex was not on the agenda. 'I like to get to know a man *really* well before I can relax with him,' she had told him. The poor man had probably wondered how many more dinners like this he'd have to sit through, how many more bottles of house red he would have to buy, before he got the cup of cocoa, so to speak. Never mind. Jude sighed. Someday her prince would come.

When you came to think about blind dating, she reflected after she and Imo had said goodbye, it was so unlikely, wasn't it, that you would meet a potential soul (or even bed) mate. There were a lot of clowns out there.

You could weed out the obvious horrors – like any man over thirty who lived with his mother, any man who had fathered more than three children, anyone who mentioned Kafka or Jung in their first letter/phone call, or anyone under five feet ten inches tall. But after that it was just a matter of luck.

Daisy waved the silver mascara wand that, after two blinks, deposited a constellation of starry freckles under each eye. Jude swiftly swept the ravaged make-up trolley out of reach. 'Let's start again, Dais,' she suggested.

When you were answering ads, you were one of many. Even if you did get to meet the man of your dreams, how would he recognise you with all those other hopefuls milling around? She plonked Daisy into the nearest chair and got to work with make-up remover and cotton wool.

'Are we going to do some face-painting, Mummy?' Daisy asked hopefully. 'What shall I be?'

'What do you want to be?' Jude chucked the cotton wool into the black bin with perfect aim. She would not join a dating agency to be catalogued, indexed, fixed up by someone un-single with a superior smile. And as for friends who had dinner parties and invited Jude and one conspicuous spare man – that was pure hell in a sitting-room.

'Anything?'

'Anything . . . within reason.' Jude arranged some colour palettes on the trolley beside her and pulled on a plastic apron to protect her mohair sweater and tartan mini-skirt from the fall-out of beauty.

Daisy was deep in thought, blue eyes troubled, fingers twiddling with a strand of her pale blonde hair. 'Mummy, what's your favourite animal?'

'A snow leopard.' She couldn't remember what they looked like. Only that she'd seen some at a zoo one time when she was holding hands (and later legs, but that was another story) with a rather tasty man called Michael who sadly turned out to have a wife, five children and a council house in Bognor Regis.

'Mine's a flamingo.' Daisy leapt up from the squidgy black chair, stood on one leg and folded her arms, hands and purple-varnished finger-nails behind her.

Oh, dear. Jude had no idea what flamingo faces were like – only that they were extremely pink. 'Tigers are nice and dramatic,' she said. 'And they roar very loudly.'

But why shouldn't *she* do the advertising? It wasn't dangerous – not these days, when you could use a box number or screen a tape. That way she would be the one doing the interviewing too. She could pay for a tape on *Heart to Heart*, ignore the messages that were in gorilla-speak or sounded dodgy, and interview the rest. Woman management . . . power . . .

A low tigerish rumble emerged from the black chair. Slowly, it gathered momentum. Jude grabbed some pale yellow foundation and began smearing it on to her daughter's eager, upturned face. Choice and control . . .

Chapter 5

'Bank statements,' Imogen said, rifling through the contents of the locked drawer. She'd put it off, scared of what she might find, not wanting to know any of his secrets. What was the point? Edward wasn't here any longer, was he, to defend or explain himself? Wasn't it better to keep her picture of him intact? It was bad enough not to have loved him as she should, it was bad enough to have lost him before she'd taken the chance to change anything about them. Without this. She dusted her hands on her jeans.

'Bank statements?' Vanessa sounded disappointed. She flicked a cobweb from the magnolia-painted wall and came to peer over Imogen's shoulder. She was wearing a simple blue dress, cut to show off her slim figure and falling to mid-calf, tights but no shoes. 'A separate account?' She scrutinised the figures through half-moon glasses. 'And a regular transfer of funds?' Over the bifocals, she looked at Imogen. 'Darling?'

Imo had already noted this, already placed a huge mental question mark. She pushed the whole pile of papers to one side. 'I'll ask about it at the bank sometime.' There was no hurry. Everyone knew the paperwork surrounding a death took an age to get sorted.

Vanessa reached over to give her a quick squeeze. 'But first you have to take a proper look at these. Forewarned is forearmed, darling.'

She was right. Again. Imo nodded, picked up one of the statements, absorbed the account number, name, the bank, the figures. A fairly large amount had been transferred elsewhere halfway through the month. She grabbed another. The same thing applied. What did it mean?

'It might not be what you think,' Vanessa said.

But Imogen wasn't sure what she thought. What did her mother think?

'But whatever it is, you have to deal with it.' Vanessa got to her feet and retrieved another piece of paper, still lodged in the drawer.

Imo could see that it was a photograph. She tensed.

'You must finalise all his affairs.' Her mother passed it to her. 'You owe it to yourself. And to him.'

To him? With impeccable timing, the doorbell rang, the knocker was crashed simultaneously against brass, and Hazel's voice rang out. 'Only me! Anyone at home?'

Vanessa touched Imo's hair. 'Buck up, darling.' She closed the study door behind her.

Imogen listened to their voices – Hazel talking too much in a semi-musical flow of long, unfinished sentences; her mother firm and monosyllabic. Only as many words as was necessary. Was that how it had been between Edward and Imogen too? Only as many words as was necessary?

Methodically, she sorted the bank statements into date order. For some reason it seemed important. And she had to *do* . . . She had to summon up all her strength. Jude was right. Her mother was right. She couldn't wallow guiltily in this empty cottage. Especially not now.

In time, when she had cleared this room, sold this furniture – the glass-fronted bookcase, the desk, the leather chair – she would redecorate, she decided. So what if they were antiques that had been in Edward's family for generations? What did that matter to her? She wanted – no, *needed* – change. And she needed it now. This room could be so different. It could be a spare bedroom, a place for her mother to stay when she was in the country. Imo liked the idea of having her firm, monosyllabic mother close to her from time to time. She was infuriating – but she had always been so strong.

Imogen picked up the photograph. Whatever his secrets, Life Without Edward was beckoning more urgently than ever.

In the sitting-room of the cottage, Vanessa and Hazel were tucking into lemon sponge cake as Imo came out to say hello. She felt dry, dusty and burned out.

'Imogen, dear.' Hazel – as pink and frothy in a pastel puff-sleeved jumper and A-line skirt as her mother was red-lipped and vital – got up to kiss her. 'You look tired. Are you sleeping properly?'

'What Imogen needs,' Vanessa declared, before she could reply, 'is for her life to get back to normal.'

Imo sank on to her cream sofa with a soft sigh. She had chosen the decor of this room – peaches and cream with a thick, oatmeal carpet and rich, russet curtains. Impractical, perhaps, but with no children, why shouldn't she be? She pulled up her knees like a child and regarded her mother. Normal? What was normal? She wasn't sure she knew any more. And as for children, she and Edward had discussed it, of course, but the time had never seemed right and they'd agreed to leave it for a while. To enjoy each other, as he had put it. Imogen repositioned a peach-and-cream-checked scatter cushion behind her head and leaned back, remembering only her feeling of relief. Sometimes she had looked at Daisy and Jude and wished things had been different. But mostly *Say It With Flowers* – begun with the money her father had left her – had been enough. And now . . . Thank God there were no children now.

'It'll take time for that to happen,' Hazel was saying in a tone steeped in experience and wisdom. She was sitting very upright in the cream armchair, as if afraid to give it her all. 'Time is a great healer.'

Vanessa passed the plate around and Imogen took a slice, more because Hazel looked as if she were warming up for a lecture about eating properly than because she was hungry.

'And time you had your house back to yourself.' Vanessa handed her a napkin and hooked her perfect dark bob behind one ear.

'Is it compulsory?' Imogen was only half serious. Her mother was a breath of fresh air. She had a knack for getting things right. In the summer she was the kind of person you longed to go out with for the day. She would arrive with goodies in hampers, chilled white wine, and a perfect picnic spot in mind.

'I shouldn't like to outstay my welcome,' Vanessa murmured, pouring more tea from the pot on the coffee table.

'Fat chance of that.' Imo put another cushion under her feet. She was never here long enough. Even in Imo's childhood, before her parents were divorced, she had been

54

aware of her mother's restlessness, her inability to sit still, her eagerness always to be out, always to be doing. And after her parents' divorce she had half-suspected her mother to be biding her time, impatiently waiting for her only daughter to fly the nest so that she could make good her own escape. Perhaps that was another reason for Imogen's marrying Edward – she had at least never worried that he would leave her. She remembered the photograph and winced at the irony. Perhaps it served her right.

'So I've booked a flight to India for next Wednesday,' Vanessa continued, sitting down again in the other armchair. 'There's a guru there I want to do a feature on. In Delhi.' She stirred her tea. 'So many senior citizens are doing yoga these days, it will strike a chord.'

'I'm sure it will.' Imogen liked the idea of all those senior citizens – complete presumably, with arthritis, rheumatism and dodgy anatomical bits – being urged into head and shoulder stands by Vanessa Vaughan and her guru. She nibbled at the icing on her cake. It was pointless to try and persuade her mother to stay. She had been here longer than usual as it was. She must be itching to move on.

'So as long as you can manage without me, darling . . .' Vanessa's blue eyes were concerned.

'What Imogen needs,' Hazel put in determinedly, 'is to find new interests. That's the way to take one's mind off one's troubles. And I should know,' she added.

'What would you suggest, Hazel?' Vanessa and Imogen exchanged a look, and for the zillionth time Imo wondered what on earth her mother and Hazel could possibly have in common.

'An evening class perhaps?' Hazel ventured. 'That dreadful thing they do at the Leisure Centre. What is it now?

Ah, bums and tums.' She squeezed her lips together in an expression of distaste. 'Or line dancing? That's all the rage.'

Vanessa laughed. 'Imo's got her hands full with *Say It With Flowers*,' she said. 'But what about you, Hazel?'

'Me?'

'It's high time you did something more with your life than baby-sitting.' Vanessa frowned. 'Now, what shall it be?'

'Heavens!' Hazel exclaimed with an extravagant wave of fluffy, pastel arms. 'I'm sure I'm far too busy to—'

'Amateur dramatics!' Vanessa clapped her hands in triumph. 'Perfect.' She put her cup down on the table and regarded Hazel quizzically. 'Either that or come with me to India.'

Imo choked on her tea. The thought of Hazel and headstands was much too much. She made a mental note to tell Jude. It was priceless.

Hazel returned home to find the first-floor flat empty and in darkness. But the lights were on in the salon so she went down to investigate.

There was nobody in the kitchenette, but as she opened the door to *The Goddess Without* a blood-curdling roar made her shriek in terror. Something on all fours – but humanish and vaguely familiar despite its yellow-and-black-striped face – leapt out of the black and chrome fitments towards her. Hazel took a step back and clung to the door handle. 'What in heaven's name . . . ?'

'Hello, Ma.' The yellow and black features materialised into those of her daughter. And she recognised the tartan mini-skirt.

Hazel closed her eyes and took a few deep breaths to

calm herself. Just as a similar – but much smaller – animal launched itself towards her with a horrible growl. This one wore acid-green leggings. 'Daisy . . .' She was sure her voice was shaking.

Jude held the smaller tiger at bay. 'We're scaring Granny,' she said. 'Hush, now.'

'But we're playing Hide and Roar,' the smaller figure objected. 'How can we do that if we can't roar?'

'Well, I'm all roared out.' Jude turned around and Hazel saw her jump as she caught sight of herself in one of the numerous mirrors.

She shook her head in despair. 'I don't know which of you is the most childish. All that yellow and black stuff is going to have to be scrubbed off tonight. And that won't be so much fun, you mark my words.'

'It's only face paint, Ma.' Jude rubbed experimentally. 'We won't need to scrub.'

'We were doing a show, Granny,' Daisy explained. 'Hide and Roar was the main game show.'

'A show, hmm?' Hazel smiled. 'Talking of shows, you'll never guess what a brilliant idea Vanessa came up with this afternoon.' She waited, but both tigers looked blank. 'I'll give you a clue.' She filled her lungs, sang, 'Laaa,' and threw her hands dramatically out in front of her.

Jude blinked. Daisy – not quite so tactful – put both fists to her ears.

'She told you to go the opera?' Jude asked.

'She told you she had a tummy ache?' This was from Daisy. Mother and daughter collapsed into tigerish giggles.

'Very amusing.' Hazel decided to leave them to their puerile goings on. Perhaps it was a good thing that Jude was so occupied with the salon; she wasn't always the best influence on Daisy – despite being her mother. 'I'm going to join an amateur dramatic society,' she said. 'And you'll both be wiping those horrid yellow smirks off your faces when you see me on the stage . . . Oh, yes, indeed you will.'

A new life, she thought to herself, as she let herself out. And who knew what would be waiting round the corner?

After Hazel had gone, Vanessa joined Imogen on the sofa in the sitting-room of the cottage. 'Do I take it that Edward might have been a more interesting man than I ever gave him credit for?' she asked, lifting her feet on to the soft fabric in a gesture that mirrored Imogen's.

That was one way of putting it. 'Perhaps,' Imo hedged. The photo was burning a hole in the pocket of her sweatshirt.

Vanessa let her hand rest for a moment on her daughter's arm. 'And you can cope with that?'

'Yes, I think so.' Couldn't she? It wasn't as if she had really loved him, was it?

'I'm glad. You know, marriage is never easy. Your father and I . . . Well, despite everything, we did love one another. For a while at least.'

Imogen knew. She watched as Vanessa got to her feet, straightened the scatter cushions on the sofa and chairs, pushed the russet curtains to one side to look into the night. It was pitch black outside. She'd heard the stories: that Vanessa had been caught trespassing, wandering across one of the Vaughan fields one day (*My best crop of barley*, Tom Vaughan had said), that she was lucky she hadn't been shot at, that she'd stayed to tea and ended up marrying the eldest son six months later. She knew that her mother had tried . . . *Up to my eyes in nappies and they didn't have disposable ones then, darling* . . . but had found herself unable to be a farmer's wife. She knew that they had loved one another still, and yet that her mother had taken a lover. She knew because she had crept down the stairs and seen them kissing one night when her father was away. Vanessa had left. She always left. Look at her now, she couldn't wait to be off.

Only when her mother had gone up to bed at last did Imogen take the photograph out of her pocket. She handled it gingerly, as if it might bite, not wanting to look properly at the face she'd so far only glanced at. Had she been too complacent about her own marriage, so satisfied with something that had never been more than second best? The comfort zone – that's what Jude called it. The tolerance that replaces love because it seems too hard to break away. Only what love was ever perfect?

She stared at the young girl pictured there, absorbed every detail of that face. And she wondered – oh, God, how she wondered.

Secrets . . .

Chapter 6

The next day, Vanessa Vaughan called Ralph. It was a relief simply to hear his voice. *Just good friends* was a phrase that couldn't begin to describe her relationship with Ralph Preston. No way. It didn't say the half of it.

'How's the little one bearing up?' he asked her.

She smiled. Little? At five feet ten? 'The little one, as you call her, has had a none-too-pleasant surprise.'

'You mean apart from the obvious?' His voice was as velvety as his eyes. He had always sounded romantic to Vanessa. Hot chocolate on the telephone line. She could listen to him for hours. Oh, yes . . . Ralph's voice had always had quite an effect on her.

'This is more of a revelation.' Should she tell him? Vanessa sat down on the small chair Imogen kept in the hall by the telephone table. She decided not. It was her daughter's secret, not hers. And rather a surprising one, she had to admit.

To his credit, Ralph didn't enquire further. 'How's she taken his death?'

'Badly.' It was never a good sign, Vanessa thought, when a girl like Imogen bottled up her emotions.

'Poor child.' Ralph sighed. 'So you'll be staying on for a while then, my love?'

Ah, if only she was. His love, that is. Though hopefully she was past all that now. Vanessa shifted in the chair. She might be feeling more tired than usual but the energy she still had to spare was mostly thrown into travelling, into dreaming up new schemes with which to hook her editors, into persuading those of 60-plus that brains and bodies did not have to deteriorate. Brains could acquire wisdom. And bodies . . . well, a spot of yoga could work wonders.

'I'd *like* to stay with her a little longer,' she told Ralph. 'You probably think I should. I *would* stay if she needed me to.' Of course she would. Even she was a mother . . . 'Though it's a bad time for me, I'm afraid.'

'So when are you leaving?' She could hear the smile in his voice. Being Ralph, he would never accuse her of maternal neglect. Being Ralph, he understood. And being Ralph, he got to hear the unembroidered truth.

'My flight's next Wednesday.' She inspected a burgundy finger-nail. Where she was going there would be no need for nail polish. 'There are things I have to do. Contracts to meet. Deadlines . . .' Her voice trailed off. 'You know how it is.'

'I certainly do.'

Yes, she could picture his smile. Vanessa held the receiver closer. The humour in those brown eyes . . . She'd first spotted it as she walked down the aisle on her father's arm towards Tom. She remembered what had gone through her mind. *God, who was that man looking at her as if he thought marriage was a joke? As if he thought her marriage was a joke?*

61

'Where are you off to this time?' he asked. She heard the rustle of a paper. Knowing Ralph, he had one ear on their conversation and both eyes on the *Telegraph*.

'Delhi.'

'A long way.'

Vanessa knew what he meant. 'Yes, but Imo's digging deep. She just needs to find some of that inner strength I've always said she has.'

'So your departure from the scene might even be a good thing.' As usual, he followed her train of thought perfectly.

'For Imo, yes.' Why not? Having a mother around – even one like her – would cramp Imogen's style, give her too much to lean on.

'Well, come to London as soon as you can. I have something to ask you. Something that needs to be said face to face.'

'Oh, yes?' Now what would that be? Vanessa chuckled. It was typical of the man to leave her hanging. But it would certainly be something to wonder about in Delhi.

'In the meantime, I shall look forward to reading the article. What will it be? "Discovering Delhi in a Wheelchair?"'

'Good idea. It would save the legs.'

He laughed. 'And give the little one my love.'

'I will.' Despite this weariness that she couldn't seem to shake off, Vanessa was smiling as she put down the phone. Love. What an all or nothing sort of a thing it was when you were young. Thank God it could slide into the background of your life as time went by. Thank God indeed for that.

LET ME PLAY FAIRY GODMOTHER TO YOUR FACE.

As a gust of wind caught her by surprise, Imogen pulled

her black, woollen coat around her more closely and stared through the Georgian panes at the sign in the window. Why not? She didn't know what Jude was up to but Imo could do with a touch of magic – especially now that her mother had flown off again. She walked in and couldn't help grinning at the spectacle in front of her. 'Is that it?'

Jude was alone in *The Goddess Without*, which was probably fortunate since she was staring into one of the many mirrors, tapping her face with the pads of the middle fingers of each hand. Sharp and light – as if she were testing the heat of an iron. 'Is what what?' She delivered a sharp slap to her lower jaw.

Ouch. Imogen winced. 'The fairy godmother bit.'

Jude shot her a brown-eyed glance of scorn. ''Course not.'

Imo wondered if it confused Jude every time she looked in a mirror. The colour transformations certainly confused *her*.

'Everyone forgets to exercise the face,' Jude went on, 'and it's dead important, Imo. Facial exercises get the circulation going. Wake up a tired skin. All that stuff.'

'A bit like cold water then.' She hung her coat on the hook by the door and slumped into the nearest black chair. It wasn't just her face that was tired. It was her imagination too. Since finding *her* – because in her mind, this was how she thought of the girl in the photograph – Imogen had not been idle.

She had talked to a couple of Edward's closest friends, a colleague at work, and to his brother who lived in Leicester. She had watched their faces for a hint, a look, a clue. She had sat in Edward's study, gone through the rest of his papers and pondered. She had made an appointment to see the bank manager – bank clerks were always so damned cagey about giving out information. She had gone to work as usual, tended the flowers as usual, served the customers, smiled, said 'Good morning', locked up, gone home to an empty cottage. And still everyone talked about everything taking time.

Imo brought the fist of her hand down hard on the arm of the chair. She didn't *have* time. She wanted to know *now*.

'What?'

'Oh . . . nothing.' Imogen let her gaze wander from the contortionist beside her, around the interior of the salon. *The Goddess Without*'s black and chrome was supposed to say 'No messages' according to Jude, blank canvas, anything goes, sort of thing. But today the make-up trolley was in the front of the salon, providing a promise of colour – from pots of eye powders, creams and gel, to tubes of lip gloss and face glitter. And there was more than a little colour in Jude's hair, Imogen noted. Still blonde today but six inches longer and sporting startling streaks of what she could only describe as geranium red.

'Cold water doesn't stop sagging,' Jude informed her. 'And it does nothing for lines.'

'Unless they retreat in shock.'

Jude clenched her fist, but not in anger; she was moving it in a circular motion just above the jaw line. 'Gum stimulation,' she said. 'For glowing gums.'

Imo decided she could live without glowing gums. She had come here to confide in Jude, to ask her advice. How do you find out a woman's identity from a photograph? Put up a wanted poster? *Has anyone seen this girl?* 'Sounds like something out of *Alien*,' she said.

Jude responded by opening her mouth as if about to give vent to a huge yawn, pulling in the sides to a perfect O, and gradually closing it.

'Mouth exercises?' Imo enquired.

'Mmm-phwah.'

'Sounds like you're rehearsing the perfect kiss.'

'And you sound like you've had a bad day.' Jude closed her eyes. 'What you need is my fairy godmother treatment.'

'Suppose you tell me about it?' She wasn't committing herself – yet.

'It's a facial.' Jude blinked her eyes open again. Ready to do battle, Imo thought. 'I've got half an hour to spare. And I want to run my new idea past you.'

'Well . . .'

'Half-price to you.'

'You're on.'

'Good.' Jude began assembling towels and oils, humming the tune of 'I'm Gonna Wash That Man Right Out of My Hair' as she did so. 'No work today?' she asked.

'Half-day closing.' Imogen leaned back in the chair.

'You're not going to give up the shop then? Now that Edward . . .' Jude's voice trailed off. Vigorously, she shook a bottle of oil.

'All the more reason to work,' Imo retorted crisply.

'Too right.' Jude removed the cap, wafted the bottle in front of her nose and pulled a face.

Imogen watched her in the mirror.

'If *I* didn't work, I'd go crazy.'

'Exactly.' Imo felt the heat on her face as Jude draped warm, sweet-smelling towels around her throat and head. At least work enabled you to forget. The black squidgy chair was soft and comfortable. Imo sank further into it. Photograph? What photograph?

Jude bent to light a candle. The fragrance was lavender – strong and sweet. Imo sniffed deeply.

'It's supposed to be stimulating,' Jude said.

'Work is?' In the mirror, Imo scanned the shelves opposite. Potions and promises . . .

'Lavender is.' Jude grabbed a chart from her facial and massage trolley and glanced at it briefly. 'I'm using peach kernel for your base. Nourishing and recuperative.'

Stimulating, nourishing, recuperative. What more could a girl want? Imo closed her eyes, only dimly aware of Jude's preparations – the mixing, the warming, the oiling of hands. Until she felt the fingertips begin their work. Soft and insinuating, gentle yet probing. 'So what's your idea?' she asked somewhat reluctantly.

'No more answering the personal ads.' Jude's voice seemed to be coming from far away as she smoothed her fingers over bumps and into crevices.

'You're giving up on men?' Imo was so surprised she almost sat bolt upright.

'Don't be silly.' Jude's fingers continued to stroke Imo's throat – upwards and out. 'If you want to acquire something, what do you do?'

'Go out and look for it?' *She* – tucked inside Imo's bag – came into mind. The tension was being massaged from her face, but her brain was still working overtime.

Jude's fingers become infinitesimally less tender. 'You advertise for it,' she said. 'And that's what I'm going to do – with your help of course.'

'My help?' Imo asked weakly. She would much rather relax back into the pleasures of the senses. Lavender and peach were in her nostrils, in her pores — hopefully unblocking all the clogged ones — and doing their recuperative bit at the same time.

'I'll be doing the advertising, the guys'll be queuing up, *I'll* interview *them*, and get to pick the best of the bunch. Elementary. Foolproof.'

Foolproof? 'You might have to go out with an awful lot of men,' Imo pointed out.

'Exactly.' Jude looked smug.

That wasn't quite what Imo had meant. But she was drifting, and Jude was droning on.

'It's all a matter of communicating,' she told her. 'Getting the message through to the right man.'

'Yes, but what's the message? And how do you recognise the right man?' Not that Imo really wanted to know. She was drugged. She was floating on the verge of an other-worldly experience. She didn't want to have to think — she wanted to forget. Thinking was Jude's bag. She could never be an ordinary anything and so she'd never be an ordinary beautician. She was probably the only one in the world who provided a homespun philosophy lecture along with your eyebrow tidy or shoulder massage.

'The message can be whatever you want it to be.' Jude seemed clear on this point and Imo wasn't about to disagree. 'It's like beauty.' She smoothed back Imogen's hairline.

'Beauty?' Imo was trapped inside her warm cocoon with the scent of lavender hanging in a haze, hot and heavy around her. Her mind was supposed to be cleansed of all thoughts. She was looking for release. OK, escape even.

Jude adjusted a towel. 'The beauty business is about finding the real me.'

'Me?'

67

'You.' Jude paused. 'And me.'

Imo regarded her in the mirror once more. She was wearing her usual black one-piece shift and her make-up was simple but stark – green eye liner with a streak of orange to the brow bone and a muddy sort of lip colour, carefully drawn. And then there was the hair. It was certainly true that Jude had made beauty individual, no losing the sense of self for her. And as for communication? Imogen smiled. She would shout her messages from the roof-tops and declare them in geranium red if necessary.

All too soon it was over and now Imo didn't want to escape at all. Her face tingled with a pleasant sort of sharpness – as if she'd just splashed cold water over it actually – but deeper. Clearly the oil had penetrated into her dermis just as Jude had promised. She was stripped bare.

Jude was examining her reflection with a critical eye. 'So what's up?' she demanded. 'This isn't just about Edward, is it?'

The photo was in Imo's bag. She could get great shock value by whipping it out, by telling Jude the story she'd invented in various forms over the past few days. And it was why she'd come here today. Jude had always been her partner in speculation. But now, Imo wasn't sure that she was ready to hear Jude's probably cynical views on the subject.

'I'm fine,' she heard herself saying instead. 'I feel loads better.' What else could she say? *Have you seen this woman?* And, *Why do you suppose Edward was transferring money from one bank account to one belonging to someone else? Every month . . .*

'Really?' Jude looked unconvinced.

'Really. How much do I owe you?' Money . . . She wouldn't think about the money.

'Forget half-price. Have it on the house.'

Did she look that bad? 'No way.' Imo grabbed her bag and dug inside for her purse. 'You've got a business to run, don't forget.'

Jude shrugged. 'And don't you forget you promised to help me with the wording of the ad.'

Had she? Imogen touched *her* – the photograph in her bag. She had to get to grips with this thing and fast. But it was scary. And most scary of all was the growing conviction that the man she'd married was actually someone quite different from the one she had always thought him to be.

Chapter 7

At *Say It With Flowers* Imogen slid open the large greenhouse
door. The location of the shop had seemed perfect when
she'd first viewed it with Edward eight years ago, particularly
because the property included a back plot on which she could
easily install two greenhouses. Imo had never wanted just to
sell flowers; she wanted to grow them too.

Edward wasn't over-enthusiastic about it, but for Imo it
was her chance to get away from a job that had become a
complete drag. And she felt in her bones that her father
would have approved of her spending his money this way.
Her mother certainly did – to Vanessa, *Say It With Flowers*
spelt independence for her daughter and she had lost no
time in telling her so.

Imo called out to her assistant. 'Tiffany!' Turning, she
was momentarily distracted by the sight of the neat rows
of hyacinth bulbs – opening out nicely, they would be
perfect for Christmas. Christmas . . . ? God, she pushed
the thought away.

'Yeah?' The voice came from the far section of the
greenhouse – obscured from view by a row of tall shrubs.

They needed a thorough clear out, Imo reminded herself. Could Tiffany be trusted to do it properly? Certainly it would have to be tackled before spring; from February she would need every inch she could find for the new cuttings. This was a far pleasanter thought – new growth, new beginnings, a whole new life . . . 'We're almost out of ivy. Can you bring some through?' What on earth was she up to in there?

As Imo moved forwards to investigate, Tiffany emerged from behind the wintering potted *leylandii*. There was one bright spot of red on each cheek – the second time in a week Imogen had caught her looking guilty.

'What is it?' Imo thrust her hands into the pockets of her indigo jeans. She'd discarded black since last Sunday; it no longer seemed appropriate somehow.

'What's what?' Defensive, too, Imo recognised the signs.

She sighed. 'Oh, nothing.' She hoped Tiffany hadn't been a mistake after all. Edward, of course, had disapproved of her . . .

'Will she give the right impression?' he had asked when Imogen first told him about the girl she was employing to help out on Saturdays and twice a week after school.

Imo had hated that. Right impression? What about what was underneath? 'Perhaps the wrong impression is valid too,' she had said, knowing she was being childish.

And that was Edward's cue to sigh. 'Honestly, Imogen, you think in riddles – it's a business you're running here, don't forget.'

Hah! As for riddles, she thought now, he could talk, couldn't he? Well, not at this precise moment in time obviously, but with all this photograph and bank statement business . . .

'Ivy?' Tiffany looked as blank as only a teenager could.

'With rings on her fingers and rings in her nose' came to mind.

'Yes.' Imogen decided against confrontation. The benefit of the doubt was something she strongly believed in. 'Ivy. Green-and-white variegated or sometimes just green. Pointy leaves, trailing, fast grower, people put it in pots and window boxes with pansies in the winter.'

'Yeah, right.' Tiffany disappeared again, muttering, 'I'm not totally stupid, y'know,' not even under her breath.

Was she right to say nothing? A sharp 'What's going on?' might just do the trick. Imo slid the greenhouse door to behind her, though it was so mild today she was tempted to leave it open. It was like that in the cottage too. She found herself wandering from room to room opening windows as if she had to clear every bit of air and start again. Ah, well. She knew Tiffany was more interested in money to buy make-up, studs and designer trainers than she was in flowers. But Imo didn't want to lose her. More than anything – particularly since finding that photo – she didn't want Edward, beyond the grave or wherever, to be proved right.

Imogen had employed Tiffany because she was curious about a girl who looked so innocent and yet was so clearly compelled to make some sort of statement. And because in her interview Tiffany had said, 'I like to watch things grow.'

That had struck a chord with Imo. She'd had her share of office jobs and admin but the truth was she too liked to watch things grow. A hobby had become a passion and a passion had led – after a year's training in floristry at the local agricultural college – to *Say It With Flowers*. What would Edward have had her do? Stick her inheritance money in a building society and work nine to five in a job she'd begun to hate?

Imogen had taken on Tiffany, body piercing and all. And so far she had not regretted it. Nevertheless, the girl had looked decidedly guilty in the greenhouse, she thought, as she re-entered the shop through the back door.

The one customer was a male browser, peering around in bemusement as if saying it with flowers was a language he'd never spoken in his life. Jude was right, Imo reflected, men rarely had any idea what they were looking for. But did Jude know what she was looking for? And how was Imogen going to help her write an ad designed to enable her to find it? Or him?

'Can I help?' He was in his twenties, she guessed. Tall, lean, and dressed in jeans and a leather bomber jacket; the kind of man they didn't see in here too often.

'Yes,' he said, shooting her an intent glance. 'I want some flowers.'

Imogen bit back a sarcastic retort. 'A mixed bunch?' She indicated some chrysanthemums, carnations and stocks – they might not last, but there was such a wonderful, heady scent from those stocks. 'A large spray?' She practically embraced the lilies – the most elegant of flowers and definitely her favourites – touched the irises whose petals were mauve velvet. 'A small arrangement?' She selected some yellow freesias.

'A small . . . ? Ah.' He smiled in understanding. His mouth was wide (Eat your heart out, Mick Jagger, Imo thought) and his eyes very blue. 'I see what you mean. Let me think now . . .'

Imogen shifted her position slightly. She knew the form – now she'd given him too much choice.

But: 'A few of those dark roses – hmm, almost purple, aren't they? – and some of this white stuff, I think.'

'Gypsophilia.'

'Some irises too.'

She moved her hand.

'No, just those dark ones.'

'Right.'

'Two of these lilies.'

Imogen selected them. She was beginning to think he had quite an eye for colour.

'Where d'you want the ivy, Imo? Out the front?' Tiffany sauntered back into the shop, armed with a tray of plants. She looked their customer up and down with some interest. 'Horny,' she mouthed at Imogen, eyes opening even wider than usual.

'Yes, outside, Tiffany, thank you.' Imogen glowered at her.

'And three white freesia stems to finish,' the customer proclaimed, as if he were ordering a five-course dinner.

'Very nice.' She wrapped the flowers carefully, named a price, he handed over the money and for a split second their eyes met. No, not their usual customer at all, she decided.

'Thanks.' He seemed about to say something more, but only nodded and was gone.

'Great bum,' Tiffany commented.

Imo watched his long-legged progress past the small shops, cafés and flint-fronted houses on South Street. It was rather. Looking away, she began rearranging cards on the stand that didn't need rearranging at all. 'I didn't notice,' she said.

'As if . . .' Tiffany joined her behind the till and nudged her with a bony elbow. 'He was blatantly giving you the eye, Imo.'

'Oh, rubbish.' Imogen put a hand to her face. Her skin

felt hot. The customer had been young enough to be of more interest to fifteen-year-old Tiffany than to Imo, who was over twice her age, she reminded herself sternly. And yet . . . the girl in the photo, *she*, could only have been a few years older than Tiffany. So young . . .

'Why not?' Tiffany draped herself decoratively over the counter. 'What're you like? You're a good-looking woman, you are – for your age, I mean. Great bones.'

Rattling bones, it felt like.

'Even Warren says he could quite fancy you.' She twiddled her eyebrow hoop.

'Goodness.' Imogen wasn't sure whether or not to feel flattered. Warren was Tiffany's boyfriend. He rode a motor bike, had long, greasy black hair and wore jeans in dire need of a good wash. According to Tiffany he was into leather in a big way (whatever that meant; it was probably safer for Imo not to know). 'Well, I don't have the faintest idea who he was,' she said, distancing herself from the thought of Warren and leather. 'But he was just a boy.'

'How old do they have to be?' Tiffany erupted into her dirty laugh. 'Looked blatantly old enough to me. Arty. Sexy. Well wicked, in fact.'

'If you say so.' Perhaps because she was ten years his junior, Imogen had always – until she'd found *her* – thought of herself as Edward's young girl.

'You didn't fancy him then?' Tiffany was disbelieving. 'Not even a bit?' She shook her head. It didn't seem to have occurred to her that Imogen's husband had only just left the land of the living. Life and the men you fancied clearly went on regardless. 'You must be crazy.'

Perhaps she was. Gently, Imogen reached out to touch the white freesias – like the ones he had chosen. They were pure as untrodden snow. Owning a florist's meant that a man would never dream of buying you flowers. Especially not practical, predictable Edward. Predictable? That was a joke. 'Of course I didn't fancy him.' Nevertheless, whoever the bouquet's recipient might be, Imo thought, that was one very lucky lady.

Alex let himself into the house with his key. 'Hiya,' he called, negotiating the narrow hallway and knocking on Sylvie's open kitchen door.

He went straight in because that was the way it was at Sylvie's — home from home. 'Happy birthday.' He thrust the flowers towards her surprised face.

Quite a nice spray, even if he said so himself; it had been a laugh to show the woman in the florist's (who clearly thought he'd never bought flowers in his life) that he knew what he was doing — at least as far as colour was concerned. An interesting-looking woman too. A kind of serenity about her . . . laughter, too, but hidden well under the surface, at least for now. He'd half wanted to stay and chat to her. But you didn't do that in shops, did you? Especially not here in the South. You handed over your money, took the goods and walked.

'You remembered.' Sylvie blushed to the roots of her tightly permed grey hair. She was what his mother would call a treasure — though in this case his mam wouldn't, actually. She would just wonder — and did, often and vocally — why the heck Alex was wasting his money living down South in lodgings, when he could be at home in Nottinghamshire with the rest of the family.

''Course I did.' He kissed her soft pouchy cheek.

'They're beautiful, Alex, lovie.' She sniffed the purple and white blooms. Behind her thick-framed glasses he thought he could see her eyes misting. When, he wondered, had he become her lovie? 'I'll get them in water right away.'

'You do that.' Alex watched her wipe her free and floury hand on the faded wraparound apron before she turned to bustle over to the old-fashioned stainless steel sink. He observed the wrinkled brown stockings and battered carpet slippers, and smiled. Sylvie was a good woman – and uncomplicated too. Since her own children had flown the nest, the most she wanted was to 'do' for a replacement. He could tell. Most women weren't like that any more, were they? They needed different things, more complicated things. They were more exciting, yes, but more exhausting too. He chuckled. According to Sylvie, most of the new breed couldn't even make custard – and weren't interested in learning either.

She ran the water till it was lukewarm, sprinkled some sugar into an old glass vase and picked the flowers up almost reverently. 'You're a good lad, you are.'

He would buy her a new vase for Christmas, he decided. 'Tell that to me mam.'

'Oh, I'm sure she knows already.' Sylvie nodded her grey head but still looked smug, bless her. She and his mam were two of a kind, Alex thought. If they were ever to meet they would be best friends or deadly enemies.

He wrinkled his nose. 'What're you baking?' Hopefully something good for his dinner. Because Sylvie, like his mam, wasn't just good at custard. She specialised in jam roly-polys and spotted dick puds that were straight from heaven.

'Just a birthday cake.' Sylvie was still fiddling away. She'd managed to all but destroy the rich velvet contrast of the purple and white flowers that the florist had created so effortlessly.

'For yourself? You should have let me buy you one from Marks.'

She sniffed. 'Thanks all the same, Alex, lovie, but no.'

He grabbed the bowl containing the mixture she'd been beating. 'Let's have a go, then. You shouldn't be making your own cake, you know, Sylv. It's bad luck. Let me finish it off.'

'Oh, Alex, honestly . . .'

But she wasn't really objecting. He knew she liked him to be here in her kitchen while she worked, to take the odd turn with the mixing and the wiping up, so long as she remained in charge. 'Who's this in aid of then?' No way would Sylvie bother to make a cake for herself. Perhaps her daughter was coming round? Alex began beating with the wooden spoon. Trixie by name and tricksy by nature – even Sylvie admitted she led her husband a merry dance.

Alex scooped the mixture from the sides of the bowl with the back of the spoon, as his mam always did. If Trixie was coming round, he'd go out with Marisa, he told himself. Deal. He should call her – they had a kind of open arrangement about tonight, but he was a bit *Should I, shouldn't I?* about the whole thing.

'Esther and Pammie.' At last Sylvie seemed satisfied with her efforts in the flower-arranging department. She stuck the mottled glass vase in the centre of the dresser, squashed between the big Toby jug and the brass donkey. Ah, well . . . 'They're coming round for a drink later,' she told him.

'Champagne, I hope?' Alex's thoughts were still centred on Marisa. He had never intended this thing to get . . . what? Serious? He could hardly accuse Marisa of that, just

78

because she had taken him to meet her mother. Naomi Gibb had proved to be a nice lady. They'd sat in the small lounge of Chestnut Close, sipping tea, and, yes, Naomi Gibb had brought some flowers home with her too. He could see her now, making small talk while she arranged them in a brown vase; could see Marisa's expression and the eyebrow raised while her mother's back was turned when Naomi had asked, 'And what do you do, Alex?' A bit of a mouse, Naomi Gibb, not at all what he had expected. But all right.

Sylvie, he realised, was watching him. Perhaps he had been beating a bit energetically. Or perhaps (again, like his mam – was it surprising he hadn't wanted to stay at home?) she was a mind-reader. But she only smiled. 'Champagne? Get on with you. It'll be a nice cup of tea and like it.'

'Anything else to go in?' He stopped beating. Perhaps he had never intended it to go on with Marisa. Once things went on they were harder to stop; a couple became an item to the rest of the world. There were expectations; someone would feel let down and hurt.

'No, that's the lot, lovie.' She pushed the greased cake tin towards him.

Alex began to dollop it in. It reminded him of childhood, of licking out the bowl, that sugary, fatty mix that had been so delicious. God knows why that should be. He frowned. And yet it might be – should be? – hard to give up a girl like Marisa. Sexy, beautiful, all frost on the outside and hot heady liqueur when you dug deep.

Sylvie took it from him and smoothed the top with a palette knife. 'So I was wondering . . .' She hesitated. 'And Pammie was asking if you'd be around, you see . . .'

'Tonight?' Alex grinned. Three old biddies or Marisa. What a choice.

'If you'd like to pop down – just for a few minutes.' She finished in a rush as she opened the oven door, her glasses steaming up from the heat.

Alex smeared some of the mixture on to his finger, but it didn't taste the way it had in childhood. What did? 'Sure I will.' He knew how much it meant to her. Anyway, it would give him time to look at a sketch he was working on, and to phone Richie later. Three good reasons . . . Besides, seeing Marisa meant complications and Alex didn't feel like any complications tonight. He felt like a generous slice of Sylvie's birthday cake and being fussed over. 'Did Pammie want anything particular?'

'Oh, don't tell her I said.' Sylvie glanced over her shoulder as if Pammie might be lurking on the other side of the custard-and-cream-coloured kitchen. 'But . . .' she turned back to squirt washing up liquid into her yellow plastic bowl '. . . I think she wants to book you for her grandson's seventh.'

Alex groaned. Seven-year-old boys were not the most receptive audience. But man could not live by art alone – well, this man couldn't – and the graphic design work promised by Richie had dried up lately.

'Don't you want the work, lovie?' Sylvie immediately looked concerned, and he regretted the groan. He had arrived in Chichester from London broke and dependent on Richie – the only person he knew around here – for part-time work that often didn't materialise. Sylvie's name (third in the lady-looking-for-lodger list obtained at Tourist Information) had come up, she had welcomed him with open arms and an iced chocolate sponge, and it was she who – on discovering that he had often entertained friends with his amateur juggling – came up with the idea of children's parties.

He had done a dozen already – combining juggling with balloon-animal making – for a selection of Sylvie's grandchildren and her friends' grandchildren. The list seemed never-ending; Sylvie must be doing a great job on publicity. And all this had apparently qualified him for the crème de la crème, namely the job of Father Christmas at Kirby's department store where Sylvie's daughter Trixie worked in lingerie. Alex grinned. So to speak.

''Course I do.' He flung an arm around her shoulders. 'I'm grateful.'

'But if you're too busy . . .'

Alex knew Sylvie well enough to recognise a reference to Marisa. He smiled. Twice last week he'd missed dinner. 'Doing what I shouldn't be doing?' he teased.

'Not at all.' Sylvie became almost prim as she rinsed her mixing bowl. 'I'm not your mother and it's none of my business.'

'Right.' He waited.

'But I have told you to feel free to bring her round.'

'Who would that be?' He was beginning to enjoy himself now.

Sylvie blushed. 'Your new girlfriend, of course.'

'Hmm. But Marisa . . .' How could he put this? 'Isn't a girlfriend exactly.'

But she only laughed and blew a soapsud in his general direction. 'Oh, I know you young lads, don't think I don't.' She finished the last pot and wiped her hands once more. 'A girl's got to be careful . . .'

Alex picked up the tea towel and started drying. If she were to meet Marisa she'd soon change her mind. Marisa was far too much in control to have to be told to be careful. Sylvie wouldn't take to her, he was sure of that much.

Neither would his mam. But the question was — had Alex taken to her? And why did he get the feeling he was being drawn — very carefully, very slowly — into a web that was very much of Marisa's weaving? He couldn't make her out. He wanted her. So why was he practically climbing the walls trying to get away from her?

Chapter 8

Independent . . . blonde . . . Which first? Jude sat back in the chair behind *The Goddess Without*'s reception desk and considered. Independence was most important to her, that went without saying. And hair colour could be found in a bottle, spray, mousse, or even a mascara wand these days. She cast a glance towards her colour and tint trolley. But was independence off-putting? Did it also say bolshie? She sighed. And so what if it did?

If it did, she reminded herself, her tape would remain conspicuously empty. First things first . . .

And then there was age. Absent-mindedly, she fiddled with the edge of one of her acrylic nails. You couldn't not say. But how specific did you have to be? She might feel young at heart on a good day, but apparently she was middle-aged in all the other places (and who could see her heart?).

Leaving her nail alone before a massive repair job became necessary, Jude took a sip of her coffee, pulled a pen out of the top pocket of her black shift and began to write. She compromised with, 'young, early-40s'.

The salon phone rang and she spoke to a client who was coming in that afternoon for an aromatherapy massage. They discussed the advantages of *The Energiser* (4 drops Tangerine to 4 drops Bergamot) over *All Systems Fortifier* (4 of Tea Tree to 2 of Lavender and Eucalyptus). Yes, she could decide on arrival. Yes, it was OK to be ten minutes late – Jude raised her eyes heavenwards – and yes, Jude might be able to fit in a rapid shampoo and blow dry afterwards. But she couldn't make any promises. She replaced the receiver. People were so selfish sometimes. It was a pity her appointments book had so many spaces, but times were hard and more women made the business of beauty a DIY job these days.

Now where was she? Cuddly or curvaceous? Jude reached for a cigarette, flicking her lighter and drawing the smoke into her lungs gratefully. Very different connotations. Comfort or sex. She frowned. Voluptuous was going too far, while generous build made her sound like an all-in female wrestler.

WLTM . . . who? She flicked ash in the glass ashtray on the desk. A knight in shining armour? All very well, she smiled, but would he be a control freak? A David Ginola lookalike? She exhaled with a sigh. Anything less than the real thing would be such a disappointment, and she doubted whether *he* needed to read the *Heart to Heart* personal ads in the *Chichester Echo*.

'Where are you, Imo?' She picked up the phone and dialled the number of *Say It With Flowers*. She couldn't do this alone.

'What are you looking for?' her friend asked. She sounded busy and distracted, as if Jude had caught her elbow-deep in liquid nitrogen or something.

'A good question.' She inhaled once again as she gave the matter more thought. 'I'm not crazy enough to expect a Mr Right.'

'You're not?' Imogen clearly didn't believe her – though whether about the crazy bit or the Mr Right bit, Jude wasn't sure.

'No. Mr Flawed-but-interesting will do. So long as he's got some sex appeal.'

'Ye . . . es.'

'But I don't want a slob,' Jude added. What she did not need were toe-nail clippings in the sitting-room. 'Nor anyone who shouts at me. I can't bear uptight, irritable men.' She stubbed her cigarette out with some feeling, thinking for some reason of her landlord, James Dean. 'And he's got to love me to bits – at first sight preferably.'

'You can hardly put all that in the ad. It'll cost you a fortune if you start rambling.'

Rambling? The cheek of the woman. 'How about WLTM someone to restore her faith in men?'

'A bit corny. And it sounds as if you've been dumped ten times in the last month.'

'Hmm.' Jude stretched out her legs. She'd been right to consult Imo; she had a fail-proof bullshit button. 'Size of parts relatively unimportant?'

Imogen giggled. 'Is that what you really, really want?'

A picture flashed into Jude's mind. 'On reflection, no. How about WLTM man to make her purr?' She put on her thirty-a-day sexy growl.

'Sounds a bit of a come on. You might get some perverts.'

'Sweetie, you *always* get perverts.' She laughed, but Imo became serious.

'Be careful, Jude,' she warned.

'I always am.' Jude shifted the telephone receiver to her other ear and glanced at the appointments book once again. How was she supposed to fill it? She did her best to drag 'em in and be sweetness and light while they were here, but all she got were clients like the acrylic nail extension refill due in . . . what? . . . five minutes. She was a pain. And always on time. Jude located her fresh air spray and depressed the push button to waft away any remaining cigarette smoke.

'Perhaps it's safer to say. "Spent last Saturday night reading Argos catalogue, this can't continue, urgent rescue required".' She broke off as her ten o'clock client opened the salon door.

'Oh, Jude.' Imo seemed to be taking a deep breath. 'Is it so awful to be on your own?' There was a silence.

Jude motioned the ten o'clock to remove her coat (brown suede, very nice, soft and classy) and sit down. ''Course not,' she said cheerfully. 'But I think it's high time you and I hit the town. Come round to the flat tonight. We'll finalise the wording of this ad and discuss tactics.'

'You're on.'

Jude knew Imo almost as well as she knew herself and realised she was trying too hard to sound cheerful. Ergo, she needed a friend. 'As early as you like,' she said. 'I've got a client. Must dash.' Onward to the land of acrylic nail extensions and penetrating pinnacle cream. Heigh ho.

Imogen put down the phone. It would do her good to go out. It might stop her brooding about Edward and photographs, secret lives and other women.

Mondays were quiet at *Say It With Flowers* and she was just wondering about tackling the late pruning out back when Warren sauntered in.

'Oh, it's you.' For some irrational reason, a streak of fear shifted across her shoulders and settled on her spine.

'Tiffaround?' he demanded.

'What?' Imo blinked. It was hard to imagine that he'd said he could fancy her. Quite worrying too.

His expression mellowed into irritated patience. 'Tiff. Is she around, like?'

'Oh.' Imogen regained control. 'No, Warren, she's not. She'll be at school, won't she?' Tiffany was only fifteen, though going on twenty. Imo tidied away some cellophane from the counter, hoping he would take the hint and leave.

'School?' His mouth (did he ever clean those teeth? she wondered) twisted into a nicotine-coated sneer. 'Oh, yeah, like yeah. At school, yeah. As if . . .'

Very intelligible. She took a cloth from the sink behind her and wiped away the debris of leaves and faint traces of sap from the last bouquet she'd wrapped.

Warren remained where he was. 'She didn't leave nothing for me then?'

Didn't leave nothing? Did leave something? Imogen was tempted to say that she was not a messenger service. But something in his expression as she shook the cloth into the bin and glanced up made her think better of it. Of course she wasn't *scared* of him – though she wouldn't like to meet him on a dark night when she was wearing her leather coat.

She gave a cursory glance under the counter to satisfy him. 'No. Nothing.'

'Sure?'

87

'Absolutely.' It had become a battle of wills that Imogen had no intention of losing.

'So what time's the tartduin?'

'What time's what?' Imogen couldn't help feeling relieved as a customer opened the door and strolled in. Hair a little long, leather jacket (but thankfully not with metal studs and silver-stitched New-Age-witchy diagrams like Warren's), jeans, big smile. Him again. Did he need more flowers already?

The man hesitated on the threshold, seeming unsure.

Imogen didn't want him to walk straight out again and leave her alone with Warren, so she leaned on the counter and beamed at him. 'Hi!' she trilled. 'Don't go away. I'll be with you in a moment.'

The man frowned at her. 'OK.'

Imo turned her attention back to Warren. He was little more than a boy. There was certainly nothing for a woman of the world (though Imo wasn't sure she really was one of those) to be afraid of in him. 'What time's what?' she repeated very slowly.

'The tart due in. Tiff.'

It wasn't exactly an insult; she'd heard enough teen-speak to at least know that. 'A quarter to four.' She moved to the other side of the counter to make it clear their conversation was at an end. 'Excuse me, please.' And if he started hanging around when Tiffany was supposed to be working, she would have words, she really would. It was coming up to her busiest time – bar Mother's Day and Valentine's – but there would always be other assistants she could find. She just had to make it plain to Tiffany that work was work and Warren wasn't welcome there.

'I'll be back,' he snarled as if she'd said all this out loud.

'Fine.' But it wasn't. Imogen felt under threat and paranoid. She certainly would go round to Jude's tonight, she decided. She needed to regain some perspective. And perhaps her friend was right. Perhaps she also needed a good night out.

Jude turned her attention to the jagged broken nails of her ten o'clock appointment. She was a stunning girl in her late-teens or early-twenties perhaps, with strawberry-blonde hair, long, curling dark eyelashes – both natural – and clear ivory skin.

Being in the beauty business, Jude – who had never had any of these natural accoutrements – could only admire. But unlike some clients to whom the intimacy of the salon was like a confessional box, this girl was a closed book. She never talked about herself. She did, however, put her hands, palms down, on the black imitation leather of the manicure cushion.

Jude tutted as she pulled the trolley closer and locked the wheels. Many clients came to her for nail extensions because they were fed up with ugly, bitten nails. But not many bit the acrylic ones. 'Been under a lot of stress?' she asked her, plugging in her tools. It took so much time when you had to reshape the tips as well as infill and build the base. She should charge extra really, but she couldn't afford to risk losing the business.

'Not 'specially.'

Cool as cucumber in an iced Florida cocktail, Jude thought, going to work with the cuticle clippers. 'How's it going then?'

'All right.'

'Good.' This would be a long job, an hour at least. Plenty

of time to chat. And yet after six months Jude still knew zilch about this girl. And wasn't it every woman's duty to confide in her beautician? So she took a deep breath. 'What do you do, by the way?' Hard manual labour, judging by the state of these. Very carefully, she began creating a fine dust on the nail surface with the arbor band.

'I model.'

The arrogance was in the understatement. Jude should have guessed. And no wonder the girl had her nails done – they were her only blemish. 'Really? That sounds terribly glamorous.' Jude motioned to her to bend her fingers slightly. Uptight or what?

The girl was staring down at her nails. 'It isn't,' she stated. 'It's incredibly draining.'

That was an improvement. She might even be human. Jude switched her attention to the other hand. 'Do you do photo shoots?' She'd bet that this girl was good at her job. Few of her clients were so expert at keeping still.

'And life modelling for artists.' She lowered the green eyes.

Artists, hmmm? Jude paused to glance across at her. She quite fancied the idea of an artist. Laid-back, expressing all that sexy, creative energy. She could see it now . . . She stuck on the first nail form . . . Someone with a beard and a wonderful bone structure flinging his arms around and being creative all over the place. He would paint her and discover the beautiful woman underneath the superficial gloss, the original vulnerable vamp just waiting to get out from under her black-corseted body stocking.

Nail forms numbers two and three. This girl was the only client who needed all ten tips redoing every single fortnight. But Jude had found out more about her this morning than she had in the previous six months, and decided to persevere. She started on the other hand. 'Married, are you?' Last nail form, all present and correct.

'No.' The girl didn't bite – only watched as Jude began to apply the primer coat.

'Can't say I blame you. Men . . .' Jude finished priming and selected a fine art brush for the acrylic cementing. 'Are they worth it? I ask you.'

Out of the corner of her eye she saw a lip curl. Jeronimo!

'It depends what you want them for.'

Ah. And what did this girl want them for? Money? The right arm at the right party? 'It must be a biological urge or something,' Jude said as she began reshaping and forming the acrylic into consummate shapes and square tips. She'd had this conversation with herself (and Imo) many times; she didn't particularly need any response and temporarily forgot her mission of achieving client confidences from Miss Tight-arsed ten o'clock. 'I mean, we know they're not good for us, we know they're just children who look a bit more grown up than the other kind, we know they can't respond to us on the emotional level we need them to. So why do we bother?' She looked at her client. Over to her.

The girl shrugged. 'You tell me.'

Jude would. 'Because we want that dizzy feeling again, that's why . . .' She waved the brush at the girl sitting opposite her – even her eyebrows were perfectly plucked, she realised – before dipping it into the powder. 'We want the excitement, the feeling that we're in love, the adrenaline rushing around all our bits. We want to believe someone loves us, would die for us even . . . we want to be thrown on to a draining board in the name of passion occasionally.'

Jude sighed. 'Of course none of it's true, but we need to believe it could be.' At last she came to a halt. The emotional temperature on the other side of the manicure trolley was sub-zero. 'Don't you ever get excited about anything?' Jude asked curiously. She was cold as cut glass, this one.

'I like sex.'

Jude's eyes widened as she concentrated on reshaping with the arbor band. So, she liked sex. On her own terms, no doubt. Had she ever been taken for granted on a shag-pile rug? Been laid on a dining-room table? Probably not. But then neither had Jude – she was always worried the table (or the man) wouldn't be strong enough to take her anywhere, let alone into ecstasy . . . 'You've got a boyfriend?'

'Of course.'

The diamond point was intended to seal in the sides and smooth the top of the nail. Jude could think of other uses for it . . . *Of course.* 'You're much too young to get serious though, I suppose?' Who was she kidding? There was no such thing as an age at which it was too young to get serious. Jude knew. She had been the original ugly duckling. She would have got serious at twelve if someone had asked her to.

'I haven't decided on my next move yet,' her client said.

Jude went to work with the baby oil. What could she say to that? Only that she wouldn't like to get in Miss Ten o'clock's way when she did.

'I was thinking of a hyacinth,' Alex said. That sounded bloody daft for a start. No wonder the woman (why had she smiled at him like that? Could it be a case of mistaken identity?) now looked surprised-with-a-hint-of-frost. Who could blame her? He sounded like a prat, and what's more he had never thought of a hyacinth in his life. What would he do with a hyacinth, for God's sake? What was he doing in here?

'Colour?' Eyes of grey. Still-warm ash. She was waiting.

'Sorry?'

She folded her arms. He thought he saw a hint of a smile pulling at her mouth, but maybe not. She was serene and she was also beautiful. 'What colour hyacinth?'

'There's a choice then?' It seemed like a game, a kind of batting about of colours and plants. A new language. Say it with flowers. Inwardly, he chuckled.

'There's always a choice.'

For a moment Alex wondered if she were teasing, but he dismissed this thought almost immediately. She wasn't the type, he sensed, to tease a stranger. She held herself in, kept something back, presented only her smooth exterior to the world. And sure enough her expansive wave of the hand indicated a display of baskets and pots opposite the counter of the shop, all containing green stubby shooting things with various additions.

'Delft Blue, City of Haarlem . . .' she smiled '. . . that's yellow to you. Anna Marie – pink – or Ben Nevis – ivory.'

'Right.'

'They come with moss, grass seed, with moss and ivy or all alone.' She seemed to be enjoying herself.

'Mind-boggling.' Once again he wondered why he had come here. Five minutes ago he'd been eating a sandwich in the Bishop's Palace Garden, walking around to keep warm. His gaze had shifted from the Cathedral tower and spire to the conifers and white winter pansies of the garden, and he had thought of her – the woman in the flower shop with the calm grey eyes and hesitant smile.

He hadn't been able to remember if she was wearing a wedding ring.

Five minutes later here he was, wondering how the hell one might *Say It With Flowers*. And what he could buy to say it with.

At last she laughed – at him probably. 'They'll be in flower in time for Christmas, I hope.'

'You grow them yourself then?' Alex wanted to prolong this conversation, not because of a passionate interest in hyacinths, but in the hope of another radiant smile.

With a finger-nail, she forked the sandy earth alongside a bulb growing moss-less, grass-less and alone.

No ring, he noted. But he thought he could detect an indentation on the third finger of her left hand. Artists were trained to notice such things.

'I do most of it myself. With a little help from Tiffany.'

Yes, he remembered Tiffany. All bleached hair, black make-up and punctures. He came across a lot of Tiffanys at the college. They were bold, strung up and confrontational, those girls. They also made him feel ancient. 'This your place then, is it?' he asked the seemingly thawing woman. It wasn't a huge shop but every square metre was in use. Behind the hyacinths was a selection of pots, bowls and plant paraphernalia. In front were the tubs holding the flowers and greenery from which he'd selected Sylvie's bouquet. Mistletoe and holly hung from the walls, pots of ivy, pansies, white jasmine and other winter-flowering plants no doubt drew her customers inside. On the other side of the narrow shop was the long counter, the gift cards and open books displaying various styles of wreaths, arrangements and bouquets. At the back of the shop was a door. There must

be a lot more space out there, he thought, if she grew and
cultivated some of the stock.

Her eyes grew wary.

Big mistake, Alex realised, to lunge in with a personal
question like that. End of thaw. Normal service resumed.

'It is,' she said. 'And although I don't want to hurry
you . . .'

Clearly, she did. He sighed.

'I have a load of holly wreaths to get on with. So . . . ?'

'Yes, of course.' Holly wreaths would be much in
demand. Christmas – like holly – was a pain in the arse
and the second shift of *Père Noël* at Kirby's was looming on
Alex's horizon like a bailiff at the front door. He picked up
the Ben Nevis with moss and ivy. *Père Noël* meant humiliation
in large doses. 'I'll have this one,' he said.

'A wise choice.'

Not sure if she was being sarcastic, he groped in his pocket
and handed her the money, but she didn't – or wouldn't –
look at him this time.

'I'll be seeing you,' he said.

'Yes, I'm sure.' But she was vague and distracted; she
didn't seem sure at all. 'And . . . thanks.'

What was she thanking him for? Alex decided not to
ask, not to wonder – though it might be something to
do with the young bloke who'd been in here earlier. But
that was her affair. Christ, his life was way too complicated
already. Tonight Alex would see Richie (sweet simplicity,
a jar down the pub, thank God for mates) and tomorrow
Marisa. Another thing entirely.

He stomped out of the shop, hyacinth in hand. It was in
a white china pot – so at least she wasn't a plastic person.
Brown plastic and he would've chucked it in the nearest

bin. But as it was . . . look on the bright side, he'd started his Christmas shopping earlier than usual.

But for now it was back to Kirby's. No time for flowers, nor for women with eyes of grey. Forget it, boy, he told himself, not even sure what he was contemplating. She was probably married with four kids. She must be ten years older than him. And? And what was he thinking of, for God's sake? Forget it? He hadn't thought of it in the first place. Anything. At least . . . he hot-footed it down South Street towards the Pallants and Kirby's . . . at least, only in passing.

Chapter 9

Jude regarded Florrie with some concern. Her fragile frame was wrapped in an enormous brown fur coat that looked as if it might have survived at least one world war. It made her seem smaller and more vulnerable than ever. 'You're cold,' she said accusingly. Outside it was bitter, and here inside Florrie's flat there wasn't much of an improvement.

'Perhaps I should get out more,' the old lady said vaguely. 'Otherwise you don't feel the benefit when you come in, do you? Only the stairs . . .' Her voice trailed.

'You'd feel the benefit if our dear landlord installed a central heating system that hadn't been around since the Dark Ages,' Jude retorted. She stalked over to the one and only radiator in Florrie's cluttered sitting-room, and felt it. Barely warm. 'Where's your thermostat? Can't we turn up the temperature?'

'It's a bit temperamental.' Florrie slipped the coat from her shoulders. 'I'm fine, dear, really I am.'

Jude wasn't so sure. And why should Florrie freeze half to death while James Dean luxuriated in some centrally heated mansion somewhere? It was a landlord's responsibility to

97

look after his tenants – however little rent they were paying.

'I'm going to have it out with him,' she said. 'Suggest he does something about the heating in this place.'

Florrie looked shocked. 'Oh, I wouldn't do that,' she said.

'Why ever not?' Jude's eyes narrowed. 'I'm not scared of him, Florrie, and neither should you be.'

'Scared?' But Jude noted she didn't deny it.

'I've spoken to the Social Service advice centre and the Citizens' Advice.' Jude patted thin bony hands. 'And there's no way he can get you out. You've got rights, Florrie. You don't have to go anywhere.'

Florrie looked distinctly uneasy. She put a hand to her white hair, seemed about to speak and then stopped herself. 'That's nice, dear,' she said at last.

Jude sighed. Didn't she understand? Didn't she realise that she didn't have to be bullied – any more than she had to be cold? Poor Florrie really had no idea and James Dean had a lot to answer for.

Downstairs, Jude put Daisy to bed and read her her favourite story about an owl mummy who left her babies all alone one night. The poor loves went through various stages of sleeplessness, hunger, neglect and rising panic, before at last she returned – with food, note – to be rewarded by Bill the youngest owl's avowal: *I love my mummy*.

'Why is that your favourite story, Daisy?' Jude pulled down the blind, trying to sound casual. There were brown owls on the blind, tawny owls on the wallpaper frieze, barn owls on the calendar, and a blown-up picture of her favourite Beanie Baby owl on the wall. Daisy liked owls.

98

'Bill's like me, Mummy, that's why.'

'In what way?' They were both neglected children? Their mummies made a habit of leaving them?

'Because he's an owl.'

'Mmm?'

Daisy treated her to the usual smile of sympathy when Jude was being slow on the uptake. 'And so am I,' she whispered.

'Oh, I see.' It was a measure of Jude's ever-ready guilt programming that this option seemed preferable to her own. She kissed her owl-daughter. 'And how long has this been going on?'

'Ever since I was born.' Daisy's eyes blinked wider. Almost owl-like, you might say. 'So I was thinking . . .'

'Hmm?' Jude tucked her in. There was an owl on the duvet cover too, along with Winnie the Pooh, Kanga and others.

'Owls stay awake in the night-time. All night. And I'm not a bit tired. So can I . . . ?'

'No.' Suckered again. Jude shook her head in despair. 'It's almost nine o'clock, and this young owl needs her beauty sleep. Trust me.' She switched out the light so that only Daisy's night lamp was burning. 'I know.'

Once Daisy had been persuaded to be a daytime owl, Jude got down to an express tidy-up. There were three smallish bedrooms (the main attraction of the flat for Jude initially) and apart from the kitchen, a tiny bathroom and a sitting-room just big enough for two small sofas and an easy chair squashed too close to the TV. The layout was rather different from Florrie's flat upstairs, Jude reflected. She reckoned someone, once upon a time, had taken the two large original rooms and made them into the four small ones that suited Jude so well. They might not have space, but at least they had privacy.

As she began shovelling toy animals, dressing-up clothes, marbles and sticklebricks into Daisy's stack of toy boxes, she noted that her mother hadn't vacuumed today.

That made two days in a row. Jude carefully picked up a three-dimensional object made of Lego from the sitting-room floor and deposited it just inside Daisy's open bedroom door. Hazel was as flat-proud as Jude was not. And Jude was *accustomed* to her mother doing the vacuuming – in the half-hour slot, otherwise known as the news, between *Watch This Space* and *Streetlife*. However something unusual had happened to the TV tonight. It was switched off. Jude stared at the blank screen. What was going on? She had her suspicions but could they possibly be true?

With half an hour before Imo was due to arrive, Jude changed into an orange ribbed polo-neck and loose lounging trousers and dialled the number on the card James Dean had given her. She was quite looking forward to this.

He answered in his clipped, no-nonsense voice and she launched straight in.

'About the upstairs flat – the heating's knackered and poor Florrie'll get hypothermia if you don't do something about it.' She tapped her nails sharply on the kitchen counter. Don't give him a chance to prevaricate, that was the way.

'Does she want me to come and take a look at it for her?' he asked. Grudgingly, Jude conceded that he did sound concerned. 'Perhaps there's an air block.'

'A new central heating system would be more efficient,' she said. 'That boiler belongs in a museum, if you ask me.'

He laughed, damn him. All right for him, Jude thought, he didn't have to live there.

'Have you asked Florrie what she thinks about that?' he asked.

'Florrie wouldn't say boo to a goose,' Jude snapped. She'd never get Florrie to complain — she was far too scared of him.

He sighed. 'Whereas you, Miss Lomax—'

'I am not a little old lady.' Jude lit a cigarette and inhaled deeply. 'And I'm not afraid of speaking out.'

James Dean muttered something that sounded like, 'You can say that again.'

'What?'

'I'll talk to her about it,' he said. 'If she'd like a new central heating system, then I'll phone a plumber. Satisfied, Miss Lomax?'

But for some reason, Jude did not feel satisfied. She felt put out. 'When Florrie can keep warm in her own flat,' she said, stubbing out the cigarette, 'that's when I'll be satisfied, Mr Dean.'

Imo arrived on time, carrying her blue-and-green-fringed hippy shoulder bag and a bottle of red wine. Under her coat she was wearing her usual blue jeans and a long, velvety shirt in deep aubergine.

'Good girl.' Jude kissed her and took charge of the wine. Pale, eyes a little red, but otherwise OK, she noted. 'Let me get you a glass.'

'Mmm, thanks.' Imogen frowned. 'What's that noise?'

Jude pulled a face. 'Ma singing in the shower.' This was also new.

'Frank Sinatra?' Imogen took the glass of wine Jude handed to her. '"My Way"?'

'Probably. And it's not a pleasant way to live with, I can tell you that.' Jude put a soft blues CD on the player in the sitting-room. 'And talking of doing things her way . . .' She practically pulled Imogen on to the largest of the two sofas. 'I suspect that my mother,' she whispered, 'has got it bad.'

From the direction of the bathroom, the sound of 'My Way' shifting seamlessly (were the tunes really so similar, Jude wondered) into 'Somethin' Stoopid' could be heard despite the bluesy sound now coming from the speakers.

'What's she got? An obsession with Ole Blue Eyes?' Imogen put her glass down on the floor and tucked her long legs under her on the sofa.

'Worse than that.' Jude rolled her eyes. 'You've heard of *Saturday Night Fever*? Well, this . . .' she paused for emphasis . . . 'is am dram fever, sweetie.' One minute her mother's idea of a perfect evening was the consumption of a Walnut Whip, a cup of milky coffee and plenty of CCC (comforting, constant companion; the TV was bright and chatty but *never* talked back). And the next? She was wandering around the flat, arms akimbo, learning lines, making plans, a future star in the making of *Mikado* or *Carmen* or something. And all the time, she was singing.

Imogen was looking decidedly shifty. 'She joined then?' And as Jude leaned closer, 'I'm afraid Mother suggested it.'

Vanessa . . . she might have known. But Jude couldn't blame her. Hadn't she herself said that her mother should have new interests? Hadn't she bemoaned TV compulsive obsessional neurosis? Hadn't she wanted a revitalised parent – albeit one who would still be around for baby-sitting?

'It was that or go to India,' Imo added.

Now there was a thought.

They both looked up as Hazel wafted into the room. She was dressed in a powder-blue kimono and singing 'You Make Me Feel So Young'.

Imogen and Jude exchanged a glance of perfect understanding. '*Who* does?' Imo whispered.

That was precisely the question Jude had been asking herself. And last night she thought she might have discovered the answer. It was about five feet four inches tall, had brown eyes rather than blue, and was Italian. It had given her mother a lift home but not come in for coffee.

'Imogen dear, how lovely to see you . . .'

Jude frowned. Was that an Italian accent? She stared at the lipstick her mother was wearing. It was vivid fuschia – she could hardly believe it. And was that a new silk scarf flung artistically over one shoulder of a powder-blue number? Her mother was undergoing a complete body image and personality change. How could Jude hope to keep up?

'Are you going somewhere nice?' Imogen asked politely.

Out? Surely she wasn't going out in that kimono thing? Jude shuddered.

'You could say that.'

Now she was looking mysterious again. Jude clenched her teeth. She was *trying* to be patient but she was in danger of becoming a serial toothgrinder.

'Just a little meeting. A sort of pre-rehearsal.' Hazel made it sound vaguely naughty. 'Don't wait up.' And off she went with a wave and, oh, God, a wiggle.

Jude refilled their glasses. Her mother was enough to turn anyone to drink. 'My ma—'

'Has found fulfilment in the world of am dram?'

'Well, she's certainly found something. And I think its name is Giorgio.'

'Isn't that a perfume?'

'If it is, it's plump, balding, and drives a red Ferrari.' Jude gulped her wine. 'A touch pretentious, wouldn't you say?'

Imo's whistle was decidedly unladylike. 'So who exactly is Giorgio?'

'One of the chaps from Trident – the am dram lot,' Jude admitted glumly.

Imo's eyes widened. 'Is it love?'

Jude considered this. Was it possible at her mother's age? 'I'm afraid it might be.'

They sat in a shared stunned silence.

'Good for Hazel,' Imogen said at last, sounding a bit dubious.

'It isn't that I mind her finding love . . .' Though Jude wasn't sure if this was really true. 'I mean, why shouldn't she?' (Because it wasn't fair? Because it was *her* turn?) 'But wouldn't it be ironic . . .' Jude could hardly bear to voice this, '. . . while I'm working my socks off to get a man, *Heart to Heart*, blind dating, computer love, you name it . . .'

Imo only nodded.

'. . . my darling mother scores instantly at the am dram society at the age of seventy. I mean, honestly, Imo. It's hardly what you'd call playing the game, now is it?'

Imogen pulled a notebook out of her bag and groped for a pen. 'Let's do it then,' she said. 'Let's create you the perfect ad.' She squeezed Jude's shoulder. 'Let's find you the man of your dreams.'

Chapter 10

Richie came back from the bar of the Three Jolly Brewers with two pints of foaming Best. 'What's up, mate?' he asked.

'Up?'

'You seem a bit down.'

'Down?' Alex stared into the middle distance behind him. This wasn't a bad place, but it was a man's place. The lighting was gloomy rather than atmospheric, highlighting nicotine-stained windows, curtains and lampshades, beer-stained tables and bar. The furniture – wooden tables, chairs and benches with hard red plastic seating – was basic, the old-fashioned glass ashtrays rarely emptied. But the beer was something else. 'Down?' he repeated. Sounded like a frigging carousel.

He liked Richie, but how much did he want to confide in him? How much did he want to confide in anyone? Alex decided to play safe. 'It's this Father Christmas caper.' He knew that even the way he talked was different with Richie. Men were different with men. They weren't supposed to brood about stuff like emotions and women and the future.

Men were men. Different languages for different people. Say it with flowers . . .

'Right, Father Christmas. How's it going? Mr Jolly, eh? Got your sleigh working yet?' Alex received the first nudge of the night. 'Is your beard nice and tickly, mate? Got all those little girls sitting on yer knee?' Slap of said knee. It was pointless, Alex realised, to tell him that these days there were strict rules about touching. None, period.

'Or do you ask their gorgeous young mothers to have a go?'

'Yeah, yeah . . .'

'I bet they love it. I bet they say: What have you got under that red cloak, Santa? Don't they, eh?' He burst into song. '"Big boy in red . . . is horny for me . . ."'

Alex waited patiently. It took Richie five minutes to use up all his Father Christmas jokes while Alex continued to enjoy his pint.

'Finished?'

Richie's expression approached something resembling sympathy. 'Can't you get yourself the sack, mate?' He grinned. 'Oops, sorry, no pun intended.'

'I need the money.' Alex glared at him. 'Because you don't find me enough work – mate.'

But he knew it wasn't Richie's fault. He was an OK sort of guy, though better before two pints than after. He didn't duck his round, he was a laugh – sometimes – and he was available at short notice. They'd had a lot in common once . . . when Alex had been heavily into computers too, when he and Richie had smoked the early hours away together. Before Richie got married to a conventional woman and a nine-to-five job. Alex supped his beer. But that was what people did.

'If you wanted to come full-time, Alex,' his friend said now, 'no problem, mate. But freelance stuff . . .' He shrugged. 'There's not a lot around. And everything slows up in December, you know it does.'

'Apart from the rate at which money seems to leave my pocket, yeah.' But Alex knew Richie would help if he could. It wasn't his fault this artist wasn't selling, that exhibitions were thin on the ground – and had to be paid for – that the college was wondering if they could afford an artist in part-time residence any more.

'I know.' Richie gnawed at the skin around his thumb nail. 'It's that time of year, innit? Beth's getting a coffee percolator.'

'What?'

'For Christmas. From yours truly.'

Alex leaned over the beer-stained table towards him. 'Bloody hell, Richie.' Were things *that* bad between him and his wife?

'It's what happens after ten years of marriage, me old mate.' Richie picked up his glass. 'You don't know about such things.' He stared into its murky depths. 'Lucky you.'

'About coffee percolators?' Alex never wanted to get to that stage. And once it would have been unthinkable for Richie too.

'About what keeps you together after ten years. The material things you share. Stuff like mortgages, pensions, joint bank accounts.' Richie was becoming maudlin. He was supping his beer as if it were the last one he'd ever get down him. 'Until you get to the crucial point—'

'Which is?' Though Alex wasn't sure he should even ask.

A muscle twitched in Richie's left cheek and Alex noticed

his glass was already empty. Whatever else had happened, Richie could still put 'em away.

'The crucial point is when the possession of a dishwasher and a microwave becomes more important than oral sex.'

Alex stared at him. 'But you and Beth – you're still OK, aren't you? I mean, you still love her and all that?' He realised that he and Richie had probably never talked like this before. And he found himself wishing they had.

'Love? What's that?' Richie wiped his mouth with the back of one hand. 'It'll happen to you too. It happens to all romantics in the end, mate.'

Alex didn't know what to say. Richie and he had a shared past and yet now he seemed like a stranger. He looked the same as ever: dark skin, straight black hair, eyes set close together. He wore jeans and white cotton shirts same as always. But he'd changed. And what made him think Alex was a romantic? Nothing was further from the truth, and he could ask Marisa if he didn't believe it.

All of a sudden Alex regretted his attempt to get serious. He clapped Richie on the back. What he needed was a good night out; that was what they both needed. A bit of male bonding . . . He laughed Santa-style. 'Ho-ho-ho. You're much too young to be so cynical, my son.'

Richie shrugged. 'It's what she wants,' he said. 'Gotta get her what she wants.'

'I guess so.' Alex was thankful he hadn't married. There had only been one might-have-been, a fellow student at art college, name of Elaine. Long hair, hippy skirts, into textiles. But somewhere along the line he and Elaine had become friends, and instead of that bringing them together, she had left his bed for that of someone more challenging.

Alex positioned a beermat on the edge of the small round

table and flicked it up, catching it neatly first time. Sign of a dissolute youth. He saw Elaine sometimes back in his home town. She helped run a clothes and candles shop in Nottingham, a little cavern of a place that took him instantly back to student days whenever he went in. When he brushed past the rails of thin silk scarves, paisley wraps, Indian hemp shirts, and smelt that familiar musty, musky fragrance of joss sticks, grass and patchouli.

With some difficulty, he brought his mind back to Richie and the here and now. Richie hardly ever went back to Nottingham. He said you couldn't go back – period.

'What about yours, Alex, me old mate?'

'Mine?'

'Your bird. For Christmas, like? Sexy lingerie or what?'

Marisa was a million miles away from Elaine. And all Alex could think of was coffee percolators, oral sex being out of the question.

Richie laughed. 'Yeah. What does this Marisa want from *you*?'

A good question. One that Alex had put to himself many times already. 'Christ knows.' The truth was, he didn't want to talk about Marisa. Neither did he want to get in too deep – but that was another story. How deep was too deep? Was meeting her mother too deep? Was lingerie for Christmas? (Perhaps he should give her the hyacinth?) Was sex in his studio too deep?

It was his round so he got to his feet. He and Marisa hadn't done normal things like going out for a drink, to the cinema or out for dinner. Courting, his mam would call it. And the thing they'd discussed the most (apart from posing positions for life drawing) was contraception. Bloody hell! Alex delved into the pocket of his jeans, registered that his wallet felt extremely thin. And he thought Richie buying Beth a coffee percolator for Christmas was sad?

'Been invited to hers for the festive day?' Richie asked as he picked up the empty glasses.

Jesus! Was everyone thinking about Christmas to the exclusion of all else? He had never known Richie be obsessed with it before. Granted, Alex had begun his Christmas shopping earlier than usual, but the hyacinth had been an accident; a kind of slip of the tongue. 'No way.' His mam would kill him if he didn't do the ritual trip to Nottinghamshire. 'It's not like that with Marisa.'

He made his way up to the bar. Like what? Not homes and gardens; certainly not coffee percolators. Though the oral sex was something else again.

Hazel swung the interior door open wide – she'd understood the advantages of maximum entrance impact since she was her granddaughter's age, and hadn't needed to join a theatrical society to learn. The chairs were arranged in a circle in the middle of the hall. Not an inspiring place, thought Hazel, adding her coat to those hanging by the door, but at least it had a stage and a piano. She slipped into a seat opposite Giorgio in order to maintain total eye contact. The effect of her new perfume could come later – when she got close to him.

'Sorry I'm late.' She noted with pleasure that on seeing her he had half-risen in his seat and that he was wearing a smart dark suit and tie. She had always liked a man in a suit. And Giorgio Manelli, whilst undeniably foreign, was a gentleman.

Gracefully, she inclined her head in his direction. It was true that she had never been one for foreigners . . . She

110

drew her knees together under the blue dress. Foreigners could be a minefield. Look what had happened to Brenda in *Streetlife*. You knew where you were with a certain sort of Englishness.

'I don't see why we have to do Gershwin anyway,' Daphne was complaining. As usual she was dressed in a blue skirt, low-heeled shoes, and a blouse and cardigan both buttoned up tight around her scrawny neck. And as usual she was seated at the piano.

'It's better than Sondheim,' Belinda sniffed, readjusting the pile of sheet music on her lap. 'Everyone does Sondheim. Singalong with, stars of, songs of, you name it.'

'But what's wrong with a nice musical?'

'Such as?'

Hazel crossed her legs and allowed herself to look a teeny bit bored. Daphne and Belinda were getting into one of their power struggles. As far as Hazel could tell, Belinda generally won, but she would presumably have to concede occasional points to Daphne since otherwise they would lack a pianist. It hadn't taken Hazel long to grasp the internal politics of the Trident Musical Comedy Society.

'*Pirates of Penzance*. Now *that's* what I call a musical production.' Daphne shuffled her sheet music around and struck a few chords as if to remind herself what she was there for. There were a few titters from the others. Daphne enjoyed a reputation as a Gilbert and Sullivan fanatic.

Hazel smiled at Giorgio — a special, secret smile which was unfortunately intercepted by Belinda, a large-bosomed woman in her early-sixties, Hazel guessed, although not terribly well preserved. Her posture was good but Jude could certainly teach her a thing or two about powder application. Hazel touched her own cheek carefully with one fingertip.

111

'Gershwin is far more original,' Belinda said authoritatively. 'And our charming Giorgio must do "Summertime".' She turned to him. 'You simply must! With that adorable accent . . .' She clasped her hands together in front of massive breasts that wobbled precariously, Hazel observed, with every sigh.

Giorgio looked flattered – well, he was a man, wasn't he? – so Hazel raised one delicate eyebrow in Belinda's direction, just to put him straight.

'Zummertime?' Giorgio made it sound soooo romantic, Hazel thought. He spread his hands and looked down modestly.

Belinda leaned forward – with enviable balancing skills, in Hazel's opinion. 'Would you, Giorgio?' she cooed, sorting through the music on her lap. She passed one of the sheets over to him.

Hazel seethed in silence. If that woman fluttered her eyelashes any more, she'd take off.

Giorgio smoothed back his dark hair (getting a little thin, Hazel noted, but still there in principle), held the sheet music at arm's length and cleared his throat. There was a swift glance in Hazel's direction (she smiled encouragingly) and then Daphne thumped out the introduction, in a manner that could only be called *sour grapissimo*.

Giorgio began, in his mellow tenor, and almost imperceptibly Hazel swayed in time. Music could be so *meaningful*, and Giorgio did give the song a certain something. Hardly the power of Pavarotti, but with bucketloads of emotion. Still, that was Italians for you.

Hazel thought that perhaps she would accept if he invited her for a bite to eat after the rehearsal. It would put Belinda's over-powdered nose out of joint for a start to see them sweeping out of the hall together. She allowed herself another smile. Modesty and mystery were all very well to start with but maybe they'd run their course.

'Does it remind you of your homeland?' Belinda asked when Giorgio had finished. She sighed and those breasts quivered. 'Garda . . .'

Hazel looked away in disgust. Garda indeed. But nevertheless she made a mental note to buy a book on Italy so she could at least keep up. She and Byron had once spent a weekend in Venice visiting — among other things — the apartment of his namesake, but a coach and boat tour wasn't exactly the height of sophistication.

Giorgio's eyes darkened with warmth at Belinda's words and he hadn't glanced at Hazel for at least thirty seconds. 'Eet does, eet does.'

'Blue skies.' Belinda was in her element. 'Smooth water rippling on the lake, olives, cypress trees . . .'

'Pizza?' Daphne provided a welcome note of discord. 'Can we get on?'

Hazel decided it was time to offer a suggestion. Trident's newest member she might be, but she was entitled to express an opinion, and there were times when one simply had to get noticed. She took a deep breath. 'Perhaps we could construct a story around our Gershwin songs?'

'A story?' She had everyone's attention now, especially Giorgio's. The word compromise hung in the very air of the room; it was something Trident needed in order to survive.

'His life story perhaps?' she went on.

'Excellent!' Giorgio clapped and beamed, flashing his very white teeth at all and sundry as if Hazel were his own discovery. 'You may be our newest recruit, dear Hazel —'

at this Hazel beamed and Belinda glowered '– but I sense an . . . 'ow do you say? . . . an instant understanding of Trident Musical Comedy Society, its aims and ethos—'

'Didn't know it had any.' Daphne swung round on the piano stool to face them. 'But I'm all for a story.'

'I could do some research,' piped up a mousey fifty-something called Patricia who worked in the library.

Better and better. Hazel glowed with pride.

'Capital.' Arthur Brown expanded his chest. 'As leading man, I—'

'Well, now.' Belinda created a hiccup in the general bonhomie. She was rearranging the sheet music on her lap and did not look a happy bunny, Hazel thought. 'I'm not sure that we should have one leading man as such.' She switched her 150-watt gaze back to Giorgio.

'No?'

There was an instant hush. Hazel guessed that such a suggestion had never been made before. Arthur was undisputed lead; he had once sung in the choir at Westminster.

'Giorgio has such a good tenor. Very affecting.' Belinda's shoulders were back and her breasts visibly heaving.

Hazel sighed. This was going to be a battle, and no mistake.

'That voice is a gift.' Belinda got to her feet, moved along the circle to Giorgio and actually put her hand on his shoulder. It was Hazel's turn to frown.

'I suggest that for this production,' Belinda went on, 'we spread the load a little. And, Giorgio, I think we should start with you.'

'Tell me about your home, Giorgio?' Hazel suggested two hours later when they were seated face to face in Mario's.

'Ah, but it is beautiful.' Giorgio looked deep into her eyes. 'You have the lake to one side, the mountains to the other. A pink 'aze in the morning, a grey mist in winter.'

'I've always adored Italy.' Hazel glanced at the menu. This was a nice place – light and airy with lots of chrome and glass, a fan on the ceiling and Mediterranean greenery, yukkas, palms, even a lemon tree. But as for the menu . . . *Minestra di pasta e lenticchie*? Hopefully he would order for her. 'How could you bear to leave?'

He shrugged. 'You adore Italy. Me, I was always 'alf in love with England.'

'Ah.' Hazel sipped her wine. White and fresh, so much more refined than those heavy reds Jude preferred. And was it her imagination or was Giorgio looking at her with those intense dark eyes as if he might already be half in love with her?

'Buckingham Palace . . . the Tower of London . . .' he elaborated with a wave of one hand.

Hmmm. Not a patch on the shores of Lake Garda, she would have thought. What would it be like there in the summertime – when, as Gershwin said, the living was easy? 'Culturally, England is very rich,' she agreed.

'I came to England when my wife died.'

Hazel gave him her most sympathetic half smile. She knew what it was like to lose a mate. Even when one knew their shortcomings like the back of one's hand, it was hard to be alone again. 'Wouldn't she have liked it?' she enquired delicately, hoping he would feel able to confide in her.

'She was a wonderful woman,' Giorgio said.

'I'm sure.' She waited for the *but*.

'But she was not . . . how can I say . . . ?'

'Culturally aware?' Hazel offered. She knew the feeling.

115

Many was the time she had trailed Byron around art exhibitions and galleries, but the poor man had died still unable to tell a Van Gogh from a Renoir.

Giorgio nodded eagerly. 'I came, meaning to stay a few months . . .' He shrugged. 'And that was two years ago.'

'Goodness.' Maybe she'd caught him just in time. 'But you miss Italy?'

'I miss the warmth.' The waiter appeared and Giorgio ordered something unintelligible from the menu. 'And for you, dearest Hazel?'

Dearest Hazel? 'Dear Hazel' back in the hall, and now 'Dearest Hazel' . . . 'You order for me.' She showed him her vulnerability. Now *that* was the way to a man's heart, she must remember to tell Jude. All this independence lark was a lot of old hooey. 'I simply can't decide.' She sighed at the pure enormity of the task.

He obliged. And, yes, she could see that he was pleased. Now all she had to do was manage to eat it.

Giorgio continued to wave his hands around and talk about Italy. Hazel noted the gold cufflinks. She liked smartness in a man too.

'So you miss the sun?' That was hardly surprising, she thought, and decided to take things a small step further. 'And what about human warmth?'

He took her hand over the table. A little premature perhaps, it was probably all that Latin blood. 'And human warmth, my dear Hazel. Ah, I miss that most of all.'

She smiled in terror – not at Giorgio's words but at the pasta and shellfish concoction that had appeared before her, delivered by the deft hands of a silent-footed waiter. But nevertheless she was also aware of a distinct – and pleasurable – kind of fluttering. Life, she felt, certainly had

116

something special left in store for her. And one couldn't deny the possibility of what one might call an Italian connection.

'So how about it, Imo?' Jude asked, emptying the last dregs of the second bottle of wine into their glasses. They had created an ad that said it all, that focused, as Imo put it, on the *him* rather than on *her*. 'Do you like women?' their ad read. 'Do you have the courage of your convictions? Like to laugh? If you're 40ish, solvent and decent-looking, you could be the man for me.' Oh, yes. Jude thought that would do it.

And now they were planning a secondary strike. 'Shall we make a move on the singles scene?' Jude continued. 'What a partnership we'll make. How about the Singles Only Saturday dance at the White Rabbit Hotel? They won't know what's hit 'em.'

'Any time, any place, anywhere . . .' Apart from sounding like a well-known advertising slogan, Imogen's speech was slurred. 'Why shouldn't I be ready? I'm more than ready. I'm not exactly a grieving widow, am I?'

'Aren't you?' Jude blinked. Was she missing something here?

'I should have left him years ago,' Imo moaned. She grabbed one of Jude's maroon scatter cushions and hugged it ferociously. 'How could I have been such a fool?'

Now they were getting somewhere. Jude sank back into the sofa next to her, ready with sympathy and a shoulder for Imogen to cry on. 'But you were happy together,' she soothed. And then, because drinking a bottle of wine compelled a certain honesty, 'More or less,' she added.

Imogen leapt on this. 'Yes, but which?' she demanded.

'What?'

'Which? More or less?'

Jude felt she was in danger of losing the thread, and Imo seemed to be in danger of losing her entire box of marbles. She retrieved her cigarettes and lighter from the floor at her feet and lit one slowly to give herself time. Edward had never seemed *enough* for Imo. But that was in the past. There was no point in brooding about it now.

'More or less?' Imo looked quite threatening. Her grey eyes were fierce and her jaw jutted in determination.

'You got by,' Jude said at last, resorting to platitudes. 'And anyway, it's all over now.'

Imo's face crumpled. 'I thought he loved me,' she wailed.

'He did. But now he's gone.' Was it her imagination or were they talking in song titles? Jude got unsteadily to her feet to search for the ashtray. ''Course he loved you.' She found it on the other side of the room, half hidden under Daisy's polka-dot-and-daisy bean bag. 'Who wouldn't?'

'And who wouldn't love *her*?' Imo groped for her bag.

Her? 'Are you all right, Imo?' Obviously not. Jude stared at her in alarm. She was crying now, great glutinous tears running down her cheeks. Anyone else and Jude would have called it self-pity. But Imo was not the self-pitying kind.

She sniffed. 'I found a photograph.' More gropings in the hippy shoulder bag. 'Where the fuck is it?'

Jude blinked at her again, this time having some difficulty in refocusing. She didn't think she'd ever heard Imo use the F-word before. Things must be worse than she'd realised. 'You're not telling me that Edward . . . ?' She was definitely off her head. If anyone wasn't the type, then Edward wasn't. Not in a million years.

'What am I supposed to think?' Imo let out a sad squeal of triumph and waved it in the air. 'This is her.'

'Her?' Jude stubbed out her cigarette and peered at the photo as Imogen collapsed sobbing into the cushions.

'It's the idea of him having a secret life that hurts the most,' she moaned.

Jude patted her arm and squinted at the photo. 'Bloody hell,' she said.

'I know — she's so young, isn't she?' More sobs.

'No.' Jude couldn't tear her eyes away from the photograph.

'No?' Slowly, Imo emerged from her sanctuary. Her hair was half-down, her eyes were red and the streaks of tears were still visible on her face.

'I mean . . . yes, she's young . . .' Jude looked from her to the photograph and then back again. Young, strawberry blonde, immaculate features and a cold smile. Oh, yes, and one more thing . . . acrylic nails. 'But it's not just that.'

'What else then?' Imo was hanging on to her every word.

Jude gazed down at Edward's secret life — her ten o'clock client. What had the girl said this morning? She frowned in concentration. Ah, yes. That *of course* she had a boyfriend, and that she hadn't decided on her next move yet. What could that mean when the boyfriend in question was dead?

'Oh, Imo,' Jude said. 'It's just that I know her, you see . . .'

Chapter 11

'"Two more days to go . . . to go and mow a meadow. Two days, one day and an elf . . ." Oh, sorry.'

If she hadn't been with Daisy, Imogen would have walked straight out of the grotto. But then again, if she hadn't been with Daisy, she wouldn't be here. She surveyed Kirby's Santa warily. His beard was looking a touch ragged and one white eyebrow was skewiff. But she supposed anyone who did this sort of job would have to be an eccentric. Children – even Daisy – weren't easy.

'Good afternoon,' she said politely. Since it was her half-day she'd been happy to help Jude out; school holidays were difficult, and this afternoon Hazel was apparently closeted with this Giorgio of hers, building a stairway to paradise – at least she thought that was what Jude had said.

'What are you doing here?' the Santa demanded.

Well, that was a bit off. Imogen bridled. 'The usual, I imagine,' she retorted sharply. Didn't he realise he had a reputation to maintain before these kids? Hundreds of children might stop believing.

'Hello, Santa,' said Daisy, apparently unaware of any inconsistency.

'Hello, little girl.' Now he sounded like a pervert.

Imogen put a restraining hand on Daisy's arm, just in case she felt the urge to leap on to his lap.

'And what would you like for Christmas?'

Peace, thought Imogen. Peace of mind particularly. Only that was one commodity that the season never seemed to provide.

'Some reindeer, please.' Daisy – a girl whose manners had been nurtured by her grandmother – replied promptly and specifically. 'Six of them.'

Six reindeer? Imogen raised her eyes to heaven, or in this case the cotton-wool ceiling of Santa's grotto. They had been in the queue for half an hour watching large quantities of tea and digestives being delivered by a man in a pointed red hat to a Santa who clearly couldn't function without them. But he was functioning so *slowly*, and if Daisy had anything to do with it, the discussion was about to take a distinctly philosophical turn.

'Ho, ho, ho.' Santa apparently had no problem with reindeer. But why did he keep looking at her like that? He was supposed to be concentrating on Daisy. 'I hope you don't mean *my* reindeer?'

'Oh, no.' Daisy fixed him with her clear-eyed gaze. 'I mean the ones in the toy department downstairs.'

'Toy reindeer?'

Daisy's expression changed to pity. 'Bean-baggie ones. Obviously. Real ones wouldn't survive in this country, would they?'

'Wouldn't they?' Santa was becoming distinctly flustered. The other eyebrow was now pointing down towards the bottom of his ear. Imogen grinned.

'Without snow, I mean,' Daisy added. 'And they're very timid, aren't they?'

Santa leaned closer. His eyes, thought Imogen, which were rather nice, very blue and slightly familiar, were beginning to glaze. 'You seem to know an awful lot about rain, dear,' he said.

Now Imogen was confused. Snow? Rain? Naturally, she was preoccupied – who wouldn't be? Jude had said that she knew *her*, said she was a client, offered to find out more information, because she *couldn't believe* that she and Edward . . . But how long would it take? She hadn't come up with anything yet. And Imo wanted to know everything.

'Can't you just give her the present?' she asked Santa. It might be abrupt but there was a long queue outside. It might sound cynical, but that's the way life was.

'Present?' he growled, as if he'd never heard the word.

'Yes.' Imogen stood her ground, frowning, trying to place him. 'Present.' This Santa was getting above himself. 'There's a lot of people waiting. And it's getting late . . .'

'Mummy *is* in a hurry,' Santa said to Daisy.

She tucked a strand of platinum blonde hair that had escaped her neat plait carefully behind one ear. 'This isn't my mummy. This is Auntie Imo.'

'Ah. Auntie Imo . . .' He seemed particularly interested in this information. And he was talking in an odd, over-gruff voice.

Who was he? Imo's frown deepened. Did stores like Kirby's check for a criminal record before letting any old Santa loose on their customers? 'So?' Free sweets and a present, it said so outside.

'All in good time. Ho, ho, ho.'

Imogen thought that in a minute she might hit him. She could see the headline: Santa Claus Assaulted By Madwoman in Department Store. *I was sitting ho-ho-ho-ing in my sloping grotto (it's under the escalator, you see) amid fake wood and simulated snowflakes, when she smacked me one . . .* That would go down well in the *Chichester Echo*.

Jude was grabbing a welcome tea and fag break and fantasising about the evening ahead. Imogen had been spot on. Their ad had already produced a feast of replies, and she was seeing the first tonight.

She stubbed out her cigarette and looked up as Florrie came into the salon. 'Fancy a cuppa?' she asked her neighbour.

'I wouldn't say no.' Florrie was looking as small and birdlike as ever in her huge, brown fur coat. 'But I was after a shampoo and set. It's cheeky, I know. I usually go to that little place in North Street.'

'But it's a bit of a way.' Jude nodded her understanding. 'And it's cold outside.'

'These weeks have flown by. I really had no idea Christmas was practically upon us.' Florrie reached up and touched her pure white hair.

That gesture held such wistfulness . . . Jude's heart went out to her as she examined her appointments book. She was fairly quiet this afternoon, she could squeeze her neighbour in. 'No problem.' She got to her feet. 'I'll put the kettle on and we'll get started.'

Florrie beamed. She was a naive old thing, Jude thought, hadn't even asked how much it would cost. She took her brown fur coat rather warily and hung it on the stand. And that was why the elderly got ripped off so easily these days; they were too innocent for their own good. Gullible. They believed most people were still basically decent. Look at Florrie's attitude to James Dean, for example. She had no idea what sort of a man he was: certainly unscrupulous, probably corrupt. Jude draped her neighbour in one of her black gowns and went out to the kitchenette to put the kettle back on. These senior citizens didn't just need meals on wheels, they needed further education – on how to become streetwise. The lessons should be compulsory, and they should come along with their pensions.

'And what else would you like me to bring in my sack when I come down your chimney?' Santa enquired.

Heaven forbid. Imogen recrossed her legs and glanced pointedly at her watch. The elf re-entered the grotto with more tea.

'A computer,' said Daisy. 'Microsoft with Windows.'

Imogen looked at her in astonishment. What did a girl like Daisy know about Microsoft Windows?

But Santa was oblivious. He was clearly the sort of Santa who expected seven year olds to be au fait with computer technology. 'It'll be my pleasure.' He beamed and rubbed his hands together in a Santa-like way.

Imogen was on her feet in one movement. 'Should you do that?' she demanded.

'Do what?' He grinned. His beard had slipped to one side and he looked more familiar than ever.

'Make promises to children that their parents might not be able to keep.' God, she sounded more holier than thou than Hazel on a bad day. She wasn't even sure why she was so cross. Only, Jude was a single parent, struggling to run a business and make ends meet. It really didn't seem fair.

Santa, to his credit, seemed to be reassessing the situation. 'No, I suppose I shouldn't. I'm sorry.'

'Auntie Imo . . .'

'It's entirely unethical.'

'Yes, er . . .'

'And irresponsible.'

'Auntie IMO . . .' By now Daisy was tugging at her hand.

But Imogen wasn't going to let him get away with it that easily. The frustration of the last weeks seemed to have turned into anger – primarily against this poor man. 'You're supposed to be Santa Claus. It's not enough to get a kick out of seeing their faces light up, to think of yourself as some sort of glorious benefactor, you know . . .' She paused for breath. 'Spare a thought instead for those poor parents on Christmas Day when their little ones . . .' (now she was beginning to sound like the vicar) '. . . expect some flash computer and end up with a Thomas the Tank jigsaw puzzle . . .'

'Thomas the . . . ?'

'Tank Engine, silly. And I know you're just a man dressed up. I don't even believe in Santa Claus.'

'You don't?' Imogen sat down again. Trust Daisy to make her lose the gist of her entire argument. But Daisy wasn't stupid, was she? She might not believe, but she wouldn't be handing her present back – if she ever got it.

'You don't?' Santa seemed crestfallen and despite herself, Imogen felt a twinge of pity.

'And anyway . . .' Daisy looked seven going on seventeen

125

'. . . I've already found all my Christmas presents at the bottom of Mummy's wardrobe.'

Oh, dear. Imo bit her lip. Should she tell Jude?

Santa's shoulders drooped alarmingly. 'She's right,' he confessed. 'I'm a complete fraud.' But Imogen would swear that his mouth was twitching.

Despite feeling drawn to him and even being tempted to sit back and have a good laugh, she found herself hardening her heart. She would not, she told herself, be putting any trust in a man again. 'Present?' She held out her hand. She had paid for it after all.

'Blue for a boy and pink for a girl.' He delved into a tub covered with more fake holly and snow and labelled *Santa's Special Surprises*, and pulled out a flat, oblong parcel. It didn't look too promising.

'A bit small for a Microsoft computer with Windows.' Imogen grabbed it and thrust it towards Daisy. 'Let's go home and find Mummy.'

'Yes.' Daisy skipped out of the grotto. 'She'll want to hear about what a lovely time we had with Santa.'

'Hmm.' Imogen wouldn't look at him. 'She certainly will.'

Jude helped Florrie on with her coat. 'I've been meaning to ask you . . .' She wondered how to say this. 'Ma, Daisy and me, well, we're having Christmas dinner at home with just my friend Imogen—'

'How lovely.' Florrie produced a small purse from her pocket. 'Do have a wonderful time.' She smiled with a touch of the mischief that Jude had glimpsed in her before.

'And we were wondering if you could join us?' Jude went on. 'I've bought a huge turkey. We'll be eating the thing cold, curried and what have you for days afterwards otherwise.'

'How very kind of you, my dear.' Florrie extracted a five-pound note from her purse. 'But I've already accepted an invitation for Christmas. In fact, I shall be away for a few days.' She looked faintly wistful at the prospect.

'Oh. Not to worry then.' Jude was mildly curious, but Florrie didn't elaborate. 'That'll be three pounds.' Jude hoped she hadn't noticed the price list. It would take some explaining. Although shampoo and set didn't feature on the salon's treatment list, a shampoo and blow dry alone was more than double that amount. But Florrie needed it more than she did, Jude reasoned. It was good to be neighbourly, and it was Christmas.

'Really?' For a moment Florrie's blue eyes met hers and Jude could swear she'd sussed her. 'That's very reasonable.' She pressed the fiver into Jude's palm. 'Keep the change, my dear.'

'Are you sure?' She wanted to ask if Florrie had enough for electricity and next month's rent, but that would be taking neighbourliness too far and was probably, Jude thought, the sort of question James Dean himself would ask. The poor woman had to retain some independence, Jude reminded herself, and her dignity. Though she might pop out to the off licence later and pick up some sherry for her for Christmas.

'You didn't handle that very well.' The salesman in the ridiculous red hat – only who was he calling ridiculous? Alex wondered – handed him a mug of tea.

'Could you do any better?' Alex couldn't believe that she – the woman from the flower shop – had actually been

127

here, in his grotty grotto. He hoped to God she hadn't recognised him.

'Couldn't do much worse,' the elf replied.

'Huh.' Alex was sick of being Santa, and hadn't asked for an elf or a cup of tea. Pity it wasn't a stiff whisky. Talking nicely to obnoxious and materialistic little kids was enough to drive the most tolerant Santa to drink. And there were so *many* of them . . .

The elf took no notice. 'Ready for the next one, are we?'

'No, we bloody well are not.' Alex pulled off the scratchy beard. Oh, the relief. He'd be better off growing a beard and bleaching it himself next year. Next year! What was he thinking of? He shuddered. Never again. He had experienced enough humiliation in the last three weeks to last him a lifetime. And then *she* had to come in . . .

Imo. He was glad that at last he knew her name.

The elf peered out from behind the red curtain. 'We're gonna have to speed it up,' he said. 'Don't bother with the hellos and what do you want for Christmases. Cut to the chase.'

The chase. Alex stuck the beard back on to his face. Why should it matter if she had recognised him? She was only a woman in a flower shop. A woman with warm grey eyes and cheekbones he longed to capture with his pencil. It had been odd to see her away from her territory, wearing blue jeans and a long black fitted coat. No longer the woman in the flower shop . . .

He got his smile ready once again. Next year? He'd rather starve.

Jude knew something was up the second they walked into

the salon. Daisy was wearing an unspeakably large amount of pink plastic jewellery and Imo was clearly stressed.

'Did you have a good time, sweetie?' Jude attempted to kiss her daughter as she cantered past but caught only fresh air. 'Granny's got your dinner ready upstairs.'

'Neigh,' said Daisy, disappearing out of the back door.

'Hi-ho, Silver.' Jude refocused on her five o'clock makeover. The client was nice enough, but at fifty probably should have known better than to select glitter and sparkle look number one. Jude frowned as she discovered a stray eyebrow hair. Still, didn't everyone deserve a touch of glamour at Christmas-time?

'How was Santa Claus?' She thought she saw Imo wince as she chucked her bag on the floor. Jude wielded the brush with dexterity. Thank goodness gold glitter blended into the eye socket was not acceptable all year round.

'Unconvincing.' Imogen sat down at the reception desk recently vacated by Hazel who had left a sprig of mistletoe dangling suggestively above the receptionist's chair.

Jude selected some tweezers. 'Just a tiny pull . . . there.' Her client winced.

'Even your daughter doesn't believe in him.' Imogen's voice rose. 'And if you saw the Santa in Kirby's, you'd have a good idea why.'

'Really?' Jude glanced up in surprise. Who had rattled her cage? Santa Claus perhaps?

But Imo wouldn't meet her eye. 'I'll put the kettle on.' She pulled up the sleeves of her lilac polo-neck and stomped off through the interior door that led into the kitchenette.

'Hmm. Good idea.' Jude dipped a cotton wool bud into some smoothing gel and stroked it along her client's eyebrows. Better . . . The man she was meeting tonight

129

was called Roger. And he sounded – oh, miracles – quite promising. She completed the makeover with a flourish of Night Silver lip ink, helped her five o'clock client into her coat and accepted the generous tip with grace. She was knackered.

Imo came back through, carrying two mugs of coffee and an ominous expression. 'I've got to see her,' she blurted.

'Who?' Jude lit a cigarette and began to tidy the make-up trolley. She knew damn well but she'd stall for time. She was stuck in a conflict of friendship versus client confidentiality, and she didn't like it one bit.

'Her. You know.' Imogen sank into one of the salon's black chairs, hands cradled around her mug. 'The woman in the photo. Marisa . . . what did you say her name was?'

Her and her big mouth. 'Gibb.' Jude pushed the trolley to the back of the salon and grabbed the broom from just inside the kitchenette. 'Imo, what good will it do?'

'It'll do *me* some good.' Imogen adopted the stubborn expression that Jude knew so well. 'It'll mean that I know who she is, I can find out what happened. Why . . .' she faltered.

'Why you weren't enough for him?'

Imogen turned huge accusing eyes on her. 'If you want to put it like that, yes.'

Jude took a deep drag, balanced her cigarette on the side of the ashtray and began sweeping. She hadn't meant to put it like that, only to put Imo off. Because this could only hurt her even more. Bad enough to find out your husband was involved with another woman – especially a younger one. But to have him die as well so that he wasn't available for recriminations, apologies, cross-examinations . . . that must be hell.

130

'Imo, I know it's hard for you.' She propped the broom against the wall, came closer, put an arm round the narrow shoulders.

'I want to talk to her,' Imogen repeated. 'Don't you see? I can speculate till the cows come home and I still won't know what it was all about. Why Edward was seeing her. Why he was giving her money . . .'

Jude straightened up. 'But you can't just go charging round there.' Marisa Gibb *might* (though granted, this seemed unlikely) be even more upset than Imo.

Imogen propelled herself out of the chair, slammed her mug down on the ledge in front of her. 'Tell me her address.' In two strides she was at the reception desk, leafing through Jude's client book.

'I can't just stand by and watch you doing that . . .'

'Then close your eyes.'

Jude did as she was told. In any case, now that she knew her name, Imo could just as easily have looked up the address in the phone book. The mood she was in, she would have called up every Gibb within a fifteen-mile radius.

Jude only opened her eyes when she felt the touch of Imogen's hand on her arm. 'Thanks.'

'Are you going to phone her first?'

'I think . . .' Imogen looked more cheerful than she had for ages '. . . I'd rather have surprise on my side.'

'You're going round there now? On the day before Christmas Eve?'

'I am.' To Jude's surprise Imogen plonked herself down on the chair again and stared at her reflection in the mirror. 'But first, you're going to make me look beautiful.'

That was a turn up. Despite her tiredness, Jude grinned. Now this she was good at. 'You're on.'

131

'And second, we're going to have a couple of very large drinks.'

'We are?' She thought of Roger. But this wouldn't take too long. Roger would wait. 'In that case,' she said, 'we might as well make that the number one priority. I'll go upstairs and get a bottle right now.'

Chapter 12

'Tonight?' Alex wasn't exactly in the mood. He only had one more Santa-day left (thank God) and then he'd be on the train heading north faster than Elvis Presley could have sung 'In the Grotto . . .'

'Yes, tonight.'

Alex shifted the receiver to his other ear. He was thinking with longing of a bath, a glass of red wine and a slice of Sylvie's Battenberg. He knew he should see Marisa but . . .

'I've got a present for you.' Being Marisa, this was said matter-of-factly without a trace of sexual teasing.

'Yeah, me too.' Actually, this wasn't true. He had nothing to give her apart from the hyacinth in his room upstairs. And it felt quite wrong to give her that because . . . well, because he'd become absurdly fond of the thing, waiting for it to blossom – any day now – watering it, treating it to as much wintry sunshine as it could get on the window sill of his small room.

Alex leaned back against the dark brown and cream flock wall that made Sylvie's hallway appear more narrow than it

133

really was. It was also very draughty and thus not conducive to long telephone conversations.

'Something exciting?' Marisa murmured.

'Hardly.' Alex had originally taken Richie's advice and bought lingerie, purchased during his lunch hour in Kirby's from Trixie who had smirked and raised the perfect half-moons of her eyebrows. But the ivory silk had seemed too personal and intimate for Marisa somehow.

He noted a patch of wallpaper in the corner by the door, that was curling and damp. It was almost as if he'd bought the silk underwear with someone else in mind. So he'd taken it back. In Kirby's he had also toyed with perfume (but which did she use?), silk scarves (not her style) and handbags (she never seemed to use one). And the result was that he'd bought her nothing at all.

'It's the thought that counts.' He heard her sigh as if she guessed all this. 'It's Christmas, isn't it, Alex? Time to exchange gifts rather than just bodily fluids, hmm?'

Trust Marisa to come right out with it. 'It's just that tonight's difficult.' Any night was difficult if he was honest. Because he shouldn't be with Marisa at all.

'Difficult?'

Alex longed for the simplicity of Nottinghamshire, Christmas dinner with the family, a Boxing Day hike in Sherwood Forest. 'Oh, you know. I'm busy and tired and pissed off being bloody Santa Claus.'

'Just come for a quick drink,' Marisa said swiftly. 'For Christmas.' *You owe me that much*, her voice seemed to add.

'All right.' Had she heard *his* sigh? It wasn't her fault that Christmas brought out the worst in him, that he had got involved and now wanted out.

He could pick up chocolates and a bottle of liqueur in

the offy on the way, he decided. Easy, impersonal gifts. He replaced the phone in its cradle. But after Christmas, in the New Year when a guy got to make resolutions – about doing half an hour's exercise every day (not including sex), drinking no more than three pints of an evening down the pub, and obeying his conscience because man must not live according to libido alone – yes, then, in the New Year, he thought, as he loped back up the stairs, it would be different.

Marisa was thoughtful as she put down the phone. Why was he backing off? Had she come on too strong? She leaned back in the rose-patterned easy chair with the plumped up cream scatter cushions and lacy upholstery protectors. Her mother's taste: old-fashioned and twee.

With the exception of Edward, Marisa had always been in complete control as far as men were concerned. Though Edward, of course, was another matter entirely.

She had never known a man who hadn't jumped to attention whenever she lifted a finger, she had never known a man who hadn't been intrigued by her, who hadn't showered her – and bothered her – with phone calls, concert tickets, flowers and attentions of one kind or another. If they got the chance.

Marisa stared at the phone. Didn't Alex Armstrong appreciate that? Didn't he realise that he was the only one she had invited into her life, into her home?

She heard her mother's key in the lock, the soft step in the hall, and then Naomi was there, standing in the doorway, face flushed from the cold. With that waiting look in her eyes again. Marisa knew what she was waiting for. But she wouldn't comply, damn it. Why should she?

'Cup of tea, love?' Naomi asked.

'OK.'

A pause.

'Has anyone phoned?'

Has *he* phoned? she meant. Marisa stretched, lazy as a cat, and glanced up at her mother. She looked dowdy and apologetic with her cloche hat pulled down over her ears, the green scarf wrapped around her throat, her complexion at once pasty and flushed. 'No.' And who could blame him? Look at her, just look at her.

Naomi pulled off her outdoor things as if aware of her daughter's disapproval.

'And before you ask, no one's called round and there's no post. Not even a Christmas card.'

Naomi did not comment on this nor on Marisa's bitterness. 'Will you be in for dinner?' she asked instead.

As usual down to practicalities, Marisa thought. One meal following another, leading to sleep, leading to more meals and then the Big Sleep. Well, that was not enough for Marisa.

'Yes.' It would save her the bother. And she wouldn't be getting dinner out of Alex. Marisa got to her feet and wandered through to the adjoining dining-room. She selected a satsuma from the glass fruit bowl on the table, dug in a perfect thumb nail and peeled the fruit. She let the peel drop on to the polished mahogany veneer, knowing that it annoyed her mother. Alex . . .

She had given him acres of space to begin with. From the beginning, she had known, *felt*, that he was part of where she was going. Alex had no idea of his full potential. Artists didn't think like that. They were another breed. They had to be nurtured.

136

Deftly, she separated the segments of the satsuma, removed a strand of pith with another perfect finger-nail and bit into the fruit. A drop of juice squirted free and landed on the table, alongside the peel. Marisa chewed thoughtfully, allowing the fruit to slip down her throat. But now . . . everything had changed, the gears must be shifted. She smoothed her free hand over the flatness of her stomach. Alex was still very much a part of her plans. The hand crept to her mouth. She chewed the thumb nail – already ragged and torn, down to the quick. The gritty taste of the acrylic was on her tongue. Now she must move more quickly than he might like. The time had come to reconsider her options.

Shivering, Imogen pressed hard on the doorbell. It was cold and it was dark – not a night for visiting strangers. When *she* – the other woman – came to the door Imogen would say . . . oh, hell, what would she say?

She heard footsteps. The door opened.

'Oh.' She found herself staring at a woman with reddish hair, a woman she thought she knew. She was wearing a plain brown dress and an expectant expression. Imogen frowned. This wasn't the first time today that she'd experienced an unexpected sense of familiarity.

'Yes?'

'Mrs Gibb?'

'Miss.'

'Sorry.' However, this was not the woman in the photo. This woman, frowning at her as if she too were trying to place *her*, looked old enough to be Marisa Gibb's . . . ah, her mother. Imo shifted her weight on to the other foot. That did rather complicate the issue. It had never occurred to her that the woman engaged in adultery with her own husband might live at home with a mother.

'Oh, hello there, it's you.' The woman in the doorway beamed and held out a hand in greeting.

Imogen felt she might be approaching an identity crisis. 'Me?' But she took the hand since it seemed impolite not to.

'You're the lady from the flower shop, aren't you?' She peered closer. 'Though you do look a bit different in this light.'

'Am I? Do I?' What had Jude done to her face? Was she unrecognisable or disguised? Stronger, stranger or just a painted lady? Imogen put a hand to her hair. It wasn't where she expected it to be at all. It was swept up and to one side, fastened with a tortoiseshell comb. Jude should never have brought that gin down to the salon. And Imogen should never have drunk it.

'Well, yes.' The woman laughed. '*Say It With Flowers*, isn't it?'

Imogen nodded. This was one of her customers, for heaven's sake. Not at all what she'd prepared herself for. She was ready for confrontation, not small talk.

'Do come in, won't you? It's such a cold night.' The woman shivered. 'What can I do for you?'

What could she say now? She hadn't done too well so far. *Can I see your daughter? I believe she was having an affair with my late husband?* 'I came to see Marisa,' she said with some difficulty. 'Is she in?' She hovered, still on the doorstep, half hoping that the girl would be out, unavailable, that all this had been in vain.

'You know Marisa?' The woman almost seemed not to believe her. Was it so unlikely?

138

'Well, um, not exactly.'

'Those lilies were wonderful by the way.' She didn't seem to notice Imogen's reticence as she gestured once more for her to cross the threshold.

How many times had Edward crossed it? Imogen wondered. Had he ever met Marisa's mother?

'Almost three weeks they lasted. I only threw them out this morning.'

'That's nice.' It was surreal to be discussing lilies in these circumstances, but now at least she remembered the woman, one of the many customers accused by Tiffany of being not all there. And if Tiffany could see Imogen now, she was pretty sure she'd say the same about *her*.

'Let me take your coat.' All smiles, she helped Imogen out of it. 'Can I get you something? A drink?'

Could she smell Imogen's breath? 'Well . . .'

'Coffee, perhaps?'

'That would be lovely.' Politeness got the upper hand. But when precisely was Imogen going to drink it? When she'd introduced herself? When she'd asked Marisa about her relationship with Edward?

'Come through. Marisa's in here with her boyfriend.'

'Boyfriend?' Imogen stopped in her tracks, assailed by a vision of a ghastly ghostly Edward hovering by the fireplace. 'A new boyfriend?' she asked weakly.

'Newish.' The woman smiled. 'You haven't met him then?'

'No.' Goodness, but she was a fast worker. It was beginning to look as though Imogen would be conducting their chat in front of an audience of interested parties along with the coffee and cakes, God help her. She took a deep breath and walked in.

*

Thanks to Imo, Jude was running late. But this made her feel virtuous. After all, her friend had always been there for her. And it had been worth it – if only to get her hands on Imo's wonderful bone structure.

Jude climbed over the double bed and flung open the doors of her wardrobe. It might be small but this was her own space, painted in pollen-yellows and grass-greens to cheer her up every morning – whether the sun was shining or not.

How was Imo getting on? she wondered. Had she tackled Marisa Gibb about Edward? And if so, how had the Living Doll reacted? Jude began to strip off her clothes. She wasn't a doll though, was she? Hardly Miss Compliant. Her heart was steel, not soft rubber. But Imo had passion on her side. 'Go, Imo, go,' she muttered.

Luckily, her favourite black top never needed ironing. She pulled it on, grabbed her black pencil skirt, climbed into it and turned to inspect her profile. OK to middling. The skirt was slimming even without the lacy 'medium control with tummy-flattening front panels' knickers she'd bought in Kirby's last week from a twiggy shop assistant with the name TRIXIE embossed on her badge. A passionate encounter might not be on the agenda, but a girl should be like a boy scout – always prepared. Because princes didn't wear crowns any more and most of them weren't tall, dark or handsome. They didn't ride horses and bikes weren't quite the same. So how were you supposed to recognise one when he came up and grabbed you? By being ever-ready, Jude smiled to herself, that was how.

She brushed her hair, added spray at the roots and a fine mist to keep it in place. No time for extensions tonight.

She checked her make-up — matt, pore-minimising and marvellous at deflecting the light from imperfections — had a final slurp of G&T and traced in her lip lines with a fine brown pencil. Being single meant always looking your best, even for trips to the supermarket, because you *never knew who you might meet* . . .

And besides . . . Jude filled in the colour (Black Toffee Treacle) and grabbed her coat . . . minimalist make-up, less is more and all that jazz was a bare-faced lie. With make-up, a girl could be who she wanted to be. Sexy, glam, confident. In Jude's opinion, the only women who willingly laid their faces bare were those lucky few who looked good in just a scrap of Vaseline and a-smile.

She glanced up sharply as the doorbell rang. It was too late for double-glazing salesmen or the meter man. Her mother wasn't expecting company — hardly, since she was flat out on her bed having a rest, recuperation and revitalising session. Might it be Imo perhaps, returned from her mission and needing a shoulder to cry on? Selfishly, Jude hoped not. She loved Imo, but she had a mission of her own tonight.

She opened the front door to be confronted by the dark unsmiling features of her landlord. 'Oh, it's you,' she said ungraciously, noting the elegant cut of his grey jacket. It was easy, she told herself, when it came to clothes, to buy a classy look. His dark hair was still brushed back but now almost touched his collar. 'The rent's not due, is it?' she asked.

He raised one eyebrow. 'I'd expect someone as organised as you to know exactly when your rent's due, Miss Lomax.' He managed to make the word 'organised' sound like an insult, and she'd swear he was eyeing her up and down. Damned cheek.

His brown eyes were inscrutable. 'Going out?'

141

'I'm not dressing up for dinner with my mother, Mr Dean.' Jude leant on the door jamb. Was he expecting her to invite him in? If so, he was in for a long wait. She was not some old biddy charmed by that intense, hungry look of his, more than ready to produce tea and sympathy at the sight of that scar. 'So what can I do for you?' Deliberately, she stuck out one hip. Men like him deserved to be teased. Might make them smile occasionally too.

But he didn't. 'I've brought you a small gift.'

'A gift?' What was he on about? Then she realised he was holding a carrier bag and looking . . . embarrassed? She must be imagining things.

'For you and your mother.' From the bag, he extracted a bottle.

Despite herself, Jude peered at the label. Hmm. A good claret by the look of it and tied with a red and glittery festive bow – a feminine touch if ever she saw one. 'How kind.' She took it. 'Have you given Florrie one too?'

'I beg your pardon?' He blinked.

Did he want her to spell it out? 'Well, I presume this is a landlord to tenant gift, and I'm touched naturally . . .'

'Naturally.' The dark eyebrow rose again as the sound of 'Embraceable You' wafted down the hall.

'But I was just checking that you hadn't forgotten her.' James Dean might want her out but Jude wanted Florrie to get her new heating *and* a bottle of claret.

His eyes hardened. 'Why should my relationship with the tenant upstairs be any of your concern?' he asked.

'Because I don't approve of landlords taking advantage of their tenants' frailties.' Jude glared back at him.

'Oh, don't you?' He was smiling now – a smile straight from the freezer cabinet.

'No, I don't. Florrie is an elderly lady who needs to be looked after.'

'Precisely,' he shot back. 'Which is why I asked you to keep an eye on her, Miss Lomax.'

Damn and double damn! Jude silently cursed her own big mouth. She'd sailed right into that. 'But she's not exactly incapable of looking after herself,' she snapped. 'And I'm on hand should she need anything.'

His mouth twisted. 'Even though you lead such a busy life? Looking after your family, working . . .' He eyed her outfit. 'Going out on the town.'

'Well!' What a nerve he had. Did he want to control the lives of all his tenants, was that it? Did he imagine he could buy her compliance in his plan to get rid of poor Florrie with a miserly bottle of claret?

'I'll let you get on,' he said, before she had a chance to let rip. 'And I'll see you on the second.'

'The second?'

'Of the month. Rent'll be due then.' He swung round before she could see the expression on that face, but she'd bet it was still smiling.

Jude slammed the door shut and stomped back down the hall into Hazel's room.

'Who was that, dear?' her mother enquired mildly. She was prone on the pink bedspread, hair turbanned in a white fluffy towel, eyelids covered with slices of cucumber, lips adorned with segments of avocado that wobbled as she spoke. 'I Got Rhythm' was playing on the cassette player now. Jude peered at the case. It was the tape of *Girl Crazy*, another Gershwin production, no doubt.

143

'Scarface.'

'Oh, I do wish you wouldn't call him that.'

Jude knew she shouldn't too. 'He's infuriating,' she growled.

'What did he want?' The avocado wobbled once more.

'He brought some wine.' Jude pulled on her coat. She would drink it but it wouldn't make her any more kindly disposed towards him, that was for sure.

'Such a nice man,' Hazel murmured. 'So thoughtful.'

Jude was late, she wouldn't stop to argue with her mother now. But it was only as she let herself out of the flat that she realised she hadn't even thanked James Dean for the wine. So now he would think her an ungrateful bitch on top of everything else. She slammed the door behind her. What did she care?

As she walked into the small living-room, the first person that Imogen registered was Marisa – mainly because she was dressed in a tight-fitting white cat suit and because she was draped (there was no other word for it) over the small rose-patterned settee in the centre of the room. Imogen was glad she'd gone for the makeover, but the fact remained that while she was wearing her old blue jeans and a sweater, Marisa looked stunning – even more so than she'd seemed in the photograph. Clear skin, strawberry-blonde hair, green eyes that were oddly transparent. Vaguely familiar. Stunning and very, very young – barely into her twenties, Imogen guessed.

And she seemed so unlike anyone Edward would have dallied with (but what did *she* know?) that Imogen could only stare.

'Someone to see you, Marisa dear.' The woman who had

144

answered the door left the room, presumably to put the kettle on.

Marisa looked her up and down. 'Who the hell are you?'

Not exactly one for small talk then. Imogen tried to stand up straight but she could feel herself drooping alarmingly. 'May I sit down?' Without waiting for a reply she chose the similarly patterned armchair opposite the settee which also happened to be the closest thing to hand. It was that or fall over.

'Alex, darling.' Regally, Marisa beckoned someone over from the far corner of the adjoining dining-room. 'What are you doing in there? Come and sit here by me.'

Imogen squinted at Alex darling as he came through the half-open frosted glass doors and moved closer. He seemed to be avoiding her eye. Tall, lean and kind of crumpled-looking. Very blue eyes, nose a bit on the large side, wide mouth, serious stubble. The man who had come into the flower shop — twice. She sniffed. Sandalwood and mandarin — an elusive mixture. She had smelt it earlier on today too. She knew who Alex darling was. 'Father bloody Christmas!'

'Spot on.' The man called Alex now met her gaze with one of apparent relief, took a step towards her and held out his hand. 'Auntie Imo.'

Marisa's boyfriend? Imo stifled an inappropriate and gin-induced giggle. His handshake was warm and firm, just the way she liked it.

But if looks could kill, Marisa Gibb would have had her stone dead on the carpet. 'Who the hell is Auntie Imo?' she snarled. 'What do you want? And how do you know Alex?'

145

'Ah.' She was quite an operator. Imogen noted that Alex had positioned himself a few feet away from the settee and out of Marisa's range. She wondered where to start. But didn't she have more reason to be on the offensive? She had a grievance and a half to offload, and this girl could have it all, it was about time. 'My name is Imogen West,' she said stiffly, just as Marisa's mother returned with the coffee.

There was a thud and a crash as the tray landed on the floor. Imogen stared at the hot liquid soaking and steaming into the grey and white pile of the carpet, Alex stared at the woman who had dropped it and said, 'Are you all right, Naomi?'

But Marisa and her mother just stared at Imogen. They both knew of her existence then. That much was obvious.

Marisa was the first to regain control. She unfolded herself from the settee. 'You're Edward's wife,' she said.

'Yes.' Imogen tried to keep the anger burning, but the room was spinning and it was hard to be self-righteous when your brain wouldn't keep still. 'I certainly am.' Or was.

Chapter 13

'How clumsy of me.' Naomi Gibb was frantically sponging the carpet, her pink face clashing madly with her ginger hair. 'How very—'

'Imogen.' Rather surprisingly Marisa, ignoring her mother's immersion in carpet-management, seemed to have warmed considerably. 'I've wanted to meet you for so long.'

To Imogen's utter amazement, she came over and planted a cool kiss on her cheek.

Imo blinked up at her. 'Oh, I betchyerhave.' She tried to lace the words with all the scorn of an injured wife. But she couldn't quite recapture the mood somehow, and the slurring didn't help. Besides, it was Edward she was furious with, Edward who had done the betraying, and Edward who wasn't here to answer all the questions she had burning away inside. Fiercely, Imogen pushed her fists into her eyes. It was hardly fair. But she mustn't cry – not now.

Marisa was doing her regal beckoning routine again. 'Alex, Alex . . .' She seemed determined that he should share in this . . . well, this whatever it was.

147

For some reason it felt like a reunion. Which was plainly ridiculous, Imogen told herself firmly. The reunion of the other women? Heaven help them all.

'Alex? However do you know Imogen?'

He fixed her with a penetrating stare from those blue, blue eyes. 'I bought some flowers from her,' he said. 'And a hyacinth.'

Imogen suppressed a wave of mad laughter. Laughter and tears were battling for dominance – doubtless the gin again.

'And then we met up in Kirby's.' He scratched his jaw.

'Almost,' Imogen put in, wondering in the midst of this weird situation whether he was still feeling the after effects of the white beard. 'Though I didn't recognise you.' She remembered how odd his behaviour had been, and knew she should bring the conversation back to Edward and Marisa, but couldn't for the moment think how to do it.

'Not very good at the Santa routine, am I?' He laughed, but still looked uneasy and far too big for this pretty, flowery room, Imo decided.

'Alex is an artist.' Marisa, sleek in her white cat suit, was all pride and possessiveness.

But if he was Marisa's boyfriend, what about Edward? 'What do you paint?' she asked Alex, allowing herself to be diverted, aware that she needed to think this through. In the meantime, Marisa's mother was still frantically sponging the grey and white carpet.

'He paints life,' Marisa replied for him.

'What, all of it?' Try as she might, it was becoming harder and harder to see Marisa Gibb as a contender for the Other Woman. Something was wrong but in her inebriated state Imo couldn't work out what it might be. Naomi had fetched kitchen towels and was keeping her head down. And Marisa . . . well, Marisa was smiling. A bit too much under the circumstances.

'Edward kept you extremely well hidden,' Imogen said sadly. 'You must think me very stupid, but I had no idea he was involved—' she hesitated. Should she say this in front of the girl's mother and boyfriend? '—with another woman.' What the hell? She deserved it.

She noted Marisa's swift glance towards her mother. Clearly, her daughter's liaison came as no surprise to her. 'Until I found your photo.'

'My photo?' The girl was all smiles again. 'Have you got it with you? Let's see.'

Imogen was aware of her own scowl as she groped in her bag. She handed it over.

Marisa perched at her feet, so close that Imo could have touched that strawberry-blonde hair. What was going on? She was behaving more like Daisy than a rival in love. 'Oh, that one. He took it when . . .'

'You're not at all what I expected,' Imogen blurted. Surely this girl could see that she hadn't come here to listen to memories, to be tortured by details of a relationship she'd never imagined could be possible?

'I'm not?' Marisa frowned.

'No. You're so . . .' What? Beautiful? Icy? 'So young,' she said, aware she was close to tears once more. Only, why so many tears when she wasn't even sure if she had loved him? 'What on earth did you see in Edward?'

'See in him?' Marisa looked utterly bewildered, her smooth brow puckered in a frown.

Slowly, Naomi pulled herself up from the floor. Her face

149

was still flushed, Imogen observed, but then she had put a lot of effort into cleaning the carpet.

'I don't think you quite understand,' she said softly. 'Marisa is Edward's daughter.' She came closer to rest her hand gently on Imogen's arm. Her eyes were full of sympathy. 'I'm so sorry.'

'Daughter?' Imogen struggled to make sense of the word. She stared at the hand on her arm, red from carpet cleaning, and shrugged it away from her instinctively. She did not want sympathy. 'Daughter?' she repeated. Had she heard right? Had she drunk more gin than she remembered? Imogen put a hand to her head. She had been so sure . . . There was the photo, the bank statements. And yet, now it all fell into place. She looked down at the girl, still sitting by her feet, head turned, half-smiling, as if waiting for her to comprehend. Marisa's age, the photograph, the money that had been regularly transferred – even the kiss on the cheek from the girl herself. Imogen groaned.

'Are you all right?' Apparently Alex was the only one here not part of the same big happy family.

'Oh, my God.' Did she feel a fool. 'Why didn't Edward tell me?' What was wrong with having had a child before they'd even met?

There was another awkward pause.

'It's a long story,' Naomi said at last, seemingly not sure of her ground.

Had they been married? Imogen wondered. Or just had an affair long ago? 'Why did he keep you such a secret?' she asked Marisa.

'Does Edward know you're here?' Marisa's mother, answering question with question, had a very strange expression on her face.

150

'What?' Imogen stared at her. 'Does Edward know? Hah!' She heard someone laughing hysterically and then realised who it was. But, oh, God. She looked from Alex to Naomi to Marisa and then back again. They didn't even know he was dead.

In the Gull and Gherkin Jude was considering whether or not to invite Roger back to the flat. She had been on the singles circuit for long enough to be aware of the safety aspect – using 141 before she returned a call left on her *Heart to Heart* tape, not giving out her address, meeting in a public place and so on. But she was so tired of it all, so needy of personal contact, a little bit of trust from time to time.

'Another drink?' he asked.

Jude considered. She didn't know that she wanted to stay here any longer. The Gull and Gherkin – despite its name – was not an old-fashioned pub. It was light and bright and boasted circular pale pine-veneered tables, high chrome bar stools and leaflets about what was playing at Chichester Festival Theatre. There was nothing wrong with the place but it wasn't high on atmosphere. 'I'm not bothered.' She threw the ball back into his court. He had been generous with the drinks, while his suggestion that she accompany him to a friend's party next month seemed to indicate an intention to stick around for a while.

'Or do you fancy coming back to my place for coffee?' He laughed as he said it. 'Don't take that the wrong way.'

Hmm. Intuitive or experienced? Jude regarded him over the rim of a wine glass that was almost empty. Pale blue eyes, fair hair, chunky body. Nothing to write home about, but she wasn't exactly God's gift herself. He was divorced, no kids, no obvious emotional baggage, worked as an electrician.

And now he had managed to put her on the spot. 'I have to get back. My daughter,' she reminded him. Her mother would be there too but she hadn't told Roger yet about her living arrangements. She had implied that there would be a baby-sitter to be relieved, of course. It was always useful to have that to fall back on.

'Yes, I see.' He hesitated.

But at least he hadn't backed away in horror the first time she'd mentioned Daisy. Jude finished off her wine. In fact he'd wanted to know more about her, so either he was a good actor or a genuinely nice guy. And nice guys, as Jude knew only too well, were in short supply.

'Your place then?'

Crunch time. He took her hand. The first physical contact between them but the earth didn't even tremble – and neither did she. 'Nothing heavy, Jude,' he said. 'But we can be friends, can't we?'

''Course we can.' That settled it. There was such a thing as being too cautious, she reasoned. How could a relationship ever take off if she discounted every man before they even got to first base? She should give him a chance. And she shouldn't be too choosy. Nobody was perfect.

'All right,' she said. 'But it'll have to be a quick coffee.' She didn't fancy him but she could always use a friend. And who could tell what might develop in time?

'It was the shock.' Naomi had fainted clean to the ground, though luckily not in the same place that she'd spilt the coffee. Now – with the help of the other three – she had come round and was sitting on the rose-patterned sofa next to her daughter.

Alex was passing round brandy on a tray. Perhaps she

152

shouldn't but Imogen tossed one back anyway. God knows she needed it. She had entirely neglected to consider the fact that the woman she was visiting might not know of Edward's death. Make that *women*, she thought. It was incredible, and yet obvious when you came to think of it. It was Imogen who had informed everyone who had to be informed, Imogen who had dealt with everything that had to be dealt with – from bank accounts to funeral arrangements. With no mention of a daughter in his will or anywhere else how could she have known?

Imo ran her fingers through what she'd already come to think of as her new hair. She'd tried to be tactful but obviously failed miserably.

Marisa was whey-faced. 'She's been waiting to hear from him,' she told Imogen as if her mother weren't in the room. 'He hasn't been here for ages. She thought he didn't want her any more.'

Want her any more? Imogen blinked at her and grabbed another brandy from the tray. What did *that* mean? That Edward and Naomi Gibb had been lovers right up until his death? She downed the brandy in one, pretending not to notice Alex's look of surprise. She had been right all along – only, she'd got the wrong woman. And despite herself, she felt a wave of sympathy for her. Naomi Gibb did not epitomise the typical mistress. She was small, plain, quiet. But there must have been something that she had given Edward, something Imogen herself had not . . .

It was what she had come here for – to find out. But now was not the time. She couldn't ask Naomi how long it had gone on, she couldn't ask her why. In fact . . . Imogen got to her feet. She couldn't stay here one moment longer. 'I'm sorry to have dumped all this on you,' she said

153

awkwardly, feeling angry, confused and upset all at the same time. 'But—'

'You were dumped on too.' Alex laid his hand briefly on her shoulder.

'Yes, I was.' Imogen felt absurdly grateful for his understanding. Though perhaps it had been a mistake to come. All she'd done was disrupt another two lives. 'I must go,' she said.

The two other women barely acknowledged her exit as Imogen got up and went to find her coat. She slipped out of the front door, took a deep breath as the fresh, cold air hit her like a slap . . . and realised that Alex was right behind her.

'Shouldn't you stay with them?' Whatever her own feelings, Marisa and Naomi Gibb had lost a man who had been centrally important in their lives – albeit a man who had also been Imogen's husband. She'd had weeks to grieve. Their time was only just beginning.

'They've got each other.' He was brusque. 'I'll take you home.'

Imo barely hesitated. 'Oh, all right.' She wasn't feeling great, what with the stress of meeting Edward's other women and after the gin and the brandy and everything. It would be good to be looked after – even if it was by someone else's man, she reminded herself. Already she and Alex seemed to go back a long way and she instinctively trusted him.

'Good.' He took her arm. Long, lean and smelling of mandarin and sandalwood, and the leather of his jacket. Imo relaxed.

'So where's your car?' she asked.

'I don't have one. Where's yours?'

Was he mad? 'At home. I've been drinking.'

'You don't say.' He grinned – it was a nice grin, and there was a lot of it. For some reason she thought of Jude, heart to heart and OHAC. Even on a cold night a grin could beat own car hands down, she decided.

'Point me in the right direction,' he said. 'And we'll go.'

'We're going to walk?'

And yet after a few minutes Imogen found the fresh air not so much cold as . . . well, bracing. The streets in town were hung with Christmas lights and most of the bars and restaurants were still open.

'And now,' he told her, 'you can fill me in. I want to know all there is to know about this husband of yours.'

Jude was filling the kettle when she felt it – the sense of a man getting closer. She had very well-developed antennae as far as such things were concerned. And a need for her own space. She froze. But as she felt his breath on her neck she swung round. That was too close. 'Roger?' She sounded as if she were sending a message by radio waves. 'Roger?'

He raised a hand in what she supposed to be apology. 'Out of order?'

She nodded. Did he have to ask? 'I thought it was friendship we were moving towards.' Only, she of all people should have known better. And she didn't much like the look in those pale eyes of his.

'Right. Yeah, of course. Friendship.' He sounded as if the word was new to him. 'So you're not into sex then?'

'Sex?' Jude decided not to risk turning her back on him at this point. The coffee could wait. 'Not until I know someone really well,' she lied, adopting her primmest expression. Or unless she fancied them like crazy, of course.

He smirked. 'And you're saying you don't know me well enough yet?'

Yet? Jude took a deep breath. 'What kind of woman are you looking for, Roger?'

'Someone soft and fluffy.' He reached out towards her.

Jude stepped smartly away, taking refuge behind one of her high kitchen stools. 'Well, that's it then.' She tugged at the black skirt, but there was no way it was ever going to reach her knees. 'The only time I get remotely soft and fluffy is when I see a traffic warden standing next to my car.'

'I bet.' He took another step towards her. The stool was between them and the cooker was behind her. Any second now she'd be trapped against it, not a pleasant fate for any woman. 'It's true,' she insisted, trying to sound more forceful than she felt.

'I reckon you're soft as anything under that . . . under that . . .' He trailed off, apparently unsure of what was on her outside. 'And I can think of lots of ways you could get to know me better.'

'I'm quite sure you can.' Seeing Roger move the stool aside, Jude took a neat side-step to her right, thus leaving him face to face with an oven hob stained with whichever pasta sauce Hazel had been practising making tonight. Whatever it was, it had included a lot of tomato. 'But sex isn't on offer here. Nothing heavy, you said. Otherwise I would never have invited you back.'

He spread his hands little boy pleading style. 'But what if I can't resist you, Jude?'

'Try harder,' she snapped. If he pushed her any further she'd make it bloody easy for him to resist.

156

'Hey — why don't you loosen up a little?' He was on to her again and Jude was getting seriously annoyed. So was he — at her lack of co-operation presumably. The thick neck above the chunky cable-knit sweater was flushed and his mouth was tight. 'What is it with you? You got a problem or something?'

'Only you.'

At this he grabbed her by the shoulders and tried to kiss her.

'Get off!' Jude turned her head and got her cheek slobbered on. Pathetic. She lifted her arm to wipe it away. 'I think it's time for you to go.'

'You prefer dykes, do you?' He tried for a lunge and lift of the black pencil skirt, but was no match for the super-cling lurex or the medium-control front panels of her new knickers which were determined to give nothing away.

'Nothing doing,' Jude growled, and kicked him in the shin.

'What did y'do that for?' he moaned, clutching his leg.

Whatever had happened to male enlightenment? she wondered. 'You'd better make yourself scarce,' she advised. 'Before I call for the lodger and get you thrown out.'

This ploy to get rid of Roger without further ado might have worked had Hazel not wandered into the kitchen at that very moment, wearing only a face mask and a white towel. As a threatening lodger, she didn't quite look the part, Jude realised, though she did, undeniably, look odd.

'What on earth is going on?'

'Jesus wept!' Roger stared at Hazel, and her mother had precisely the effect that Jude had been hoping for.

Roger ran.

*

Alex Armstrong didn't know what to make of Imogen West. He had never known a woman's moods change so rapidly, and when she'd turned up at Marisa's earlier . . . Well, he'd thought his eyes must be popping out of his head. Not just because she was the ultimate in unexpected visitors, but because she'd clearly been drinking (before this he'd had her down as perfectly in control at all times whether running a flower shop or visiting Santa Claus in a department store). She looked different too – beautiful, sophisticated but distant; he'd never felt such an urge to paint a woman. And as for her agenda . . . He had soon known that he had to find out more.

'I don't know why I'm telling you all this,' she'd said, veering to the left to walk down a driveway half-blocked by a small Vauxhall Nova and apparently belonging to a cottage set back from the road. 'I don't even understand half of it myself.'

The exterior security light flicked on to reveal a mixture of old and new – flint walls, a heavy oak door but double glazed and immaculately painted – all in the best possible taste. It made him feel strangely uncomfortable. This Edward must have been pretty well-heeled.

'Because I asked?' He took the key that Imogen was waving ineffectually in front of the solid front door. 'Here, let me. Is there an alarm or anything?'

'Thank you, Marisa's boyfriend,' she said.

Alex winced as he inserted the key. 'Alex, please. You see, she's not really my . . .' No, he had no right to say that. Not yet. 'Alarm?'

'Yes, but I always forget to switch it on. Edward used to get so cross . . .'

He pushed the door gently and stood back.

'I would invite you in.' Imogen had taken a step inside and was hanging on to the door as if she might fall. 'But I'm in no fit state for visitors. And . . .'

'And?' He wanted to kiss her. What the hell was happening to him? He wanted to take her in his arms and kiss her.

'And I need to go to bed.' She wrinkled her nose and he wanted to kiss her even more.

'Will you be all right?' Yes, he wanted to kiss her, but he wouldn't take advantage of this woman. Quite the opposite. Alex was surprising himself. He actually wanted to take care of her.

'Oh, yes, I'll be fine.' She closed her eyes, seemed to drift away from him and then snapped them open again.

He couldn't see in this light but he knew they were grey. Warm ash. But they were sad too, and she was almost too thin – her ankles and wrists so slender. He could probably encircle her ankle with one hand . . .

'You're sure?' Why the hell had Marisa's father ever bothered with Naomi Gibb when he had this woman waiting at home? Alex asked himself. They might not have been blissfully happy – she had asked Alex if he'd ever been in love and looked sort of wistful when he said, no, he wasn't sure he knew what love was. But she hadn't walked out on this Edward chap; she had stayed. Was that why tonight's revelation seemed to have hurt her so much?

'I'm sure.' She seemed very serious. She wasn't smiling, but neither was she shutting the door in his face.

'Take care of yourself then.' But he couldn't leave without touching her. Gently, Alex ran his fingers down one cheek. Her skin was soft and cool from the night air. His fingertips touched the corners of her mouth.

She stared at him.

They stayed motionless, his fingers on her face, her eyes still and unblinking. For what seemed like minutes . . .

Until she broke abruptly away from him and at last slammed shut the heavy oak door.

Chapter 14

Christmas Eve — hardly a day for coping with revelations about one's late husband. It was at times like these, Imogen thought, as she hastily brushed crumbs from her kitchen table, straightened chairs, and chucked the remainder of a granary loaf in the terracotta bread bucket, that a girl needed her mother.

In the hallway, she grabbed her black woollen coat from the banister. This time of year should be renamed the festering season. Imogen sighed. Some people had started in October, for goodness' sake. A greedy article was Christmas — everyone consumed more than was good for them while IT consumed the rest of the year; August to January wrapped in tinsel, bows and silver paper.

She switched on the answerphone. No matter that at thirty-five a girl was a girl no longer. Where was that mother when her daughter was trying to cope with infidelity and a hangover from hell? Doing head stands in Delhi or heading for darkest Darjeeling on a narrow-gauge track into the Himalayas? Imogen picked up her bag and opened the front door of the cottage. She'd prefer to go back to bed.

161

But it was no use feeling sorry for herself, she had a shop to open.

What with the head and everything, she needed all her concentration to negotiate Chichester's early-Christmas Eve traffic, before turning into the tiny car park behind South Street. She locked up the Nova and walked round to the front. It was milder today and thankfully not raining.

'Good God.' Tiffany was waiting outside *Say It With Flowers* – never been known before – nails and hair beglittered, five tiny Santa studs in one ear and three snowmen in the other.

'Shouldn't take the Lord's name in vain, my mum says.' She caught Imogen's look. 'What? Nothing wrong with being Christmassy is there?'

''Course not.' Though the Santas made her think of Alex. And the thought of him probably made her face look Christmassy-red with huge Christmas carrier bags under the eyes. But no one could accuse Tiffany of not looking interesting. She even had a plum pudding stencilled on the back of one hand.

Very interesting . . . No sooner had Imogen unlocked the door than Tiffany bolted out back. 'Where d'you think—'

'I need to check the greenhouse.' She was gone.

Imogen frowned. She switched on the heating, began to check the flowers, and then Warren strode in.

'All right?' Big, greasy and beleathered, he didn't seem to expect an answer.

So she gave him a question. 'Bit early for you, isn't it? Tiffany'll be back in a mo. She's just gone out the back.'

While Warren lurked by the chrysanthemums, Imogen began preparing the cut flowers. They and the red and cream poinsettias would sell well today – everyone wanted fresh

162

flowers in the house for Christmas. She stripped off the lower leaves. Especially the white lilies, the red and white carnations, the freesias. Christmas . . . Oh, God. Once again, it all threatened to sweep over her. Imogen glanced across at Warren who was scratching an acne-infested chin, and felt even worse.

A guilty-looking Tiffany returned. She gave a start at the sight of Warren, promptly retreating with him to the far corner of the shop where they began whispering furiously by the potted ferns, glancing every so often towards Imo. Interesting, hmm? Right now she would prefer plain old boring and reliable.

Imo gave them two minutes – and that was generous, she felt. Then: 'When you two have *quite* finished . . .' She would swear she saw Tiffany pass him something. But what? 'There's a lot to do this morning, Tiffany.'

Warren stuck his hands – and the whatever it might be – into his pockets as he and Tiffany sprang apart. 'Yeah, right.' he said, articulate as ever. She supposed he had more than twenty words in his repertoire but you'd never guess.

'Sorry, Imo.' Tiffany pulled off her denim jacket and replaced it with green overalls with a white poppy embroidered on the lapel.

Imogen was stripping off more leaves than strictly necessary. Calm, be calm, she told herself. Get in the Christmas spirit – but she'd had more than enough of that last night. 'What's going on?' She handed Tiffany a heap of carnations. 'A quarter-inch off the stem, please. At an angle.'

Tiffany blushed to the roots of her bleached and glittered hair and shuffled her feet. 'Nothing.' She was wearing high black patent wedges that made Imo feel uncomfortable just looking at them. And when teenagers said 'nothing' in that defensive tone, you could be sure there was something. Imogen decided to try the reasonable approach. 'Tiffany, I like you.' Positive reinforcement was meant to work wonders. 'But I have a business to protect here.' She grabbed a bucket from the drainer, put it in the sink and turned on the tap.

Tiffany looked outraged. 'I blatantly wouldn't do anything to hurt the business, Imo.' She stopped snipping and gave Imogen the wide-eyed innocent treatment.

Imo spoke louder to compete with the running water. 'I don't like Warren.' Perhaps she was being childish, but she had certainly felt threatened by him before and she was sure he was up to no good. She turned off the tap sharply. 'And I don't want him in the shop, OK?' It was her shop, her decision, her right. And if nothing was going on then Tiffany would leap to his defence.

She didn't. 'OK,' she agreed, without so much as a whisper of a fight. 'I'll tell him.'

OK? 'And if there's anything you'd like to tell *me* . . .' Imogen let this hang, took hold of the bucket with both hands and heaved it out of the sink towards the cut flowers. She should use a hose but somehow she could never be bothered. She would make the time today to have a good look round that greenhouse, she decided. Could Tiffany be hiding something there for Warren? Something stolen perhaps? Or was Imo's imagination working a night shift?

'I love it here, Imo,' was all Tiffany said. Followed by, 'Can I help you with anything?'

With her back to the shop door, as she positioned the bucket for the chrysanthemums, Imogen hadn't realised anyone had come in. She swivelled round and looked up to meet the clear gaze of Marisa Gibb. Oh, hell. It was too early for this. She hadn't got her aching head round the events of last night yet, let alone those of this morning.

'Imogen . . .'

'Marisa.' So, they knew one another's names. Big deal. How should she handle this? Imo had no idea. This girl who was cool, so cool, was virtually her step-daughter. Virtually? Hellfire. She took the flowers laid by Tiffany on the counter and began placing them in the bucket. At least, she *would* have been her step-daughter if Imogen had met her when Edward was alive. Was that how it worked? What happened to step-daughters when the step bit was no longer operative? When the father had gone?

'I wanted to apologise.' Today Marisa was dressed all in black, she noted.

And why shouldn't she grieve? She had lost her father, Imo reminded herself. And yet even the grieving seemed contrived. It was all so carefully chic – the skintight black leather trousers, two-tone fleece jacket, black silk-chiffon scarf, perfectly manicured (by Jude presumably) nails – although one hand remained gloved, she observed. She could see from Tiffany's scathing expression what she thought about this vision of perfection.

'There's nothing to apologise for.' Running out of chrys-anthemums, Imo picked up a vase of freesias and moved them into the display area of the shop. Theirs was a delicate scent, but they were part of the whole. Fragrance, Imo thought, was a matter of balance. And apologies? Look at her own behaviour. Apart from being the pur-veyor of bad news, she had practically accused Marisa of having an affair with her own father. And . . . Imogen thought of Alex. No. She wouldn't think of Alex – bad idea.

165

Marisa brushed this impatiently aside. 'You weren't to know.'

She had to ask. 'How is your mother?' Edward's mistress, Edward's other woman, that awfully nice customer who had come into her shop – so tentative, so polite – to buy lilies.

Marisa's face hardened. 'She'll survive.'

'I'm relieved to hear it.' But Imogen looked away. She didn't like this girl. She had thought it last night, but blamed the gin, and she thought it again now. She didn't like this almost-step-daughter with her hard eyes and cold way of dismissing her own mother. Imogen wanted nothing more to do with her. Only – was it possible now? Despite Edward's death they seemed irrevocably connected.

'Will you come to see us tomorrow?' Marisa asked.

'What?' Her jaw must have dropped practically to the floor. 'But tomorrow's Christmas Day.'

'I know.' The clear eyes flickered. 'But we'd like you to.'

Imogen found this hard to believe. Marisa perhaps, but . . . 'Your mother too?'

She nodded. 'There's a lot we'd like to know – if it isn't too painful,' she added. 'A lot she wants to ask you.'

The feeling was mutual. But on Christmas Day? 'It must have been a terrible shock for you both,' Imogen murmured.

'My mother feels awful about the whole thing.' Her voice was emotionless. Imogen could almost imagine her reaching into some mental compartment to check her script. *Have I said all the right things? Can I leave now?* 'She loved him, of course,' Marisa added. 'Always has.'

'Of course.' Imogen paused in the act of separating

gypsophilia. Hang on, though. Why, *of course*? He had married Imogen, hadn't he? 'I'm not sure it's a good idea,' she said. In fact, it was a ridiculous idea.

'Please?' Marisa moved closer, so close that Imo could smell her perfume – subtle and expensive. She probably always got what she wanted in life, and that would mean nice things. But how? And where did Alex fit in?

Imogen shivered. No, she mustn't think of Alex. She must concentrate on this slice of ice here in front of her. A more unlikely daughter for Edward and Naomi, she couldn't imagine. Edward and Naomi . . . The horror of it was that the two of them seemed as if they would have been ideally suited. She closed her eyes.

'A quick drink? My father would have liked that.'

Oh, come on . . . 'Would he?' More likely he would have been horribly embarrassed. Imogen became aware that Tiffany was staring at them. She gave her a get-on-with-your-work kind of look. And hesitated. She had to admit she was curious. There were so many unanswered questions. 'All right, I will.' Why did she feel this was one of her crazier decisions?

Marisa gave a small smile of triumph, blast her. 'Good. We'll expect you at eleven.' She clicked the heels of her well-polished boots together – Nazi-like, Imo couldn't help thinking – and was gone.

'She's his what?' Jude shrieked. She pushed hair spray, wax and mousse aside and plonked a cup of murky coffee on the black ledge in front of Imogen. Her greener-than-emerald eyes opened wider.

'His daughter,' Imogen repeated patiently. She had only dropped in to the salon on the way home from work to give Jude the lowdown on what had happened the night before. Oh, all right, and because she wasn't too keen on going home to an empty cottage on Christmas Eve.

'Bloody hell,' Jude said. 'Talk about dark and devious.'

Imo was glad that she'd caught her during a cigarette and coffee break. 'Before my final pre-Christmas brow tidy and lash tint,' she'd told her when she walked in, straightening her black shift and shooting Imo a wink.

Imogen took a deep breath. 'And I'm going round there again tomorrow.'

'What the hell for?'

'To discuss things.' She knew it sounded mad. It *was* mad. Warily, she sipped her coffee. A drink of the alcoholic variety would be more welcome – but after last night she didn't know if it would kill or cure.

'I won't stay for long,' she told Jude. 'I'll be with you by one at the latest.'

'I'm not thinking of myself, sweetie.' Jude flicked some ash from her cigarette into the glass ashtray. 'I'm thinking of what a happy Christmas you'll be in for – meeting up with Edward's daughter and his bit on the side. I mean, honestly.' She smoothed back thick auburn hair.

Imogen almost choked on her coffee. Anyone less like a bit on the side than Naomi Gibb she couldn't imagine.

Jude inhaled fiercely. 'You need your head examined. You said yourself you don't even like the girl.'

'I don't.' It was difficult, Imo found, to admit that she wanted to talk to her husband's lover. Especially when Jude was in one of her cynical moods. A thought struck her. How could she have forgotten? 'What happened with Roger?'

Jude's ferocious green glare told her she was right.

168

'Nothing happened with Roger and nothing will be happening with Roger. Not now and not in the foreseeable future, OK?' She slammed her mug down on the reception desk. A splash of coffee jumped out in protest and landed on the appointments book. She ignored it.

'Another one bites the dust?' Could this be the reason for today's transformation? Imo wondered, resolving to get it out of her friend tomorrow after Christmas dinner and a few slugs of brandy.

Jude wagged a finger at her. 'Don't change the subject. We were talking about your strange desire for emotional masochism on a day when everyone else in the Western world is getting drunk and pretending to enjoy themselves with Auntie Edna.'

'That's me.' Imogen shrugged. Her only hope was to make light of it. 'Always one for the difficult option.'

Jude got to her feet, picked up her ashtray and disappeared into the kitchenette. 'Just be careful,' she warned, as she emerged, drying her hands.

'Of Marisa? Or of Naomi?' Imogen laughed.

'Of getting sucked in.' Jude nodded in a worldly-wise sort of way that didn't suit her in the least. 'That's the danger, Imo. They want to suck you into their lives. I know. I can feel it in my water.'

Imogen refrained from debating the powers of Jude's bladder. 'I won't let that happen.'

She watched as Jude began to prepare her instruments of torture. Jude was her best friend, and she was probably right. But Imo had decided. She would do what she damned well pleased.

As Imogen drove through the one-way streets of Chichester

back to the cottage, it began to rain and she found herself thinking not of Naomi or Marisa, but of Alex. She couldn't resist the thought of him any longer. It was a long time since a man had touched her like that. Edward had never done it; touched her with curiosity — as if he wanted to know what was underneath, as if he were marvelling at the way skin and bone were formed to create what was on the outside . . .

In the darkness, even with street lamps and Christmas lights, Priory Park on her left was just a lumpen mass of blackness. In the summer the park, with its majestic trees and cool expanse of green, was playground for bowlers, cricketers, summer lovers . . . Oops, there she went again. Of course, Alex probably hadn't been thinking anything of the kind last night. He was probably marvelling at the amount of make-up she had allowed Jude to put on her face. Or counting the lines.

As she stopped at the traffic lights, Imogen raised her hand slowly to touch her cheek. It was different, today's face — devoid of the slap and colour, it felt naked and vulnerable. She glanced into the rear-view mirror. Behind her, a young, impatient driver was revving the engine of his red Porsche. Making a statement? Imogen smiled. Was Jude right? Did women wear make-up in order to find a sense of self? To be someone different? Imo shook her head in affectionate despair. Jude and her theories on beauty, women, men . . . But she was a special person, and she deserved to find a special man. *If* that was what she wanted. Imo tapped her finger-nails on the steering wheel. *Was* that what she wanted? What could have happened with Roger? Imo wondered, putting a hand to her face again, trying to recapture the Alex-feeling. But his touch was elusive tonight.

What rubbish. The lights changed, the driver behind her hooted angrily. Momentarily mesmerised by the rain sweeping across the windscreen, Imogen shoved the Nova into gear and accelerated – hard. Such rubbish. He was so young for a start. Practically a boy. And she was a thirty-five-year-old woman, even if she was behaving like a teenager – something she'd never done before. She shivered, and turned up the heating. Hot air blasted out at her. How old was he? Twenty-five at the most. And he was also the perfectly lovely Marisa's boyfriend. Imo increased the speed of the wipers with the flick of a finger. She was imagining things.

She passed the fire station – all the lights were blazing, two engines parked and ready to go – and turned into Bracken Street. Why had she told him everything? It wasn't only because of the booze, it hadn't just been the way he'd asked, the way he'd listened . . .

More rubbish. But would he be there tomorrow? She hoped so. She hoped not. Oh, hell . . .

Imogen swung the Nova into the drive, switched off the ignition, got out of the car and tensed. The rain was falling harder, the exterior light had come on. But there was another light. A light on in the cottage.

She locked the car, ran round to the front door and groped for her keys. Her fingers were already cold and dysfunctional, rain had splattered her coat and crept inside her collar. But it was all right. It had been so dark this morning, that was all, she must have left that light on. These winter days . . . so dingy, so gloomy. And she certainly hadn't been with it when she'd left the cottage with her hangover from hell.

Imogen slammed the door behind her, took a step forward

171

and listened. Someone was in the sitting-room. She froze. Only . . . burglars wouldn't switch on the radio, would they? And only one person she knew was hopelessly addicted to Radio 4.

She flung open the door. 'Mother!'

Vanessa was standing by the cream sofa. Imogen grabbed her and enveloped her mother's small-boned frame in a huge hug.

'What a marvellous welcome.' Vanessa seemed to be struggling for air. There was a strained look about her – jet lag probably. 'Let go of me and let me look at you, darling.'

Reluctantly, Imogen released her and they drew apart. She could hardly speak, she was so ridiculously pleased to see her.

'I'm sure you've lost weight, darling. Have you been bothering to eat proper meals?' Vanessa narrowed her almond-shaped eyes. She almost sounded like a proper mother, Imogen thought. 'Truth now.'

'Better meals than you've had, I should think.' Imogen pulled off her coat, flopped into the sofa and leaned back against the cushions, patting the seat beside her.

Vanessa clicked her tongue. 'India is not merely the place to acquire a tapeworm, darling,' she remonstrated. 'There are plenty of other things in its favour, let me tell you.' She sat down next to her.

'Please.' Imogen smiled. Christmas suddenly seemed a much brighter prospect. 'And when you're done, have I got some things to tell you . . .'

Chapter 15

'We were childhood sweethearts,' Naomi said. She was sitting on the rose-patterned easy chair, hands clasped, knees together. As she spoke, her sad expression changed into almost-smiling and far-away.

'I see.' And Imogen could see – how she might have been as a girl with her calm voice and gentle eyes. She had been wrong to think Naomi plain. Her clothes were ordinary, inexpensive and even unfashionable, like the brown waisted dress she wore today. But her pale skin and light red hair gave her an undeniable quiet appeal.

'At seventeen I was so naive.' Naomi shook her head in wonder, glanced across at Marisa who had separated herself from them by sitting on the small rocker in the far corner of the room. 'It never occurred to me that Edward and I wouldn't be together forever. You know how it is?' She looked to Imogen for confirmation.

Imo nodded though she hadn't known it, she realised with a small shock.

Naomi twisted her hands together. 'I don't want to upset you.'

'You're not. Please go on.' Imogen wanted to hear it all. It might help her find a way forward. And it didn't quite seem as if Naomi – sitting here in this pink and flowery room that made few concessions to the time of year; a small silver artificial tree, a few cards strung above the mantelpiece – could be talking about *her* Edward anyway. There were now two Edwards at least.

'I looked up to him,' Naomi went on. 'I suppose you could say . . .' she hesitated '. . . he was everything to me. My world.' The sadness in her eyes returned.

Imogen thought of Marisa's words: *Of course she loved him* . . . She could see that now. Whereas Edward had never been everything to *her*, she realised with a pang of guilt. So what had gone wrong between them? 'Didn't he feel the same?' she asked. Edward was always so self-contained, so compartmentalised. It wasn't easy seeing him as a man to whom Naomi Gibb – or anyone else for that matter – could be everything. He wasn't exactly a you-are-everything kind of man.

Naomi laughed softly. 'Oh, he cared for me,' she said. 'I was an easy sort of girlfriend to have in those days.'

Imogen shook her head. 'Don't say that.'

Marisa looked up. She was wearing black again today, a soft, cashmere turtleneck and long woollen skirt. 'She always puts herself down.'

And so do you. Imogen sipped her sherry. She had never liked the drink – it was too sweet and sickly for her taste. But she needed fortification and she hadn't been given an alternative. Yes, Marisa was very good at putting her mother down. A pity really that she was here at all. And a good thing, Imogen decided firmly, that Alex was not.

'I was, though,' Naomi protested. Her fingers moved to

174

her hair. No rings, Imo observed, twisting her own tiny amber stone. She had taken off her wedding ring the day after she'd found the photograph – a small gesture but an important one, she had felt. 'I never complained if he was late for a date or forgot to phone me.'

'I can imagine,' Marisa said dryly. 'Doormat,' her eyes added. Imogen replaced her glass on the table beside her and licked the sweetness from her lips.

Naomi shrugged. 'You can't change who you are,' she told her daughter. 'I couldn't have played hard to get, or whatever you like to call it, even if I'd wanted to.'

Imogen smiled in sympathy. Not everyone saw love as a game with rules, strategies and one clear winner, thank you very much. Like Jude did. 'But what went wrong?' she persisted.

'Nothing at first. We drifted along for some years. We were saving.'

'To get married?'

'Oh, yes. Or at least, that was what I thought. I had a ring. I always assumed . . .' Her voice trailed off. 'Until it happened.'

Imogen waited, though she could guess the rest. It was old as the hills and twice as corny.

Naomi's expression changed once more. She glanced at Marisa. 'We never took precautions,' she said. 'It was silly of us, I suppose. but Edward said he'd take care of it and . . .'

'And he didn't,' Marisa provided. She was sipping orange juice, seemingly unmoved, the chair rocking gently as if she hadn't a care in the world.

Naomi shifted uneasily. It must be difficult for her, Imogen thought.

'I got pregnant.'

Imogen glanced from mother to daughter. The innocence bit surprised her. Edward had never seemed in the least innocent to her.

Naomi shook her head. 'I assumed it wouldn't make much difference; we'd just get married earlier than planned. Only . . .' she hesitated. 'When I told Edward, I realised for the first time that he wasn't ready to settle down at all.'

It was hard for Imogen to imagine. When she'd met Edward, he'd been thirty-four, and – according to Vanessa – already old before his time.

Naomi looked into the distance as if she were remembering. 'Don't misunderstand me,' she said. 'Edward was *prepared* to marry me. He was always a loyal man. He took his responsibilities very seriously.'

Imogen too had thought him loyal – until she'd found out about his other women. But she let this pass.

Naomi sighed. 'But I could tell, you see, that he actually didn't *want* to marry me.'

'Ah.' Imo was beginning to understand. She stared at one of the Christmas cards – a huge, red Santa driving a sleigh – and thought of Alex.

She was brought back to the here and now by a snort of derision from the far corner of the room. 'As if that mattered,' Marisa said. Her voice was clipped and cold. 'I don't know why you expected him to be overjoyed. Wasn't it enough that he was willing to do the decent thing?'

Naomi cast a despairing look towards her daughter. 'She doesn't understand,' she told Imogen.

'What is there to understand?' Marisa snapped. 'What I do understand is that you deprived me of a father for my entire childhood.' Bitterness was clear in the curl of her lip.

Imogen tried to see things from Marisa's point of view, but despite the fact that she should hate her, it was Naomi she felt sorry for.

Marisa looked around the small room as if she were about to enlarge on the subject of deprivation. 'Just because he didn't leap up and down cheering when you got yourself up the duff,' was what she actually said.

Imogen had a clear and shocking mental vision of this. Hastily, she reclaimed her sherry.

'Perhaps you're right,' Naomi said. 'Perhaps I shouldn't have been so proud.' But even now, sitting there so upright, clearly grieving deeply, Imogen had to admire her dignity.

'You let him back out?' she asked.

'Better than that,' Marisa answered for Naomi. 'She told him she wasn't pregnant after all.' She recrossed her legs and stared straight at her mother. 'And then she left him.' The rocker creaked into startled action.

'Goodness.' Imogen could see that must have taken some courage.

Naomi smiled in acknowledgement. 'I didn't want him, you see, if it was half-hearted. What would have been the point? He meant too much to me for that. I couldn't have stood it.'

Imogen's heart went out to her. Better to risk everything and have the chance to have it all, she thought. She had been right to come. The love story Naomi was telling her had confirmed what she had always known, deep down. She might have imagined herself in love with Edward, but perhaps it was more a case of being in love with love. 'So you hid it from him?'

'I went away.' She seemed to sit up even straighter. 'Edward was shocked. And the strange thing was—'

'He never guessed?' Imogen knew how dense men could be. Either that or they were experts at sticking their heads in the sand and waiting for the bad things to go away.

'That's right.' Naomi smoothed her dress. 'I went away thinking . . .' she glanced at Marisa '. . . perhaps wrongly, that I didn't need him. That I could look after my baby alone. That she would never want for anything.'

Imogen noted that Marisa wouldn't quite meet her mother's eye.

'And then I didn't see him for twelve years.'

They sat in silence for a few minutes. Twelve years. That made him thirty-seven by Imogen's reckoning. She and Edward would have been married for two years by then. Imogen was relieved. That meant that when they were first together, first married, then – at least – there was no one else. And now she sensed it was her turn to speak.

'I met him when he was thirty-four,' she said. 'He came along at exactly the right time and seemed to do all the right things. I thought I loved him. I wanted to be loved.'

Naomi sat up straighter, seemed to be holding back her grief. 'And he did love you. He told me you were the most beautiful thing he'd ever seen. That he could hardly believe it when you agreed to marry him.'

Imogen bowed her head. 'That isn't enough,' she said.

Marisa put it more directly. 'You two are like chalk and cheese.' She tossed her hair from her face. 'Having both of you must have been a dream come true for Dad. Adore and be adored, the best of both worlds.'

Imogen looked at Naomi who had loved him so selflessly. Yes, she could see why Edward had wanted this woman in his life.

'We met again by chance.' Naomi took up the story

once again. 'In Hereford – that's where I was living by then.'

'Hereford?' Imogen tried to recall a trip Edward might have made there. Surely she should be able to remember something so significant? But, no.

'We literally bumped into one another in a department store.' Naomi shook her head. 'We had tea. I was with Marisa. He asked me her age, I saw his mind going into overdrive, and then he said: "You didn't waste any time, did you?"'

Imogen could almost hear him. 'How long before he guessed?'

'Not long at all.' Naomi put a hand to her head. 'I think it was her looks that gave it away.'

Imogen scrutinised Marisa's perfect features. She had Naomi's colouring but there was not a freckle to be seen on her clear skin. Her hair was lighter too – blonde with just a hint of red. On Edward the eyes might have been a little softer, the chin not quite so firm. But it was true, she was like her father, and Imo understood now why the girl in the photograph had seemed familiar. Familiar and yet very different. He had been attractive; she was stunning. But he had never been so cold.

'Was he angry?' Imogen asked her. 'That you'd lied to him?'

'Shocked. Baffled.' Naomi frowned at the memory. 'Yes, and angry too.'

'And who the hell could blame him?' Marisa jumped to her feet and stalked to the window. It looked out, Imogen could see, on to a small patch of winter garden. Neat square borders, pruned shrubs, a dampness visible in the grey air and the heaviness of the grass.

179

'What happened next?' Imo turned her attention back to Naomi.

'We wrote occasionally. He asked us to move back nearer Chichester. He wanted to be able to see Marisa.' She leaned forward in the easy chair. 'There was nothing between us. Not at first. But he did offer us financial help.' Once more she glanced at Marisa. 'It wasn't easy to say no.'

She didn't need to explain that Marisa wanted things. She was the sort of girl who would always want things. 'It was your right,' Imogen murmured.

'Well, I felt it was only fair to her—'

'Hip-hip-hooray!' came sarcastically from Marisa by the window.

'There was nothing to keep us in Hereford.' Naomi shrugged. 'Marisa seemed to have taken to him. So back we came.'

She got to her feet, placed a hand gently on Imogen's arm. 'I was never looking to take him away from you, my dear,' she said. 'Not in any shape or form. I told him that he should come clean to you, tell you about us. It was all such a long time ago. There had been no contact between us for so long . . .'

'But you still loved him?' Simple as that.

Naomi barely hesitated. 'I still loved him. He came round often – to see Marisa. He said he didn't want to upset you because you'd not had any children of your own. He wanted everything to be kept separate.'

Compartmentalised. That made sense.

'He was kind. And he seemed to need something.'

Marisa hooted in derision.

'It was too easy to fall back into,' Naomi admitted. 'He had a way of looking at me – as if he really saw

180

me. It made me feel *known*.' At last her eyes filled with tears.

'Although he was married?' Imogen couldn't resist the barb. Naomi might have had him first but she was still the other woman.

'I didn't let myself think about you. I believed him when he said that we weren't hurting you, that he would never hurt you.' Naomi crossed to the window and placed a hand on her daughter's shoulder. For a brief moment they formed a tableau of togetherness. Two women alone and grieving at Christmas-time. Edward's women . . .

'I'm sorry,' Naomi said again. 'I shouldn't have agreed to it. But it was him telling me that—'

'Yes?' Imogen braced herself.

She paused. 'That I gave him the comfort he needed. I couldn't deny him that, you see.'

Chapter 16

'Well, that's one word for it,' Jude said with some scorn. 'Comfort, indeed.'

Imo could almost see the dark fingers of a grey sky stretching out to consume what was left of the daylight on this Christmas afternoon. There were only a few intrepid walkers in Christmas scarves and gloves braving the City Wall walk. Like Jude and Imogen – who had left Vanessa, Hazel and Daisy back at the flat playing Cluedo – they were probably trying to walk off an indulgent Christmas lunch, Imo thought, as they cut along Canon Lane towards the Cathedral.

The past half an hour had been spent discussing Roger and what an arrogant prat he had turned out to be. 'He could have forced me,' Jude said, eyes blazing. 'D'you think we should consider self-defence classes?'

Imogen had steered her away from this by changing the subject to Naomi and Marisa Gibb.

'Why not just call it a good screw and be done with it?' Jude continued now, wrapping the lime-green-and-purple scarf Daisy had given her closer around her neck. 'Comfort? I ask you.'

Imo shot her a sidelong glance. Today her auburn hair had streaks of ash blonde and was tied in a pony-tail, cheerleader-style. Her eyes were bottle-blue, and with the scarf she wore multi-coloured Mr Men gloves. 'It's not as simple as that.' Though Imo was no expert – her marriage had hardly been a hotbed of passion.

They linked arms as they turned up St Richard's Walk. On either side of them the built-in turreted flint walls loomed high, bordered by winter flowers: crimson pansies, late-flowering white daisies, a few over-eager spring bulbs already pushing their shoots out of the earth, Imo noted. Would they survive a heavy frost?

The heels of Jude's clogs clacked on the paving slabs. 'How bad did it make you feel, hearing the whole grisly story? Honestly?'

'Worse than I expected.' Though for different reasons. Imo looked up at the Cathedral, towering in front of them, a lighter grey than the darkening sky. She had ended up feeling like an obstacle to true love.

'And what about the money from the bank account?' Jude was never one to avoid getting down to the nitty gritty. 'What was that all about?'

'He paid maintenance – for them both, I suppose, though Naomi was working until recently, and Marisa . . .' Who knew? 'I do some modelling,' was all she'd say. 'And he paid the mortgage on their house.' Naomi had been reluctant to tell her all this but Imogen had prised it out of her over another small sherry and a mince pie.

Jude spun round to face her as they reached the cloisters. 'Jesus!' She flipped the scarf back in place.

'What?' Imo kept walking, knowing what was coming.

'I know you too well, Imogen West. You're thinking

183

of carrying on paying the mortgage and the maintenance, aren't you?'

Imogen thought of the black leather trousers, the soft cashmere, the manicures. 'Marisa isn't a child. I don't think she needs to be maintained. She's doing just fine by herself.'

'And the mortgage?'

'Ah.' That was a different matter. Imogen paused for a moment, wanting to savour the atmosphere of the cloisters which was all the more potent today of all days. The paving slabs were uneven here, in different colours, shapes and sizes, worn down by time; the battered flint walls broken up by arched windows and tiny old doorways, plaques, carvings and bronzes. On the other side of the passageway huge arched windows looked out on to what Imo knew was a former burial ground, known as Paradise. Paradise? Hah! She'd be lucky . . .

'Naomi's lost her job,' she explained to Jude. 'If she can't pay the mortgage, she might lose the house too.'

'*You're* not responsible,' said Jude fiercely.

'A girl could take that two ways.'

'Shut up, Imo. You know exactly what I mean.'

But she was responsible, wasn't she? And she needed to think things through. She needed some time alone – to go walking alone instead of waiting for Jude to examine another of South Street's window displays. There were plenty of places to walk. Chichester was thought of as a seaside city but most of it was inland. Even the canal was over four miles long and came out in the harbour opposite Bosham Hoe.

'I might walk down to the harbour tomorrow,' she told Jude, whose mind seemed to be on a three-piece suite cut down to half-price and labelled *Sizzling Super Saver*.

'Don't change the subject,' she said, rather unfairly, Imo thought. 'I told you you'd be sucked in.'

They arrived back at *The Goddess Without*, walked down the side alley and up the black spiral stairs. In the living-room, the discussion was becoming heated.

'Granny wanted to be Miss Scarlet,' Daisy was complaining. 'So I had to be Colonel Mustard – again.'

Jude sniffed and regarded her parent. 'Miss Scarlet's a bit teenybopper for you, isn't she, Ma?'

'Not a bit of it.' Hazel moved the candlestick into the ballroom. 'You're as young as you feel. Now . . .' she smiled sweetly '. . . I accuse Reverend Green . . .'

'Oh, hell,' said Vanessa, moving herself from the conservatory. 'I was heading for the secret passageway.'

'Isn't that blasphemy?' Imogen enquired mildly, sitting on the edge of her mother's chair.

'Tell her she's not responsible for them, Vanessa,' Jude demanded. She wandered over to the window and peered out into the gloom. 'You know, earlier on, I'm sure I saw—'

'Tell who what?' Vanessa peered at her cards for inspiration. 'Can't help you, Hazel darling. Sorry.'

Honestly, sometimes Jude was like a dog with a bone, Imogen thought.

'The Gibbs.' Jude disappeared into the kitchen and returned with a plate of M & S mince pies. She took one and nibbled it absent-mindedly. 'Scarface wasn't here today, was he, Ma?' she asked, an odd expression on her face.

'James?' Hazel made them sound like the best of buddies. 'No, dear, why would he be?'

'Thought I saw his car earlier, that's all,' Jude mumbled. 'But you're right. No doubt he's tucked away in some posh country mansion doling out champagne to his wife and family.' She snorted her dismissal of her landlord and turned back to Imogen. 'You can't evade the issue, Imo. And you mustn't do anything without talking to your solicitor.'

'Mmm.' But Imogen didn't agree. To her, it was a question of doing what felt right.

Jude switched on the living-room wall lights. 'Miss Scarlet seems to have acquired a ghostly pallor since lunch,' she said. 'Are you all right, Ma?'

'Tip-top.' Hazel tapped her cards. 'With a rope,' she declared.

Jude frowned. 'Have you been using my new foundation?'

'New foundation?' Hazel peered at the card offered to her by Daisy. 'I don't know what you're talking about.'

'Barely Frost.' Jude stood hand on hip.

'Hint of Snowdrop, actually.'

'Hah! Caught you.' Jude thumped the table in triumph. Colonel Mustard, Reverend Green, Miss Scarlet and Co. all jumped to attention.

'I was in the library,' Vanessa complained. 'One never has time to read these days.'

'One would if one didn't go off gallivanting here, there and everywhere,' Imogen put in, watching the game with amusement. Unnoticed by anyone else, Daisy was assembling a set of suspects. Imogen threw her a wink.

'I rather thought it suited me.' Hazel sounded wistful, but Jude remained unmoved. 'And I thought you told me I could use any of the samples?'

'You can. But—'

'I accuse Miss Scarlet,' Daisy said.

'And so do I,' Jude agreed. 'It's a bit, well . . .'

186

'What?'

'A bit Snowdrop?'

'In the ballroom,' Daisy said.

'There's nothing wrong with Snowdrop.' Hazel looked most put out. 'Snowdrops are charming.'

'In the right place,' Jude muttered.

'With a dagger.' Daisy leaped to her feet and did a passable improvisation of a fiendish murder. As she thrust the dagger deep into her mother's breast she simultaneously checked the secret packet on the Cluedo board and then whooped with glee just as the doorbell rang.

'Well done, darling.' Remarkably unharmed, Jude went to answer it, followed closely by Hazel.

'Hello, hello, hello.'

'The police?' In the living-room Vanessa teased Daisy.

But it was Giorgio who came through, half hidden behind a huge bunch of red and gold chrysanthemums.

Not from *Say It With Flowers*. Imogen examined them surreptitiously for signs of wilting. With her practised eye she guessed they were a week old – at least. But chrysanthemums could take it. They went on forever.

Giorgio was exactly as she'd expected, smooth and yet effervescent, smiling with very white teeth and kissing everyone on both cheeks. In the meantime Hazel fluttered quietly in the background.

'Charmed,' Vanessa told him when the introductions were made by Jude. Imo hid a smile.

At last Giorgio turned to Hazel with skilful dramatic timing. 'My darling.'

'Giorgio.' The Snowdrop fluttered a bit more.

Jude exchanged a cynical eyebrow-lift with Imo.

'I'm so glad you could come.'

'Ah.' He practically threw the chrysanthemums into her waiting arms.

Imogen winced. She always became very protective when there were flowers around.

'I would go to the ends of your earth for my English rose.'

Hazel's blue eyes flashed 'Told you so' at Jude.

Jude leaned towards Imo. 'Utter crap,' she muttered. 'English tea rose – white and windblown.'

'Stop it.' Imo dug her in the ribs. It was all very well being brittle and cynical – and who could blame her after Roger? But this was Christmas Day and Jude was overdoing it. 'Offer the man a drink, for goodness sake.'

Further games of Cluedo were clearly out of the question. But it didn't matter. There was tea. And later – better still for some – Christmas being what it was, there was an old Disney movie on the television.

'Does your mother know what she's doing?' Vanessa enquired mildly of Jude as they stood by the front door of the flat about to leave. In the living-room, Hazel and Giorgio could be heard singing an impromptu duet from *Porgy and Bess.*

Jude winced. 'You tell me.' She grabbed Imo's arm. 'And you tell your mother about the Gibb thing.'

'All right, all right.'

'And . . .'

Imogen sighed. There was more?

'Don't forget our night out.'

'Night out?'

'The singles dance at the White Rabbit. You promised. I'm not a grieving widow any longer, you said.'

'Did I?' Suddenly the singles dance at the White Rabbit held scant appeal.

'You've got to come, Imo.' Jude leaned closer. 'You see, I've got this funny feeling . . .'

Not again. She'd had her fill of Jude's funny feelings.

'That I'm going to meet him.'

'Him?'

'Oh, you know, Imo.' Jude smiled. Roger might never have existed. *Heart to Heart* had been chucked out of the window. Jude – being Jude – had bounced back and moved on. 'The one I've been waiting for,' she said with a flick of the pony-tail. 'My prince, the man of my dreams.'

'So what do you think?' Marisa demanded.

'What about?' Naomi was washing up, Marisa drying – a job Naomi knew she loathed. But that was not her present concern. She was keeping busy, trying not to face it. Edward, dead. It seemed unbearably harsh that she'd rediscovered him only to have him taken away. As if even with that extra time she hadn't bargained for, there still had not been enough. And not even the chance to go to his funeral, to say goodbye.

'I don't need to tell you, Naomi,' he had once said, quite soon after she and Marisa had come back to Chichester. (Had he ever doubted that they would?) *What* hadn't he needed to tell her? she had often wondered. That he loved her? That she was as comfortable as an old slipper and just as easy to slip into? Gosh, that was crude. She added another plate to the meagre stack of washing up and glanced at Marisa. But thankfully she hadn't spoken aloud.

'It's always been so good between us, Naomi.' He had said that too.

189

Yes, always good. But, 'No. How can we? You're married, don't forget.'

'In name only.'

'Oh, Edward.' How many husbands had said that? How many affairs had begun that way? It was enough to make you laugh, only she couldn't because her stomach was churning and she was suddenly afraid she would burp or fart or do something so unacceptable that he would run away again.

'In name only,' he insisted. 'And missing . . .'

Her? Was he missing her? She'd been missing him for years. Never got over him, in fact.

'Warmth,' he said. 'And comfort.'

Ah, yes, warmth. Well, that she couldn't deny him . . . Naomi sighed as she added more water.

'What do you think about *her*, of course.' Marisa flapped the tea towel. She was impatient, but then she often was. 'His wife. This Imogen.'

Imogen. Naomi swished the water around to create more soapsuds as, mentally, she played with the three syllables. Im . . . o . . . gen. And Na . . . o . . . mi. Despite everything, Imogen was someone she didn't mind thinking of.

She had been staggered, of course, that the tall, grave lady from the flower shop (and Naomi had almost asked about a job!) should be Edward's wife. And no sooner had she made that discovery than – well, she'd lost him again. Story of her life, but this time with no going back.

Never had him, Marisa would say. Not really. But she'd had a part of him. They couldn't deny her that.

She took a deep breath. 'She seems nice enough.' Marisa was so hard to please. Often, she wondered why she bothered, frequently she had no idea what her daughter wanted from life. Other times she knew only too well.

'Yes, she's *nice*.' Marisa made it sound like a character flaw. She dried, using only the precise amount of energy required. Wipe round, wipe under, place in pile, transfer to cupboard. 'But do you think she'll help out?'

'Help out?' Naomi was rather in the habit of echoing Marisa. In a sort of amazement at some of the things she came out with. Like this. What did she mean – help out?

'With the house, of course.' Marisa deposited the plates on the shelf and rubbed thumb and forefinger together like Shylock.

Had she raised a Shylock, Naomi wondered.

'With some dosh.' And at her mother's shocked expression: 'That's what you've been getting into a stew over, isn't it?'

'No.' And yes. Mostly she had wondered where he was. Had Edward had enough warmth and comfort in his life?

'We don't want to lose the house as well as Edward, do we?' Marisa demanded. 'So what d'you think? Will she help? I can't carry on—'

'We couldn't possibly ask her.' Naomi didn't want to hear what Marisa couldn't carry on doing. She focused on her scouring cloth.

'Oh, yes, we can.' Marisa blew bubbles from a saucepan and smiled her cat's smile. 'I can.'

This thought filled Naomi with horror – house or not. She had not been prepared to like the wife that gave Edward neither comfort nor warmth, but she liked Imogen West. And there were two sides to every story. 'No,' she said.

Marisa ignored her. 'Now that I have Alex . . .' She put the pan away in the rack and pushed her hair from her face.

191

Her eyes behind that sleek strawberry-blonde curtain were surprisingly dreamy. Oh, yes, you're beautiful, thought Naomi. But did her daughter have Alex? She rather thought not.

'I have to be careful.'

Of what? Naomi rinsed the roasting pan and let out the water. It gurgled obligingly, small droplets of oil shining yellow on the surface. Naomi had come to know him a little and she liked him. But Alex Armstrong certainly wasn't Marisa's usual type. 'What is it about Alex?' she asked. She felt reckless tonight. Sad and reckless. Perhaps her daughter was in love for the first time. Perhaps she might even grow a little nicer, develop a little understanding of others.

'I'm going to make him famous.' Marisa said it in such a way that Naomi almost believed her. 'He has potential. He has a great talent.' She hung the damp tea towel over the oven door handle.

'But no money,' Naomi put in, continuing on her reckless path. She cleaned the sink with long sweeps of her cloth.

'For now.' Marisa's eyes narrowed. 'But Imogen's money . . .'

'What of it? What does it have to do with you?' They had taken too much from her already, Naomi felt.

Marisa sighed. 'Sometimes, Mother, I despair of you. What it has to do with me is that it happens to be my father's money. And I'm his only child.' She spoke with some pride.

Naomi pulled off her apron. This was dreadful. What on earth was she going to do?

'If he could afford to pay the mortgage on this place . . .' Marisa sniffed to indicate the house's low status in the general scheme of things '. . . without her even noticing, then there must have been plenty to go around.'

'Marisa, please.' But it was hopeless. When had her daughter ever listened to her? Naomi took a step closer, made to touch her arm. 'We'll move. We'll manage.'

Marisa glared at her. 'We bloody well will not. Our days of managing are over.'

Naomi didn't reply. But she was terribly afraid that Marisa might be right. She wasn't sure she felt capable of managing at all.

Chapter 17

Imogen watched Jude sashay back to their table. The flickering lights were making her dizzy and the music pounded in her head before vibrating through her entire body down to the floor.

'He's a poet,' Jude announced loudly. She rested her arms on the table and stuck out her backside.

As far as Imogen could see, one had no choice but to stand up and kind of lean over it as Jude was doing. There were no chairs, only carpeted ledges – some way from the tables – that could be pulled out on a hinge from the wall. Modern, yes, but extremely uncomfortable. In the centre of the room was a small circular dance floor. And a lot of lights – some moving, most flashing.

'Really?' Imogen regarded the man at the bar with whom Jude had been dancing. If you could call it dancing . . . Talk about rubbing people up the wrong way. Would he be brave enough to take on a woman like Jude? Seductive, exhibitionist, straight to the point.

Imogen looked sadly at her pineapple and vodka cocktail which also left a lot (vodka mostly) to be desired. She was getting cynical. The White Rabbit Singles Club, as joyfully proclaimed over the door tonight, was only bringing her down.

'Yes, really. C'mon, Imo.' Jude wiggled her hips. 'Get in the mood.' She was wearing a startlingly sequined number in black and silver, with a low neckline and a high hem that left about the same – nothing – to the imagination. Her blonde hair was highlighted with fluorescent purple and her eyes were bright, though their colour couldn't be identified in here. Was the White Rabbit Singles Club ready for Jude? Imo wondered.

In her close-fitting backless grey jersey dress that had seemed elegant before she left tonight, she felt overdressed and about ninety. It wasn't so easy to get in the mood, especially when you glimpsed the predatory males clustering in safe groups at the bar, lurking at the edge of the dance floor, ready to lunge at the first bar of a slow song.

'We're gonna have a ball.' Jude leaned closer to make herself heard. Was she drunk? Not on these vodka-pineapple cocktails, she wasn't. Imogen realised she even had sequins on her temple. 'Look at that . . .'

Imogen looked. And so did the predators. Female, pin-thin and dressed in crimson with stilettos to match. 'Hmm.'

'Where does she put her internal organs, I'd like to know?'

Imogen tried to grin, but her pineapple-coated lips were stuck tight. What was the matter with her? Why was she being such a drag? Why did each and every man here fill her with a primitive kind of terror?

Jude turned her attention back to the one she'd been smooching with. 'Relax, Imo. He's got a friend.'

A friend? Relax? Imo tensed as she examined the two men

fast approaching their space. Number one, the poet, looked suitably wild and Heathcliff-esque enough to impress even Jude. But number two, though an improvement on most of the men here – at least he was under fifty – was blond. Imogen had always distrusted blonds. And: 'He's a midget,' she muttered into Jude's shoulder.

'Vertically challenged.' Jude giggled. Nothing was going to bring her down tonight. 'Take off those high heels and you'll be perfectly matched.'

'Roll over and die.'

'Chunky, though,' Jude shouted in her ear.

'Sounds like dog food,' Imo growled.

'Probably works out.'

'Or eats like a pig.' As the two men reached their pit-stop of a ledge, Imo smiled and floated away with a, 'Time for the ladies, I think.'

In the cloakroom, she re-applied lipstick in the cruel glare of a score of 100-watt naked bulbs and contemplated the fact of the poet. Jude's lack of romantic success was reaching almost legendary proportions. And this might be THE ONE. Imo blew herself a wistful kiss. On balance – if it would help Jude – she thought she'd better be nice (but not too nice) to the friend.

He was called Nigel. 'Imogen,' he yelled in her ear. 'That's an unusual name.'

'Oh, God.'

'Pardon?'

'I said, oh, got to . . . get a drink.' She smiled. 'I'm so thirsty.' And oh-so-fed-up with smiling. She felt as though she had a coat hanger stuck in her mouth.

'Let me go.'

'Well . . .' She was no good at this. Here she was feeling guilty – guilty, God help her – about accepting a drink from a man who was not going to get anything in return. Help! She was a throwback to the seventies, she had never matured, emancipation had passed her by, she was . . .

'How kind,' she yelled back at him. She could at least accept gracefully. Although it was hard to do anything gracefully over this number of decibels.

Back at the ledge, Jude and the poet had finished grinding and gone on to heavy snogging. Imogen tried not to be shocked, but she didn't know where to look. She focused on the poet's bum – Jude had one hand on it, but apart from that it seemed safe enough.

'So what do you do?' she shouted at Nigel when he returned with another vodka-pineapple cocktail.

'Insurance,' he shouted back. 'Are you divorced or what?'

'What,' Imogen told him.

'You're an unusual woman,' he informed her.

Imo's heart sank further. 'You should meet my mother,' she shouted.

He seemed to take this for encouragement. 'Can I take you home?' He glanced over towards the writhing Jude-and-her-poet. They didn't seem to need to breathe. 'Those two are getting on pretty well.'

Imo hesitated. 'Okay, but I don't want you to think . . .' Had she learnt nothing in thirty-five years? Was she as inept at dealing with the opposite sex as she had been in her pre-Edward days?

'I don't think anything.' His eyes were blank. And for some reason she believed him.

'Let's share a taxi,' she compromised, as the final slow

song was announced and the pack hit the remaining single women on the dance floor en masse. She was an independent and capable woman. He was harmless – he was in insurance, for heaven's sake – and shorter than she. She was safe. 'And we'll drop these two off on the way.'

In the taxi, Jude and her poet were still glued together.

'I run a beauty salon,' Jude was telling him. 'That's creative too, you know.'

'All creativity is a precious gift,' he whispered into her hair. 'Believe me.'

Precious being the operative word. Imogen couldn't believe that Jude was taking this seriously.

'Most people don't realise that.' Shamelessly, she fluttered her (fake) eyelashes at him. 'And some people . . .' Was it Imo's imagination or was this directed at her? 'Some people think beauty is only skin deep.'

Funny, but Imo had thought that was the point.

'I create a look,' Jude told him. 'It's not easy.' She glanced at Imo again. 'In fact, with some people it's bloody difficult.'

'You are absolutely amazing,' the poet said – with commendable use of alliteration, Imo noted.

'I am?' Jude grinned.

Imogen sighed.

'And intensely imaginative, I bet. A natural, I can tell.'

Imogen shifted in her seat. They were crawling through the one-way system and she wished the driver would get a move on. She couldn't listen to this drivel much longer. Any minute now he'd start talking in iambic pentameters.

At last she peered out of the cab window. 'Just here,' she told the driver, since Jude had apparently forgotten where she lived. 'By these trees, please.' Oh, no. Now she'd caught it. Rhyming slang. 'Jude? Home time.' After what had happened with Roger the Dodger (there she went again) she half expected her friend to go in alone.

But: 'Come on in, Mattie,' she said to her poet.

Mattie?

'I'll look after you.'

And Imogen imagined that she probably would. Clearly Jude had lost what little common sense she'd had at her disposal earlier tonight. Look after him? She'd eat him for breakfast, more like.

Chapter 18

'I thought you might fancy a walk.'

Imogen stared at Alex Armstrong. He was loitering on the doorstep of the cottage as if it were the most natural place in the world to be. And she felt the heat of a blush — remembering the things she'd told him about her marriage. The expectations, the broken dreams, the feelings of . . . was this all there was?

'Why should you think that?' she said.

Alex shrugged. 'It's New Year's Eve.' He was wearing denim jeans and walking boots, a dark snuggly charcoal fleece jacket only half-zipped.

And she should open up the shop. She was late already. 'What does New Year's Eve have to do with it?' She peered past him. It wasn't raining for a change. In fact the day was looking rather promising. The sky was clear and a determined sun was doing its best to warm things up a little.

'Your last chance this year?'

Hmm. Very clever. 'I hardly know you. We're not exactly friends . . .' She was prevaricating and they both knew it.

They could very easily be friends — and more than. 'You may be Marisa's boyfriend . . .'

'Or I may not.' Mouth tightened, jaw jutted. A mouth, she thought, that looked better when he was smiling.

'But I'm not sure I want to have any further connections with Marisa.' Her almost-step-daughter. Though there was the small question of guilt and responsibility. 'Or with her mother come to that.' Imo shivered. It was true that she had instinctively liked Naomi. But it wasn't done — was it? — to like the other woman? With Edward dead there was no need for jealousy, but once things had been officially arranged there would be little reason for friendship either.

'I'm relieved to hear that.' Alex sounded very formal. 'I feel exactly the same way about them myself.'

'You do?' Why had he come here? she wondered. Why was she so drawn to those fierce blue eyes? Why did she want to run a finger along the angular planes of his face? Why did she want to smile when he smiled? It was ridiculous. She didn't get it. And he almost had a foot in the door already.

'Look . . .' He shifted position. She could slam the door on him now, but she didn't. She opened it wider. An inch, but an inch was as good as a mile.

'Yes?'

'I wanted to see you. I thought we could talk. I've been—'

'Away?' Imo didn't want protestations of any kind. Up until this moment she had put her lack of appetite down to Christmas — everyone else was overindulging and she felt contrary right now. It was silly to keep thinking of him — a customer in her flower shop, a Santa in a grotto, a stranger in someone else's sitting-room. A man whose face might almost be ugly if it weren't for those eyes, that smile . . . But she thought of the predatory faces last night at the White Rabbit's Singles evening, the nothingness of it all, and suddenly was glad he was here.

He nodded. 'In Nottinghamshire. Family.'

'A good Christmas?' Still she hesitated.

'Bearable.' He grinned and then he was in the door and Imogen was wondering where she had put her walking boots. Besides, his face wasn't ugly so much as interesting. She brushed past him, not quite touching, and was assailed by mandarin and sandalwood, the scent that had been haunting her all week.

'Country, sea or town?' she asked him. 'If I agree, that is.'

'It'll be pretty windy on the coast. And tramping fields is a hell of a lot better than pavements.'

She thought of Jude and the thinking time she'd promised herself. This wouldn't exactly be quiet thinking time unless he proved to be a silent walker. And she hoped not – she probably wouldn't be able to stand the tension. 'Ever been to Kingley Vale?' she asked him.

'Nope. A yew forest, isn't it?'

He'd heard of the place at least. She nodded. 'Oldest in Europe. The burial place of ancient kings.'

He raised one eyebrow. 'Dwelling in the past?'

'Not at all,' she countered. 'You said it yourself. A new year's about to begin.' Heaven help them all.

Her mother had swanned off to London this afternoon to stay with her friend Ralph in Knightsbridge. But they'd had a week of catching up. Imogen had brought her up to date on the revelation that had rocked her life, and Vanessa had regaled her with stories of India – about how she'd claimed a place on the famous 'toy' train that climbed 6,000 feet to Darjeeling, for example. Apparently, she had shoved a bedding roll through an open window and simultaneously waved a 20-rupee note at the guard . . .

Such nice brown eyes. And there we were, shuddering up the Himalayas, darling. Complete with children and goats — half of them incontinent. You should have been there.

Imo smiled. Thanks, but no thanks.

And now she was with Ralph. Imogen had sometimes wondered . . . Ralph had been one of her father's oldest friends but that wouldn't have stopped Vanessa, she felt. Fleeting affairs of the heart had been somewhat of a hobby for her mother in those days.

So . . . Imogen looked at Alex and he looked back at her. Tiffany wasn't due in, and they were unlikely to have many customers. The sun was shining and the man was smiling. To hell with it. He was just too tempting. She grinned. The shop could wait.

'Black and platinum streaks?' Jude peered into the mirror at the client sitting in front of her. She tried not to screech. 'Are you completely bonkers, Ma?' She was beginning to think the whole world had gone mad.

'I saw it in one of your magazines.' Hazel frowned and then immediately smoothed it from her brow with a fingertip. 'Coal and ash. It looked awfully elegant. And, well, different.'

'It'll be different, all right.' Jude could accept that she might have been wrong about the Snowdrop foundation, but with black and platinum streaks in her grey hair, Hazel would look as if she were rehearsing for *Macbeth* not *The Life of Gershwin.*

'You promised you'd do a tint.' Hazel put on her stubborn face. 'And the article said subtle highlights create mystery.'

Mystery was one thing, Jude thought, total incomprehension another. 'Well, don't ask me to strip it out again,' she said. 'Because it would take forever.'

'Drama,' Hazel murmured, half-closing her eyes. 'That's what I need.' She wagged a finger at Jude. 'And you're not going to stop me getting it.'

'I wouldn't dream of it, Ma.' What *she* needed after last night's disaster was some good sex. And the sooner the better.

As if in answer to her prayer, the phone rang and Jude picked up. 'Mattie . . .' In the background she heard her mother sigh. She knew she had not been forgiven for trying to seduce Mattie in the hall last night. 'Tongues practically down each other's throats,' her mother had muttered at least three times today. What Jude hadn't told her — since Hazel preferred not to discuss sex, it not being in the Nice Girl rulebook, Jude supposed — was that she had got nowhere with Mattie. Only disappointed.

'About tonight's event . . .' he began.

'Yes?' Jude tried not to sound too eager.

'It's at the community hall in Ross Street. Do you know it?'

'Uh-huh.' It was a couple of miles down the road, and not very promising. She'd encountered it previously in its mother and toddler days, and heard a rumour once about line dancing. But Jude had never been one for following a trend and even when Daisy had toddled, she'd avoided other mothers and toddlers like the plague.

'So, are you coming?'

Jude eyed her mother. She wanted — needed — to see

Mattie. She shifted her weight on to the other clogged foot and thought cold showers and stone floors. (Ouch!) 'Is it a party?' she asked hopefully. No one had parties any more – too much money for too much mess, she supposed. There would always be some joker who threw up or stubbed cigarettes out on your best rug.

'A session of liberation,' he said.

Jude reached in her shift pocket for her cigarettes, lit one and took a deep drag. She had no intention of being one of the millions who tried to give up tonight. 'Liberation from what?' It sounded even less promising than the community hall as a fun venue. Did she want to be liberated – or just chucked to the floor in the throes of passion? Did she need to be liberated on New Year's Eve when other less enlightened people were simply getting drunk and enjoying themselves?

'It's a real letting go sort of experience, you know? Meditation and expression. Freeing the soul.'

Jude took another drag. It didn't sound quite *her*. But she mustn't be hasty. This man could still be the one of her dreams. 'What happens exactly?' she hedged, sitting down, crossing her legs and slipping her feet out of the clogs. 'When you get liberated?' And what would he say if she asked him to come round to the flat for some good old liberating hanky-panky instead?

She noticed her mother reach for a magazine and start flicking through the pages. Jude wanted to go on talking to Mattie but if she didn't get back to her soon, God knows what other bright ideas she might come up with.

He laughed. 'You'll see. It's a commitment thing.'

'Oh.' Jude wondered if she should add Mattie to the list of people going loopy around her. She decided not. She still had high hopes, and an even higher level of frustration. Last night she had coaxed, teased and seduced till she was blue in the face. And then she'd fallen asleep. Goodness knows what time Mattie had left the flat. Jude inhaled deeply and decided she needed more black coffee. It was ironic really after Roger. Perhaps Mattie did need liberating after all.

'The event evolves from the dynamics of the group,' he said.

Group dynamics? It sounded worse by the minute.

'Some poetry, music, maybe some yoga.'

'Will there be any booze?' Jude tucked a stray strand of hair back into her pony-tail. It was all a bit Girl Guides gone New Age to be honest. A slow-burning camp fire and Bob would be their close relative. 'It is New Year's Eve after all,' she added, just in case he thought she was an alcoholic.

'Sure.' She could eat that marshmallow caress in his voice. 'It's just a group of like-minded people . . .'

Hippies 'n' drugs, thought Jude, who had experienced her fill of stoned zombies sitting around, all too paranoid to share their thoughts let alone any other part of themselves. If that was liberation, she was stuck in prison doing life. 'Sounds cool. I can't wait,' she said gamely. She whispered goodbye, put out her cigarette and returned to her mother's hair. She should open up her life to new experiences, she reminded herself. She mustn't be shuttered and cynical. Mattie was different from any man she'd met before – and since most of them were rats, that had to be a good thing. He was sensitive and sweet and, let's face it, she could do with some poetry in her life.

'Black and platinum streaks?' she murmured to her mother, her mind not really on the job. 'Coal and ash?' She fetched the book and flipped through. Thick streaks, had she said? A thought occurred to her. 'You can baby-sit tonight, can't you, Ma?' It was selfish perhaps but she was treating her mother to this tint. And at Hazel's age surely New Year's Eve wasn't crucial?

Because this could be special. Once again Jude felt hopeful. This could be the start of the romance she'd been looking for. A new year, new opportunities. She pulled on her plastic apron and gloves, mixed the colour with hydrogen peroxide, working quickly from the trolley, wanting to get this over with as soon as possible. Daisy would be back from her friend's house in an hour, and besides the smell of the bleach was making her head throb.

'Ma?' She would even try out her new, *never let them see you shine* base coat in honour of the occasion, she decided. If there was dancing she wouldn't even glow. She wasn't sure how it fitted in with liberation, but what the heck.

'Well now . . .'

'Well now what?' Standing here over her mother gave Jude a sense of power that was probably an illusion. A quick flick of the wrist, a grab for the scissors, the make-up tray, the bleach . . . The possible transformations were limitless.

'You did say that you and Imogen might just stay in and . . .' Hazel paused. 'How did you put it? Get plastered to high heaven was the expression, I seem to recall.'

Jude remembered. She teased out a strand of her mother's hair, put it on the foil and painted on the tint. 'But that was before I met Mattie,' she said, pressing down the foil.

'Ah.' Hazel wagged that irritating finger once again. 'But we can't let one man change our lives just like that, can we? We can't run every time he whistles.'

That was rich, coming from her. A more sudden switch

to Italophile Jude had never encountered. She adjusted her mother's black gown. 'I think they're showing a double episode of *Streetlife* tonight,' she wheedled, easing out another strand. 'And afterwards your Giorgio could come round and . . .'

'No!' Hazel sounded quite vehement. 'We want to go out. It's all planned. Giorgio is *not* coming round to the flat tonight.'

'And *Streetlife*?' Jude slapped on the tint. To think that she had once tried to persuade her mother to retune to Melvyn Bragg.

Hazel sniffed. 'It's only a TV programme,' she said. She turned the page of the magazine on her lap. *Looking Spritely at Seventy* ran the headline. 'And it doesn't pay to take television too seriously.'

Grrr! Who could Jude get to baby-sit? The only person who sprang to mind was Imo, but how could she ask her friend when she'd half-promised to meet up with her tonight? Jude continued to plaster the thick glutinous mixture on to her mother's crowning glory and wondered how to get out of the hole she'd dug for herself. Was she being selfish? Should she forget about seeing Mattie tonight?

'I want to seem independent and decisive,' Hazel was telling her reflection. 'But not obvious. That wouldn't do at all.'

No, she couldn't ask Imo. Jude gritted her teeth and weaved another foil.

In no time at all, Hazel's head was covered in rows of foil squares. Jude checked her watch, waited the required processing time – and a bit more because she was desperate for a quick smoke – and then took her mother over to the basin to rinse off.

Hazel was still wittering on, apparently not noticing Jude's silence as she rinsed – and rinsed, and rinsed, but it made no difference – as she swathed her mother's head in a towel, patted and patted and patted her hair dry. She began to panic. Heaven knows what she'd been thinking of. Ash on ash allowed the undertones to come through. And the undertones of ash were . . . oh, hell.

Imogen parked the Nova near the little downland church of West Stoke, changing into her thick socks and walking boots while Alex got out of the car and watched her through the passenger window. Uncomfortably aware that she was all thumbs this morning, Imo finished the lacing, got out, locked the car and led the way out of the car park.

She climbed over the stile first – thus not running the risk of his holding out a hand to help her – and they started down the farm track that led to Kingley Vale. It was certainly brighter than it had been all Christmas. The air held a crispness that made Imo catch her breath, and the sun kept glinting through the clouds, irritatingly accurate at picking out the lighter strands of Alex's thick brown hair. Imogen concentrated on the trees bordering the track.

'Where did you and Edward used to go?' he asked as they stomped on towards the Vale. 'When you went away for holidays?'

Imo thought of Hereford. No, he had never taken her there. 'To France,' she told Alex. '*Gîte* holidays in France. Every year.' It sounded terribly conservative. And the more she thought about it, the more she realised that conservative was exactly what Edward had been.

'Ever go further than France?' Alex asked. 'To . . . I don't know, India? Africa? Australia?' With his boot, he scuffed at the chalk on the path.

'No.' That wasn't Edward's style at all. And to be fair, she'd never suggested it. Even before Edward, when friends were back-packing various trails around the world, Imogen had stayed in Sussex, drifted from one office job and nice but ordinary boyfriend to the next. Travelling was her mother's forte, as if Vanessa had done all Imo's exploring for her.

Out of the corner of her eye she saw Alex push back his hair with one flick of the wrist. He was an angular, graceless man – he was taking the farm track in huge, leggy strides that she could hardly keep pace with. And yet his hands . . . They moved constantly, as he talked, as he walked. His hands, she thought, were strangely compelling. 'And you?' she asked. So far, so good. Polite small talk seemed safe enough.

'I'm in limbo,' he told her, stuffing those hands into the pockets of his fleece as if that was the only way he could stop them moving. 'I've got a friend called Richie who promises me work as a graphic designer that should keep me happily drowning in mortgages and dishwashers for the rest of a very sad life.'

She couldn't imagine that somehow.

As the track narrowed they moved fractionally closer together. Whereas Edward and dishwashers were more interchangeable, Imo reflected. Both were reliable, efficient and predictable. She smiled. Both had neat compartments; everything with a place. Both removed clutter and mess, were clean, and created a look with polish (if you used the right rinse aid). And both could apparently be turned on by someone other than Imogen.

Alex was still talking as they approached the nature reserve and the yews. He was young but good therapy, she decided. 'And sometimes all I want to do is make it as a painter.'

That would be the bit Marisa liked, Imogen guessed. How long before she got him in Armani suits and Calvin Klein underwear? Or was the bohemian artist look more appropriate to her plans?

'Santa Claus is being dumped then?' She could still see him in that ridiculous red coat and white beard. Still smell the mandarin and sandalwood . . .

'You bet.' Alex laughed. 'Other times I just want to get out of here. To travel. To explore the world a bit.'

They passed the wooden shed providing information on the reserve. Imogen had followed the trail once, answered such questions as: *Are the two large yew trees male or female?* Today she had not dissimilar things on her mind. 'Can't you paint and travel?' It seemed pretty obvious. 'You're young.' Yes, far too young for her. 'No ties.'

He shot her a dark look. Which bit had he objected to? she wondered. In silence they tramped along the path. The yews were dark and brooding, their sweet scent damp in the air. *How many species breed here?*

Alex trailed his hand (no, she wouldn't look) along the bark of one of the oldest yews. As squat as a toadstool itself, she saw that a ring of fungi was growing around the vast circumference of its trunk. Like a magic circle.

'What about you?' he asked.

'Me?' Imogen turned, took a breath in as the path began to slope upwards, climbing the side of the great natural amphitheatre that housed the yews and grassland of Kingley Vale. 'I go on with the shop, with my life. I may not have a husband any longer but I have my friends and sometimes my mother.' She sounded a right twit, she realised, and pulled a

211

packet of mints out of the pocket of her green waxed jacket to offer him one.

'And you're free.' He took one, put it in his mouth.

Imogen looked away. Was she? They walked on in silence until they reached the top of the Vale. In the distance she could make out the coastline, the dark stretch of sea, the farmland spreading out below them, and Chichester itself – almost invisible today except for the cathedral spire. Was she free? Was it as simple as this man seemed to think?

He touched her hand. For a moment she allowed herself to take a quick tiptoe towards those blue eyes. Then back again – even quicker. No way, Imo.

'You are if you want to be,' he said.

She shot him a quick look as they headed left towards the wood, leaving the few other walkers in the Vale way behind them. 'Tell me about you and Marisa?' She didn't trust the silence between them, and small talk no longer seemed appropriate somehow.

'I'm not proud of the way I've behaved.'

'Oh?'

He told her briefly and unemotionally about an open invitation that had turned into something more. 'One minute it was an uncomplicated diversion . . .' Alex held the gate open for her.

'You mean sex?' She didn't look at him. Dangerous word, sex.

He nodded. 'And before I knew what was happening . . .' The gate swung back behind him. He secured it, looked at her, shrugged.

Imogen thought of Marisa. 'She is beautiful.'

He seemed to brush this aside. 'Pretty, yes. Perfect, even. But, God, I was a stupid bastard.'

212

Imogen risked another quick glance. 'Men are so inno-cent,' she teased.

'And that makes them susceptible to the wiles of women?' he countered.

'Not all women have wiles.'

At this he paused, taking her arm, linking it with his as they walked on.

Imogen flinched but in fact it felt natural; it was easier to leave it there, she decided.

'Do you?' he asked. 'Have wiles, I mean.'

'I'm better at just letting things happen.' Imogen smiled. 'I'm not too hot in the wiles department.' Didn't have the brains for it, Jude would say.

He stopped walking again. At this rate they'd never make it to the pub. And she could almost taste the tension between them. It was in the dryness of her mouth, the cold air around their bodies, the compelling fierceness of his eyes.

'Is that right?' She couldn't read his expression as he spoke, slowly, every word measured. 'You just let things happen, do you?'

Chapter 19

It was New Year's Eve and Vanessa was feeling hopeful as she took off her gloves and rang the bell of Ralph's flat. Gosh, it seemed cold after India, she thought. 'It's me,' she said into the intercom. As always, she was so looking forward to seeing him, and waiting to hear what it was that had to be said face to face.

'One moment, my love.'

Vanessa's overnight bag was light, so she took the stairs. It was silly to be tired; there were only two flights and one had to keep fit.

Ralph was waiting by the lift when she emerged. She tapped him on the shoulder, aware that she was more out of breath than she should be.

He kissed her cheek. 'You always did try to surprise me.'

'And succeeded more than once.' Vanessa allowed him to take her bag though it was only a few steps to his front door, and remembered the first time she'd tried to seduce him. He'd come round to the cottage one wet night when Tom was away and she'd been so desperate for the company that

she'd practically dragged him inside. God, those days . . .
Imogen was a baby, Vanessa was finding her feet as a mother
and discovering they were chained to the kitchen sink.

Ralph had teased her, she remembered, said, 'What did
you expect – that something magical would turn you into
a real mother overnight?'

She had laughed, offered him a drink, and when he left,
tried to kiss him. But Ralph, of course, would never have
taken advantage. Vanessa smiled.

Inside the flat, the decor was grey and white, minimalist
and yet soft. Ralph took her coat and she sank into one of
the grey leather sofas that always reminded her of elephant
hide. She slipped off her shoes and smiled up at him. 'How
are things?'

'Dull without you.' He fetched them both a glass of
sherry. He hadn't changed much over the years, she thought.
The humour was still there in the dark eyes, though his hair
was greying and his shoulders slightly stooped. 'How long
can you stay?'

Vanessa hesitated as she took her glass from him. 'Only
overnight, I'm afraid. But do you feel up to Trafalgar
Square?' This had become a tradition for the two of them
and she realised she'd never questioned it before. Perhaps it
was her growing sense of her own mortality that increased
her concern. But she had always worried about him. She
remembered his voice when he had told her that Tom had
died. *Our Tom – he's gone, my love.*

It didn't matter that she and Tom had been separated for
years. It didn't matter that she hadn't seen him for longer
than she cared to remember. Tom was what had brought
them together and Tom was what had kept them apart.

'I'm game if you are,' Ralph said now.

'Of course.' Though now she was here, it was rather tempting simply to stay in this sofa. To relax with the one man with whom she felt able to. But no, she'd come here to celebrate in grand style with Ralph, and celebrate she would. Vanessa tucked her hair behind her ears. Trafalgar Square at midnight made her feel young – people, pigeons and all.

'Pity you can't stay longer.' Ralph fiddled around with some papers on the bureau in the corner and tossed a broadsheet on to her lap. 'There's a new exhibition on at the Courtauld – looks interesting.' He was wearing baggy grey corduroy trousers, so that he blended in with the room somewhat, Vanessa thought with a smile. And a dark crew-neck sweater, with the customary neckerchief tied loosely around his throat.

'Maybe I'll come back for it then. When is it?' Vanessa looked down. *The Italian Set*. She thought of Hazel who was certainly hooked on her Italian and laughed.

'What?' Ralph was heading towards the kitchen.

One could never keep him from the kitchen for long, Vanessa thought. He was a wonderful cook; he loved to be stretched by visitors and Vanessa was happy to oblige. She didn't think she'd ever been served the same meal twice, though that could be because Ralph made things up as he went along, and by the time he'd finished, he'd drunk too much red wine to remember the recipe.

'Hazel's got herself a man,' she called out.

'No!' Ralph reappeared in the doorway, now sporting a William Morris print apron and holding a wooden spoon as if about to present some Pre-Raphaelite cookery programme. 'What can he be like?'

Vanessa grinned. Hazel and Ralph had met only once but neither had understood the other in the least. The only thing

216

they shared was a bafflement that Vanessa could possibly be friends with them both. 'The smooth and slippery type.' She pulled a face. 'Italian and charming.'

He raised an eyebrow that was bushy enough to be called forbidding, but had never seemed so to Vanessa. 'And what does your Hazel have to offer a man like that, may I ask?'

'He says she's his English rose.'

'Wishy washy. More like alyssum, I'd say. Cotton wool pretty.' Ralph looked Vanessa up and down appreciatively. 'Something you absolutely are not.'

Was that a compliment? She decided to take it as such. He retreated once more to the kitchen and Vanessa leaned back into soft grey leather and closed her eyes. He hadn't been quite so forward in the past.

She remembered the second time she'd tried to seduce him – at a friend's wedding, during a slow waltz played by the band. Imogen was a bridesmaid, Tom had gone home early with a headache, saying, 'Look after the girls, will you, Ralph?' And Vanessa was trying to keep him to his word.

She wasn't so much attempting a seduction as telling him how she felt. Beginning with, 'I don't suppose you have any idea how I feel about you, Ralph darling, have you?'

'Friendly?' His mouth had twitched at the corners. He was enjoying her discomfort, she realised.

'Very friendly.' By now, Vanessa was fairly accomplished in the art of taking a lover. Since she'd been married, she'd managed three, all discreet, all hidden from Tom. She never intended to hurt him. He had always been dear to her. But sometimes she felt she was dying of boredom. And worse, she was becoming reckless; she almost wanted him to find out, so that she might be free.

217

Ralph narrowed his brown eyes at her. 'What's happened to the last flame then? Have you blown him out? Has he done a runner or has Tom shot him at dawn?'

'You knew?' She could feel his hand, light on the small of her back. Other couples (not married – or at least not to one another) were allowing a head to rest on a shoulder here, a hand to linger on a waist or hip there. And why not? Married life needed to be spiced up a little if it were to stay alive. Not by Ralph, though. He maintained a respectable distance, damn him.

He laughed. At her? Vanessa couldn't say for sure. He led her into a different step and the chiffon pleats of her yellow dress flared out into a fan. 'I know when you go out man-hunting,' he teased. 'And I know Tom hasn't a clue, poor sod.' His expression changed.

Vanessa pouted. 'You don't understand . . .'

'Ah, but I do.' Lightly he touched her hair. 'But it's not Tom's fault he's not enough for you, lovely.'

She moved an inch closer. 'You're the one I want,' she whispered. 'You always have been. You know that.'

He looked sad. 'I couldn't, my lovely,' he said. 'I just couldn't.'

And Vanessa couldn't see how she could change his mind. Loyalty . . . pah!

She opened her eyes now to see Ralph standing in front of her. Familiar and dear. That wedding could have been yesterday.

'I have a proposition for you, lovely,' he said.

'Oh, yes?' She reached for her sherry.

'But first of all, I have food for you. Lemon sole with roasted peppers, a kind of dill sauce and a rocket salad. How does that sound?'

'Like manna from heaven,' Vanessa said. And as for love . . . Thank God they had remained friends instead.

'Then where is he?' Marisa was trying to keep calm, but this woman was nothing if not irritating. Why ever did Alex want to live with a landlady? Not for long, she told herself. Oh, no, not for long. But why didn't he just get himself a flat? She clicked her heels together. She would suggest it. They needed somewhere else to go, an alternative to that draughty studio of his.

'I couldn't help you there, I'm afraid.' The woman facing her folded floury arms and stared right back. She had on one of those wraparound pinny things that Marisa remembered her own mother wearing. Afraid? She didn't *look* in the least afraid. 'I'm not his keeper,' she said.

But she'd probably like to be. 'He came back from Nottinghamshire last night, though?' Marisa persisted.

'Oh, yes.'

'When exactly?'

'Nineish.' She'd swear the woman was smiling as if she were glad Alex hadn't picked up the phone, rushed round to Marisa's straight off.

She straightened her back, focused on Alex's landlady. She had always been able to make people do what she wanted, and she'd realised from an early age that this was a gift. A girl with her start in the world – a girl with no father, no money, no hand to help her up the ladder of life – had to use every gift as a weapon if she wanted to get on. 'And he didn't go out again?'

'He was tired, poor lad.'

She was old enough to be Alex's mother but probably had a king-size crush on him, Marisa thought. Women of a certain age. Nothing better to do. Look at her own mother . . .

'All he wanted was a hot meal, a bath, then bed.'

Okay, but why hadn't he at least rung? Marisa averted her eyes, took in the flaking paint around the front door, the flocked wallpaper within. What a dump. And as for Alex . . . Next to no contact over Christmas and now not even a phone call. The problem was he didn't appreciate any of the sacrifices Marisa had made for him. She turned her attention back to his landlady who clearly had no intention of inviting her in although she must be cold standing on the doorstep without a coat, despite the winter sun. Oh, yes, Marisa had made sacrifices aplenty. Half of which he knew nothing about, and some he'd never know . . .

She pulled her jacket more closely around her and eyed the woman over her designer sunglasses. There were changes to be made if Alex Armstrong had any hope of achieving what she had planned for him. And she would tell him so.

'Never you mind, lovie.'

What? Marisa's thoughts might have run away with her but she recognised pity when it smacked her in the face. And this old bag's 'lovie' she most definitely was not. Marisa drew herself up to her full height. 'I *don't* mind,' she said crisply, pushing the shades back up again. 'But I do need to find out where Alex is now.' She was repeating herself, she knew. She'd lost track. But where *was* he? Not in his studio, she'd already checked.

'All he said was he'd be out all day.' *Patience of a saint, I had*, she'd say to him later, the old cow. Oh, yes, she was enjoying herself, Marisa could tell. 'He said not to do him any dinner. He said . . .' she smiled once more and Marisa noticed the web of fine lines around eyes and mouth, the well-worn creases on brow and cheek '. . . to expect him when I saw him.' And then she softened. 'They don't know how important it is to us women.'

Us women? She had some nerve.

'You know what men are like.'

Yes, Marisa did. She knew a lot more than Flour-fingers here. And she also knew she had two choices. She could insist on waiting for him here. Or she could go and look for him.

Marisa turned on her heel. She had no intention of being left alone on New Year's Eve. It was unthinkable. She would find Alex Armstrong if it killed her. And then she would make him pay.

'So you just let things happen,' he said again. It seemed to Alex that they were all alone in this place. Woods and fields, chalk and winter grass. Bleak, bleak farmland, the yews behind them; just fields and a dirt track that led (she'd told him, peering at the map) to the pub. But before they got there . . . Jesus, how he'd like to sketch her here al fresco. Should he suggest it? It would scare her, he knew. Perhaps better not.

'Well . . .' She hooked a stray strand of nut-brown hair behind one ear and it immediately flew out again.

He loved her uncertainty, the way she had of chewing her bottom lip when she worried and wrinkling her nose when she laughed. And those eyes – they told him nothing and everything at the same time. God, the woman had got to him. Over Christmas he'd thought of nothing else. He must see Marisa, he knew, to make it right between them. He'd never meant to behave badly; he'd just lost sight of his own intentions, taken a while to

221

realise that where Marisa wanted to take him, he did not want to go.

'It's easier to let things happen,' Imogen said.

Too right. An almost-invitation.

He kissed her. Easy, because she was close beside him, uncertain with cold lips and warm eyes. And because . . .

He tasted her. Wanted more of her too, but she jumped back from him like some startled animal.

Had he gone too fast? He grabbed her hand, not wanting to lose her, feeling that she mustn't get away. 'Did you just let that happen or did you want it to happen?' It was important to know.

'We must get back.' She pulled her hand away from his, hurried on down the track.

She might not have feminine wiles, Alex thought as he followed her, but she was bloody good at avoiding awkward questions.

Driving – too fast – back to Chichester, Imogen asked him if he wanted to be dropped off anywhere. Everything seemed so strange – as if the world had been turned upside down. She almost didn't know what to do with him.

'Your place will be fine.'

Her hands tightened on the wheel. She should say something, do something. Her place wasn't fine, damn it. She hit the dash and he jumped.

'What?'

'Nothing.' Was that the best she could do? Nothing?

She swung the Nova into the drive, got out of the car and heard the phone ringing. A lifeline? She fumbled for her keys. Don't stop, don't hang up . . .

'Hello?' She sank on to the chair by the phone, saw him come in the front door behind her. Oh, hell . . .

'Imo?' It was Jude, thank God. Imogen shrugged off her waxed jacket.

'Yes?'

'I've been trying to get you all day.'

'Oh?' She watched as Alex walked straight past her and into the kitchen.

'I wondered if you wanted to come round to the salon this afternoon. For coffee and a chat?'

'Er . . .' Imo heard the sound of water running. He was filling the kettle, making a cup of tea in her kitchen. She pulled off one shoe with her free hand. 'The salon?' It seemed like another planet. She was still stuck on the farm track in Kingley Vale where Alex had kissed her this morning. She was in a time warp. She pulled off the other shoe, kicked them under the telephone table.

'Yes, the salon.' Jude sighed. 'What's going on, Imo?'

'On?' He walked back into the hall, glanced across at her, took off his own shoes . . .

'Imo, why are you talking like a zombie?'

She tried to pull herself together. For goodness' sake, he was only a man. 'Sorry,' she muttered. 'But I don't think I can make it right now.'

'Hmm.' She could almost hear Jude lighting a cigarette. The click of the lighter, the inhalation. 'I've been phoning the shop all day.'

'The shop?' She watched as Alex strolled into her sitting-room. Through the open door she saw him sit down on her sofa. He shrugged off the fleece jacket. Underneath he was wearing a dark red shirt, she noted. Any moment and he'd switch on the TV, he seemed so much at home.

223

'Your shop, sweetie. Flowers? Remember? That's what you do usually? Only, I thought you said you were opening today?'

So she had. That seemed like centuries ago. 'I changed my mind.' Jude, more than anybody, would understand that.

'Playing hookey?' There was laughter in her voice. 'Well, I don't blame you. I've had to contend with my mother all morning.' Her tone changed. 'God, what a disaster.'

'A disaster?' Imogen tried to concentrate.

'I'll tell you later. She wanted her hair done to impress Mr Pasta. Seems to be playing some sort of mind game with him. I can't get my head round it at all.' She drew breath. 'So where have you been all day?'

'I went walking,' Imo told her. *They* had gone walking . . . But she wouldn't tell her friend that. Not yet.

'Oh, you and your walks . . .'

Despite herself, Imo grinned. Typical Jude, dismissing her day in one clean sweep. 'It was good,' she protested, watching the long, lean, crumpled figure stretch out on her sofa. More than good. She felt the wonderful tiredness that followed a long hike on a winter's day. All she wanted now was to settle into the sofa next to Alex, with maybe some tea and crumpets to follow that marvellous lunch at the Hare and Hounds.

'Now about tonight . . .' Jude became brisk.

Imo never liked it when Jude became brisk. She sat up straighter. 'Tonight?' she asked weakly.

'New Year's Eve, Imo, you know.'

Alex had his feet under the coffee table. What was she going to do with him? He was young. He was a bohemian artist with a sense of adventure to match her mother's.

224

He was her almost-stepdaughter's boyfriend. What was she doing? 'What about New Year's Eve?'

'Mattie's asked me out.'

Oh, yes, Mattie. She'd almost forgotten. Imo made a big effort. 'So how did it go last night?'

'I can't remember much about it, sweetie.' Jude laughed but she was being evasive, Imo knew the signs.

She recalled their vague plans and sniffed. Surely she could smell something cooking . . . 'Then you must go. I'll be fine.' She didn't acknowledge Alex who was shooting her an inquisitive look.

'Well, the thing is . . .' Deep drag of the cigarette? If they brought in video-phones she'd know for sure. 'Ma was going to baby-sit. But strangely she doesn't seem to want Mr Linguini in the flat. I tell you, Imo, she's behaving very strangely.'

She wasn't the only one. Alex got up, came into the hall, raised his eyebrows at Imogen and disappeared into the kitchen again. She heard fridge-type noises and he must be pouring the tea. 'Shall I baby-sit?' she asked. Jude was offering her a straw and she must grab it – though she'd prefer to drown.

'Baby-sit?' Jude shrieked.

'Yes. It's not as if I'm doing anything else tonight.'

Alex came back through with a tray. He'd even found the tea cosy, and the hot buttered toast smelled divine. 'Hope you don't mind,' he mouthed at her as he passed.

'Oh, Imo, I couldn't possibly ask you to. Not on New Year's Eve,' Jude said in a tone that suggested that indeed she could – if pressed.

'I don't mind.' She did, she did!

'Oh, Imo, sweetie! I'd love you forever.'

225

'I'm glad to hear it.' Imo shifted the phone to her other ear.

'What time can you come?' Jude – being Jude – quickly got down to practicalities.

Imogen looked at Alex who had put the tray down on the carpet and was now shifting magazines from the coffee table. 'Any time,' she said. She had the feeling that despite all this activity, he was listening closely.

'Eightish? And Imo—' A brief pause. 'Don't say a word to Ma about her hair. Just pretend you haven't noticed.'

'Fine. I'll be there.' She put the phone down, took a deep breath, walked into her sitting-room.

'Running away?' he asked her, patting the seat beside him.

'Doing a favour for my best friend,' she corrected. But he was right. She sat down in the chair opposite. 'Can I have some tea?'

'Imogen.' His eyes were to fall into. 'As far as I'm concerned, you can have whatever you might desire.'

In the flat above *The Goddess Without*, the doorbell rang.

'I'll get it. And will you please stop apologising?' Hazel's fury was spent. She knew the damage done by her daughter had not been intentional. Tentatively, she put up her hand. Her hair now fitted her head like a skull cap. And it still looked terrible. Every time she passed a mirror, the sight of her reflection made her jump. She plucked a tartan scarf from the hook by the kitchen door, draped it over her head and round her neck, and opened the front door with a flourish, managing a plaintive hum of 'Somebody Loves Me . . . I Wonder Who?' as she did so.

The eyes of the man she'd last seen kissing her daughter

in the hallway widened at the sight of the tartan scarf, and then Jude brushed past in a haze of Opium.

'Have a good time,' Hazel said, shutting the door thankfully behind them and whipping off the scarf.

She had known from the expression on Jude's face in the mirror, as she stood there inanely patting the towel turbanning Hazel's head, that something was very wrong. But nothing had prepared her for the thick black and purple streaks that grew more prominent the drier they became.

'Get it out,' she had told her daughter, refusing to listen to her garbled explanation about the undertones of ash being purple. 'Get it out, right this minute!'

'Gold would counteract the purple,' Jude was muttering as she consulted that horrid book of hers. 'But that'll make the black even darker.' She bit her lip. 'I could bleach out the black, do an overall tint and bring it up to a warm colour . . .'

'Like red?' Hazel snapped.

'More of a copper really, but it'll take at least three hours and . . .'

'Cut it off!' Hazel shrieked. Three hours she didn't have. And she didn't want to be copper, damn it. Copper was ridiculous at her age.

'If I cut it short, it'll only enhance the two-tone effect,' Jude began. 'It'll be more obvious.'

'Cut it off.' All Hazel knew was that there would be less of it.

The cut was good. And the hot sweet tea Jude made had allowed her to recover a little of her equilibrium. But it had still been one of the worst days of Hazel's life.

She began on her eye make-up – one had to compensate. Jude, of course, though apologetic had no conception of the seriousness of the situation. Declarations didn't appear out of the blue. They required the projection of a certain image, the maintaining of certain standards and a degree of manipulation. Romance was about the unattainable, as Byron knew – the poet, that is, not the husband. He understood; hence his success with women – any woman, even relatives, she'd heard. And if a woman played the game, in return she might expect a degree of security. It was a question of adopting a basic survival technique. You'd think in Jude's business she'd understand that.

Hazel sighed. Her taxi was due in twenty minutes and still no Imogen. But on cue the doorbell chimed and Hazel hurried to let her in.

'Hello, dear.' How nice. Imogen had brought a friend. A man. Tall, ungainly – and dressed in jeans. *How long has this been going on?* she wondered in true Gershwin style.

'You don't mind, Hazel?' Imogen's gaze was momentarily transfixed by her hair, and then rapidly it flicked away, shooting some sort of warning to the man by her side. 'Me bringing, er, someone?'

'Not at all.' She beckoned them into the bright hallway and squinted at him. Tall, nice smile, she noted.

'Alex, Hazel.' Briefly, Imogen made the introductions. 'Are you going somewhere nice?'

Anywhere so long as it was out, with no risk of Italian hands wandering towards her breasts, Hazel thought. This rose was not an easy picking, and in her experience men rarely stopped at breasts. '"It ain't necessarily so,"' she sang.

'Pardon?' Imogen glanced at her friend and then looked quickly away again.

'Gershwin, dear,' Hazel told her. 'There's a charming Italian restaurant in Little London. Giorgio knows the owner.' There would be champagne, no doubt, and hopefully the little something that Giorgio had hinted at last night.

'Lovely.' Imogen didn't seem quite all there tonight. Was she drunk? Or was it some sort of delayed grief?

As Hazel ushered them into the maroon sitting-room Daisy appeared in her nightie. 'Auntie Imo!' They hugged. 'Can we play Jenga by candlelight? And can I stay up really late? Till midnight even?'

This time, Hazel noted, Imogen did not look at her companion. 'Of course, darling,' she said.

The man called Alex only grinned. He said, 'You can't run away forever, Imo.' Or something like that. Whatever could he mean?

Hazel glanced at the mirror in the hallway and winced. Still, it was New Year's Eve and, despite her hair, she had never felt so hopeful.

Chapter 20

They were sitting in a circle on the floor of a draughty hall talking about stones, runes and ley lines. Jude stifled a yawn. Any second they'd be entering the realm of the occult — ouija boards perhaps, or some other form of knocking on heaven's door. What then? she wondered. Black cats? Sacrifices? Blood? On a more practical note, she hadn't had a cigarette for an hour and she wasn't used to sitting on hard floors.

She adjusted her long black velveteen dress with the gold stars, shifted uneasily and sneaked a look at Mattie. He was just as attractive under the garish lights of the community hall. But the poetry that had been appealing after a few glasses of wine the night before was not quite so appealing tonight.

A drink of the alcoholic variety and a bit of action would be more appropriate. Jude stared at the magnolia walls and bare floor and wished she was in a pub. A crowded pub with noise, laughter and a glass of wine. Whatever had happened to fun? They certainly hadn't heard of it here.

'Anyone for more camomile tea?' asked an apparition

entitled Suki. Pale face, yellow hair, no make-up, and with a name like a poodle. 'It's very cleansing.' She directed this at Jude – possibly because she'd been the only one brave enough to request an alternative. But Jude didn't want to be cleansed – she'd rather get legless.

A few murmurs and the pot (of tea, no sign of drugs as yet) was passed ritualistically around the circle. Could this be the start of a pagan ceremony? Jude wondered. OK, she had no particular religious leanings, but the closest she ever got to paganism was incense, aromatherapy and therapeutic massage oils. And that was plenty close enough, thank you. She didn't need to incur the wrath of anyone. She already had enough wrath in her life. Mainly from her mother right now.

'And next . . .' A tall scrawny individual called Magic rose to his feet and flapped the sari-like thing he was wearing for silence. 'Let's talk about loneliness.'

Bloody hell. Jude sighed. This lot sure knew how to enjoy themselves.

On a rear end that was crying out for mercy, she slid closer to Mattie and placed a hand firmly on his thigh. She hoped this might lead him to consider alternative options to their current pastime.

If it did, he didn't show it.

'We've all been lonely,' Magic told them. 'But how many of us have admitted it to our innermost souls, to our loved ones, to the members of the group?'

Voices demurred, agreed, whispered . . . And one said, 'Are we going to stay here all night?' That voice was Jude's.

Mattie moved fractionally away. Not a good sign. She sighed and let her palms rest on the cold floor.

231

'Now that we are cleansed, we are able to admit our private thoughts . . .'

Gimme a drink. That was Jude's.

'Our private weaknesses . . .'

Should she admit to a need for male penetration in her life? Probably not. The feminists in the circle would attack her mob-handed and the men wouldn't understand.

'And personal vulnerabilities.'

For the right man, Jude reckoned she could be as vulnerable as the next woman. But was Mattie the right man? She was beginning to doubt it. It seemed, rather, that he was the only man. At least . . . she shifted uncomfortably . . . he *was* a man.

Loneliness was not a subject that had concerned Jude up to now. With the salon, her mother, Daisy and her multiple personalities, it was pretty hard to be lonely. Life and work seemed to get in the way. In fact she wouldn't mind a little *more* time alone.

'Poetry,' Magic said, closing his eyes and beginning to sway, 'has long been a vehicle for the expression of loneliness.'

Wordsworth. Jude nodded. She tried to remember the first verse of the lonely cloud sonnet. Something about daffodils dancing in the breeze? She wished she could dance right out of here but she was a long way away from the door and if she ran for it she might bring out their pagan tendencies and end up as a sacrifice on the fire. She tried to catch Mattie's eye, but his gaze was fixed on Magic as if he were the new Messiah.

One by one, the New Year's Eve revellers stood up to reveal painful moments of misery, loneliness and intense embarrassment. It was awful. If Jude had ever been lonely, the last thing she would do was tell these drongos about it. She'd rather drown in camomile tea.

So what in God's name was she going to say when it got to her turn?

It was five minutes to midnight and Alex and Imo were playing drunken Consequences. On the other side of Imogen, on the maroon sofa, Daisy dozed fitfully, blissfully unaware of her role as chaperone.

'Please let me stay up till midnight,' had progressed to, *'Lemme stay up?'* by nine, *'Lemme stay?'* by ten, finally reduced to a heart-rending, *'Stay?'* at eleven – by which time she'd already fallen asleep twice.

'Of course you can, darling,' Imo had repeated, ignoring Alex's mouthed 'Running away.' What did he know? Quite a lot apparently.

The Consequences had been to amuse Daisy when they all tired of Jenga and TV. Adjective, noun, verb, adjective, object noun, adverb and so on, first having to explain to Daisy, 'It's a doing word, darling,' and, 'A describing word; it's a word that tells you something about a thing and how a thing is doing something.' Clear as mud.

Daisy fell asleep (again) and Alex opened another bottle of wine, although the champagne thoughtfully provided by Jude – who had no doubt been feeling guilty and expecting Imo to be drinking it alone – was staying cool in a bucket full of icy water. The Consequences became more risqué. *A rampant lesbian seduced some huge mussels desperately* . . . They *must* be on the same wavelength, Imo thought. And they became threaded through with conversation. It had been half an hour since the last one and the format had changed.

'Talking to you is like . . .' Alex began, reading the first line '. . . watching paint dry?'

Imo giggled.

'Well, what's yours?'

'If I'd met you when I was eighteen, I would have spent my time . . .' she unfolded the paper '. . . drinking Buck's Fizz?'

He grabbed hold of her hand. 'Talking to you is like drinking Buck's Fizz,' he insisted, looking both wild and serious at the same time. Imogen suddenly found it quite difficult to breathe. 'Somehow you know that part of it's gonna be good for you,' he went on. 'It might make you into a better person—'

'Oh, yes?' But Imogen found she was touched. Touched in the head probably, to believe it. 'And the other part?' She wasn't sure she should even ask. But then, she wasn't sure that she should have brought him here in the first place.

'It's fizzy, frothy, exciting.' He drew her closer to him. Mandarin and sandalwood assailed her senses.

'And it gets up your nose?' she whispered.

'Strangely, I've never had that problem with champagne.' He held her face. Closer, closer. Mouths almost touching. Imo could feel the warmth of his skin, his face close to hers, his hands holding her still. Then . . .

'Boom!' The clock struck once, twice . . . They had left the radio on for Big Ben's chimes.

His mouth was only centimetres away, Imo closed her eyes and Daisy sprang, as if pre-programmed, into action. 'Champagne,' she demanded.

Imo jumped. She couldn't speak and her heart was hammering louder than Big Ben itself.

'Ready and waiting.' Shaking his head in disbelief, Alex

234

did the honours, up-ended the bottle, sent the cork flying, gave the sleepy Daisy her own small glass.

'To 2001,' Imogen said with what she knew was hardly sparkling originality.

'And to us.' He spoke so softly that afterwards she wondered if he'd even said it.

'God be with you,' Daisy contributed. She took a gulp and almost choked.

'Steady . . .' Imogen slapped her gently on the back. 'And now − bed.'

'Already? Lemme stay . . .'

'No.' This time Alex and Imogen were united.

Ten minutes later Imogen was back on the sofa next to Alex.

'If you had met me when you were eighteen,' he began, 'what would you have done?'

'Not a lot.' Imogen felt relatively sober now that she had done the teeth and loo routine with Daisy. 'You would've been a baby, for starters.'

'I was always mature for my age.'

'Not that mature.'

He spread his hands. 'So what's a few years between friends?'

A few years? Imo refrained from looking at his mouth. A decade, more like. Practically a generation. And friends were one thing, lovers something else again. Lovers . . . She shivered.

'If it feels good . . .' His voice was like a silk stole being draped over her senses. Imo could feel the tantalising touch of it. Help . . .

He moved closer. Dangerous proximity. She could drown

in mandarin and sandalwood, she thought. Dispense it into her bathwater and while away the hours. But in the meantime, his fingertips were doing something addictive to the nerve endings in the shoulder area.

She glanced – briefly – at that mouth, and had a wild, fleeting urge to throw caution to the wind. He was right. What did it matter if he was a decade younger than she? What difference did it make that he was a bohemian artist who wanted to travel the world while she owned a flower shop in Chichester? So what if they'd boogied to different music and used different slang when they were teenagers? And was it really that important that he was her almost-step-daughter's boyfriend?

After a bottle of wine, it didn't seem that important at all, Imo decided. She deserved to live a little. What were a few barriers in the high-barbed-wire obstacle course of life?

She snuggled closer. 'Oh, Alex . . .'

Another sound broke the spell. This time it wasn't the radio. It was the sound of a key in the door.

'How could you do that to me?' They heard the plaintive cry from the hall. Definitely not Jude's voice, Imo decided. Jude couldn't be plaintive to save her life. A door slammed and once more Alex and Imogen moved apart.

'Maybe I should be asking you that question,' Jude snarled. 'How the bloody hell could you take me to a dump full of crazy people – and on New Year's Eve too?'

That was more like it. Imogen knew Jude very well and she could almost feel the passion rising. Passion . . . Hers had been cut off in mid-flow, though their hands were still touching as if they couldn't quite let go.

'They'd better not wake up Daisy,' Imo whispered. She

raised her free hand and touched his face, tracing the line of his eyebrow, her thumb caressing his cheek.

Alex caught her hand, kissed her fingers. 'If they danced on her bed it wouldn't wake up Daisy.' They both smiled.

'And with no booze, for Christ's sake,' Jude continued.

No booze? Imogen chuckled. Gosh, no wonder she was angry.

Irate, Jude-like footsteps thumped into the kitchen. 'Where's the bloody corkscrew?' Her language had really gone down the pan tonight. Imogen coughed loudly to remind her that she and Mattie were not alone.

'Oh, Imo, are you still here?' she called, obviously sharing Alex's view about the likelihood of Daisy waking. 'I'll be right in.'

'But how could you *say* that?' the plaintive voice reiterated.

'What? Imo have you got the corkscrew?' Jude called.

'Yes.' She found it on the floor next to two empty bottles of wine.

'How could you say that the worst moment in your entire life was in that hall tonight when you discovered the only drink available was *fucking* camomile tea?'

Imogen looked at Alex and Alex looked at Imogen. The silent laughter bubbled up within her and spread to him, until they were clutching one another for support.

'Because it was *fucking* true!' Jude was well away.

'But it trivialised the whole purpose of the event, the cleansing, the expression . . .'

'I don't give a shit.' Jude stomped into the sitting-room. 'Something amusing you, Imo? Oh.' She stopped in her tracks, eyes narrowing as she surveyed Alex.

Imogen managed to regain some control, though tears

were streaming down her cheeks. She introduced Alex without looking at him once. Instead, she smiled sympathetically at Mattie who looked exhausted. Jude – in her black and gold strapless dress – just looked angry, as only Jude could. From lilac eyes she was also giving Imo a look. A *Who the hell is this, why didn't you tell me about him and isn't he rather young?* look.

'Good time?' Imo asked, to distract her.

'I'll pretend you didn't say that.'

'Er . . . We'll be off then.'

'Hang on a sec.' Jude looked torn between wanting to get both sloshed and Mattie into bed as soon as possible, and wanting to find out everything (and she always meant *everything*) about Alex.

Imogen would not give her the opportunity to choose. 'I'm exhausted.' She yawned very loudly. 'Sorry, Jude, gotta go.'

They walked back through the wide pedestrianised streets of Chichester city centre, past the pubs that had now closed up for the night, past Market Cross which was lit up, the stone almost yellow, the light gusting up the centre of the edifice and providing an illuminated background to its small spires. Gangs of people were still clustered around it, in front of the clock face that now showed almost one a.m.

They walked on arm in arm past County Hall. Talking, laughing, stopping every few minutes to kiss, until they reached the City Wall, until they turned into Imogen's street, along and up the drive that led to the cottage. She felt about sixteen.

She had strung fairy lights outside. They lit up the greenery of the clematis and Virginia creeper that wound and interwove their separate ways up to the roof of the cottage and beyond. Until they became one. 'I'm mad,' she said as she opened the front door.

'But I still like you,' Alex reassured her, shutting it firmly behind him.

And he must have. Because before ten minutes had elapsed, they were in bed. And she was loving every last bit of what was happening to her there.

Chapter 21

Vanessa was humming to herself as she put her key in the lock. It had been a pleasant – not to say illuminating – New Year's Day. 'Only me,' she sang out. 'Imogen, darling?'

Noises from upstairs. Muffled and surprised and hurried noises from upstairs. Vanessa sniffed and raised a delicate eyebrow. Well, well, well. She knew those kind of noises. She moved through the hall past the telephone table, noted the coats hung carelessly over the banister. The cottage seemed different.

'Mother . . .' As Vanessa stood at the bottom of the stairs, Imogen appeared on the landing, looking what could best be described as *déshabillé*. She was barefoot, wearing only her towelling robe, her hair was tangled around her shoulders and her colour was high.

Vanessa smiled. About time. 'Am I interrupting something?' she asked mildly, taking off her own red coat and cashmere scarf.

'I have no idea what you mean.' Imogen flounced away, shutting her bedroom door with a sharp click.

Very well. If that was how she wanted to play it . . .

Vanessa deposited her things in the understairs cupboard and went into the kitchen to make coffee. She'd bought Imogen a percolator in silent rebellion at the excuse for coffee she drank – how could anyone half-civilised not have one? But she knew that her daughter never used the thing. When Vanessa was out of the country it got tucked into a cupboard; the rest of the time it was left out to gather dust.

This was an instant generation, Vanessa thought. And yes . . . the jar of instant was out, without a lid – Vanessa clicked her tongue as she screwed it back on – with a dirty teaspoon beside it. A small puddle of stale milk completed the tableau. Vanessa sighed. She herself had never been so overcome with lust that she couldn't even make a decent cup of coffee at some point in the proceedings. But she supposed that this was a good sign.

She went as far as the open doorway. 'Coffee?' she called up the stairs.

More indeterminate noises.

'Please,' Imogen shouted down at last. 'If you're making some.'

'One or two?' And she wasn't talking lumps of sugar. Vanessa tapped her foot on the kitchen's quarry-tiled floor. It was a shame, she thought, that Imogen had always been so conventional. She took after Tom, of course.

'Pardon?'

She'd heard. Vanessa sighed. 'One or two cups, darling?'

'One,' Imogen snapped. 'Really, Mother.'

Ah, well . . . She wasn't to meet him then. Vanessa retreated and closed the kitchen door to allow her daughter to say goodbye to her visitor in private.

It was all very well, she reflected, having a key to this cottage and coming and going as she did. But Imogen was

241

far too old to have a mother interrupting her every move. Besides, Vanessa wasn't cut out for the role. She rinsed a cloth and wiped the work surface clean of milk and coffee stains. What Ralph had said yesterday – with a certain look on his kind face that she hadn't seen before – made a lot of sense. She had felt tired in India. Maybe she was getting too old for all this travelling, at least of the third-class variety. Maybe she should even have that check-up he'd nagged her about. She would still travel, of course, whenever the urge overtook her. But she would slow down.

Imogen came into the kitchen ten minutes later. By that time the coffee was poured and already cooling. 'Why did you shut the door, Mother?' she asked suspiciously. She looked charming – flushed skin, bright eyes, a bruised look to her mouth – far more beautiful than Edward had ever made her look, Vanessa observed. She had the feeling that at last her girl was finding her wings.

'For the sake of privacy,' she said.

'Oh?'

'Yours.' She added milk to Imogen's coffee.

At this Imo crumpled rather. 'How did you know?' She sank down on to the nearest chair, her huge grey eyes desolate.

Did she think her mother was born yesterday? Vanessa shook her head in despair. 'It's a question of atmosphere, darling,' she said. 'This cottage has acquired that lived in and loved in feeling all of a sudden. Very pleasant, actually.'

'Mandarin and sandalwood,' Imogen said, for no apparent reason. 'I think I'll take a bath.' She cradled the mug in her hands, but instead of drinking, she sniffed, long and hard.

'And talking of cottages . . .' For there was no time like

the present and Vanessa had made up her mind. 'I'm thinking of buying a flat myself. Maybe in Brighton.'

'Brighton?' Imogen made it sound like a hot-bed of vice.

'I'm going to cut down on all this rushing around,' her mother said by way of explanation. 'I think at long last I need a home rather more than I need a base.' She wouldn't mention tiredness and check-ups. No need to worry her daughter unduly.

'You'd live alone?'

'As a matter of fact, no,' she admitted. 'I've been propositioned – in a manner of speaking.' She smiled, remembering that certain look of Ralph's. She had never felt quite like this before. Ralph had always been special. She had thought it would never happen. And for it to happen now, after all these years . . . But why not? They had always got on well, shared similar interests and the same sense of humour. And he had always understood her. Why not indeed?

'Propositioned?'

'I'm going to share my home with a friend. A man friend. As a matter of fact, I'm going to live with Ralph Chambers.'

'Ralph Chambers?' Imogen heard herself asking. She rose to her feet.

'He's always been very dear to me,' Vanessa told her.

That was no surprise to Imogen. 'Do you love him?' she asked. She was still immersed in the sensual pleasures of the night before, still feeling Alex, smelling him, loving him.

'As much as I ever loved any man,' Vanessa said, looking up at her. 'More, in fact.'

'I see.' That hurt rather. What about her father – always

243

Imogen's rock, her stability? To distract herself, Imogen turned to search in the terracotta bread bucket for something that would pass as supper.

'It's not exactly what you think,' Vanessa went on. 'We love one another, yes, in a way . . .'

Was there more than one way? After the night and day that Imogen had just made love through, it didn't seem possible. There was only one, all-consuming way.

'And although it's a very creative and . . . energetic relationship—'

Imogen pulled a face, not sure if even her own recent experience allowed her to dwell on images of her mother being energetic with a man. She sawed a slice of bread from the stale offering in front of her and chucked it in the toaster.

'But actually he's gay.'

'Gay?' That was something Imogen had never considered. She had, she realised, been way off beam. 'You're going to set up home with a man who's *gay*?'

Vanessa tucked her neat dark hair behind her ears. 'Why not?' She smiled almost dreamily. 'Like I told you, darling, I love him.'

The toast popped up and Imogen absent-mindedly removed it, spread butter and then jam, sat down opposite this amazing mother of hers. She had always, hadn't she, loved to be different?

'Have you known for a long time?' she asked, mouth full.

'No. He kept it very quiet until after your father died,' Vanessa said. 'It was a shock.' She paused. 'I always had a bit of a thing for Ralph.'

'Did Dad know?'

244

'About my feelings for Ralph?'

'About him being gay.' Imogen took another bite, suddenly realising she was ravenous.

'Oh, no, I don't suppose it occurred to Tom.' Her mother seemed very cheerful all of a sudden. 'Ralph is gay and unlikely to reform.' She leaned over and poked her daughter in the ribs. 'So don't worry, darling,' she said. 'No hanky-panky to concern yourself about.' Her smile was wicked. 'That's apart from your own, of course.'

A brand new year . . . Imogen selected some fern for the wreath she was preparing. Although it was Sunday, she'd decided to come in for a few hours because there was so much to do. She'd neglected the shop and she'd neglected Jude. Imogen wove the greenery around the paraphernalia that would, she hoped, hold everything in place. Jude had phoned at least four times yesterday. The first conversation ran:

'What's going on, Imo?'

'Nothing.'

'Who is he?'

'No one.' *Sorry, Alex.*

'God, he's not still there?'

And he was.

He was still there for the other three phone calls and still there until Vanessa had swanned in at five in the afternoon – what passed for breakfast, lunch and other things besides, having all been enjoyed in bed.

And, 'I think I'm falling in love with you,' he had said at one point in the night or morning, Imo wasn't sure, it had all blurred into glorious Technicolor oneness.

Wow. 'You can't – it's much too soon.' But it didn't feel

too soon. And how could she stop that huge smile spreading through all her bits?

'"Love, all alike, no season knows, nor clime,

Nor hours, days, months, which are the rags of time",' Alex said, grinning all the while.

'Gosh.' No one had ever quoted John Donne to her before. And it was one of her favourite poems too. That had to be a good omen.

But then her mother had shown up, and Alex had left Imogen with nothing but a warm glow of heat somewhere in her very core. And a super-sensitivity of touch, so that when she pulled on her silk underwear she felt a frisson of excitement, when her lambswool sweater brushed against her arm she felt a play-back of the last . . . *oh-my-God, that was so good*, and when she thought of Alex, she was lost completely. It was hard to retrieve any kind of reality. The only reality that she was interested in contained the man she'd had in her bed all night and all day.

Imogen jumped as the phone rang. She scrutinised the wreath with mounting horror – it looked more like a wedding bouquet. She'd have to start all over again. 'Oh, hell.'

She reached for the phone. '*Say It With Flowers?*'

'Got you.' It was Jude.

Imogen laughed. 'You got me yesterday – at least four times I seem to recall.'

'Ah, but then you were otherwise engaged.'

Imo flushed.

'And I bet you're blushing.'

'Don't be ridiculous.'

'I don't believe you.' Jude laughed. 'I presume this Alex chappie isn't with you now?'

'No.' At the mention of his name she could feel herself getting hot and bothered again. This was insanity. This was wonderful. 'Unfortunately not.' She had a brief but hectic vision of deflowering in the greenhouse, and had to sit down rather abruptly.

'Then stay there. Don't move.'

'Why not?'

'I'm coming right over.'

Imogen laughed. 'Okay.' Jude was bound to get it out of her sooner or later.' Besides, she couldn't go on hugging it to herself like a special secret. If she didn't tell someone soon, she would explode.

Chapter 22

Before heading off for *Say It With Flowers* with Daisy, Jude decided to pay Florrie a visit. She had only come home last night and Jude wanted to check she was OK.

They found her clearing out her cupboards. 'Spring cleaning,' she told Jude. 'Never too early to start.'

Jude couldn't pretend to agree. For her, too much housework was any housework, and this sitting-room of Florrie's was so stuck in time, with its sepia photographs, delicate china ornaments and assorted paraphernalia cluttering every surface, that any kind of spring cleaning seemed impossible – unless Florrie was planning to sweep the whole lot into black bin bags.

'Take it easy,' she advised.

'I'm bursting with energy.' And Florrie certainly looked well. Her white hair was brushed and shining, her cheeks were pink and her faded blue eyes held the distinctive gleam of health. 'I've been sitting around for days being waited on hand and foot as if I were an invalid.' Carefully, she removed a wooden box from the shelf and wiped it lovingly with her duster. 'And now I'm ready for action.'

'Are these dressing-up clothes?' Daisy had discovered a pile of garments on the bottom shelf. She held up a sparkling, black sequinned number, her eyes like dinner plates.

'I can just see you in that, Florrie,' Jude giggled. 'And those,' as a pair of high-heeled evening shoes were exposed to view.

'Happy days.' Florrie held the fabric of the dress close to her breast before passing it back to Daisy. 'Try it on, dear. Anything you want from this pile is yours.'

'Florrie,' Jude remonstrated, 'Daisy will trample all over your memories.'

'Oh, no, dear.' Florrie opened the wooden box to reveal a stack of shining grey metal balls. 'Bagatelle,' she murmured. 'My memories are mine alone to trample on. These . . .' she gestured towards the clothes, the carrier bags full of treasures she hadn't even opened yet '. . . are just *things*. And if your Daisy can get some fun out of them, I'll be content with that.'

'You're very kind.' Jude watched her daughter struggle to get the sequinned dress over her head. It would look a picture with her orange joggers and lime-green trainers, she thought. 'I'm going out this afternoon,' she told Florrie. 'So I wondered if I could get you anything? Tea, coffee, biscuits?'

Florrie gave her a knowing look. 'Thank you, my dear,' she said. 'But I've been well provided for. I'll show you.'

Intrigued, Jude followed her back into the kitchen. Florrie opened her old-fashioned larder door to reveal a hamper stacked with goodies. Bread and crackers, cheeses and jams, a bottle of sherry and tins of salmon, tuna, pineapple. Next to the hamper was a basket of fresh fruit.

'Lovely.' Florrie was certainly being looked after by

someone, and Jude was thankful for that. If she knew who it was, she might contact them and warn them about James Dean and his plans to evict her poor neighbour. A picture of his dark, brooding face flew into her mind and she brushed it irritably away again with a mental broom. Cool, calculating, unsmiling. And then pretending to be concerned for Florrie's welfare. Well, he needn't think *she* was so easily fooled. 'A Christmas present, was it?' she asked.

'Yes, it was.' Florrie turned away with an enigmatic smile.

It was funny, Jude thought. Florrie could talk for hours about the old days – the dances she'd attended, the beaux whose attentions she'd enjoyed. But when it came to the here and now, she was surprisingly reticent.

'Why don't you leave Daisy with me for an hour or two?' Florrie continued as they returned to the sitting-room.

'Please?' Daisy begged. 'It's magic in here.' She had found the old bagatelle board and was rolling the shining metal balls with her fingertips.

'Isn't it?' Florrie drew her fawn cardigan closer around her thin shoulders. 'And a bit later, I'll make us some tea and toasted scones.'

As Jude left, she heard the unmistakeable notes of Gershwin's 'Sweet Embraceable You'. Clearly, Hazel's singing had sparked off some memories. What *was* she going to do with them all?

'Tiffany!' Imogen hadn't seen her assistant for a while. A long while. In fact she'd last spotted her heading purposefully towards the big greenhouse in order to restock the greenery in the shop. So where *was* the greenery?

'Tiffany . . . Jude's coming over. Can you look after the

250

shop while I take a break?' she hollered from the back door. No answer. No sign of her.

With half an eye and ear still on the shop, Imogen ventured further outside and found her – lolling against the greenhouse door. 'Tiffany?'

'Mmm?' Tiffany straightened – but slowly. And smiled. It was not, Imo thought, a sensible smile.

'What's the matter? Are you OK?' How long had she been out here alone? This was what Alex was doing to her already, Imo thought, making her forget her responsibilities.

Tiffany twirled a strand of bleached blonde hair around her little finger. 'Er, yeah, I'm um . . .' She didn't seem sure what she was. But she did seem happy about it.

Imogen peered at her more closely. Her pupils were dilated, her eyes bloodshot and her luminous pink lipstick smudged. 'Tiffany, have you been doing something you shouldn't?'

'Nah! As if . . .' With a sudden burst of energy, Tiffany headed back towards the shop. She was grinning from ear to ear. 'You want me to look after things, yeah? That's cool.'

Imogen was having doubts. As she caught up with her, she sniffed. A sweet, smoky scent clung to her assistant's *Say It With Flowers* overalls. 'Have you been smoking?'

'Smoking?' Tiffany flushed, giggled, fiddled with her eyebrow hoop and went pale.

'I thought you didn't – that's all.' But if she wanted a quick ciggie outside, that was fine. Only . . .

'Um . . .'

Young people today were so vague, so inarticulate. As Imogen shut the back door and hurried through, an awful thought occurred to her. Did that include Alex? He was pretty young – compared to her anyway. 'These carnations need shifting and sorting,' she said.

'Shifting and sorting?' For some reason, Tiffany seemed to find this hilarious.

Imogen frowned. 'Are you sure you're OK?'

'Whaddya keep on asking me that for?' Tiffany rolled her eyes and managed to stop grinning for about five seconds. 'I've blatantly never felt better.' She located a chocolate bar in her overall pocket. 'A bit hungry p'raps.' That was nothing new – Tiffany was always hungry.

'And a bit unco-ordinated too.' Imogen watched with concern as Tiffany – having demolished the chocolate bar in three bites – grabbed a vase and began filling it under the tap. Water splashed over her hands, her overalls and the shop floor. Tiffany smiled happily, rolling up her sleeves to reveal a flock of butterflies heading for a palm tree just above her elbow.

Imogen wasn't sure what to do next. The girl looked drunk, but how could she be? It was only midday, there was no tell-tale smell of alcohol on her breath and she didn't appear to have a vodka bottle stashed about her person. So what exactly *had* she been up to?

It was one of those glorious, unclouded winter days that Jude loved. When the sky was brittle and blue, the wind sliced into you like a knife, and yet the sun continued to shine, drawing people out in their hundreds, she noted, to Chichester's sales, to the restaurants and cafés that were doing a brisk lunchtime trade.

She walked quickly, hands tucked in her coat pockets because she had forgotten her gloves, her new green and purple scarf wrapped around her neck, her feet cosy in

252

her black suede ankle boots. She was about to cut through the Pallants to avoid the crowds when she glimpsed a face through the window of a restaurant. A Thai restaurant, she registered. James Dean.

She lingered, watching him as he smiled at his companion. She was dark and pretty – young too. Jude bit her lip. His wife, maybe? But what was it to her? Nothing at all. Only, it wasn't somehow the sort of place she'd envisaged him frequenting. Rather bohemian in fact.

Oh, well . . . Realising she'd been standing and staring like a brainless idiot, Jude walked away. Imagine if he'd looked up and seen her gawping at him. God knows what he would think.

But the sight of him had darkened her day somehow. She was no longer so eager to get to *Say It With Flowers*, to hear Imo's news. Instead, she found herself thinking of Florrie, so full of energy today, so hopeful. She didn't deserve bad treatment from anyone. And if she were forced to live in an old people's home, where would she put all her precious memories?

Jude clenched her fists inside her coat pockets. Just let him try.

Jude strolled into the shop just as a grinning Tiffany knocked over a vaseful of gypsophilia. 'Ooopsie!' she sang.

'Morning all.' Jude looked from one to the other of them.

'Hiya.' Scowling at her assistant, Imogen bent to gather the delicate flowers.

'Sorreee.' Tiffany moved to help her, slipped on the water she'd spilt and promptly skidded to the floor. 'Ouch!' She began laughing hysterically.

253

It was the last straw. Imogen sat back on her heels. 'Are you drunk?' she demanded.

'No.' Tiffany looked briefly indignant. Then giggled.

'Stoned more like.' Jude fingered the purple freesias that were in a glass vase by the till. 'Have you been smoking wacky baccy, Tiffany?'

Tiffany murmured something indecipherable, thrust her fingers through her blonder than blonde hair, and smiled benignly at them both.

'Wacky . . . ?' Imogen got to her feet. 'Go home,' she said.

'But Imo!' Tiffany's eyes widened. 'I was only—'

'Go home.' Imogen was so cross she was shaking. And what she was most cross about was that Edward – damn him – had been right.

Tiffany managed to get out of her overalls without further incident, although negotiating the sleeve of her coat proved more hazardous, while Imogen had to stop herself from yelling: *And don't come back!*

'We'll talk about this tomorrow,' she said instead, with what she hoped was appropriate menace.

'All right, Imo, keep your hair on.' Tiffany was still giggling as she left the shop.

Imogen turned to her friend. 'She'll have to go.'

Jude was standing, hands thrust in the pockets of her outsize rust-coloured wrap-around coat, watching the small figure weave erratically down South Street towards Market Cross. She shrugged. 'Put a card in the window. You'll be inundated with teenagers by the end of the week. And if you take my advice . . .' she leaned closer '. . . which you never do, you'll choose someone who wears low heels, no make-up and a thick fringe this time.'

The words 'pot' and 'kettle' sprang to Imogen's mind. 'A bit boring,' she protested. Though Edward would no doubt have approved.

Jude wagged a finger. Her hair was still brown, Imo noted, though shorter, and her eyes were cat's green. 'Boring maybe. But unlikely to be a druggie.'

A druggie? That was going a bit far, surely? 'But Tiffany's never done anything like this before.' Imogen went to get a mop from the back of the shop to clean the floor. 'I never trusted her boyfriend. But Warren hasn't even been in. I barred him.'

Jude laughed. 'So if he was *barred* as you put it . . .' She bent down to sniff the Christmas roses '. . . then where did she get the *stuff*?' She flicked her scarf over her shoulder and wiggled her eyebrows at Imo.

'I haven't the foggiest.' But Imogen remembered the time she'd seen Tiffany hand Warren a small package. She'd been suspicious then, hadn't she?

'Perhaps she's growing it in one of your greenhouses,' Jude suggested cheerfully, undoing the belt of the wrap-around. 'Imo's Utopia. Flower Power returns to Chichester. The sixties revisited . . .'

'Oh, for heaven's sake.' Imogen squeezed the mop out over the sink. But what about Tiffany's guilty expression when Imogen had caught her lurking in the greenhouse? She'd even wondered – why, oh, why hadn't she *done* something? – what was hidden there.

'Stay here,' she told Jude. 'Look after the shop for me.'

'But I can't sell flowers,' Jude wailed. 'Where are you going?'

'To look for a marijuana plant,' Imogen whispered. This

was serious. This was scary. She hesitated by the door. 'What does it look like anyway?'

'Oh, honestly.' Jude flipped the *Open* sign over and shut the latch. 'I'll come with you. What sort of a florist can't even recognise a dope plant?'

'An innocent one.'

'You're not joking.' Jude took her arm. 'Don't you even know what little goodies you have in stock?'

They found them. Yes, them – there were eight plants – in the far corner of the big greenhouse. Imogen almost had a fit.

'Hell's bells . . .' She stood goggle-eyed. Her hand flew to her mouth and she glanced guiltily over her shoulder, half expecting the appearance of the drug squad, armed police, or at the very least a sniffer dog.

'They seem healthy enough,' Jude pronounced approvingly. 'She's been looking after them. Giving them plenty to drink. And they're in full sunlight.'

'Well, thank goodness for that. Otherwise what on earth would we have done?' Sometimes, Imogen despaired of Jude ever appreciating the seriousness of a situation. Couldn't she see that Imo could be arrested for cultivation or drug dealing or harbouring criminal activities or something?

'She's harvested one.' Jude poked the shorn plant. 'That's probably why she was testing the goods.'

Harvested? Did that mean that Tiffany was a dealer? Imogen shuddered. How long had she been growing and incubating and harvesting on Imogen's premises? How *could* she?

Jude proceeded to sniff the leaves. She seemed very calm to Imo – but then, what did *she* have to lose? It wasn't her place that had been used for illicit purposes. 'She must have dried them out somewhere,' Jude said. She looked up at Imo. 'Any ideas?'

Imogen frowned. She had no idea of the procedure involved. But she supposed it would work the same as dried flowers and herbs. 'The old oven?' She grew flowers for dried arrangements and used an old Baby Belling in the drying process.

'Perfect.' Jude rubbed her hands together, clearly enjoying this. 'Lead on.'

Imogen led the way back into the rear of *Say It With Flowers*, to the workshop area where she did the messier work of plant rearing and flower arranging. 'Here.' She glared at the oven as if it were somehow responsible for Tiffany's misdemeanours.

Jude shrugged off her coat to reveal a mustard-coloured sweatshirt, orange mini-skirt and black tights. She opened the oven door and sniffed long and hard. 'You could get high in here,' she giggled, sniffing again.

'Don't you start . . .' Imogen pulled her out none too gently. 'Wait till I get my hands on that girl,' she muttered.

'It's pretty harmless though.' Jude lit a cigarette. 'Only a bit of grass, sweetie. We've all done it.'

'What – grown it?' Imo stared at her.

'No, smoked it.' She glanced back at Imogen and seemed to realise at last how upset she was. 'Tell you what . . .' She touched her arm. 'I'll go back to the greenhouse and destroy the grisly evidence.'

'Destroy it?' Imo had visions of a huge bonfire. All of their neighbours opening their windows and getting high as kites. Turning up their hi-fis, rediscovering their love beads.

Tuning into their inner selves. Free love on the streets. Mass orgies in Chichester city centre.

'Snip-snip.' Jude made a scissors-motion. 'Well, you don't want to keep them, do you?'

'Of course not.'

'And you're not going to let Tiffany have them?'

'You must be joking.' The only thing Tiffany would be getting was a rollicking.

'So . . .' Jude shrugged. 'No police, I presume?'

'No way.' Whatever Tiffany had done, Imogen wouldn't wish that on her. And the last thing she wanted was to have officious policemen nosing around. Besides, would they believe her if she said she simply hadn't noticed the plants? Like Jude said, she was a florist, she was supposed to know about these things. They might think she was a silent collaborator.

'Then I'll give them the chop.' Jude seemed to be looking forward to it. There was quite a gleam in her eye. 'I could take care of them for you.' She pulled up the sleeves of the mustard sweatshirt. 'Shame to waste them on the compost, sweetie.'

Imogen shivered. 'Not on your life. They're going in a black bin bag and being dumped. Today.'

'Spoilsport.' But Jude grabbed a fork and some shears from the shelf. 'You'd better open up the shop and put the kettle on.'

'And then?' Imo felt quite shaken. It wasn't every day you discovered your place of work being used as a . . . as a . . . well, whatever.

'And then . . .' Jude grinned. 'You are going to tell me everything about this Alex character.'

'There's absolutely no future in it.' But Imogen couldn't

258

help smiling. Once again, it sort of crept up on her and spread. But she was doing well. She hadn't thought about him for ten whole minutes.

'Good God.' Jude shook her head in despair. 'Look at you. Anyone would think you were in love.'

Chapter 23

'Marisa Gibb's fella?' Jude was agog. 'What happened then?'

'Well, we . . .' Imogen was clearly distracted. Her hair had escaped the confines of the tortoiseshell comb that was supposed to keep it up and back, and there were dark rings around her grey eyes. 'Um . . .' She snapped a bud off one of the white lilies and didn't even seem to notice.

'You went to bed with him,' Jude reminded her.

'Er . . . mmm.' Dark rings apart, all of a sudden Imo looked as dewy-eyed as a Mills & Boon heroine.

'I don't believe it.' Jude took a deep breath as the shop door opened with a ping. 'You mean, you slept with your step-daughter's boyfriend?'

Imogen jumped. 'Hello, can I help you?' she asked brightly, tucking one of the stray wisps of hair behind one ear.

There was a touching vulnerability about her today, thought Jude with a pang of envy. And she guessed that it had little to do with discovering illegal substances in her greenhouse.

The customer selected roses and stocks and went on her way with only a brief curious glance behind her.

'Did you have to say that?' Imogen hissed as soon as she was out of earshot. She began rearranging the white lilies once again.

'But he *is* Marisa's boyfriend. And you did go to bed with him.'

'Well, if you put it like that . . .'

'How would you put it?' Jude was amazed. This whole thing was so unlike Imo. She was so level-headed, so sensible, so innocent (look how shocked she'd been over the marijuana plants). So how on earth had she managed to get herself into this mess? 'A meeting of minds?'

Imogen shrugged. 'It just happened.'

And how many times had she heard that old chestnut? Jude paced the floor, desperate for a cigarette but knowing Imo would shoo her outside if she lit one. 'How old is he?' she demanded.

Imogen hesitated. 'What does that have to do with it?'

'Nothing. Only asking.' Young though, she'd seen that much.

'Twenty-five,' Imogen mumbled.

Jude whistled, taking by surprise a grey-haired senior citizen slowly making his way towards them.

'Do you have any African violets?' he asked Jude.

'I'm afraid I don't.' She indicated Imogen. 'But this lady might be able to help you.'

Twenty-five . . . Jude didn't know whether to commiserate or congratulate her. But on balance she would have clapped Imo on the back, she decided, if her friend hadn't been busy explaining the difference between what was clearly a white flower and equally clearly a purple flower to the senior citizen in the mac.

'Isn't it awful?' Imo said when he'd finally left the shop. She went over to the sink and brushed the soil from her hands.

'Awful?' Jude wouldn't have put it quite like that. 'It'll do you good, Imo,' she laughed. 'If you're going to have a one-night stand, you may as well have it with a young—'

'It's not . . .' Imo's voice trailed off as yet another customer entered the shop. The wreath and a cheque exchanged hands.

'Not what?' But Jude knew what she was going to say.

'Not a one-night stand.' All of a sudden, Imogen strode over to the door, shut it firmly, closed the latch and turned the *Open* sign. She took Jude by the hand, dragging her out back to her little working area and planting table.

'So you're going to see him again?' Relieved to be able to smoke at last, Jude dug into her bag for her cigarettes and lighter. She could see the temptation, but doubted the wisdom. To be brutal, she also doubted that Imo would get the chance. Jude knew Marisa, and she knew men. Experience told her that Imo wouldn't stand a chance, poor love. And if that were the case then Jude must stick around to pick up the pieces.

'I don't think I can help it.' Imogen rolled up the sleeves of her green *Say It With Flowers* overalls and plunged her hands into the tub of compost on the work bench in front of her. 'I want to see him.'

'Ye . . . es?'

'And he keeps phoning me.'

'Really?' Jude tried not to sound surprised. She drew in the smoke and exhaled with a sigh. Perhaps a reassessment was required. After all, Marisa Gibb was a cold fish. And Imogen was warm, serene and one of those rare women who could be beautiful even without make-up, she thought wryly.

'He says it's over with Marisa,' Imogen remarked carelessly.

'Uh-huh.' Jude watched Imo as, with practised hands, she filled some pots with earth. How could she stand all that filthy soil trapped under her finger-nails? Ugh!

'And he says that age doesn't matter.'

Did he indeed? Jude found she was quite enjoying her Aunt Marge routine. She flicked ash into the waste bin in the corner. 'And what do you think?' she asked.

Imogen looked up from the compost and faced her squarely. 'I think he might be right,' she said.

'Bloody hell.' Jude squashed her cigarette into an old glass ashtray usually reserved for Imogen's seeds. Poor old Imo. She really had got it bad.

'Now then, Alex.' Sylvie Price poured out another cup of tea. They were in her comfy kitchen, the scent of baking in the air, warm, soothing, normalising. But was he no longer her lovie? Alex wondered. 'Have you got in touch with that young lady of yours yet?'

Sylvie, he could see, meant to have an answer. 'She's not my young lady,' came to mind. But Sylvie wouldn't be satisfied with that. 'I tried earlier.' Gloomily, Alex helped himself to another piece of treacle tart. 'And there was no reply.' Clearly Marisa was lying low.

'You tried to phone, maybe,' Sylvie corrected. Her eyes behind the thick lenses were faintly sceptical. 'But you haven't been round there yet, have you?'

263

'Not much point if she's not there,' Alex said, mouth full of treacle and pastry. What was it to Sylvie anyway? He looked up as she moved away, standing by the sink now in her Marigolds, sleeves rolled up to the elbow, lines of disapproval and laughter contouring her face. Life lines.

'There's something wrong with that girl.' Sylvie stacked cups and plates, neatly, side by side ready for washing.

Why did she do that, Alex wondered, if they were all destined for the washing-up bowl, higgledy-piggledy, anyway? But order was important to Sylvie, just as it was to his own mam. If things could be put in order, they could more easily be dealt with and controlled, he supposed. Anything – from errant sons and lodgers to washing up.

'Something's happened,' Sylvie went on. 'You can tell by looking at her.'

Alex shrugged. What had happened to Marisa was that she hadn't got her own way for once.

'And you could at least make more of an *effort*.' This last word was clearly the important one. With some *effort* Sylvie splashed in the cutlery, planted her feet apart, firm and balanced, hands working nineteen to the dozen with *effort* on the washing up.

Wonderful! Alex reached for the sketch pad and pencil that were never far away. Perversely, he began with the saggy green slippers. Faded and shapeless, thick wrinkled ankles sprouting out of them like stalks of broccoli. 'You don't even like her,' he reminded his landlady, adding a little shade. And Sylvie had always struck him as a woman of extremes. No shades of grey for her. How would she respond to Imogen? he wondered. Imogen . . . There were life lines in her face too – faint and fine. And a new lease of life for Alex?

264

'Liking doesn't come into it. You should go and see her.' Sylvie got into her rhythm. Wash, rinse, plop into tub on the drainer . . . wash, rinse, plop . . . wash, rinse . . . 'Right is right.' Plop into tub on the drainer.

'And left knows best,' Alex mimicked, making strong, sure strokes with his pencil. No waist. Sylvie's aproned figure was a blurred rectangle. Waste not, want not. He chuckled. But she was a fascinating subject – this wasn't the first time he'd caught her in full cleaning regalia. She was one of those women, his mam's generation of women, often to be found in full cleaning regalia. That was, he supposed, what wraparound pinnies were for.

'Cheeky bugger!' Sylvie marched over, snatched his plate, dripped on to his sketch pad.

'Careful.' Alex pulled it away. 'No need to damage a valuable masterpiece.'

'Valuable, my foot,' Sylvie said with confusing logic. 'You didn't see her face – there's something wrong with that girl, I tell you.'

Lack of expression? That was his main complaint when painting Marisa, though it made her something of an artistic challenge. There had to be something more, something naked and raw, hidden under that inscrutable cool. But lack of expression meant the artist had to dig so deep, sometimes it didn't seem worth the effort. Now, you couldn't say that about Sylvie. Not only expression but years of experience on that face and in those eyes behind those thick lenses of hers. Years of lovies and honesty and right is right. And she was too. 'I'll go round and see her later,' Alex promised.

'You do that, lovie.' Sylvie noded, almost satisfied. Returned to the sink, muttering, 'What do you want to

265

be wasting your time drawing old women for anyway? When you could be . . . could be . . .'

'Drawing dolly birds?' Alex suggested, knowing she was secretly flattered. 'Like the gorgeous Marisa, for instance?'

Sylvie sniffed, turned on the tap, squirted in more detergent. 'A new young lady is it, then?' She turned and shot him a glance from the gimlet eye that might be short-sighted but had seen everything.

Carefully, Alex drew it.

'Keeping you out all hours?'

'You're worse than me mam, you are.' He made the Marigolds super-big and started to hum.

'And your mam would tell you the same as I'm telling you.' Sylvie pointed a yellow finger. 'Sort it, that's all I'm saying.'

Alex drew the finger and a word-balloon, SORT IT, in caps.

The doorbell rang. 'I'll get it.' He should be off. Things to deal with before term started. Imogen West was turning him into a dreamer. And what he was dreaming of was her.

But Sylvie was away from her sink and into the narrow hallway before you could say . . . *take off them Marigolds, lovie.* She didn't answer the door, though, just scrutinised the outline of the figure on the other side of the frosted glass. 'She may not be at home,' she said to Alex.

'Mmm?'

'Because she's here.'

The penny dropped. Alex went to open the door on the second ring.

She stood there, not angry – he'd expected angry – but beatific. Stunning too – he'd almost forgotten. 'Marisa . . .'

266

She reached up and kissed him very firmly on the mouth. 'Alex, darling,' she said. 'At last.'

'Do you really think it's so awful of me?' Wide-eyed, Imogen stared at her friend.

Jude gave her a quick hug of reassurance. 'Don't listen to me – I'm just jealous. If you think it's right then you go ahead.' The floodgates had opened and for the past thirty minutes Imo hadn't seemed able to stop talking about Alex Armstrong. And that, Jude reminded herself, was what happened when you were in love – though it had been so long that she could barely remember.

'He quoted John Donne to me,' Imogen said, with what Jude privately considered to be a sickening smile. 'But I suppose you're used to men reciting poetry?'

'Nope.' And anyway Jude had gone right off poetry just lately.

'From Mattie, I mean.'

'Mattie only quoted Mattie,' Jude told her. 'And Mattie is in the past.' She wasn't sure why she had bothered with him in the first place. Her bullshit antennae had been well off beam there.

'It didn't work out then?' Imo put a hand on Jude's arm. A hand covered in soil, she noted.

'Mattie was looking for someone to write about. Some-one to make him feel complete.' Or so he had said, shortly before Jude had given up and gone to sleep. She brushed a few specks of earth from her yellow sweatshirt.

'Nothing wrong with that.' Imogen firmed the compost with the heel of her hand and grabbed another peat pot from the pile on the shelf above the work bench. 'Is there?'

'I'd rather he was complete before I got anywhere near

267

him.' Jude watched Imogen knead the soil between her fingers. Mattie had said *she* was like the soil – well, like the earth actually. She thought she knew what he meant, but couldn't help feeling he could have tried a bit harder in the simile department. And in others actually.

'So what's wrong with Mattie?'

'Well, for starters, he takes himself too seriously.' Like most men, she thought sadly.

Imogen smiled. 'You could sort him out if anyone could.'

'But that's just it . . .' Jude sighed. 'I honestly can't be bothered. I know he's not right for me.' Why did she need to keep trying? What was so perfect about coupledom? She and Daisy were happy as they were. Why rock the boat? She groaned. 'I'm a member of the Blind Date world-wide internet introduction service. It has thirteen thousand members, and I still can't find a nice man.' She glanced at Imo. What did she have that Jude lacked – apart from a slender figure, clear skin, cheekbones to die for and a notable lack of cynicism? 'Where are they all, Imo?' Only her friend wasn't exactly the right person to ask. She had apparently found one without even trying.

'You could join a church.' Imo's mind was clearly not on the job.

Now she'd heard it all. Jude dusted a chair with her hand and sat down gingerly. At *Say It With Flowers* you could never be quite sure what you were sitting on and she was very fond of her orange skirt. She watched Imogen flicking through her seed packets with long fingers, scrutinising them closely to check dates. 'You don't honestly think

I'm likely to meet my ideal partner in a church, do you?'

'Or you could start hanging out in bookshops or art galleries,' was Imogen's next offering.

'I have a salon to run.'

'Evening classes?'

'Forget it.' She had made up her mind. One more from her shortlist and then she was done. If that was another miserable failure, then she would drop it. And neither would she wait patiently for her prince to come. Jude lit another cigarette. No, she'd go out and buy a vibrator and to hell with it. At least she wouldn't have to wash anyone's dirty socks for the rest of her life.

Whereas Imo . . . Jude narrowed her eyes. Look at her, so *saturated* today, so *glowing*. 'What was he like between the sheets then?' she asked, realising belatedly that this was the one bit (the best bit) that Imo had left out.

Imogen blushed. 'Pretty good, actually.' She grinned. 'And Mattie?'

'Terrible, since you ask.' Jude really wasn't keen to remember. 'He said he felt challenged.'

'Is that good or bad?'

'In this case bad. Truth was he couldn't manage it at all.'

Imogen sprinkled some fine compost on top of the seeds. 'Oh, dear, poor Jude.' She hesitated, and Jude just knew she was going to say something absolutely awful.

'Come on then, out with it.' She sighed. 'Say what you've got to say.'

Imo grinned. 'Mattie wasn't a performance poet then?'

Hah-bloody-hah. Definitely time to go. She grabbed her

269

coat. As for Imo, it was all very well throwing caution to the wind and falling in love madly, truly and deeply. But Jude had the feeling that Marisa Gibb would have something to say about that.

Chapter 24

'Whoever can guess what this is going to be . . .' Alex manipulated the rubber of the balloon between his fingers '. . . gets to keep it.'

'Big deal,' said some kid in the front row with long hair, buck teeth and a Bart Simpson jumper.

Little brat. Alex was not feeling well disposed towards the world. And kids were supposed to like animal balloons. They were supposed to watch open-mouthed – and quietly – as he magically created sausage dogs, long-eared rabbits and the odd giraffe. He moved closer to the semi-circle of children and squeaked the red rubber as close to the Little B's face as he dared.

'Gerroff!'

The kids laughed. Gotcha. Alex roamed from one side of the room to the other, in the hope that if he kept moving he'd keep them with him. And at least in this annexe of the church hall (hung with balloons and banners but unmistakably a church hall) there was more space to swing a cat-balloon than in the average sitting-room.

'A dog!' someone called.

271

'Correct.' He ran off another four assorted animals, keeping up a patter of corny jokes. *What game makes you hoarse? Stable tennis.* And, *Why did Cinderella get dropped from the football team? Because she kept running away from the ball.* 'Who wants to try some juggling?' He offered the skittles to the Little B in the front row.

'I bet you wouldn't juggle with knives,' the Little B jeered. 'Too chicken to do that, eh?'

Why did the chicken cross the road? Alex would have used knives – if he could have got the Little B to have a go. The children, he sensed, were getting restless, starting to whisper and giggle.

Smoothly, he began with three skittles. Glossy red to contrast with his black tracksuit. Get into the rhythm, keep up the jokes, that was the way. And don't panic. So, *How do you stop a skunk from smelling? Hold his nose.* Alex added more skittles. Easy does it.

Behind the Little B was a grave-faced child whose eyes were fixed on Alex. She seemed very familiar though it was hard to say when she was only on the edge of his peripheral vision. Hell's bells. Daisy.

Alex dropped the lot.

Vanessa leaned towards Hazel. 'Is anything wrong?' she asked. They were sipping Earl Grey in Kirby's Wedgwood blue, Edwardian-style tea room. But Vanessa had been practically summoned here today, and Hazel was not looking her usual ebullient self. She was wearing the kind of black hat one might wear to a funeral, and her face was as pale as if she had indeed just attended one.

Hazel replaced her china cup in the saucer with an uncharacteristic rattle. She was wearing a black coat too, black scarf, black stockings, black court shoes. 'Does anything seem wrong to you?' she asked intently.

Vanessa repressed a sigh, looked around her, tried to be soothed by the elegance of the wood panelling, the pleasing geometry of so many straight lines. Games . . . Perhaps that was why she found Ralph so invigorating. They had agreed from the start that game-playing, once fun, now bored them. There didn't seem time enough left for it, she supposed. They had known one another for so many years and it was wonderful not to have to pussy foot around. A spade could be called a spade and dirty too. 'Not particularly.' Vanessa waited.

'I can't wear a hat in Italy,' Hazel said. 'It'll be much too warm.'

'A hat?' If there was any logic to Hazel's remark then it was lost on her. 'Italy?' she added for good measure. With luck she'd get there eventually.

Hazel peeled off the said hat with a sad and dramatic flourish.

'Oh.' Vanessa blinked. Her friend's hair was very short. And the colour was . . . copper? Bright, new, bottom-of-saucepan copper.

'It was the streaks,' Hazel explained, looking surreptitiously around the tea room. Only a middle-aged man rustling a paper, two elderly ladies and a fifty-something female immersed in a book were within range. She replaced the hat. 'Jude had to bleach out the black and then do an overall tint.' She shuddered. 'It took three hours and it was pure hell.'

'Three hours?' Streaks? Confused, Vanessa pushed away the disconcerting image of a naked copper-haired Hazel racing across a cricket pitch.

273

'And the tint brought it back to copper. It was that or go black.'

'Back?' To Italy perhaps? Vanessa refocused on her gloves, lying neatly by her side plate. Kirby's was very civilised, she reflected, and Hazel was normally predictable. But not today.

'Black.' Hazel pointed to her hat, or at least to what was hidden by it.

'Ah, black.' Vanessa nodded, unfastened the buttons of her red coat. Logic was always there if you searched hard enough for it. Most people acted with reason.

'What do you think of the new colour?' Hazel seemed to be aiming for nonchalance as she sipped more tea.

Vanessa, however, was tired of games. 'Not one of your wiser decisions,' she said.

Cup and saucer clattered together once again as Hazel emitted a low wail. 'Feel it,' she demanded, releasing a copper clump from the constraints of the hat band. 'Just feel it.'

Reluctantly, Vanessa did so. It reminded her that she needed more hand cream.

'Well?'

She frowned. 'A good protein conditioner might help. I use eggs when I'm travelling.'

'Eggs?' Hazel repositioned the clump. Out of sight, out of . . . 'Eggs?' Her voice seemed to be rising towards hysteria.

Vanessa tried to defuse the situation. 'I love the cut,' she said. 'Very chic.'

'Giorgio hates short hair.' Absent-mindedly, Hazel picked up Vanessa's eclair and took a large bite. 'He thinks women should be women.'

274

And not have the vote perhaps? But Vanessa realised that this must be the Italian connection. 'You're going to Italy with Giorgio?' she said brightly, trying to cheer her up.

Hazel nodded miserably. 'He asked me on New Year's Eve,' she confided. 'Just after his *crema e granita al caffè.*'

'For a holiday?' Vanessa made her voice brighter still.

'He wants me to meet his family.' Hazel took another bite and Vanessa waved at the waitress to fetch her another one. 'I'm supposed to be on a pasta diet,' Hazel went on.

'Pasta diet?'

'I only eat when I'm with Giorgio.'

Goodness. 'And you're worried he won't like your hair?' Vanessa tried not to sound incredulous. After all, there were women to whom a good hair day meant a day when all was satisfactory with their world and a bad hair day meant they might as well have stayed in bed. This was merely an extension of the same concept though Vanessa would have hoped that intelligent women had grown out of such insecurities by the age of sixty. And as for diets . . . Extension? A thought occurred to her. 'How about a wig?' she whispered.

'Oh, you weren't that bad,' Trixie said brightly.

But Alex knew that Sylvie's daughter was just being kind. He had never dropped all the skittles before. And he never really recovered. With the Little B and Daisy Lomax in his audience, his act had disintegrated into farce. He'd even resorted to toilet humour. *Why did the lobster blush? Because the sea weed*, to regain some respect. Before long, the kids were wandering off to find the food, and Alex had decided that enough was enough, and this was too much.

'Nice of you to say so.' He began collecting up his stuff. 'But I was hardly on top form.'

'We all have our off days.' Trixie looked doubtful. Whatever her mother said, Alex knew she wouldn't be recommending his services to any more of her friends.

But it didn't matter. Alex wouldn't be doing any more children's parties. He'd made up his mind. No more Santa Claus, no more juggling. He'd gone off children in a big way.

'*I* enjoyed it, Alex.'

He glanced up to see Daisy standing beside him. She looked charming in her pink party frock and blonde plaits with pink ribbons, and he didn't trust her an inch. 'Hello, Daisy.' Now how could he put this? 'I'm glad you had a good time.' He dropped nonchalantly to her level and met her steady blue gaze. 'But I don't think Auntie Imo would be interested in hearing about it, do you?'

'Oh, but she would.' Daisy sounded confident. 'Auntie Imo loves anything that makes her laugh.'

'Does she indeed?' Alex groaned. He was unlikely to score any Brownie points with this afternoon's disaster.

'Oh, yes.' Daisy blinked. 'And she might feel sorry for you too.'

'Might she?' Alex brightened at this.

'Mmm. She'll think you're really sad.'

And that was supposed to make him feel good?

'Do you love Auntie Imo?' Daisy went on conversationally.

Alex felt about twelve. He gulped. 'Love? That's a big word.'

'It's only four letters.' Daisy was waiting.

'Auntie Imo is a lovely lady,' he said. That seemed safe enough. Though with this child, who could be sure?

'I thought you did.' Satisfied, Daisy turned on her black

276

patent heels. 'Wait till I tell my mummy. She'll be *really* interested to hear that.'

At *Say It With Flowers*, Imogen was in the front of the shop trimming fern when she glanced out of the window to see Marisa Gibb walking up South Street.

Help! Instinctively, she ducked behind the counter, still clutching the fern. She wouldn't be coming here, would she? Imo prayed for her to walk on by.

But the shop door opened with a ping, and . . .

'Imogen?' Marisa's tone demanded attention.

She couldn't face Marisa. She really didn't think that after New Year's Eve and Alex . . . She couldn't talk to her. But neither could she stay where she was so, slowly, Imogen rose to her feet. 'Oh, it's you. Hello.' She tried for pleased and surprised, and probably only managed guilty.

Marisa looked wonderful. She was wearing chocolate brown jersey trousers and a cream fleece. Her clear green eyes were knowing. Imogen swallowed hard, put the crushed and forlorn fern on the counter, wiped her hands on her green overalls. Did Marisa know? Could she know? Surely Alex wouldn't have told her?

'Imogen.' Her nod was cool.

Imo grabbed some more greenery from the pile by the till and began cutting furiously. 'How can I help you?'

'I just wanted a little chat.' Marisa glided over to the white roses, bent and sniffed. 'My favourites,' she said. 'Alex often buys me white roses.'

'Does he?' In Imogen's hand, another innocent fern was crushed to a pulp. She rubbed at the green stain on her fingers. And at the thought of him – just the thought of him – her heart did a bungee jump. 'How is . . . er . . . Alex?'

she asked carefully. It proved harder than she'd expected to drain the name of all emotion. 'Have you seen him?'

Marisa considered. 'Not over Christmas,' she said at last. 'He had to go back to Nottinghamshire to see his family. We hate to be separated. But he had to let them know what was going on.'

Imo put the fern to one side before she destroyed the lot. Her bungee-jumping heart had coiled into a knot of unease. 'Going on?'

Marisa moved in closer. For the kill? Imo wondered. 'There were things he had to tell them, you see. Things that couldn't be said over the phone.'

Imo stared at her. 'Things?' She half-hoped Marisa wouldn't elaborate. What things? She grabbed a packet of Staybright flower food – wishing *she* could – spooned some of the powder into a large watering can and marched over to the sink. Having her back to Marisa for a while, she reasoned, would give her valuable recovery time.

'Mmm.' Imogen didn't have to look at her to sense the girl's small smile. 'I've seen him since he got back, of course.'

Of course. The tap continued to gush. The watering can filled, overflowed, and still Imogen stood there, as rooted as one of her perennials.

'Hadn't you better turn it off?' Marisa swished over and twisted the tap.

Imogen blinked. First Tiffany and now her – both trying to flood the shop.

'Something the matter?' Marisa asked. She unzipped the cream fleece to reveal a matching sweater of soft lambswool.

'No, nothing. I was miles away.' Imogen wished she

was. 'I was dreaming.' Yes, dreaming of a better life. One in which people were honest and men had values. Where women had no right to look as good as Marisa Gibb and still get the man, damn it.

She began a tour of the shop, providing fresh water for her flowers. Anything to keep moving. Alex had seen Marisa since he'd been back, that was all she could think. Before or after she'd gone to bed with him? Did it matter? Yes, actually. It mattered a lot.

She straightened. 'Why are you here?' It was time to be direct with this girl. Edward's daughter she might be, but with or without Alex, there could be nothing between them. Imo didn't want there to be anything between them. She didn't even like her.

'Because I like you,' Marisa said.

Oh, hell.

'As soon as I met you . . .'

Imogen gulped. This wasn't what she'd expected to hear. And it was certainly not what she wanted to hear. She repressed a twinge of guilt. She'd never considered herself a boyfriend snatcher, particularly when it was from someone sixteen years her junior and beautiful to boot. But it hadn't been, had it, a case of snatching? More – as Jude had hinted – a one-night stand.

'I sensed a sort of bond between us.' She flicked back her strawberry-blonde hair.

'You did?' Imogen sat down on the chair next to the counter. Was that the sort of bond that meant they liked the same things, the same men? she wondered.

Marisa nodded. 'My mother and I . . .' Her voice trailed away. 'We don't get on.'

Imogen considered this. She could see that this girl had

279

problems that had never been resolved, and having heard the story, could even understand some of her bitterness. But despite everything Imo had been drawn to her husband's mistress and found herself disliking their daughter.

'She's allowed us to be left with nothing,' Marisa continued.

'Nothing?' Imo tried to focus on the meaning behind the words, the emotions under the cool exterior. She got to her feet and began tidying the counter. Anything to keep busy. To stop thinking, though that was impossible.

'So although it's been awful for you too . . .'

Imo watched her warily. 'Yes?'

'Finding out about me and my mother. Missing my father . . .'

'Yes?' Imogen frowned. Was it so heartless of her to find comfort in the arms of another man when she'd only buried her husband a month ago? Was it so heartless when she'd found something that Edward had never been able to give her in ten years of marriage? Oh, Alex . . .

'And although everything of my father's is yours by right . . .'

'Yes?' Imo braced herself, knowing there was more to come.

'I'm not asking for money.' Marisa paused. 'What I want more than money, more than you'd imagine possible . . .' she smiled '. . . as I said to Alex only this morning, is for you and me to be friends.'

'A wig?'

Vanessa flinched. Hazel obviously didn't realise how well her voice carried. It must be all that rehearsing for the Gershwin show that had made projection an unconscious

280

part of her daily routine. The elderly ladies and the middle-aged man all looked curiously around in the direction of Hazel's black hat. Even the fifty-something's eyes flickered.

'Or a hair extension,' Vanessa whispered. 'Jude must have . . .'

'Judith . . .' Hazel spoke sternly '. . . is never coming near my hair again.'

Vanessa realised that this was like a jigsaw puzzle to which she needed all the pieces to comprehend the whole. 'Can't you just tell Giorgio about the hair gaffe?' she asked Hazel. 'Have a bit of a laugh about it?'

'A bit of a *laugh*?'

Vanessa sought the sanctuary of her tea-cup. So Hazel and her Italian couldn't even laugh together? Inwardly, she despaired. Why *did* she keep up with Hazel? Was it simply force of habit? She was fond of her but never ceased to marvel at her priorities. 'Still, it's only a holiday.' She wondered whether or not to say what she'd like to say. In the end, she couldn't resist. 'And it'll grow out.'

Hazel glared at her as she swallowed a mouthful of eclair. 'It's not only a holiday. It's more of a . . .' She fiddled with her teaspoon. 'A reluctant sojourn.'

Vanessa had never seen her look so embarrassed. 'Don't you want to go to Italy?'

Hazel pressed her lips into a thin line. 'It's not Italy I object to,' she said. 'It's what Giorgio will want to *do* in Italy.' She sighed. 'Italians are very hot-blooded, you know. It must be all that sun.'

'Ah.' Vanessa considered this. 'Has he proposed? Why didn't you say? We could have gone to a restaurant and had champagne.'

'No.'

'No?'

'The proposal was not one of marriage.' Hazel seemed to be struggling to recover her poise.

Vanessa smiled, took a sip of her tea and placed the cup carefully back in the saucer. First Imogen, now Hazel. 'Then what was it? Nights of passion on Lake Garda? A naughty weekend in Venice?' Hardly Hazel's style, she thought.

Hazel gave a dismissive wave of the hand. 'Hardly. But one has to move with the times. Perhaps marriage is a touch outdated. What do you think?'

What Vanessa thought was that she didn't believe her. And sure enough Hazel's expression was wistful as she glanced down at the third finger of her left hand. 'He said he had a little something for me,' she said. 'I had hoped . . . nothing gaudy, a solitaire perhaps. You know where you are with a solitaire.'

'Perhaps that will come in time,' Vanessa soothed.

Hazel did not seem convinced. 'He told me that Italy is perfect for lovers,' she said, as though that settled it. 'I could see the meaning in his eyes.'

The waitress – dressed in black with a frilly white apron, red lips and a big smile – brought another eclair. Vanessa thanked her, removed some surplus cream with her little finger and licked it off. 'You could just let yourself go and think of Italy.'

Hazel frowned. 'It's dangerous to do any such thing without the security of knowing one is looked after,' she said.

'Is it?' Vanessa raised an eyebrow.

Hazel wasn't the most sensitive of women, but even she seemed to catch a whiff of disapproval. 'I don't have a lot,' she reminded Vanessa. She wiped her mouth with her ivory linen napkin. 'And I can't afford feminist ideals. I'm not in a position to pick and choose.'

Vanessa refrained from saying that one could always pick and choose. That when you lost the ability to do that, you may as well lie down and die. But she understood now about the hair. It was all so — thank God — different from her relationship with Ralph.

She bit into her eclair, enjoying the texture of the pastry as it gave way to thick cream. How refreshing not to have to pretend, she thought again. Ralph had seen her during some bad times, and yet he still wanted to spend time with her, he still found her interesting. Tom had always been the one for him, they both knew that, but he would be happier with Vanessa. There would be no angst, no jealousy or frustration. He even loved her in his own way. Not with passion, but Vanessa had experienced her fill of that. The time had come for something more stable, more lasting, more reliable.

'Though of course . . .' Hazel was still speaking '. . . who knows what the future will hold?' Once more she projected with ease and the middle-aged man on the table next to them cleared his throat, as if about to tell them.

'And is it a flying visit to Italy?' Vanessa pressed.

'It might be longer.'

If Hazel were to play her cards right. Vanessa nodded as another piece of the jigsaw fell into place. 'How did Jude take it?'

Hazel became very interested in the teapot. 'More tea?'

'No, thank you. Well, Hazel?'

'I haven't exactly told her yet,' Hazel muttered, refolding her napkin into its neat rectangle and placing it by her cup and saucer.

Vanessa had thought as much. 'And when *exactly* are you planning to go?'

Hazel brightened. 'After the show.' Her eyes grew soft. '"The man I love . . ."'

'Giorgio?'

'Gershwin.' Hazel looked over Vanessa's shoulder into a land no doubt peopled only by Gershwin and Giorgio. 'Giorgio wouldn't leave before the show's finished its run.'

Vanessa sighed. She made it sound like the West End. 'You must let me have some tickets. I'll bring Imogen along.' Amateur dramatics, operatics, musical comedy had, after all, been Vanessa's scheme in the first place. Though she'd had no idea Hazel would get so involved, let alone meet the man of her dreams and be whisked off to hot nights of passion in Italy.

'You'll be here then? Not zooming off somewhere?' Hazel sounded as excited as a girl at the prospect of this show of hers. A spot of pink appeared in each cheek.

'Not zooming off at all. My zooming days are over. I'm settling down.'

'Really?'

Vanessa shrugged. 'After a few days in its company the zebra is only a donkey with stripes, darling. And when you've seen one mosque, you've seen them all.' Of course it wasn't as simple as that. She was tired. Her eye no longer as fresh as it once was. There was her health to consider, too, and wasn't travel writing best left to those who were seeing something for the first time? Sometimes she felt so jaded. As if she'd not only seen it all, but from every blessed angle.

But Hazel had the scent in her nostrils. 'Settling down with Imogen, you mean?'

'No. With Ralph. You remember him?'

'Goodness.' Hazel looked her up and down as though wondering how anyone who didn't bother with foundation on a regular basis could possibly have found herself a man. 'You too?' She began humming 'Love Is Here to Stay'.

Really, Vanessa thought, the sooner this Gershwin show was over, the better.

'Do you love him?'

Women the world over, Vanessa concluded, would always ask the same question. 'He's very special,' she told Hazel. Would she understand? 'And he has always interested me.' That was much more to the point. 'It isn't a sexual relationship . . .'

'Lucky you,' Hazel said with some feeling.

'But not a dependent relationship either.' How could dependence be a good thing, when it gave one a tendency to turn into Mrs Blobby? Vanessa had never been so glad in her life as she had been when Tom left Imogen enough money to become independent.

'And have *you* told Imogen?' Hazel teased, quite cheerful now.

'Oh, yes. But she doesn't need me.'

The waitress brought their bill and Vanessa scanned it briefly before reaching for her purse. 'My treat,' she said, as she always did.

'Is it your turn? Well, thank you, dear,' Hazel said as she always did. She collected her things together. 'But as for Imogen, I met her young man, you know, dear. And he's *very* young.'

Vanessa shrugged. She had wondered how long it would take Hazel to get round to that subject. But who cared how old he was? 'If he's *enough* for her,' she said firmly, 'that's all that matters.'

'Friends?' Imogen repeated in a daze. How could they be friends? And *this morning?* Marisa had seen Alex this morning?

'Alex wasn't so sure . . .'

'This morning?' she repeated. No wonder he wasn't sure.

'He didn't want me to come and see you.'

I bet he didn't, Imo thought. The rat. Playing one off against the other. Pretending it was for real.

'He said you'd probably tell me where to go.'

Imogen drew herself up to her full height and looked Marisa straight in the eye. 'But you came anyway?'

'I persuaded him . . .' the expression in Marisa's green eyes left her in no doubt of the kind of persuasion involved. '. . . that you were the perfect person to confide in.' She beamed.

'Confide in?' If Alex had been around, Imogen would have throttled him. He had touched her more than she'd thought possible. And now this. Marisa wanted to confide in her. Marisa! Her almost-step-daughter. The girl whose boyfriend she had gone to bed with. It was all ridiculous. Whatever the confidence was, she didn't want to hear it. But Imo couldn't stop it. She couldn't say a word. If she opened her mouth – other than to play Miss Echo – she would say it, she would tell Marisa what she'd done. But if she really concentrated . . . 'I'm not the right person,' she said. 'I'm not a nice person—'

'Oh, I don't want a *nice* person.' Marisa grabbed her arm. 'The thing Alex had to tell his parents . . .' They were so close now, Imo could feel the softness of the cream fleece as it brushed against her skin. And she could smell her perfume. Crisp and dry. Not the vegetable oil but Estée Lauder.

'. . . is that I'm pregnant,' Marisa said.

Chapter 25

The next couple of hours passed in a blur for Imogen. She switched on the answerphone and was tempted to close the shop. But she wouldn't. She wouldn't admit defeat.

Alex left two messages that she erased immediately. The sound of his voice gave her a play back that she'd better start erasing too. Only she couldn't erase the longing. She sorted her flowers, checked tomorrow's orders, swept the floor three times and paced it more like twenty. What did Alex think he was doing? Didn't he realise he had a pregnant girlfriend? Didn't he know that this changed everything?

And then Tiffany turned up. It was four o'clock. She sloped in, dressed in black bootleg jeans and a ribbed poloneck that made her look more skinny than ever.

'Recovered, have you?' Imo snapped. Any more acid and she'd be nicknamed Vinegar Features.

'I'm blatantly sorry, Imo,' Tiffany said forlornly, twiddling her nose hoop. 'For getting so out of it, I mean.'

Apart from red eyes and smudged make-up, she didn't look too much the worse for wear, Imogen thought. She stood the broom up against the far wall and folded her arms.

'I found the plants,' she said. 'Is there anything else I should know?' Cocaine hidden in the plant food perhaps, ecstasy tabs hoarded in the bottom drawer under the counter?

'Warren dumped me.' From Tiffany's expression it was at least the end of the world.

'Good riddance,' Imogen said tartly. She stalked to the sink, rinsed out the cloth and turned to wipe the counter. She knew about being dumped. She'd been dumped practically before she'd been taken on – in a manner of speaking. Alex might keep calling but having a pregnant girlfriend in the background didn't help his bachelor nice-guy image. And besides her sympathy levels were at an all-time low.

'I know you never liked him.' Tiffany shrugged and stretched in one typically teenage movement that lifted the polo-neck and revealed her jet black belly stud.

Imogen shuddered. Nails, noses, belly buttons, what next? 'He was an animal.' She decided to start packing up. She'd had enough for today. Grabbing her mist spray, she began on the carnations in the corner. Warren was bad news. For all of them as it had turned out.

'It was his idea, you know? To plant the seeds.'

Imogen could see she'd have to explain in words of one syllable. 'I don't doubt it, Tiffany.' She adopted her responsible, *I am an employer* face, though she wanted to go home, get drunk and scream – not necessarily in that order. 'But I employed you, not Warren. I trusted you, not Warren. You had a responsibility to me.' She misted the roses and freesias.

'And I blew it.'

Imo nodded. 'End of story, OK? I'm not calling the police,' she wouldn't have the energy, 'and Jude's got rid of the stuff.' She rolled her eyes. God, she sounded like a character out of *Police 999*.

'Got rid of it? What, all of it?' Tiffany's eyes became saucers. 'You mean . . . ?'

'Chucked it out, not smoked it. Yes, the whole lot.' She didn't care if Tiffany's high-as-a-kite routine had been due to losing Warren, an attempt to get back at him or an experiment she intended to repeat. It didn't matter now. She liked Tiffany, but the girl had let her down.

To Imogen's surprise, Tiffany giggled. 'Warren'll go ballistic. He said he was coming for the rest of the gear tomorrow.'

'Warren can go to hell.' Imo was surprising herself. She slammed the mist spray back on the counter. Assertive? She was verging on the aggressive. She might want to burst into tears, but they would be powerful tears.

'Are you OK, Imo?'

'I'm perfectly *fine*.' She pinged open the till and started cashing up. It had been a quiet day – in some ways. 'And if he says anything to you about it – anything at all – you can tell him to have it out with me. I'll deal with him, no problem.' And, yes, right now she felt that she could deal with anything.

The phone rang. The answerphone picked up. 'Imo?'

Anything except Alex. She sighed.

'You're not at home. You're not at the shop. Have you gone into hiding? Don't. And call me.'

Tiffany's eyes became dinner plates.

'Anything else you forgot to tell me?' Imogen asked her, pretending she hadn't heard the message. How could a man's voice keep giving you goose-bumps, she wondered, even when he had become King Rat?

Tiffany shook her blonde and pink head. 'So I'm fired then?'

''Fraid so.' Already Imo half-regretted it. Then she caught a flash of Tiffany's studded tongue as she yawned. It was all too much. And this was the best way. 'You'll be finishing school soon anyway.' Though God knows she was hardly ever there. 'What are you going to do after that? Not work in a florist's, surely?'

'Art college if I can get in.' Tiffany surveyed the kingfisher tattoo on her arm. 'They do everything. Body painting, textiles, the lot.'

Art college . . . Alex. 'And nudes,' Imo added. Was everything from this moment on going to remind her of him?

'Well, yeah.' Tiffany looked confused – as well she might.

Imo stuck out her hand. 'No hard feelings, Tiffany? Keep in touch.'

'No hard feelings, Imo. You did what you had to do.'

Police 999 had moved seamlessly into *The Good, the Bad and the Ugly*. They shook on it and Tiffany headed for the door, tattoos, multiple body piercing and all.

Imo sighed. She would miss her. Tiffany was sparky and fun. OK, she was also a liability. And a criminal, if you wanted to be picky. But *Say It With Flowers* would be a duller place without her.

In the doorway, she turned. 'You're blatantly right about Warren,' she said. 'He is an animal. Well shot, aren't I?'

Imogen smiled. 'Blatantly.' Tiffany would learn. Maybe she already had.

'And good luck with that guy with the nice bum.' She nodded towards the phone.

'Huh?'

'I'd recognise that voice anywhere.' She gave Imogen an

admiring look. 'Who would have thought it, eh? All that time I spent here with you and I never realised you were such a fast worker.'

'A Slow Delicious Screw with a side twist, please,' Jude said to the young hunk behind the bar.

'Certainly, madam.' He threw ice into a tall cocktail glass and began with vodka.

'Honestly . . .' Jude threw a despairing look at the man in trendy baggies and loose dark jacket by her side.

'The names they think of,' he agreed. 'I'm Philip, by the way.'

She knew; she had recognised the rolled-up *Independent*, so much more subtle than a carnation. 'Jude.' Though she had to admit, few would recognise her tonight. She was wearing a plain black top and long skirt. Her hair was light brown (she'd washed out all the remaining colour mousse yesterday), its normal length (two inches below the ears) and brushed lightly back from her face. And that face . . . well, apart from a light dusting with powder foundation and a slick of mascara and lip gloss, it was naked. Even her eyes were pale blue, though she had drawn the line at specs. For *Forty-five but looks younger, great sense of humour and average IQ* as described on her tape, she had laid herself bare. Testing out some of Imo's theories perhaps? Beauty is as beauty does? Could someone love her for herself alone?

'What do you do?' he asked her. 'You said you were a career woman.'

Jude watched the barman deposit the side twist of lemon on the rim of her sugar-frosted glass. 'I own a beauty salon.'

'Really?' He seemed surprised.

292

Understandably, Jude thought, considering her appearance tonight.

'That must be, er, fascinating.'

'Mmm, it is rather. I have themes,' she elaborated. 'A kind of thought for the day.' It had originally been intended to attract passing trade, but over the months had become a joke between her and Imo. Every time Imogen visited the beauty shop she tried to dream up a new one for next time. And she hadn't run out yet.

As Jude had expected, he was interested in this. 'What's today's?'

She smiled at him and took a tentative sip. Not bad. This place was flashy and overpriced, nothing but chrome, glass and black imitation leather, but what the hell? Sometimes a girl had to slum it. 'Is your skin falling apart?' she asked him.

'Pardon?'

'That's today's thought.'

'Ah.' He twirled his umbrella cocktail stick. 'Skin damage. I see.'

Jude nodded gravely. She'd known from the moment she first spotted him at the bar that he'd be on her wavelength.

'Bad diet perhaps?'

'Or lack of sleep.'

'Emotional stress,' he contributed.

'Sensitive? Dry? Oily?'

'Mine can't seem to make up its mind.' He retrieved an ice cube and crunched noisily. 'So what's your professional opinion?'

Jude peered more closely at his face. 'Nothing aggressive,' she said. 'A gentle facial perhaps. I do a special. First aid for faces.'

'Sounds good,' he said.

'Here, I'll give you my card.' She thrust a hand into her bag. 'Ring me.'

'I will.' He smiled as if he'd made a friend for life. 'Another Slow Delicious Screw?'

'No, thanks.' A girl could have too much of a good thing. Jude slid down from the bar stool. 'No offence.'

'None taken.'

Sometimes, Jude reflected, you just knew it wouldn't work out. She leaned closer to him for a second as he helped her with her coat. He smelt of citrus with an undertone of pear. He was taller than she and his blond hair was immaculately layered, gelled and slicked away from his face. But: 'I'd cut down on the bronze highlighter and eyebrow tinting if I were you,' she whispered in his ear.

Ah, well. Life was full of such ironies.

Outside *Say It With Flowers* it was mild, damp and already dark, though South Street was illuminated by street lamps, pubs, cafés and clubs, not to mention the Christmas lights that were still up, Imogen noted. She took huge gulps of air. She was suffocating – at least on the inside. Her blood was pumping, her heart was thumping and she couldn't breathe. Was this heartache? Was this a panic attack? Was this merely the severe stress that followed a romantic interlude?

Pulling her black, woollen coat more tightly around her, she loitered briefly outside The Green Man. A drink would be nice but it was only 5.15 – forty-five minutes before her personal watershed – and anyway, she didn't much like drinking alone.

'Are you all right, Imogen?' It was a gentle voice.

294

She spun around. Naomi Gibb. The entire family was haunting her today. 'I'm fine. You?'

'I'm fine too.' Equally a lie and Naomi's faint self-parody of a smile acknowledged it as such. In truth she looked pretty terrible. Her face was washed free of colour, her pale ginger hair was lank, and her eyes were red-rimmed and sad. Edward . . . could he have inspired all this? Imo wondered.

She made a sudden decision. 'I was just about to go in here for a drink. Would you join me?' She wanted to talk some more with this woman. She felt a rapport with her, sympathy, and to her surprise no hint of jealousy.

'Well . . .' Naomi glanced at her watch.

'Please?' Imogen took her arm. To hell with watersheds. She was being power-woman today, wasn't she? 'I need a drink. Don't make me go in there on my own.'

Naomi made no further protest and together they walked in. The Green Man was one of Chichester's small, rather arty wine bars. The decor was predominantly purple, the furniture old pine. Tonight it was, as Imo would have predicted, very quiet.

'Have you had a bad day?' Naomi asked.

'The worst.' Imo considered telling her, but thought better of it. She could hardly mention Alex, and Naomi might well be shocked at the cannabis story. Imogen was shocked at the cannabis story.

So she played almost-safe. 'I saw Marisa,' she said when they had taken off their coats and were seated in a small alcove nursing a big glass of red wine (Imo) and a small shandy (Naomi). 'She came into the shop.'

'Oh?' Naomi fiddled with the sleeve of her bottle-green cardigan.

'She's looking . . .' Imogen hesitated '. . . well.'

Naomi's glance was a perceptive one. 'You know then?'

'Know?'

'That she's pregnant.'

Didn't she just? Imogen ran her finger round the top of the wine glass. All right, she had been angling for information, though she wasn't exactly sure what. But it struck her that very little would get past Naomi Gibb. There was a lot more to her than she'd thought. Had Edward seen that? She supposed that he must have.

'Is she pleased?' Imogen asked.

'Oh, my dear, like a cat that's got the cream.'

Imogen looked up in surprise. And yet Naomi was right. That was exactly how Marisa had seemed. 'But surely it wasn't planned?' she blurted.

Naomi sipped her shandy and eyed Imogen thoughtfully. 'Not by Alex, I'm sure. I'm certain that he wants something quite different.'

A rush of heat began in Imogen's toes and – inch by inch – suffused the rest of her body. She shifted in her seat. They could do with some air conditioning in this place.

'But let me tell you something about my Marisa. There isn't a single thing she does that isn't planned.'

'I see.'

'You might think me disloyal?'

'No.' Imogen sipped her wine. She strongly suspected that Marisa would drive anyone to disloyalty – even her own mother.

'But she is a law unto herself. Always has been. And sometimes . . .' Naomi's voice faltered '. . . sometimes she frightens me.'

Imogen frowned. So Marisa had decided to have Alex's

baby. Oh, Alex . . . 'Why?' she whispered. 'Does she love him?' It was odd, she thought, that it seemed so natural to be having this conversation with Naomi Gibb.

Naomi shrugged. 'I wouldn't know about love. But she wants to marry him.'

'I see.' But it was so old-fashioned. Heavens . . . Imo would have thought the concept of the baby trap to have gone out with the advent of the contraceptive pill. And why did Marisa want to marry him anyway? He had no money so it must be love. This time she gulped her wine.

Naomi seemed to be reading her mind. 'Getting yourself pregnant can still be an effective way of getting a man,' she said. 'Guilt is a powerful weapon. And not usually connected with love.'

'I know.' Imo didn't need lessons on guilt. But Alex . . . She was bewildered. He had told her that it was over with Marisa, a message that was a million miles away from the one Marisa was sending. A thought occurred to her. 'D'you think she's told Alex she's pregnant?' she asked Naomi. The words tipped out in one breathless shovel-full.

Naomi nodded. 'I thought so.'

'So she has?' Imogen was desolate.

'No, my dear.' Naomi patted her hand. 'I don't know if she's told Alex. What I meant was . . . I rather got the impression that you and Alex had become . . . friends?'

Imogen stared at her. What on earth must she think? 'How?' she whispered.

'When you were with us on Christmas Eve. I thought I was imagining things – it was rather a dramatic evening, to say the least.' She looked down at her lap. 'But sometimes you sense a spark . . .'

Imogen nodded. There had been a spark all right.

297

'Then you left together. Marisa didn't like it. And . . .' she smiled '. . . you're not terribly good at hiding your feelings, my dear.'

Imogen thought of Jude. *I can read you like a book.* 'There was something. Or I thought there was.' She forced herself to be brisk. 'But it doesn't matter now.'

'Doesn't it?'

'What matters is Marisa and the . . .' she swallowed hard, '. . . the baby.' She thought of the papers at home. Bank statements. Money. Her own feeling of guilt about this woman. And now there would be a child too. Another one. 'I've been thinking, I know it must be hard for you to manage without . . .'

Naomi raised her eyebrows. 'Edward's money?'

'Well, yes. And so, to be blunt . . .' Imogen took a deep breath '. . . I'd like to go on paying your mortgage.' There, she'd said it. It wasn't so hard. Jude would create but this had nothing to do with her. This had to do with Imogen's sense of responsibility, with doing what Edward would have wished.

For the first time tonight, Naomi seemed flustered. 'Oh, no,' she said quickly. 'I couldn't possibly let you do that.'

'Why not?'

'It isn't right.'

'But I want to.' Imogen wasn't giving up that easily.

'Because of Marisa's baby?' Naomi shook her head. 'No, no. She's brought it on herself. It's nothing to do with you.'

'Not because of Marisa's baby,' Imo told her. Though she had to admit that was part of it. 'Because of Marisa. She's his daughter. He neglected her enough as it was. So this is what Edward would have wanted.' She had thought

298

long and hard about it – even before Marisa's bombshell. This was what Imo had to do to make things right.

Naomi laid her hands flat on the table in front of her. 'I don't think I ever knew,' she said, 'what Edward wanted.'

Imogen smiled. 'Me neither.' A tidy life, she had thought once.

'No, I can't let you do this.' Naomi was firm, stubborn even. 'And you mustn't mention it again.' She finished her drink. 'Let me get you another.'

Pride, Imo thought. How could she get round that one? Ah, well, one more drink and then . . . what the hell? She'd take a taxi home and collect the car tomorrow.

When Naomi returned from the bar, the atmosphere between them seemed to lighten, and Imo found herself telling her about Tiffany and the marijuana plants. They both laughed, Naomi told her a few stories about Marisa as a teenager, and Imo began warming to her even more. Naomi, she discovered, wasn't as shockable as she'd first appeared. Already they seemed almost friends. What would Edward say, she wondered, if he were looking down on them? It would, she supposed, surprise anyone, and yet Imo didn't care. She would take friendship wherever she found it. And no one could say they had nothing in common . . .

'So I've lost my assistant,' she said, tucking a stray strand of hair behind one ear. 'I'll have to advertise, I suppose. Jude says stick a card in the window, but I need more than a schoolgirl.' The shop was gradually getting busier, and without a full-time assistant she had no time for the part of the job she liked best: the planting of seeds and cuttings, the creation of wreaths and wedding bouquets that were, she hoped, that little bit different.

'I'm sure lots of people would love to work in a flower shop,' Naomi said.

Inspiration struck Imogen between the eyes. 'Would you?'

'Oh.' Naomi blinked. 'Yes, but I wasn't trying to—'

'I know. But you have to admit, it's a great idea. We get on. I like you. You like flowers.'

'Edward . . .'

'He's gone,' Imogen said firmly. 'You should be practical. We both should. You need a job. I need an assistant.'

Naomi clapped her hands together. 'I'd love to work for you.' She beamed.

'With me,' Imogen corrected. She'd cracked it. She'd had another idea. Red wine, she decided, must be good for her creative juices.

'Well, yes, with you, of course . . .'

'As a partner.'

Imo could see Naomi was about to object again, so she rattled on. 'I'm not saying there's much money in it but you won't need to put any in either. And it's some security at least.' She glanced at Naomi. No, that wasn't enough. 'I need more than an assistant,' she explained. 'What I really want is someone to share the responsibility with, someone to understand, someone who can take over when I need a holiday. I need . . .' she grabbed Naomi's hands '. . . you.'

'Are you sure?' She still seemed doubtful.

'Never been surer.' It was the perfect solution for them both, she felt. 'Besides,' she said, tongue very firmly in cheek. 'it'll keep Edward happy, knowing we're looking after each other.'

*

An hour later, back at home, the telephone rang and the answerphone picked up. 'Imogen?' Alex . . . again.

Fortified by the wine, she grabbed the receiver. 'You know Marisa's pregnant?' she said into it.

She put it down before he could reply. If he hadn't known before, he knew now.

And as she'd expected he didn't ring again that night.

Chapter 26

She wouldn't let Alex say goodbye.

Marisa stretched out her feet until coral-varnished toenails were almost touching the bedroom wall. This conviction had been drumming in her head since yesterday. All night it had hovered on the edge of her dream-consciousness, a frayed refrain of: *I won't let Alex say goodbye.*

Since she'd rung his doorbell and seen it in his eyes . . . the goodbye look . . . Marisa allowed her gaze to drift around her bedroom. Her mother had given her the biggest and best room when they'd moved in, talked about young people needing space in which to breathe, feel free in. But Marisa didn't feel free, only hemmed in by this lifestyle to which she'd never believed she belonged. But now – the goodbye look?

She got out of bed, stared out of the big bay window that looked out on to Chestnut Close, wrapping her arms around herself though the heating was up high. Someone had sung about that once. Not someone from *now* but someone from the sixties or seventies, her mother's era. It was so frustrating, she thought, watching the postman swing a leg over his bicycle, pedal off down the street, that so many of those crap lyrics and naff tunes from some bygone year had stayed in her head – jumping into voice every now and then as though her mother had force fed her from cradle on.

And so she had in a way, Marisa recalled. The transistor radio had always been playing until Marisa had got so bored with it, she'd flung it in the sink one day, smiling as some prat of a DJ (they might be presenters now, but on the stations her mother tuned in to they would always be DJs) lost his voice at last.

Of course, Naomi had said nothing, merely replaced it with an updated model – twin speakers but still tranny in nature, Marisa thought, with a curl of the lip. Her mother had never blamed, merely excused her actions. The *single parent, only child*, thing.

Anyway, Marisa had rung Alex's doorbell, waited an age for him to let her in. And seen it in his eyes . . . The goodbye look. But maybe she'd seen it before that, because it wasn't unexpected when it came.

And she wouldn't let him do it. This was her script, her meticulous planning. The more she thought about it, the more convinced she was that someone had stepped in. So *when* had they stepped in and *why*? And more to the point, *who*?

Although she was still naked, Marisa flung aside the net curtain and yanked open the sash window. The cold wind slapped at her skin, turning it to goose-flesh. She didn't flinch. Down below, she saw Henry from next door bringing his rubbish out to the front. He turned to go back inside, saw her at the window, his jaw dropped open. Marisa only laughed, put her elbows on the sill and stretched forward so that even more of her breasts was visible, the nipples hardening in the chill winter breeze. Henry scurried inside as though he'd been burned, silly old sod.

Marisa frowned. It had, after all, been going so well, with Alex hooked and being drawn in close . . .

So *who*?

She had seen the existence of someone else – lurking behind that goodbye look. Marisa selected soft velvet trousers in a shade of pale ecru, a flame coloured polo-neck, and a simple gold cross.

If it were someone in Nottingham then she wouldn't have known where to start. But would he have come back to Chichester so soon if so? No, she answered herself. He would have stayed there all the holiday. And if it were someone here . . . then it had to be her father's wife! Imogen West. Impossible but true. Who else could it be? There had been no time. And she'd suspected as much when Imogen had first stumbled into the sitting-room at Chestnut Close. All that Auntie Imo and Santa stuff.

And so she'd gone to the florist's and now she was sure. Marisa clipped her strawberry-blonde hair back from her face. She was sure. And she was angry.

'So what are you going to do?' Jude demanded.

'Never mind me. What are *you* going to do?' Resolutely, Imogen changed the subject – or was it the object? She had told all – almost all anyway. She'd left out some of her finer feelings. End of story.

'Do you mean, how will I manage now I'm going to be a proper single parent with no resident child-minder? Or do you mean, how will I manage without advertising for a man?'

'Both.' Imogen watched Jude clear up the debris of her

latest wedding makeover. What with Jude doing the make-up and Imo providing the flowers, the more weddings in Chichester, the better off they were. So why did she feel miserable at the sight of another happy bride-to-be tootling out of *The Goddess Without* and into Real Life?

'I'll manage the same way that every other single parent does,' Jude said vaguely, slotting brushes into her brush cleaner. 'On both counts.' She flicked back long honey-blonde hair and shot Imo a fierce look from blue-as-the-Mediterranean eyes.

'How's that?' Imogen didn't know much about children but she knew they weren't easy. She sat down in one of Jude's squishy black chairs and stared dismally at her reflection.

'After school club, tea with friends. And Daisy can hang around here for that matter, she's no trouble.'

'And in the holidays?'

'Play schemes.' Jude was consulting her appointments book. 'Bikini line and half legs.' She glanced at her watch. 'Eleven o'clock but she's always late.' She went to retrieve a different trolley from the back of the salon, and began laying out more instruments than a dental surgeon.

'Half legs?' Imogen shuddered.

'Up to and including the knee.' Jude waved at her own black-stockinged calves under the short black shift. 'Going somewhere nice and hot probably, lucky cow.'

'Why do we bother?' Imo thought of Alex.

'Body hair is animal.' Jude grimaced. 'Hairlessness is angel. And whoever saw a model with hairy legs?'

Imogen got to her feet. 'You'll miss her,' she said. Though she might enjoy the space. Space . . . It was wonderful, Imo reflected, to stretch out in your room, in your bed, with no one to touch you, no one to turn away. It had become Imogen's bed, not the bed she'd shared with Edward, and now she could choose to share it — chance would be a fine thing — or claim it as her own. Oh, Alex . . . She sniffed. No one to turn away, but equally no one to turn to.

'Perhaps I'll take in foreign students.' Jude plucked a black towel from the pile on the shelf, laid it out carefully and selected a wax treatment. Imo blanched.

'No pain, no gain,' Jude said.

Would that be hot wax, foreign students, or the thought for the day? Imo wondered. She peered into the window — she'd been too distracted to notice when she arrived. 'Create the perfect pout? Oh, Jude, honestly.'

'It's an instant mood booster.' Jude waved towards the make-up trolley. 'Better than buying new clothes. You don't have to get undressed to try them on.'

Imo took a look. So many to choose from. 'Lots of purples,' she murmured. The beauty business, she concluded, was something she simply couldn't get to grips with.

'Not just *purples*, sweetie.' Jude tidied and rearranged, picked up a tub of aloe vera moisturiser and dropped it into Imogen's bag. 'I despair of you, I really do. Deep Purple, Blackcurrant Bliss, Air of Aubergine, Blueberry Fool, Hot Heatherberry . . . you name it, I've got it. Once you find a colour you like you can never have too many shades.' She surveyed Imogen critically. 'Which one would you put on *your* lips?'

Imogen selected a brown. 'Coffee Bean?'

Jude grabbed it from her and put it back. 'And the worst possible reason for choosing a lipstick is because you like the colour.'

'It is?' Imo was more confused than ever.

'You have to think skin tone, sweetie. Eyes, hair, clothes, the whole bit.' She chose Dawn Mist and got to work with her lip brush. 'Come to think of it, you must be the only female who comes in here without buying anything. Even a lipstick. You're really rather weird . . .'

'Arvegorloadsoflipstaready.'

'Don't talk.' Jude began filling in the colour. 'Most women can never have enough make-up. They're always up for it if the packaging's classy enough.' She stood back. 'That's the lips, but we really have to do something to your eyes.'

'No, Jude.' Imo held up a warning hand. 'Your eleven o'clock will be here, and—'

'Just a touch of kohl. Stay still.' She grabbed a grey eye pencil and treated it to a blast from the hairdryer fixed to the wall. 'To soften it,' she explained. 'Open . . . close.'

Imogen obeyed.

'A little smudge and there you are. Now go and face the world, woman.'

Imogen peered from the trolley to the mirror, sucked in her cheeks and tried to look nonchalant. The trouble was, she was unwilling to face the world. And she would be late opening – again. 'But what's the use?' she wailed. If love was blind then how could people fall into it at first sight? And if beauty was in the eye of the beholder, then why bother with salons like *The Goddess Without*?

'How d'you mean, *use*?'

Too late Imogen realised this was rather like asking a fish why it needed water. Or was it? How necessary was make-up for survival? Even Jude's survival? Come to that, how necessary were men?

'Do you mean its *use* as a fashion accessory, or its *use* for attracting the male of the species?' Now Jude was laughing at her. '*Use* as in vital ingredients in the pursuit of true lust?' She narrowed her very blue eyes. 'Or are we talking lurrve?'

'Well, um . . .'

But Jude was off on one. 'Or do you mean its *use* in developing women's self-respect, confidence, esteem?'

It was hopeless. Imogen wasn't sure she had any of those any longer. And the Dawn Mist lipstick and grey kohl made not a jot of difference.

'So tell me, Imo.'

'Mmm?' At last Imogen made it to the door. She had to get out of here.

'What are *you* going to do?' Jude demanded.

Imogen slipped out of the salon without replying. It was a good question. Just a shame she didn't know the answer.

Marisa decided to ring Shelley Finn. They hadn't spoken for a while. Shelley and her escort agency belonged to a part of her life that Marisa mostly kept hidden.

'I want to give up work,' she told her.

'Completely?'

'Yes.' She wouldn't be able to continue for long anyway. And it was too risky. There was always the chance she'd be recognised by someone when she was with Alex.

'You're not even going to do a bit part-time?' Shelley cajoled.

'No.'

'Not even . . .' She heard Marisa hesitate. 'Not even Bertie?'

It was tempting. Easy money too, for just talking. But: 'No.' She must be firm. It was in Shelley's interest to persuade her to continue. It was in Marisa's long-term interest to give up.

'Win the lottery, did you?' Marisa could imagine Shelley making notes, perhaps spinning round on that low chair of hers, and flicking through the filing system. Shelley wasn't a computer person. She always said — with a throaty laugh — that she preferred hard copy, and that glamour could not easily be transferred to disk.

'No.' She knew that Shelley would guess what was coming next. In her line of business she must hear it pretty often and be sick of it, frankly. 'I've met someone,' Marisa said anyway.

'A client?' Shelley asked quickly, probably thinking of her percentage.

'Oh, no.' Marisa examined the nails of her right hand. It was time to pay *The Goddess Without* another visit, she decided. As for the clients, Shelley had to be joking. They were old and faceless.

'Same old story, eh?' Shelley sighed. 'That's how I always lose my best ones. And when it's over? Will you want to come back then?' For Shelley, love was finite. At some point it was always over.

'I'm pregnant too.' Marisa hadn't intended to tell her this, but she had the urge to spread the news. And she'd always liked Shelley.

There was a sharp intake of breath. Now she *had* surprised her. 'Do you know it's his?'

'Of course.' Was she worrying about insurance or something? Marisa drummed her one remaining acrylic nail on the coffee table.

'Not like you to be careless,' Shelley commented.

'I wasn't.'

'Right.' Another intake of breath.

What was wrong, Marisa would like to know, with forward planning? A girl had to look after number one. Men could never be trusted. Men let you down – hadn't she learned that the hard way? From her own mother?

'You don't do things by halves, do you?' But Shelley chuckled. 'So it'll be a while before you're back.'

'I won't be back.' That was not part of the plan.

Shelley continued as if she hadn't spoken. 'If you're ever on your own again and saddled with a kid you'd find the money useful. I'll keep you on file.'

Marisa had to admire her practical streak. And Shelley was about the closest thing to a friend that Marisa had right now. She'd always been a loner, different from the girls at school – all settled in their happy families, thinking they were rebelling if they had a fag after school or let some boy finger them in the park. Marisa wasn't interested in rebellion for the sake of it, rebellion that ended in conformity. She was only interested in change. And besides, she'd grown up years before those other girls. 'I'd prefer that you didn't,' she told Shelley. She'd much rather slip anonymously away – it was so much safer.

'Hmm.' Would Shelley do as Marisa asked? she wondered. Probably not.

'So what makes this one different?' Shelley asked.

Marisa pondered. Where to begin? 'He's an artist . . .' That was where it had started. Perhaps because her art teacher at school had introduced her to sex. Similar to Alex in a way – bohemian life-style, scruffy jackets, hair always a little too long. Joss Browne had seen her potential as a woman when she was only fourteen, even while he was dismissing her as an artist. His scathing comments were branded on to her very soul, *Why bother to do what's been done before? Especially if you're going to do it with such little imagination, my dear* . . . Because an artist was what Marisa had most wanted to be.

'An artist?' Shelley didn't sound too impressed. 'No money, then, babe?' She might have added that this was out of character for Marisa, but she didn't.

'Not yet – no.' Marisa was clear on this point. 'But he's talented.'

'Even talented artists often don't make it till after they're dead,' Shelley put in.

'This one will.' She had seen how he'd drawn her. Somehow – and this was the amazing thing – he'd managed to see right through her and out the other side. In his sketches she was exposed – naked, vulnerable and hurting. He was the only man who'd ever had an inkling of the way she felt. Ergo, she would have him. More than that, she would *make* him.

'Look at Lucien Freud,' she told Shelley. 'And David Hockney.'

'He's that good?' Shelley sounded disbelieving.

'As far as I can see they're no better than scores of other artists,' Marisa said scathingly. 'You're only as good as the critics say you are. Because these days galleries don't want representations . . .'

'You've lost me, babe.' Shelley was beginning to sound bored.

'. . . they want vision.'

'Ah.'

'And to make it . . .' Marisa was determined to finish this '. . . to make it, you've just got to get the right image, be in the right place at the right time. You've got to make the right contacts, paint the right stuff. Artists can't do all that.'

311

'Why the hell not? Look, babe, I'm sorry to lose you, but I've gotta . . .'

'Because they're artists,' Marisa said simply.

Shelley made a noise somewhere between a snort of amusement and a grunt of contempt. 'But you *can* do that, I suppose?' she said.

'Oh, yes. You bet your life I can.' Marisa was smiling as she put down the phone. She could do that. That was her talent. And that was why she couldn't let Alex say goodbye.

Chapter 27

Alex slumped further into the blue settee with the wavy pattern embossed on its fabric. Its cushions seemed to suck up his flesh, limb by limb, as if he were drowning. Rather apt, he thought. And as he sank, he listened – sort of – to the tune of Richie and Beth bickering.

Bickering. It was a good word, Alex decided. Their conversation – about men and housework, or more precisely about Richie and housework; he didn't do any – never developed into argument or full-scale in-your-face row. But neither was it discussion or debate since there wasn't any listening to the other's point of view. Rather it rose and fell with soft insinuation; it simmered with bad feeling and the suggestion of worse left unsaid. Alex closed his eyes.

'This'll happen to you one day, mate,' Richie told him, reaching for the cashews and shooting Beth a knowing glance at the same time.

What would? Bickering with a woman he'd once loved?

'Yes, it will.' Beth spoke this time. They were at last in accord so Alex must have done something right.

He sank further into the sofa, wondering if Beth had fixed it so that it would take a full pound of flesh.

'He'll come over all domesticated.' She looked triumphant. 'Perhaps you're already considering it, Alex? With what's-she-called?'

He had noticed that women always hesitated to use another woman's name until they'd met her. But the main thing was that now Beth was smiling.

'Marisa,' he supplied.

Alex glanced at Richie in time to see him waving his arms lunatic-like at Beth.

'Oh, have I said the wrong thing?' She giggled.

'No.' But Alex stifled a sigh.

'You're not exactly Mr Commitment. Was she getting too serious?'

Pregnancy was pretty serious – as things go. Alex shrugged. 'Not exactly.'

He'd had plenty of time to think about it since Imo had blurted the information out over the phone, though admittedly a good portion of that time had been spent in states of inebriation and hangover respectively. What game was Marisa playing? And how was Imogen feeling about it all?

His first reaction had been to find Marisa and get the truth out of her. But on the way he'd slipped into the pub for a quick pint of Dutch courage and found Richie – looking for company, probably trying to escape the vacuuming. The idea of seeing Marisa – a necessity at first – had become less compelling as the evening progressed, in direct correlation to the amount of beer he'd consumed. Alex sighed again.

'Can I use your phone?' He struggled to his feet. The sofa resisted valiantly.

'Sure.' Richie was expansive. 'Make yourself at home. You gonna call her?'

How much had he told Richie last night? Alex wondered. Probably too much.

He dialled the numbers, hoped he wouldn't get Naomi. 'Marisa?'

'Alex, darling . . .'

He repressed a groan. 'I need to see you.'

'Of course.' She was all sweetness and light. 'When?'

'Tonight?' Might as well get it over with, he decided. 'I'll come to your place,' he said. 'We can go for a drink.' That was safer, he decided. 'In half an hour?'

Imogen, Vanessa and Jude had excellent seats at the front of house. It wasn't exactly the Festival Theatre, Imo thought to herself, but it was nice enough with its old-fashioned red velveteen tiered seating, Victorian-style wall lamps and plush drapes hiding the stage. It was warm and cosy, small but intimate.

'What part's Hazel playing?' Imogen scanned the programme and tried not to think about Alex. What he was doing, how he was looking, even what he was thinking. Had he tried to see her today? When he found her — if he found her, if he was looking — what would she say to him?

'They're not playing parts as such,' Jude explained, crossing her legs. 'It's Gershwin's life story, but built around the songs.'

'With a narrator.' Vanessa tapped the programme. 'And with Hazel's Giorgio as Gorgeous Gershwin himself.'

'Anyway,' Jude snapped the programme shut, 'let's wait and see.'

Imogen leaned closer. 'What's up?' Jude had been very quiet tonight. All three of them were, by agreement, dressed up to the nines, but Jude – blonde hair in a French plait and sporting a slinky black dress with deep side slits and a low neckline – did not seem in the mood.

'It just hit me.' Jude sighed as the house lights went down, the red curtain opened and black and white images of the Gershwin brothers (Ira the lyricist seated at a bridge table; George the composer at his piano) were projected on to the white backdrop.

Hazel appeared on stage with two other women. A different Hazel – seeming taller, more elegant and striking in her long sparkly frock and stage make-up. And copper-coloured hair, Imogen observed.

The orchestra struck up *Rhapsody In Blue*, the saxophone drawling out its first bluesy notes.

'What hit you?' Imogen hissed.

'I'm about to lose my mother.'

In a way, they both were. Imogen reached out and squeezed Jude's hand. Their mothers had succeeded where they had failed. Was that a sign that they should stay single until they hit sixty? Despite herself, Imogen smiled as Hazel began to sing.

'It's time we had a chat.' The door to Marisa's room had been open and Naomi was in a determined mood.

'Not now.' Marisa was seated at her dressing table. She gave her strawberry-blonde hair a last brush and surveyed the effect. 'Alex is coming round.'

Ah, Alex. And what had been resolved? Naomi wondered. 'Is he going to marry you?'

Marisa shot her one of her looks, its derision not in the

least diluted by its being a mere reflection. 'I only said he was coming round.' She laughed softly.

'Marisa . . .' Naomi tried again. This was her daughter, it was her duty to try. 'Do you love him?' As she spoke, she placed a hand on her shoulder.

'Love?' Marisa was staring into the mirror as if transfixed by the sight of her own face. 'He's right for me – that's all I know.'

Right for her? She knew nothing. It was there in her expression – Naomi could see it as she watched her. Marisa was a butterfly, a flitter. Maybe she wasn't even capable of love. Some people weren't. They loved themselves too much for even the smallest sacrifice.

'I don't want you to do something you can't live with. Something you'll regret.' She wasn't sure if she meant the baby, Alex, the other thing (she couldn't think too much about the other thing – Marisa's work, of which she knew so little), or all three.

'Oh, don't you?' Marisa's scorn radiated from her reflection once more.

She had learnt to be oh-so-scornful at an early age, as Naomi knew to her cost. She persisted. 'I don't want you to be unhappy, to make a mistake . . .'

'Like you did?'

Naomi had to move, had to get away from her. She walked to the bay window, tweaked the curtain, looked out into the darkness outside. The moon was almost full, there were street lamps on Chestnut Close, houses lit with cheerful squares of brightness. Although the night sky was now clear, it had been raining and the road shone. No clues there. Naomi turned. 'Of course I've made mistakes.' The sharpness of it surprised even her. 'I've never pretended that

317

I haven't.' And Marisa had made damn sure to point out any she'd missed. 'It's called learning from experience. And I want to—'

'Give me the benefit?'

How could she compete with such scorn? Naomi sighed.

'Save it.' Marisa turned her attention back to her reflection.

As Naomi wandered back past her, she caught a sight of herself in the mirror: brown dress, ginger hair, pale complexion, a study in middle-age. Nothing to offer, her daughter must think. Strange how their roles had reversed over the years, how the child eager to please – but had Marisa ever been that? she wondered – had become she who must be obeyed.

'Please yourself,' she said. Because it was pointless. And because she would anyway. Naomi had no authority; it had drained away under the onslaught of teenage years, teenage rebellion, teenage confidence that had never died. And yet she still loved her daughter. Mothers always did.

'Oh, I will.'

Naomi's eyes narrowed. She made her voice brisk. 'And there's something else.' She told her about the partnership. It had been simmering away inside her, the pleasure of it. It felt like the right thing to do.

'You're going into partnership?' Marisa had turned from the mirror. She was giving Naomi the whole force of her darkest look. 'With Imogen West?'

'I thought you liked her?' Naomi couldn't resist that. Well, Marisa had used Imogen's looks, Imogen's status, Imogen's youth to taunt her since Christmas Eve. *No wonder he married her. I mean, just look at her.*

Marisa's lip curled. 'I like her money.' So matter-of-fact, so damned pragmatic. 'But I hate everything else about her. And now you've let her insinuate herself into our lives, we'll never be able to get away from her. She'll always be there, always be—'

'Part of *my* life,' Naomi corrected.

'What?'

'My life.' She too could separate herself. 'And that's what I want.'

'Tell her to stuff it.'

For the first time Naomi noticed a hunted look about her daughter, and for the first time she felt no need to protect her. 'I will not.' She needed this. This was her chance to make some changes in her life.

'What did you say?' Marisa, she knew, was not used to being contradicted.

The doorbell rang. 'That'll be Alex,' Naomi said. 'I'll tell him you're just coming, shall I?'

As she went downstairs to open the door, Naomi felt free. It was a good feeling. If she were twenty years younger she'd slide down the banister, she really would. She could love Marisa, she realised, and not be responsible for her. She could let her go and watch from a distance. She could let her learn for herself.

Naomi opened the door. 'Don't let her bully you,' she said to Alex's surprised face. 'She will, you know.'

Marisa tripped down the stairs, all honey and cream but with a small frown of worry on her brow.

Did she recognise a turning point when it slapped her in the face? Ah, well . . . Naomi left them to it. Their life. She had her own to think of now.

*

In the interval, Jude and Imo made a dash for the bar while Vanessa found a table.

All of a sudden, Imo felt Jude's body stiffen beside her.

'Miss Lomax. Hello.' Some tall, dour, broad-shouldered stranger was giving Jude the full force of his piercing dark eyes. And from their expression he rather appreciated what he saw.

'Mr Dean.' Jude was equally formal. Until she added, 'What the hell are you doing here?'

The man raised one dark and bushy eyebrow. He too was dressed up, in a dark charcoal suit and pale grey shirt, enlivened by the splash of colour that was his scarlet tie. 'The same as you, I imagine,' he said dryly.

'Hmph.' Jude tried to squeeze past him but he stayed with her. 'Well, my mother's in the play, you know.' She turned to Imogen. 'What d'you think of it so far?'

'It's great. Hazel is really good.' Imogen could see Jude was proud. Hell, even she felt proud.

'She certainly is,' the stranger – who was clearly no stranger, Imo thought – agreed. 'She was a strong voice. Carries well.'

'Must be all that practice she's been putting in.' Jude, Imo sensed, was softening. 'Are you on your own? I suppose you could join us for a drink,' she added ungraciously.

The man almost smiled, but not quite. However, Imo would swear those eyes warmed up a bit and the mouth definitely twitched. 'I should have been delighted,' he said, 'but I'm with a friend.' From his expression, Imo concluded he didn't want the friend to see them, or didn't want them to see the friend.

'Oh, I bet you are,' Jude snapped back, with what Imo considered to be unnecessary acidity. 'I think I spotted you both the other day in town.' She squeezed further into the crush at the bar, not giving the poor man a chance to reply, magically got served, and when Imogen turned around again, the mystery man had melted into the background.

Imogen nudged her sharply in the ribs. 'What's going on? Who was that?' She had never seen Jude quite so offish.

'My landlord,' she hissed. 'Can you see who he's with? I don't want him to know I'm looking.'

Curiouser and curiouser. Imogen craned to see, but the man had disappeared. 'No sign of him,' she told Jude.

She pretended indifference. 'You'd never have guessed Ma was capable of it, would you, from all those sessions in the shower, hmm?' She grabbed their drinks, green eyes still looking from left to right. '"Stairway to Paradise" was brill.'

It was true. Imogen agreed that the number that had closed the first act, with all the singers dressed in black climbing a silver staircase, had looked like something out of Broadway. Trident Musical Comedy Society had done themselves proud. 'And what did you think of Giorgio?'

'A bit like Gershwin.' Jude grinned and handed Imo her wine and Vanessa's gin and tonic. 'Very slick, very dapper, very sure of himself.'

'A womaniser?' Imo had never realised George Gershwin was such an interesting character. Yes, he was arrogant — apparently, as soon as he wrote a song, the first thing he did was show it off at a party. But there was also a melancholy side to this man who'd managed to make the transition from popular songwriter to serious composer in such a short life. According to the programme, she saw that his *Porgy and Bess* opera would come in the second half of the show. She found herself looking forward to it.

321

'He might be,' Jude conceded, leading the way towards the table Vanessa was saving for them. 'But don't worry, Imo. My mother can run rings round a man like him, no problem.'

'I'll drink to that.' They clashed glasses.

Jude peered at her. 'Have you seen him yet?' she whispered before they joined Vanessa.

Imo knew who she meant – and it wasn't the landlord. She shook her head. She didn't even want to think about it.

'Can't put it off forever, sweetie.' Jude squeezed her arm. 'I tell you what. When Mother's taken herself off to the Land of Linguini, I'll throw a shag party, just for you.'

'You'll throw a what?' Jude was, Imo thought, getting more outrageous than ever.

'A shag party. SHAG. Only men who conform are allowed to darken the doorway. Single, heterosexual and gorgeous. That'll soon make you forget him.'

'Yeah, sure.' They joined Vanessa, and Imo handed over her mother's gin and tonic. Forget him? Somehow, Imogen didn't think it was going to be quite that easy.

Chapter 28

There was no physical contact between them at all as they walked down the street. Alex was struggling with his emotions, Marisa could tell. And he was angry. She pulled her fleece jacket closer around her as if it could protect her from more than the cold night. It was dangerous, she reminded herself, to care.

'Is it true?' he asked her.

Marisa listened to the sound of her own footsteps on the pavement. So she'd told him then. Suspicions confirmed. Imogen West was the enemy – and her mother's new business partner, it seemed. 'Yes.'

He exhaled as if he'd been waiting for this but she could see in the band of light from the street lamp that his face was clenched. 'Why the hell didn't you tell me?'

As they approached the Market Cross, illuminated yellow in the darkness, its clock shining white as the moon, Marisa was only too aware that they weren't walking in step. Far from it. There was an arm span between them. As usual, he was dressed in jeans and his battered leather jacket, hair curling around the collar. His step was long and ungainly –

as if he had a lot of space he needed to cover; every few metres she had to half-run to catch up. 'What would you have done?' she taunted.

'We could at least have discussed it.'

'You haven't been around,' she reminded him coolly.

Alex was silent as they approached the pub – one she knew was busy enough to be anonymous in. He marched up to the glass-fronted mahogany bar, ordered drinks, led the way to a far corner table.

She began to breathe more easily. 'I haven't known for very long,' she said softly, watching his hands as he lifted his glass, wondering what passed between the artist's eye and those hands, and whatever he held – pencil, brush, charcoal. What it was that made the vital difference.

'You knew yesterday.'

'It wasn't the right time,' she said. 'You were too busy talking about how things weren't working out between us, remember?'

'Yeah, well . . .' He took a slug of the light frothy beer, wiped his mouth with the back of his hand almost viciously. 'If I'd known . . .'

'You know now.'

He blinked straight back at her. 'Are you sure it's mine?'

'Alex!' She was surprised. For a moment she even thought he knew about the others. And then she realised it was one of those things that men said at these times. Some men at least. 'I'm surprised at you, Alex,' she said mildly, sipping her tomato juice. 'Why on earth would I be having sex with anyone else?' Because she did it for money, that was why. Or at least she did escort work which sometimes amounted to the same thing.

But not any more. And why should he ever have to know?

Alex only shrugged. 'You've always made it clear that ours isn't exactly a committed relationship. I was hardly expecting you to get pregnant.'

Marisa smiled faintly. 'Neither was I.' In fact, she and contraception were old friends. It was easy with the mini-pill to take control – though of course she'd always used condoms with clients; they even found them sexy if you put them on the right way. It was funny, because she'd miss it. Not the condoms bit, the whole thing. She didn't think of it as prostitution but as providing a service, selling a valuable commodity, taking control. And Shelley, at least, had always understood the appeal of that. But if you started to care, well, forget it, you could kiss control goodbye. Marisa had no intention of doing that again.

Behind Alex, the bar with its low amber and green lighting, rush matting and lacquered mirrors was beginning to fill up with the theatre crowd. She spotted an occasional familiar face. A neighbour of theirs from Chestnut Close, the woman who ran *The Goddess Without*, and . . .

She grabbed both of Alex's hands. He looked surprised but didn't withdraw. Perhaps she was holding him too tightly. Perhaps he realised that he owed her. 'Think what it's like for me, Alex,' she urged. 'Imagine how I felt when you told me to get lost the other night. With your baby growing inside me . . .'

His expression changed. It grew softer and his blue eyes were kind. 'I didn't think. Sorry . . . I know it's difficult for you too. But, Jesus!' He looked pleading.

What did he want her to do? Wave a magic wand and take the baby away? Marisa didn't release his hands. And she didn't look over towards the bar. She kept her gaze firmly fixed on his face. 'You know now,' she said again. The next move was his.

'What are you going to do?' he asked at last – a little grudgingly under the circumstances, and sadly she noted the *you*.

She took a deep breath. 'I'm going to keep it.'

'Bloody hell!'

As a reaction to news of prospective fatherhood, it wasn't ideal. Marisa sighed. There was still an awful lot of work to do.

'Stop it, Imo,' Jude ordered as they entered the bar.

'What?'

'You're humming "My Man's Gone Now" from that *Porgy and Bess* sequence.'

'Was I?' Well, he had. And Imogen was beginning to wish she'd never met him. She had no desire whatever to go to a SHAG party (or any other party). She needed Alex. Edward had called her the Snow Queen once. It had hurt, the implication behind the words. But Alex . . . He'd unlocked her freezer cabinet – she shivered – and surprise, surprise, the sell-by dates were within reach, just iced up a bit. And now that she was well and truly thawed – even HOT, God help her – her temperature simply wouldn't go down. She felt as if her entire body were on hold, waiting for him, ready to dissolve into a squelchy puddle at his feet. This was worse than mixed metaphors. This was serious stuff.

She woke up to the fact that Jude was standing right in front of her, blocking the bar. Not very sociable of her when a girl needed a drink. 'What're you doing?' She looked kind of fierce too. Fierce and protective.

'Alex,' Jude said.

Imogen got a pain as sharp and insistent as indigestion. 'Yes?' she squeaked.

'Has he got messy dark brown hair and a tatty ginger-coloured leather jacket?'

'Untidy hair,' Imogen corrected. 'And the jacket's sort of golden tan.' Wild hair. Ideal for running your fingers through sort of hair actually. 'Why?'

'Big mouth? Sort of lean and hungry-looking?'

'Mmm, yes.' Imo had heard enough. 'Why?' She pushed past her.

'Because Marisa Gibb is sitting over in the corner,' Jude hissed. 'With a man. A man who . . .'

A man who . . . ? Imogen was past her before you could say baby boom. Her mouth went dry. Yes, it was Alex. And, 'They're holding hands,' she said.

At five minutes past midnight, Imogen was in her nightshirt (big, baggy, unappealing and due for the wash) and halfway through cleaning her teeth, when the doorbell rang.

She stood rooted to the white bathroom floor tiles, almost swallowed the toothpaste, spat, stared at herself in the mirror. Her face was white and greasy – thanks to soap and a large dollop from the tub of aloe vera moisturiser Jude had unloaded on her the other day. Her hair was damp and in that half-up, half-down state that looked as if she'd been dragged upstairs by it. And her eyes were red and pinched in their sockets. She looked about ninety and she had a spot. Worse, the only person she could think of who might ring the doorbell at midnight, was Alex.

Hell's bells. She couldn't ignore it because her mother

would eventually wake up and answer it anyway. But she couldn't answer the door looking like this.

It rang again – more insistently this time. Imogen stayed where she was. Not only rooted but putting out supplementaries. What was happening to her? Why did she care what she looked like? Was she becoming obsessive? What about beauty being in the eye of the beholder – even if hidden by a film of aloe vera? And besides, she reminded herself, Marisa was pregnant.

At the third ring the Vanessa-noises coming from across the landing got her motivated. She wiped her toothpasty mouth – and on second thoughts, her entire face, so she just had a very healthy glow. And she grabbed her towelling robe which was big enough to cover a multitude of cellulite. She ran down the stairs. Fiddled with the lock and chain. Had a sudden fear it wouldn't be him. Who then . . . ?

'Hello, Alex.' She sounded quite normal, considering.

'Imo.' He moved into the hall quicker than a rat up a drainpipe. And he was a rat, she reminded herself. King-size. 'Did I get you up?'

'Yes. No.' Nice to be decisive. She caught the Alex-smell as he drew closer. Mandarin, sandalwood, leather. Careful, Imo . . . 'What are you doing here?'

'It's good to see you.' He went for an embrace but she was far too quick for him.

What could she say to him? She couldn't think. Something intelligent, something to put him in his place and establish hers? Something . . . 'My mother's sleeping in the spare room.' Oh, yes, brilliant, Imo, that said it all. He was bound to be riveted by their sleeping arrangements.

But Alex didn't seem to notice that her brain cells were deteriorating at the speed of light. 'Can we talk?' He took a few more steps. Towards the bedroom? Yes, please, her treacherous body yelped. No. Kitchen.

She followed him. 'I suppose so.' Did that sound grudging enough? 'Drink?'

She'd meant coffee, but he glanced longingly at the half-empty bottle of red wine on the counter. 'I could murder one.' Yes, and she could murder him. But he looked weary and untidy and gorgeous, and she longed instead to put her arms around him and wish it all away.

'What do you want?' This time she meant, *Why are you here?*

'Anything so long as it's alcoholic.'

Hmm. Their ability to understand and communicate with one another appeared to be going downhill fast. She poured wine for them both.

'I had no idea she was pregnant,' he said, a statement not liable to be misinterpreted. 'I need you to know that.'

Need? What did he know about need? 'Oh.' She sat down at the kitchen table and he sat opposite her. Did his ignorance make her feel better? Not really, she decided.

'It was exactly what I said it was between me and Marisa,' he went on, rubbing in salt with wild abandon. 'It was casual, you know, a fling. Nothing more.'

Not for Marisa apparently. And they had been holding hands . . . 'It doesn't make any difference,' Imogen said bleakly. 'We should never have . . .' No, it was hopeless. She couldn't say it.

'Made love?' His eyes were eating into hers. He had that way about him, didn't he? The gaze – he held it like a baby. Or a lover. As if he were turning her slowly inside out and then back again. Would she still fit? Was she still herself? Did she even care? She remembered what Naomi had told her once about Edward, trying to explain his appeal perhaps. *He saw me . . . He really seemed to know me.* She understood now what Naomi had meant.

'And we did, didn't we? Make love.'

She nodded, aware of the danger but unable to stop.

'It meant something, didn't it? It was special?'

She nodded again. Oh, to be a no-woman. To fight – like Jude – and overcome. Perhaps she'd had too little sex for too long. So that now it had arrived with such intensity, it seemed necessary to existence, like water to the morning hangover, and unfortunately tasting just as sweet.

He grabbed her hands. 'So it doesn't have to finish because of a—'

'Baby?' She snatched hers back again. He'd been holding Marisa's hands just like that too. 'Of course it does. Don't be stupid.' He was young, wasn't he? Too young. This must be her punishment for trying to switch generations in the hope that no one would notice. 'It's your responsibility as much as hers, you know that.'

'Shit!' He banged his hand down hard on the table. Their glasses shivered and came to rest. Their eyes met and locked inescapably once more. 'Why the bloody hell did this have to happen? Why now?'

'Will you marry her?' Her words squatted on the raft of his anger and sailed right away. Weak, she knew, but how could she help it after what Naomi had said?

'Of course I won't bloody marry her.' His anger seemed directed at her now. Perhaps he would prove to be a mad axe-man, a psychopath. It would be a relief then, presumably, the knowledge that she wouldn't be seeing him again.

'How could I marry her?' he said. 'I don't love her. I never loved her, I told you.' A huge sigh.

330

Imogen wanted to comfort him. Once more, she wanted to feel his face with her fingertips. She held back with difficulty. This was what willpower was all about.

'And, yes, of course I'll support whatever she wants to do — what choice do I have? I'll get a *proper* job . . .' his mouth twisted '. . . and give her money and stay as far away as possible and she'll hate me and I'll loathe her and I'll feel guilty as hell and . . .'

She touched his arm. She could do that at least because he didn't seem able to stop. 'Tonight?' she asked him. 'In the bar?'

'You were there?' He slumped further in the chair even as she realised what she'd seen. Not them holding hands. Marisa holding his hands, Marisa's supplication.

'She said she was going to keep it and I said nothing would change.'

Nothing would change? He had to be joking. Marisa was grafted on to his life now like one of Imogen's root cuttings.

'I can't stay with her when I don't love her,' Alex said. 'It wouldn't be right. It wouldn't be fair.'

'No.'

He got to his feet, stood behind Imogen, laid his hands on her shoulders. Soft, but pressure nevertheless.

She closed her eyes. She felt as if she'd been waiting for him to touch her all her life. But it was OK, he couldn't see her, she could close her eyes. No one would know.

'Because I love you.' His hands were inside the collar of her robe, warm on her skin.

What was he saying? Had he forgotten that he was young, he didn't want responsibilities, he wasn't looking for love? And she had never asked for the big L word. But still, she couldn't open her eyes. She felt that if she could just stay here in this dream-like state, feeling his hands wash all over her skin, rinsing away her doubts, her worries, then – somehow – it would be all right.

His thumb was resting on her collar bone. The – what did you call it? The clavicle. A faint pressing on the ridge of it, his fingertip tucking into the hollow beneath. She couldn't move. She could smell fragrance-of-Alex again – she was drunk with it. And her body screamed out: Touch me, touch me! Take me, take me! She moaned, very softly. Willpower-woman? Who was she trying to kid?

His lips brushed lightly across the back of her neck. She felt the wetness of his tongue. She knew every inch of her body was covered in goose-bumps. But the Snow Queen was long gone.

'It doesn't have to be over, Imo.' His voice was urgent, hot breath whispering in her ear. 'Does it?'

No, no, you're right, it doesn't, every sense shouted back gleefully as they dragged him upstairs in a happy haze of seeing, touching, hearing, smelling, tasting . . . In your dreams, girl.

His hand was moving towards her breast. Another second and she'd be lost. Not Willpower-woman but fallen woman. Having succumbed – a lovely word which said it all really – to the father of someone else's child. And she'd already done that, with Edward. Because of her, Marisa had never had a proper father. And now, because of her . . .

'Yes, Alex,' she said quite clearly, surprising even herself, and disappointing those senses – every one of which was swollen and fit to burst. 'It has to be over.'

Chapter 29

'I can't see . . .' Imogen paused for breath, legs dangling off the exercise bike '. . . why you're making me do this.'

There was no reply.

Imo looked behind her – not easy in her position – to where Jude was pushing weights. It looked like hard work so she decided to stay put. Indeed, Jude was fully focused – in a most un-Jude-like way since there were two men on the far side of the gym. Her hair – chestnut brown with red highlights – was damp with sweat; her eyes – hazel – grim with concentration.

'It's not as if I want to lose weight,' Imo complained to no one in particular. And then to Jude again, 'You used to tell me I was a bag of bones.' Or was that a bag with bones?

But, 'A new year means a new start,' Jude had declared mid-January – when the show was over and Hazel had left for Italy on the arm of Giorgio.

Imogen wasn't so sure. 'Start of what exactly?' She was wary. *Don't be a fool like you've been in the past . . .*

Jude had merely wagged her finger knowingly and begun scribbling ads for foreign students. ('I'm not lonely, but

the flat needs people – paying people,' she'd said.) Big
Venezuelan Monica managed to crack Jude's bath tub;
perspiring Paloma from Spain – luckily, as it turned out
– never took one; and Brigit from Germany barely spoke.

Even more radically, Jude had started a diet that specified
no chocolate and no cigarettes. This had not lasted, on the
grounds, Jude said, that extreme stress was known to shorten
and decrease the quality of life. In this case, Imo's as well as
Jude's, Imo thought privately, as Jude re-embraced both and
hatched another plan to revitalise their lives and limbs.

This time Imogen too was enrolled, only getting to argue
about it when the deed was done and money had changed
hands. Jude had chosen T'ai Chi (yang short form if anyone
should be interested, which Imo wasn't) backed up by a
Wednesday night meditation group. This scheme hit rock
bottom for Imogen, literally, when she sprained her ankle
attempting a high kick with added twist, and for Jude when
two of her clients complained about her chanting threatening
mantras during a bikini wax and eyelash tint.

Somewhat the worse for wear, March had meant another
new start for Jude and Imo in the form of focusing their
minds (a healthy mind means a healthy body, Jude insisted)
by investigating opportunities they might be missing (thank
the Lord, Imo said) in the lands of open universities, business
colleges, and even computer technology for the terrified.

Having ploughed through dozens of prospectuses, Jude
observed as the weather warmed that being stuck inside
some institution in their spare time wasn't as attractive a
prospect as it had seemed. Things changed. A healthy body
means a healthy mind; we don't have to bother with all
that learning stuff, we're in the university of life. Hence,
they were in the gym. Hence, Imogen was wary of new

334

beginnings. If she made any more, she'd be finished before she was forty.

'We're not here to lose weight,' Jude informed her as she dashed and Imogen staggered downstairs, to take full advantage of their membership by having a swim.

'What are we here for then?' Imogen was confused. 'To meet men?' Since those were Jude's two main aims in life it seemed a fair assumption to make.

''Course not.' Jude swung open the door of the changing room. 'We're here to get fit and rebuild our bodies.'

Taken aback, Imo wrinkled her nose. It was so distinctive, that smell of not-quite-clean flesh mixed with chlorine, dusted over with talcum powder and laced with the short sharp shock of a deodorant spray.

Jude hung her grey marl sweatshirt on an empty peg and threw her Nike bag on to the narrow slatted bench. 'And anyway, who needs men?'

Well, Jude generally did . . .

'Granted, you get some pretty beefy-looking guys in the gym.' She looked thoughtful. 'It kind of goes with the territory.'

'Hmm.' Imogen wasn't into beefy. She preferred interesting. She preferred men with long bodies and untidy hair to be found mainly just at one end of them. She preferred lean to six packs and thighs sturdy as the Rock of Gibraltar. She preferred a certain look and an uncertain smile . . .

'And don't pretend you didn't notice them.' Jude stripped off her leotard and tights and plucked her cossie from the bag.

Imo watched her. Was it her imagination or was Jude looking more well-toned and healthy already?

'I'm dying for a fag,' she said.

Perhaps not. 'I noticed them,' Imo conceded, rescuing her own leggings from the gully of stale water that broke up the rubber pimply floor. 'But I didn't fancy any of them.'

'Yes, well, Alex Armstrong wasn't there, was he?' Jude said, unnecessarily cruelly, in Imo's opinion.

'And is there any particular reason why *you're* not after any of the fitness freaks?' Imo demanded, hopping out of her knickers. Jude wasn't exactly dying of a broken heart, was she? She'd had her share of bad experiences, but she'd emerged unscathed.

'There is.'

'There is?' Imo was agog.

'I've entered a no-man zone.'

'A what?'

Jude sniffed. 'I've given up men.' She stepped into her all black sporty Nike number whose little tick somehow managed to underline her words.

Well . . . Imo felt way too feminine, and unfocused too, in her blue and yellow floral costume. 'Honestly?' She'd believe that when she saw the proof. It might be another one of Jude's *beginning again* schemes. Or she could just be lying.

'Absolutely.' She wasn't quite meeting Imo's eye.

'Er . . . Any particular reason?' Together they headed for the locker room.

'You mean, apart from the fact that men are bad news, screw you up, bring you down, and then persuade you to come back for more?'

Imo had to laugh. 'Got a 50p?' She opened the metal door and shoved in her own supermarket carrier bag. She was not convinced. Jude had been man-hunting so long she wouldn't have the least idea how to stop. It had become a way of life.

'Anyway, I'm much too busy,' Jude said. They negotiated the blue disinfected puddle at the entrance to the pool, discarded their towels and headed for the water.

Imogen cautiously lowered herself in, flinching as cold water splashed on to her overheated skin as a result of Jude's surprisingly graceful dive from the side. Perhaps it was true. Perhaps the new health-conscious Jude was too busy with the salon, with Daisy, and with her latest foreign student to go out looking for a man. And at this rate – for Jude, she noted, had done almost a length already – she wouldn't have the energy.

He was a charming man, Hazel told herself firmly as the water-taxi glided across the smooth surface of Lake Garda from the quaint lakeside town of Malcesine to the equally charming Limione. And if romance had not yet led to a ring, it had at least led to poetry. Ah . . . Hazel grew wistful. Giorgio was so much more poetic than Byron – the husband, not the poet. And attractive. She looked across at him. Not quite as attractive perhaps as when he'd been playing Gershwin, in that dapper suit with a cigar and baton always to hand . . . oh, she had been the envy of the entire female contingent of Trident then. Hazel chuckled. She could almost hear Giorgio's splendid tenor ringing out across the stage and into the auditorium. And still picture Belinda's thin-lipped smile. Oh, how she'd loved it!

Hazel gazed across the balmy water. Italy was glorious, and it was so warm for March, sitting here on deck basking in the last of the late-afternoon sun. But it would be a shame really not to return to England in time for Trident's next meeting, for rehearsals for the next show . . .

Perhaps she should have been an actress. Hazel closed her eyes and let this pleasant fantasy skim across her mind. She could see herself as a young woman . . . Long hair, blue eyes, petite, graceful. People had said she was pretty. Stunning even. Especially men. She'd certainly had more than her fair share of attention. Hazel sighed, becoming for a moment Elaine Paige singing 'Memories'.

Anyway, it was pleasant now to play the part of the English lady, although so far it had not turned out quite as she'd expected. Perhaps she was imagining it but there had been a few sly smiles.

There was a couple, both Italian, who lived just south of Malcesine along the lakeside road, in what she had to say was a rather tatty apartment, considering they were friends of Giorgio and all. They had made her welcome after a fashion, though she had anticipated more in the way of open arms, Mediterranean exuberance and exclamations of delight that Giorgio had found his English rose.

The woman, Francesca, had been quite surly when the men went into another room to chat – perhaps because she spoke no English. Hazel had not felt comfortable at being left alone with her. But she'd thought nothing of the sly smile on the woman's face until she'd seen it again – this time on the face of a man who came to see them at the villa.

And the villa . . . Hazel opened her eyes briefly to see Giorgio leaning on the side railings, talking – did the man never stop? – to another Italian. The sun was going down at last, the cypresses were tinged with pink, the waters of the lake shimmered in the evening haze. The villa – although exquisite in every detail, with wonderful views across Lake

Garda towards the mountains that Giorgio had described to her so vividly – apparently belonged to his brother, Gianfranco. And yet Hazel could swear that Giorgio had laid claim to it before they arrived. She could hear him now. *You must come to visit my villa on Lake Garda . . .* So?

It was confusing, particularly because Gianfranco had not seemed overjoyed to see his brother. There had been heated differences of opinion between the two of them since their arrival, though Giorgio said she was mistaken, and really, how could one argue the point when all conversations were in Italian and she didn't understand a word? There was no doubt about it, Hazel might be playing the English lady in her own mind, but she was at an obvious disadvantage when it came to communicating with others.

There were however – much to her relief – also English people living over here, and it was in order to visit two of these that they were heading over to Limione tonight. Thank goodness. At last she would be able to spend a relaxing evening secure in the knowledge that she was with her own. Hazel exhaled slowly.

'Are you feeling well, my love? Is it getting a *leetle* chilly for you?'

Hazel's eyes flicked open at the interruption. Giorgio had placed one hand on her thigh and, well, it might be very English and repressed of her, but one didn't always want to be pawed in intimate places. It could be most irritating. 'I'm perfectly fine.' She tried not to snap because he couldn't help being Italian and hot-blooded.

So far she had managed to repel his advances. They had been given separate rooms – Gianfranco's wife had seemed clear on this point, and Hazel had ignored Giorgio's raised eyebrows and torrent of Italian, taken the proffered towels and tried to ensure through body language to Marianna that, yes, this was precisely what she'd expected.

'Per'aps I should buy a place in Limione,' Giorgio said thoughtfully as the boat made its approach.

'Hmm.' Best to remain non-committal. Though, *What's happened to your place in Malcesine?* one might well ask. Hazel looked around her as they disembarked. They began a leisurely stroll along the waterfront. This was certainly a charming town with its lemon trees, narrow streets and tiny restaurants. But somehow she couldn't raise much enthusiasm for living here. One would tire – wouldn't one? – even of cypress trees and lemons?

'So what's the new student like?' Imogen asked as they floated lazily in the deep end, twenty minutes later. Imo had managed a couple of lengths, Jude must have done at least a dozen.

'What did you say?' Her eyes were closed and she looked . . . well, unusually peaceful.

'Your new student.'

Jude opened one eye. 'The trouble with Brazilians,' she said, 'is that they always spoil Daisy something rotten. So she adores them and begs me to go out just so she can be baby-sat.'

'Sounds perfect to me.' And this wasn't bad either, lying here with the water gently slurping around her neck and shoulders as another swimmer rippled past in the next lane. Jude was right – swimming was so relaxing, she'd forgotten how good it made you feel.

Jude turned on to her front and trod water. 'Almost,' she agreed, shaking back hanks of chestnut hair. 'I just have to keep a watchful eye on the telephone.'

'What's her name?'

Jude was heading towards the side. She mumbled something foreign and indistinct. 'Are you ready to get out?'

'OK.' Imo followed her up the steps. There was, she sensed, a new resolution about Jude these days.

After a quick coffee they left the Leisure Centre and headed back to the car park and Imo's Nova. Ten minutes later, she was pulling up outside *The Goddess Without*.

She noticed someone standing by the side entrance that led to Jude's flat. 'Hang on a sec . . .' She grabbed Jude's arm. A tall dark denim-clad young man seemed to be letting himself in. 'Who's that?'

'Oh, er, let's see . . .'

What was wrong with Jude? She could be a little security-conscious, for goodness' sake. Imo pressed the heel of her hand firmly on the hooter. They both jumped at the sound. 'D'you think he's a burglar?'

'Don't be daft, Imo.' Jude's voice was crisp, though she was looking a little shame-faced. 'That's Roberto.'

'Roberto?'

He – and everyone else in the street – had looked up at the sound of the blaring horn. He peered towards the car and began grinning and waving. And now, yes, here he was, loping towards them like a great big hairy wolfhound. 'Who the heck is Roberto?'

'My Brazilian student,' Jude hissed.

'Judy, Judy,' he sang.

Judy? Imo felt an irrepressible giggle rising in her throat. The woman sitting beside her had never been and never would be a Judy . . .

'Roberto, hi.' Jude began to struggle out of the door.

At the same moment he opened it with a flourish and she fell – very conveniently – into his arms.

Brazilian student? As in tall, broad-shouldered, dark-skinned and smouldering . . . late-teens perhaps? Early-twenties? So perhaps Jude hadn't been exactly lying when she'd said she was giving up *men*.

'What are you staring at?' Jude practically slammed the door in Imo's face.

Undeterred, she opened the window. This was too good to miss.

Jude was attempting to drag him across the pavement – perhaps that was why she needed to build up her muscles? – but there was an awful lot of him, and most of it was standing still.

'I was looking for you.' Roberto's eyes were liquid sex appeal. Imo knew that Jude would never be able to resist. 'My back – it is bad again,' he said mournfully.

Bad back, hmm? Imogen rested her hands on the steering wheel and strained to hear Jude's response. Whatever it was, she was smiling.

'Ah, yes. That is exactly what I need.' Roberto was smiling too. He had more teeth than a crocodile but they were very, very white. 'Another one of your specials. Hands on sports injury massage.'

Hands on? No wonder Jude had been looking so peaceful in the pool. Her problem, Imo thought, would be how to keep her hands *off*.

Chapter 30

'I'm off now, Imogen.' Naomi's voice broke into her thoughts and Imo saw it was almost three – time to emerge from her sanctuary, potting on seedlings out back, to face the shop, the telephone, customers . . .

'Okey-doke.' She resealed the pack of potting compost, rubbed the dusty earth from her gloves and pulled them off. It was a complicated arrangement, she knew, but women were good at complicated. Term-time, Naomi came to work in the shop from ten till three, picked Daisy up from school and took her back home, to Jude's or to *Say It With Flowers*, depending on everyone's itinerary and when Jude was free to take over. Admittedly, half-term had proved chaotic until they realised that Daisy loved gardening, and would be happy for hours pottering about with a tub of compost and some seeds.

It had seemed strange at first, Imo reflected, pulling down the sleeves of her overalls, but they had become quite a community, working well, one for another. She shifted the seed trays so they would get maximum light. Only . . . it didn't seem to be enough. Picking up her planting fork, she stabbed it into a pot of earth on the bench. What was the matter with her? Was she cracking up? She raked her fingers through her hair – immediately regretting the action. Her hands were encrusted with earth that had crept through the holes in both gloves.

'Are you all right, Imogen?' Naomi had come through and was watching her, arms at her sides – steady, calm. She had taken off her green overalls and put on her camel coat.

Imo knew she could confide in her, if she was so inclined. Their relationship had progressed into friendship despite all the odds. But she didn't. She said, 'Of course.'

'Sure?'

She was tempted to snap, 'Don't fuss.' But Naomi was a godsend, a natural. She was the link holding all this together; the strongest of all three of them in a way. She had proved expert at dealing with people, she'd picked up the way the business was run in super-quick time, and she was flexible. Women were good at that too.

'I should have taken you on years ago,' Imo joked. But she couldn't confide in her and she couldn't ask her – about Marisa, about Alex.

As Imogen began dealing with an order for a bouquet, and Naomi set off for Daisy's school playground, Marisa was scanning the newspaper column once more.

The first time she'd made a number of strong strokes with her red pen. This time she studied detail. Every word counted. Every word would tell her something. Because she had no intention of wasting her time. Time was money, as Shelley would say.

This time round, a new wiggly line dismissed a couple of her previous possibilities. Bohemian was almost as dodgy as eccentric and surely meant no money. And a girl in her position had to be wary of rented . . . Rented was a long way from ownership in *her* opinion. Ambition was a favourite one; romantic should be avoided at all costs. Intelligent was so-so. But it was what was being sought that was most important by far. Beauty for starters. Marisa smiled. She could do beauty.

This was an investment for the future. If she'd stayed working for Shelley, what would she be at thirty? Worn out, through and through. She had seen those girls. Shelley wanted them to go on forever. Well, Shelley would, she was running a business. But Marisa had more sense.

Slowly, she dialled Alex's number. He was usually back from college early on Wednesdays. She called him most days . . . thought of him all the time.

Jude was humming as she let herself into the flat. She broke into song in the hall, a Spanish ditty about senoritas who could sway the night away, that was always being played on the radio.

Naomi would have dropped Daisy off at her friend Hannah's house by now, and Jude didn't have to pick her up till 6.30. She turned up the central heating. Her last client (a nutrivital facial treatment to hydrate, nourish and balance) had just left. Jude had given the salon a rapid brush-over and wipe-down, her face an even more rapid check-over – a touch more eyeliner, powder top-up and lip in-fill – and she was there. Or rather here. And she knew exactly what was waiting for her.

She paused mid-chorus. 'Coo-eee.' Too late she realised she sounded like her mother.

He emerged from his bedroom – Hazel's room, to be

precise, but her mother would never know – wearing only a pair of bum-hugging denim jeans.

Jude leaned against the wall to stop herself from falling over. He was gorgeous. And at her mercy. OK, he was young too, but so what?

'Hello . . . Judy.'

She pouted. She could be a Judy. She could be anyone she liked. True colours could change with the wind and hell was losing your make-up bag. 'Roberto – hi. Er . . .' She surveyed his torso. Wide shoulders, narrow waist. Dark brown skin, masses of thick and curly black chest hair. 'How's the back?' She grinned inanely.

'How do you say? Desperate?' He grinned back at her. Also inanely.

'Well, we do say that sometimes, yes.' She dumped her bag on the floor, pulled off her outsize coat. 'But I'm not sure it's exactly the right word here.' The heating had kicked in. She took off her sweater and got down to the little black shift that she liked to work in.

He flexed his biceps in response. 'Could you . . . Would you . . . ?'

The pleasure would be hers. 'Coconut oil, I think.' She fetched some from the bathroom, led him back into her mother's bedroom.

He followed her like a lamb.

'You'd better take off those jeans.'

He didn't need asking twice. She peeled off the duvet and he peeled off everything but a pair of black boxers.

'Down here.' She pointed.

He lay prone on the bed, face down. A lamb, yes. A lamb to the slaughter. She would fix his back – and how.

Jude straddled him – her favourite position, his bum

346

between her legs – rubbed some oil between her palms and began the massage. Slowly, slowly . . . 'You're very tense today.' The skin was tight, the shoulder muscle knotty, and she kneaded gently to start with, working the oil deep into his brown skin with her fingertips.

But after a bit he seemed to relax and she began to put everything into it: pummelling, stroking, pounding. Talk about healing hands . . . She was a star. The oil was sweet and fragrant. It reminded her of summer days, hot bodies and foreign beaches. Holidays and pleasure and . . . Under her hands his body grew warmer and his skin grew softer and sweeter and hotter and . . .

'Ooh . . . aaah,' he said.

She'd give him ooh, aah. She rolled the flesh of his waist between her thumb and fingers, used the heel of her hand for added pressure under the shoulder blades. With her oily fingertips, she traced each knob of the spinal cord. In turn. Slowly . . .

'Aah . . .'

Yes, from the neck down. Slow, sensual, rhythmic, teasing.

He broke out in a spate of Brazilian. That was better.

At last she finished. If she went on any longer with this heat charging between his back and her hands, one of them might combust spontaneously. 'That's it. Done.' She slipped off and sat on the edge of the bed.

More Brazilian. God knows what he was saying, but it sounded enthusiastic enough. It didn't matter a bit that he spoke almost no English. They could communicate perfectly well without words, she decided.

He turned over. It was impossible not to notice that he

347

was several sizes larger than when he had first laid down – in some departments anyway. Jude stared.

'I wish . . .' he said, eyieng the black shift, one strap of which had slipped off her shoulder '. . . that I could do that for you.'

'Be my guest.' She slipped the other shoulder strap free. 'And if you . . . er . . . get stuck, I'll remind you what to do next, OK?'

Jude lay down on the bed that was still warm from Roberto's body and he sat astride her, his weight on his knees.

'Ooo . . . er . . . mmm.' She could feel him – a lot of him – pressing on top of her in a rather delicious way.

'We must take this dress down. We must not let it spoil,' he said.

'Absolutely.' Jude wriggled to accommodate him as he eased the shift down to her buttocks.

'Now we begin.'

She felt the warm oil seep into her skin. His hands travelled slowly down her back. They stopped just below the sternum, and then began again from the neck. 'Aah.'

The phone rang. It probably wasn't important, but since Daisy wasn't safely at home, Jude couldn't ignore it. She reached for the extension.

'Is this a good time?' James Dean's dry tones drawled down the line.

'Not exactly.' Roberto was working on her shoulder blades now, and since she'd raised herself up to answer the phone, he was getting dangerously close to her left breast.

'I won't keep you a moment then.' He sounded terse. 'I just wanted a quick word about Florrie.'

'Florrie?' Jude protected her breast with her spare hand

and pushed Roberto's marauding fingers away. Now was not the moment.

'I can't get round there . . .'

In the background, Jude could hear soft music playing. No, he was probably *far* too busy. 'The rent's not due, is it?' she snapped.

'No, I'm just worried about her—'

'Worried?'

'Concerned.'

'That she won't be able to pay it?' Jude felt reckless. 'That she's going to spend it?'

Roberto reached a certain point just below her armpit that was particularly ticklish, and she collapsed on to the bed. 'Oof.'

'What's the matter?' He didn't sound as if he cared. 'What are you doing? And this has nothing to do with the rent.'

The receiver was now stuck between her mouth and the pillow, digging into her neck. Jude wriggled in an attempt to get more comfortable. 'What then?' she demanded. 'Still worried that she can't look after herself? Still think she should be in a home?' But even as she spoke, she was aware of a twinge of guilt. How long was it since she'd last called round to see Florrie? Four days? A week? She shivered as Roberto's probing fingers discovered the niceties of her lower spinal cord. Too busy thinking of her own pleasure.

'I think you and I should discuss this matter face to face.' James Dean's voice was colder than ever now – in polar opposition to Jude's burning skin.

Was he mad? 'Oh, do you indeed?' She almost sat bolt upright, until she remembered where she was and who with.

'I do.' He sounded very forceful. 'I suggest we meet up for a drink.'

A drink? 'Won't your wife object?' she muttered.

'I'm not married.'

'Girlfriend, then.'

'Not guilty.'

There followed a silence so intense that Jude swallowed very hard and was sure he must have heard it. 'I don't really think . . .' she began, wondering why her heart seemed to be flipping around her ribcage like a demented frisbee.

And then Roberto lunged.

'Aargh!' She fought him off but he was strong. He whispered, 'Is that good, yes? Just there, yes?' into both her ear and the telephone receiver.

'And I can tell you're extremely busy.' James Dean, the original Mr Iceberg, spoke very deliberately. 'I do apologise for disturbing you.' He rang off.

'Shit.' Jude said.

'More?' Roberto asked.

Jude shook her head. 'No more.' Somehow, she was no longer in the mood.

Brian and Phoebe were – much to Hazel's relief – extremely ordinary.

Their house was charming, not ostentatious in the least, and although Hazel spotted a pool, it was small, secluded and tucked away in the modest grounds to the side. The place was set back from Lake Garda, almost embedded in the mountainside.

Brian was very English and respectable, Hazel observed, in his casual trousers and a navy blazer. And Phoebe wore a turquoise cocktail dress with pearls – real ones, she could tell.

They provided a most welcome sherry before dinner

and after the starter – mozzarella cheese with avocado and plum tomatoes – came an English and understated breast of chicken in some sort of creamy sauce. The pudding was Italian ice cream which even Hazel couldn't complain about. Some things, she had to admit, the Italians did best.

And they spoke English! They were pleasant and intelligent and Hazel could understand every word. It was heaven. She found herself drinking perhaps a touch more Bardolino than she should. But what did it matter? She was with friends here. At last.

With coffee, liqueurs and still more wine, Giorgio started telling funny stories about Trident. He could be quite amusing – Hazel had almost forgotten. And he was clearly at home here in this house. The dining-room in which they were seated was small with white ceilings and walls and white drapes at the windows. The furniture was sparse and certainly not what Hazel was used to but what there was, was tasteful.

Phoebe giggled. 'You haven't changed, you naughty man!' She recrossed her legs.

Hazel sat up straighter in the bamboo chair. How old would she be? Sixty-five if she was a day. Brian was older – distinguished and grey, but still an attractive man. Rather debonair and very . . . sound, Hazel decided dreamily.

'What is the point of life,' Giorgio demanded, 'if you do not enjoy eet?' He surveyed Hazel over the rim of his glass.

Here we go again, she thought.

Phoebe intercepted the look. 'Lucky you've got Hazel here to keep you under control.' They all laughed uproariously. It wasn't a particularly funny remark – Hazel didn't think so anyway – but it was just one of those evenings. Laughter

351

and wine flowing, good food, pleasant company. So . . . well, so normal.

Brian refilled her long-stemmed wine glass. 'Marvellous to be with like-minded people.'

'Oh, yes.' Hazel knew exactly what he meant.

'We're so tucked away here.'

'Mmm.' There were streaks of silver in his hair, she noted. 'Have you been living here long?'

'Since my retirement.'

She nodded. As she'd thought. 'Nice to get away from the English climate, though.' In winter, anyway.

He raised his glass. 'And to find some freedom,' he said with feeling. 'To freedom and self-expression.'

'To freedom,' Hazel echoed, not sure what he was talking about.

They clashed glasses.

'And how long have you been married?' Hazel asked Phoebe, thinking to tease her. A lifetime, no doubt. She put her drink down carefully on the glass-topped table.

'Oh, we're not married, darling.' Phoebe laughed again. 'We both were once – but to other people. Living in sin, that's us.'

'Really?' Well, of course, Hazel reflected, everyone got divorced these days – look at Vanessa. And like her friend, not everybody wanted to go through another marriage. It was understandable, she supposed. Though . . .

'And why not?' Giorgio too had consumed vast quantities of Bardolino. Were there really four empty bottles on the table? Hazel squinted but couldn't keep track, the silly things seemed alive.

'An outdated institution, isn't that what they say?'

Hazel smiled vaguely. It was certainly what she'd said to

Vanessa over that tea in Kirby's, which seemed like a lifetime ago. The trouble was, she didn't really believe it. She waited for someone to make the joke about the institution.

'And who wants to join an institution?' Phoebe obliged. She might be English but she was a bit of a pain, Hazel decided.

'Absolutely,' Brian agreed. But Hazel divined a lack of enthusiasm here. *He* wasn't the type to flout convention, she guessed.

Phoebe turned to Hazel. 'Don't you think so? Or are you trying to convert our Giorgio?'

Hazel sat up straighter. 'I have no intention of making Giorgio do anything he doesn't wanna do,' she said, aiming for prim and sounding sloshed instead. Heavens, was she drunk?

At this point, Giorgio – perhaps thinking that her defences were down – put a hand on her thigh *again*. She squirmed.

'Unlike me.' He squeezed the flesh – harder than necessary, surely? She would have slapped him if they hadn't been in company.

'I want to make you do everything you don't want to do, hmm, my love?'

Everyone laughed again, including Hazel who didn't immediately grasp that he was discussing their sex life – or lack of it – with two strangers. When she did realise, after the laughter had died down, she hissed, 'Control yourself, do,' and shoved his hand away with considerable force.

Brian got to his feet. 'How about a game of cards?' he suggested.

Hazel smiled at him gratefully. He was exactly the sort of man who could be relied on to break a spot of nasty tension, to change the subject discreetly and smoothly when conversation took a turn for the worse.

'Lovely.' She clapped her hands. There was nothing like a nice game of cards. It was so ordinary and so English. To finish dinner, clear the table and indulge in a few hands of whist . . .

Phoebe smiled. A sly smile? Goodness, Hazel was seeing it everywhere now. 'The usual?' she asked.

'What else?' Giorgio had become quite animated. He even helped Phoebe clear the table. Neither of them appeared to be any the worse for drink – they weren't swaying anyway.

Hazel put her hands on the edge of the table to steady herself. She was swaying and she hadn't even stood up yet.

Brian went off to fetch the cards. 'Shall I deal?' he asked when he returned.

'Gin rummy?' Hazel asked. 'Newmarket? What do you usually play?' She hoped she wouldn't let herself down. Only coffee from now on, not a drop more wine.

'Poker.' Brian's smile was ordinary, English but not very reassuring. 'You can play poker, can't you, Hazel?'

Chapter 31

As per the instruction on the invitation to Jude's party, Imogen was made up to the eyeballs. Tiffany – who had come round to tell her she'd got a place at the local art college starting in September – had added some of her own cheekbone glitter and one of her stick-on beauty spots. Imogen had drawn the line, though, at a fake dragon tattoo.

'Not that you need it,' Tiffany said, sticking on the beauty spot and admiring the effect. 'You look well groovy, Imo. What kind of party did you say it was?'

Imogen hadn't. 'SHAG.' She shrugged in response to Tiffany's exclamation of disbelief. 'One of Jude's hare-brained schemes.'

'Hey, blatantly wild.' Tiffany rolled up both sleeves to reveal a tasteful daisy imprinted on each wrist, the name DAVE inscribed in capitals below. Imo hoped he was an improvement on Warren. 'Can anyone come?'

'Absolutely not. You're far too young.' Jude had been explicit on that point too. Only women of a certain age, she had specified. The rest of them – according to Jude – were too busy having fun already.

To celebrate, Vanessa and Ralph had planned a day out at the seaside in Brighton. A morning of strolling the prom had been particularly enjoyable, Vanessa thought, as Brighton front had two levels and the underpass was home to some charming craft shops, bars and tiny art galleries. This was followed by a traditional lunch of fish and chips and an afternoon spent shopping in The Lanes, which left them ready for an evening being pampered at the Grand Hotel.

'If your answer is still yes, my lovely,' Ralph said as they sipped their champagne cocktails in the Grand's elegant conservatory, 'then we should consider location.'

'I rather like it here.' It had been a marvellous day. And now, sitting here with Ralph – who was dressed in style in grey suit and cravat – Brighton seemed the obvious choice. A compromise perhaps, Vanessa thought, being a short journey by rail from both Chichester and London. And yet in its own way it had it all. Galleries, shops, character and culture. 'And there's a marvellous festival,' she added. That was a temptation. Brighton Festival was second only to Edinburgh these days.

'Something about the place, isn't there?' He patted her hand. She was wearing her mother's garnet and diamond ring in honour of the occasion.

'Mmm.'

'Then why not?'

Vanessa smiled. Darling Ralph, so easy and so impossible to please. 'Perfect,' she said.

'I'll contact some estate agents, shall I? Make a start?' His eyes creased as he smiled back at her. That face might be lined, she thought, but he still had it – whatever it was, inside.

'It is spring after all,' she agreed. The urge for change was in the very air. Vanessa adjusted the folds of her favourite long black dress. She wouldn't tell him about the test results yet, she didn't want anything to spoil a perfect day. And besides, the doctor had assured her that the lump could be dealt with easily, having been found in time. One breast or two, Vanessa knew it would make no difference whatever to Ralph. She would tell him. But not tonight.

'And you can leave the little one?' He was watching her carefully, his eyes concerned, as if he knew without being told.

'As I said to you once before, Imogen is a survivor.' Rather unfortunate perhaps for her to have fallen for a man who was about to become a father. But . . . Vanessa twisted the garnet ring. She had a feeling that Imogen was indeed stretching her wings and ready to fly. So she wouldn't be telling her either. There would be time enough.

'To us.' With his free hand Ralph covered hers once more. With his glass he touched hers. 'Together at last.'

'To us.' Vanessa closed her eyes for a moment and felt the warmth of this man she had always wanted. Once, physically, but now . . . for his humour, his companionship, his values. Still, she couldn't resist a small smile, as she flicked a speck of dust from his jacket and said, 'I always knew you'd see reason eventually.'

Imogen arrived early to help Jude get things ready. Daisy was staying the night with Hannah. And no, Jude said, she had not told Hannah's mother what kind of a party it was.

Imo noted the sign in the Georgian-paned window of *The Goddess Without*: MAKE THE MOST OF YOUR MASK. CREATE YOUR TRUE (IMAGINED) SELF, and laughed.

357

She ran up to the flat . . . and succumbed to Jude's critical eye.

'Not bad. You see, you can do it if you try hard enough.' Jude was dressed in black. Black silk shoe-string-shouldered top, black silk pencil skirt – ankle-length but with a split to the thigh to reveal plenty of black-stockinged leg. Her hair was raven, her eyes the deepest shade of violet Imo had ever seen (could you get contacts that colour? she wondered) and her lipstick dense blackcurrant.

'You look as if you've flown out of an Anne Rice novel,' Imogen told her. It was a kind-of compliment. Anne Rice's books might be about vampires but they were generally rather beautiful and erotic ones.

'And you look like a cross between a female Gary Glitter and Liz Taylor. But you'll do.'

Imogen stuck out her tongue, grabbed a wooden spoon, and turned to scoop tuna mayonnaise into a bowl. She carried it through. 'Have you invited lots of men?' she called as she went. Not that she was interested for herself, though Jude would keep saying that the party was in her honour. Imo smiled. Maybe that should be a party for her to lose what little honour she had left . . .

'That's the general idea.'

Naomi arrived and joined in the last-minute preparations. She wasn't exactly made up to the eyeballs as specified, but she had made a concession to their hostess by adding blusher and mascara to her normal lipstick and powder. She was wearing a jade green dress which emphasised her curves and suited her colouring perfectly.

Yet again, Imogen could see the attraction she must have held for Edward, and yet again she was tempted to ask her about Marisa but she bottled out.

'How's that daughter of yours?' Jude had no such scruples. She also had no tact.

'She's done a disappearing act.' Naomi got busy with the pasta salad, though the flush that swept up her neck and face betrayed her emotion. 'I got back from work last night to find . . . well, just a note stuck on the mantelpiece.'

'Where's she gone?' Jude asked.

'London.'

'London?' Jude and Imo stared at one another.

Fifteen minutes later Naomi was still mixing pasta as if her life depended on it. She wasn't sure how much to tell them. She was still trying to take it in herself. It was a shock to contemplate living without her daughter but at heart her overriding feeling was one of relief.

Imogen re-entered the kitchen. 'With Alex?' she asked bleakly.

'Alex?' Naomi met her gaze.

'Has she gone away with Alex?'

'Oh, I see.' In the past months Naomi had grown very fond of Imogen. She had helped Naomi change her life more constructively than Edward ever had, and Naomi loved that life – the shop, the plants and flowers, even looking after young Daisy. 'Surely Alex told you that it was over between the two of them?' she asked Imogen now. Perhaps she should have said something before. Only she was wary of interfering in other people's lives – especially people like Imogen who had plenty of reason to resent the ways in which she had interfered before.

'Well, kind of. Only . . .' Imogen's voice trailed off. She looked hopelessly towards Jude (currently dealing with

359

Coronation Chicken) who sighed, shook her head in mock despair and carried the bowl through.

'You didn't know for sure?' Naomi clingfilmed and moved on. Granted, Marisa had continued to pursue Alex. Naomi had caught her once or twice phoning him, giving him a hard time, no doubt. In the end she'd told her sharply to give the man a break. Yes, Naomi smiled to herself, she could do that now; their relationship had not been the same since Imogen had entered their lives. 'You can't make someone love you,' she had told her daughter. 'Push too hard and you'll drive them away.' But Marisa would never be told. And now she'd launched herself into another . . . episode.

'There's still the baby,' Imogen said. She looked so forlorn standing there cradling a plate of Caesar salad that Naomi simply had to go over and give her shoulder a quick squeeze.

'But you see, as it turns out, there is no baby.' She said the words with some difficulty. This was not the time, she'd told herself before coming to the party tonight. This was a night for having fun. For two pins she would have cried off but she knew how much Jude was looking forward to the evening, and it was a party for Imogen after all . . . But now, seeing Imogen's expression, she had to tell her. 'And Marisa has apparently realised there's more to life than having an artist as a boyfriend. There's also money. Money that's available now – not at some vague time in the future.'

'No baby?' Imogen's eyes grew wider. 'You mean . . . ?'

Naomi nodded. 'It was in the note.' And it had given her such a jolt when she'd read the words. Irresponsible though Marisa was, Naomi had been looking forward to being a grandmother. Perhaps her daughter might even get it right this time, she had found herself thinking.

'But why? How?'

'I don't know.'

Jude had obviously caught the gist of the conversation as she re-entered the kitchen, and now Naomi had the full attention of them both. She took a deep breath. 'I don't think there ever was a baby,' she said. Any alternative to this she didn't care to contemplate. Marisa had gone away last weekend, but that wasn't unusual. Marisa did lots of things, including going away. And then she had met this man — how or where heaven only knew — who, according to her, had money and knew someone who ran a modelling agency in London. Life wasn't actually like that, was it? Though, granted these things did seem to happen to her daughter. Whatever the truth of it she had her own route to follow and Naomi was damned if she was going to feel guilty for the rest of her life after making one bad decision. She exhaled loudly. She would always worry. But: 'Marisa has grabbed her portfolio and run,' she announced.

'Hmm.' Jude was the first to move. 'I'll cancel all her nail appointments then, shall I?' She whizzed her plate through and rushed straight back again. 'Was that tactless? Sorry.'

'Not at all.' Naomi tried to be brisk. 'Marisa is a mixed blessing.' That much was certainly true.

Jude switched her attention. 'Come on, Imo, stop dreaming. If you're that desperate to speak to AA . . .'

'AA?'

'Well, it's not Alcoholics Anonymous and no one's broken down. Yet.' She groaned. 'So if you're that desperate, why not take the initiative and call him?'

'Call him?'

'Well, why not?'

Imogen hurried her plate through. Why not? She could think of a hundred reasons why not. He was too young, he was irresponsible, he . . . Heavens, she'd run out of reasons already.

'I told him to get lost,' she reminded Jude as she came in to change the CD.

'Maybe he didn't believe you.'

Not very likely. She'd blown it with Alex Armstrong. Clearly it had never been meant to be, though it had been pretty wonderful all too briefly. 'Maybe I'll meet someone single, heterosexual and gorgeous tonight,' she said, trying to be brave.

Jude gave her a knowing look and blew her a kiss. 'That's the general idea,' she told her.

Roberto emerged from his room in a tuxedo. Imo noted Jude's reaction. 'At your age,' she teased.

'I may not be as young as I was, sweetie . . .' Jude leaned closer confidingly '. . . but who said youth is the only thing worth having?'

'Er, Dorian Gray?'

'Well, he was talking crap.'

'He was?' Imo was lost here.

'I know my strengths,' Jude informed her.

Imogen grinned. 'So what are you offering? Beauty?'

'Beauty is not my only commodity.' Jude pulled a scary face. 'And what I'm offering is neither here nor there.' She put an arm around Imo's waist. 'Because I'm doing the selecting.'

'I see.' Though Imo wasn't sure it was that simple.

What happened if the person you selected didn't want
to know?

'Choice, Imo,' Jude said.

'Choice?'

'Now *that's* worth having.'

Chapter 32

Jude decided to nip up by the outside spiral staircase to check Florrie was okay with the noise level. She'd warned her about the party. Her neighbour hadn't seemed to mind in the slightest. 'It'll liven the old place up a bit,' she had said, somewhat wistfully. Jude wondered if she was remembering her own dancing days, those male attentions she had once enjoyed.

Florrie didn't answer her knock, so Jude, shivering despite having thrown her big coat around her shoulders, tried the kitchen door. It was open.

'Florrie?' She slipped inside. The light was on in the hallway so she went through, heading for the sitting-room. It was only just after nine, Florrie was bound still to be up.

'Florrie?'

She was sitting on her old sofa, surrounded by photo albums, one foot on a stool in front of her. 'Jude, my dear . . .'

'Is it too noisy for you?' The pounding of music, laughter and voices could be heard pretty clearly from up here.

'No, no. My hearing's not as good as it was. Nothing keeps

me awake these days once my head hits the pillow.' She nodded. 'I'm quite happy, my dear, you enjoy yourselves.'

And she did look happy, Jude thought, surrounded by her memories. She knelt at the old lady's feet. 'Can I see?'

Florrie pointed to a faded sepia photograph. 'Dancing at Frobisher's.'

Jude saw an elegant woman with fair hair piled into a chignon, a wide smiling mouth and a long sparkling dress. She was arm in arm with a handsome young man in uniform. 'An admirer?' Jude asked. The features seemed vaguely familiar; there was a dark intensity to the face and eyes, a tightness in the wide mouth that was both attractive and a little scary at the same time.

'My brother Jacob.' Florrie turned the bottle-green paper – like a cross between parchment and blotting paper, Jude thought, touching it with a fingertip, noting the slits that held the photographs in place. 'This is his wedding.'

Jude let her gaze wander from photo to photo. In these snapshots Jacob seemed transformed, the dark face lit with a wide smile rather like Florrie's own, presumably due to the girl by his side, his cheerful, dimpled bride with her mass of dark curls. Jude grinned. She was looking up at him as if she'd indeed found her Prince Charming. 'They look so happy,' she murmured.

'Oh, they were.' Florrie continued to turn the heavy pages. 'It took them a while but eventually they had a child – look.'

Jude peered at the tiny bundle wrapped in a white shawl, held close to Jacob's wife's breast. The black and white snap was blurred, but the emotion on the faces was clear enough.

Abruptly, Florrie closed the book. 'Both gone now, I'm

365

afraid, my dear. They died within a year of each other. It's hard, you know . . .'

'And the baby?' Jude hugged her knees.

'Oh, he's my absolute rock.' Florrie's expression changed once more. 'He nags me, of course, thinks he knows what's best for me.' She sat back, wincing in pain.

'Florrie, what is it?' Jude leaned forwards in concern.

'Just my ankle.' She looked rueful. 'I had a bit of a slip earlier on. Silly really, my eyes play me up . . .'

'Let me look.' Gently, Jude lifted her foot and touched the swollen ankle. 'You've twisted it, I think. But at least nothing's broken.' She hesitated, thinking of this nephew Florrie had spoken of. 'Is there someone I should call?'

'No need.' Florrie's faded blue eyes looked, Jude thought, more penetrating than usual. 'He'll only say what he always says, won't he?'

'Will he?' Was Florrie trying to tell her something? Why was there something nagging at Jude, some sense that she was missing something here?

'I could help get you to bed,' she offered. 'We could see how you are in the morning . . .'

'I don't want to keep you from your party.'

Jude thought of Imogen, Naomi, Roberto and all the others downstairs. 'It's OK,' she said quietly. 'I wasn't having the greatest time anyway.'

'Very well.' Florrie allowed Jude to help her up.

Supporting her weight, Jude headed for the small bathroom. Florrie sat on the edge of the white tub while Jude filled the washbasin with warm water and fetched Florrie's flannel.

'He says, not a home,' Florrie told her. 'He says, live

with him so he can keep an eye on me.' She snorted. 'A fate worse than death that would be, I can tell you.'

'Your nephew?' Jude was distracted, concentrating on soap, flannel, toothbrush and paste.

'I want to be independent, I say.' Florrie accepted the soapy flannel. 'A warden-assisted flat then, he says.'

Jude found that she had some sympathy for him. The poor man was obviously trying his best to help his aunt from afar. 'It wouldn't be so bad,' she offered. 'To have someone on hand if you needed them.' She rinsed the flannel and returned it to Florrie.

'He's trying his best,' Florrie agreed. 'Does my shopping, sometimes cooks for me too.' She eyed Jude once more with that curiously penetrating gaze. 'He's a good lad, you know.'

'I'm sure.' Jude only wondered how come she'd never seen this paragon. She handed Florrie the towel.

'And now he tells me I've got to come clean.'

'Clean?' Jude put the towel back on the rail and squirted toothpaste on to Florrie's yellow toothbrush. 'How's that?'

'But I told him . . .' Florrie accepted the toothbrush, but hesitated. '"James," I said, "I don't want her to be inhibited knowing the landlady lives upstairs. This is my place and I want to stay here for as long as I possibly can."'

Jude gaped at her as Florrie stuck the brush into her mouth. 'James?' she said. Everything was falling into place. '*The* James?'

Florrie nodded.

'James Dean?'

She nodded again.

'James Dean our landlord?' Frustration welled as Florrie continued brushing her teeth. Jude grabbed her arm and

367

propelled her to the basin so she could spit out. *'He's* your nephew and he's *not* the landlord? You mean, you . . . ?'

'I fear so.' Florrie wiped her mouth. 'It was my idea to remain incognito, I'm afraid. Originally – before you became the tenant, my dear – James thought it would be safer for him to act the part. Made it easier for him to keep an eye on me as well. But now . . .'

'Now?' Hands on hips, Jude regarded her sternly. When she thought of what she'd said to him, how she'd accused him of trying to chuck Florrie out on the streets, how she'd assumed he'd only been interested in upping the rent for his own gain, his own greed . . . she could die of shame. No wonder he'd wanted to meet up to explain things. No wonder he had been so angry.

'Now, it seems, he doesn't want you to harbour any more illusions. For some reason . . .' Florrie paused, eyes glinting with mischief '. . . he doesn't want you to think badly of him, my dear.'

Jude felt the heat rush to her face. 'I see.' She took Florrie's arm to distract herself, and led her towards the bedroom. 'So all this time I've been protecting you from a wicked landlord, *you've* actually been my landlady?' Which also meant presumably that it was Florrie who was rolling in it – not so poor she couldn't even afford a decent shampoo and set after all.

'Exactly, my dear.' Florrie squeezed her arm. 'And may I take this opportunity of telling you what a charming and helpful tenant you have been? I've grown very fond of you, you know. And that's why I can't help hoping . . .'

Jude flushed again. God, how embarrassing. How would she ever face him again?

*

The party was in full swing when Jude got back downstairs, still reeling from the shock of what Florrie had told her, and from her own tangled emotions.

As Jude paused in the hallway, Roberto appeared in the doorway of the sitting-room where most of her guests could be seen shaking their funky thing (Daisy had informed her this was the correct expression) to the Rolling Stones' rather appropriate 'I Can't Get No Satisfaction'.

He pounced.

'Jude!'

Jude and Roberto sprang apart as if she were thirteen again. So much for adulthood, she thought wryly. So much for liberation. The front door was open and her mother was standing in the hallway.

'Ma! What on earth are you doing here?'

'I live here, don't I?' Hazel snapped. She dropped her case and overnight bag to the floor. She looked tired and not a little upset. 'Who is this . . . *youth?*'

'Er . . .'

'And what's going on?'

Jude thought of Roberto's gear in Hazel's room and began to panic. Where to start? But she must remember two important facts. One, this was her flat, and two, she was over forty years old (on a bad day). So, 'We're having a party,' she told her mother firmly. 'And this is a student who's staying here at the moment.'

'In my room, I suppose?' Hazel's eyes flashed blue steel. She looked as if party pooping was right up her street. She looked as if she would simply love to throw them all out single-handed.

Naomi had always preferred the Beatles to the Rolling

369

Stones. In her teenage days that was the way the world was divided — at least the bit of it that she and her friends inhabited. And these days it was Pavarotti who got her going, though she wouldn't admit that to anyone tonight. Jude's living-room — or more precisely the music, unmistakably Stones rather than Beatles — reminded her of a certain Jez Webster.

She smiled at the memory: blond greasy hair, bluer than noon-sky eyes. Jez had ridden a motor bike, been the school heart-throb and, predictably, only dated girls in the Stones camp. Ah, yes, she remembered it well, that wild side of life that she'd always been a bit scared of and a bit envious of too. She'd always had the feeling that the Stones girls might *go all the way*.

And hearing the music now, in some secret part of her, Naomi knew that she too might well have taken that path — if it hadn't been for Edward. But it was certainly too late to take it now, she reminded herself, as she escaped from the thrust of Jagger's voice and the throb of Richards' guitar, came into the hall and realised immediately what was going on.

'Can I help?' she asked Jude, who was looking harassed.

'My mother's come back from Italy,' she wailed. Not very tactful of her but in the circumstances Naomi took her point. And as for that student of hers . . . He might be young, but he really should learn a thing or two about timing. Now was definitely not the time to be doing whatever he was trying to do to his landlady's neck as she batted him away with the back of one hand.

'Well, thank you very much. A nice welcome, I must say.'

Hazel had never in her entire life felt more like bursting into tears. Well, once perhaps, not so long ago . . .

It had been two hours after Brian got out the playing cards that she and Giorgio had finally taken their leave, though Hazel had found it hard even to speak by that point. She blushed now as she thought of it: how she had sat out most of the games, in a combination of fury, misery and embarrassment. She would have left alone if she'd had the slightest idea how to get back. And that awful woman . . .

'Till next time,' Phoebe had called after them. 'Don't be strangers.'

Giorgio had waved but Hazel couldn't bear to look back at them. Poker? Brian was wearing only his tie and Y-fronts, while Phoebe was naked but for her pearls.

Hazel shook the memory away though she guessed that final picture would stay imprinted on her mind forever. She tried to concentrate on what this red-haired woman was saying. She looked respectable, and now she was taking Hazel's arm, being kind, explaining that she lived alone and would welcome the company if Hazel would care to come and stay with her for a while.

'I love you!' Jude shrieked at the poor woman. Goodness, what could be the matter with her? Hazel wondered. She'd obviously been travelling a downward spiral since Hazel had left. And as for that awful youth pawing at her all the time . . . he looked suspiciously foreign, and after her Italian experience she could tell Jude something about foreigners.

'I'll order a taxi and take you there now, shall I?' Naomi said.

'But what about the party?' Jude cried.

'I'm quite ready to leave now, if you don't mind.' The

371

woman – Naomi – was most understanding. Firm too. And very English.

Whereas Jude was hopeless. 'Where's Giorgio anyway?' she demanded, scanning the space behind Hazel as if she expected him to jump through the letter box.

'In Italy where he belongs.' And if Jude dared to say 'I told you so', Hazel would tell *her* a thing or two.

'Is it all off then?'

Really, Hazel thought, her daughter took so long to grasp the point sometimes. 'It most certainly is.' She had begun to doubt the wisdom of marrying Giorgio, even for security, well before the dreaded incident in Limione. She just thanked God she had found out the truth in time. No wonder there were sly smiles flying about here, there and everywhere. Marianna had told her later, in broken English, that Gianfranco had lent Giorgio substantial amounts of money on condition that he didn't return to Malcesine. Thus it was hardly surprising that his brother hadn't been overjoyed to see him. So – no money and a dubious reputation, not to mention the strip poker . . . It was a miracle she had emerged with her virtue intact.

'And where on earth is my granddaughter?' she demanded, on seeing a scantily clad female emerge from Daisy's bedroom. She should never have left them alone for so long. They were clearly incapable of managing without her.

'Staying at Hannah's.' Jude laughed, rather hysterically, Hazel thought.

'So long as the poor child hasn't run away to a nunnery.' Hazel turned, yanked open the front door and stared at the young man – yes, another one – standing on the doorstep. But this one she recognised. 'Come in, come in,' she said. 'I expect she's around somewhere.'

'Before you go, Ma . . .' Jude smiled at the man and moved aside to let him pass. She put a hand on her mother's arm. 'Some woman from Trident's been phoning you.'

'Oh?' Hazel paused majestically in her tracks. She hardly dared hope. And yet . . .

'Something about some theatre somewhere showing an interest in that Gershwin thing. The possibility of a tour.'

'Oh?' Hazel felt her spirits lift. 'They were after me? Not Giorgio?'

Jude smiled. 'You, I believe. Phone Belinda. She said she has all the details.'

Belinda? 'I will.' Hazel was glad she'd come straight back to England. She was beginning to think that Vanessa had been right all along too — about dependency. One could achieve, couldn't one, in one's own right? And goodness, it did feel satisfying. 'I'll phone her tomorrow.' She began humming cheerfully before she was even out of the door: 'Nice work if you can get it . . .'

Alex found Imogen just as Steely Dan gave way to the Commodores.

'I don't suppose you remember this music,' she said, after her first blink of surprise.

'You'd be amazed what I remember.' What he remembered best was the night he'd spent in her cottage, in her bed, in every detail — it woke him up sometimes.

'I remember too.' She seemed to understand his meaning. They were in tune.

Somehow they started dancing. Their bodies fitted together. His arms felt right on her waist; hers round his neck seemed to be inviting. And very warm.

'I want my life to change,' he whispered in her ear.

373

She raised one eyebrow and her nose wrinkled in just the way he remembered. 'Don't you do small talk, Alex?'

'And I still want you.' Her perfume – whatever it was – was heady stuff. Her hair was piled up on top of her head, but as usual a few stray tendrils had escaped. And what was that black thing on her face? A beauty spot. He smiled.

'Are the two incompatible?' she asked him. She was soft and weightless in his arms – the most graceful woman he had ever known. Tonight she was wearing a silver-grey dress. It sparkled and clung to her slender body. It was the colour of dawn and the colour of her eyes.

'Come away with me,' he urged. He didn't know where the hell to or how long for. He just wanted change, he needed a new perspective in his life and this woman by his side. He'd already given in his notice. Now he just had to get the girl.

Imo had closed her eyes. She was moving dreamily to the music. There was a slight smile on her face as her long fingers brushed against his neck.

'Imo?'

'I might.'

It wasn't long before Imo came to find Jude. 'You phoned him, didn't you?'

Jude spread her hands. 'Naomi gave me the number. And if we'd left it up to you . . .'

Imogen hugged her. 'He wants me to go away with him,' she whispered. 'I might – for a while – if Naomi could hold the fort at the shop.'

'You need a break.' Jude prolonged the hug. 'Where will you go?'

374

She felt the shake of Imo's head. 'I don't know yet. I just know I want to be with him.'

Slowly, they drew apart. 'Is he the one, do you think?'

Imo, bless her, was glowing. 'Ask me when I get back.'

That was the kind of beauty that looked good on a woman, Jude thought.

Imogen slipped out of the front door, Alex close behind her. He began to speak and Imo kissed him. Mid-sentence. Attagirl. Jude grinned. Sometimes it was the only way. He blinked back at her as if he'd just been woken up.

Jude stood watching as they walked away in step. *For now*, she thought, wishing she didn't have to be cynical and bad. Was there a prince for everyone? She thought not.

'Keep smiling.' She waved to Imo. 'Remember, a good sense of humour is always essential.' Imo would come back. But would she come back with Alex? And when she came back – how far would she have moved on?

As she closed the door, Jude thought of Roberto. One sign and he'd be ready and waiting for her. She'd always known if she disobeyed the Nice Girl Rules often enough, she would get her reward. But it wasn't Roberto. Give him five minutes and he'd find a younger, prettier replacement. And besides, he would never be prince material.

Rules?

She dialled the number Florrie had given her.

'James?' she said when he answered. 'I'm not sure if it's against the rules but I'm having a party.'

'It sounds like one hell of a good one from here,' he said, not seeming surprised at her call.

'It's not bad.' She paused. 'And when I consulted the land-lady she told me to go ahead and enjoy myself, so . . .'

'So?'

'So I guess we can keep it going till the small hours.' Now it was up to him. Selection was all very well, but a girl could only do so much. She waited.

'Is anyone invited?' he said.

'You qualify.' She held her breath.

'I'm on my way.'

Jude put down the phone and exhaled before she burst. Single, heterosexual and gorgeous. Princes? What the hell. The choice – in the end – was a blatantly simple one.